# Planetfall

L.E. Howel

ISBN:-13:978-0615968490 (Howel Works)
ISBN:- 10:061596849x

Cover Design: Malcolm McClinton

# DEDICATION

TO MY FAMILY

"THE MIND IS ITS OWN PLACE,
AND IN ITSELF CAN MAKE A HEAVEN OF HELL,
A HELL OF HEAVEN"

# Planetfall

# ONE

In the space of our imagination there is adventure, there is hope, but above all there is the promise of a brighter future. In this dark corner of reality, however, there was nothing. The cold emptiness of space remained unaltered, an impassive witness to the events that would never take place in its void. Even the brightest stars shone only dimly here, their light and warmth diminished to single pinpricks by the distance. This was as close to nowhere as anywhere could be. Yet it was here that it first approached, small at first, but growing ever larger. A ship, a massive hulk, not beautiful, and yet somehow an ugly, majestic tribute to the great things that small hands could accomplish, if they had the spirit to imagine.

Through the silent darkness the great vessel approached unnoticed. Four huge, carbon encrusted cylinder engines throbbed noiselessly below an almost delicate smaller structure fixed to them. It was a ship, a tiny ship that might have been a parasite, long since dead but still clinging through memory to the mighty engines whose energy had once sustained it. Now even the memory seemed to have faded and all that remained was this lifeless shell. Like all parasites it had met with a greater force intent on its destruction. The icy fingers of space had reached out and swatted it. It was dead now, and the four immense engines, fired by little more than the vapors of its former hopes pushed the dead mass on to its unknown goal.

***

Feeding time at the zoo. It was an early June morning and the fresh, clean air of spring had yet to be replaced by the oppressive summer heat. In the days of his youth this might have seemed like a day of opportunity, like the forerunner of a long, glorious summer ahead. Even now these memories echoed somewhere in his head as the laughter of children sprinkled the air through the buzz and bustle of the crowd. A silent orange balloon bobbed rhythmically in the air, anchored to a noisy child, who was pointing excitedly from one animal to the next. A young baby cried and was consoled by its mother. A father demonstrated a greater knowledge of animals than he truly possessed in his explanations to his wide eyed young daughter. Everywhere excitement and a sense of freedom pervaded the grounds as the sun glistened lustily on the roofs of the dew kissed enclosures.

Chief Keeper Edwards passed through the throng, unaffected by their optimism, spirit, or enthusiasm. His ears did not hear their laughter, his eyes did not see their smiles, and his soul was untouched by their joy. His world was a different place. Something had broken loose years ago, and he had drifted further and further from the experience of others until now he was utterly alone in both thought and deed. He could share nothing with them, and so he walked among these people as through a mist or fog that had the appearance of reality, but no substance.

He couldn't remember when it had all begun. This had all been the reality of his dreams once: this job, this position, this life, but now they had changed into the phantom of his nightmare existence. He had worked hard for this, but when he had reached the very summit of his life he had only found the panorama blighted. Whatever he had been looking for wasn't here. It never had been. The happiness he had expected to find had somehow eluded him, and his weary eyes could find nowhere else to look.

And now it was feeding time again, and the animals' calls for food were drowned by the baying of the crowd, hungry for its entertainment. Edwards had felt a habitual duty to both, and so, despite his position, he had made public feeding a part of his daily schedule. Back at the beginning of things he had seen this as an important part of keeping him from losing touch with both patrons and protected under his care. He wasn't sure that either really mattered any more, and now he was hardly aware of the noise that surrounded him as he pushed the cart of food toward the first enclosure. It was a daily routine and his mind was on other things.

His thoughts were running down the same dark channels they always followed. He rarely strayed from them now and deep ruts of habit had formed so that he could hardly escape them if he had wanted to. There was something wrong with him, he knew that, but he didn't know what he could do. He couldn't even say what it was, but he knew it was there, and he also knew instinctively that no one else must know. It wasn't normal. It must have been something inside him. A spark, or something else, wasn't quite there anymore and it had been replaced by darkness. Life continued the same as ever, on the surface it was better than ever, but still a hunger-like emptiness remained, gnawing, demanding, waiting to be filled, but by what? That was the trouble, knowing what.

Edwards reached down for a bucket on his cart. His own emptiness, so unknown an experience until recent years, seemed mocked by this ritual of feeding time. Animal needs were so easily satisfied, he thought to himself as he poured the food into a meager dish. He eyed the contents dubiously.

"Such food, such vile food," he muttered to himself, and yet he knew that just the smell of the stuff would be enough to start a ripple of unbounded excitement in the enclosure. This had always disgusted Edwards, such joy from such a simple thing, and yet it was this that fascinated him most of all. He was even vaguely aware that if he looked deeply enough within himself he would have found an odd admiration, even envy of this simple desire and the pleasure its fulfillment seemed to bring to his animals.

Placing the bowl within the first cage Edwards shuffled away on the rest of his rounds. At least someone would be happy today, he thought to himself as he started toward the next enclosure.

***

The ship persisted on its unknown course. With throbbing engines muted by the vacuum of space it glided past a small, dark sphere, a dead world of rock, cold, lifeless, and desolate. Unwavering, the craft moved on, soon encountering a second planet. In contrast with the first its shimmering atmosphere seemed to glint welcomingly, to invite further investigation, but this also went unheeded by the travelling monolith as it proceeded silently toward its goal.

Inside, the same quiet embraced a single, dark room in a perfect state of nonexistence. No sight, no sound, no awareness. This was the interior of the smaller ship, the delicate parasite that had once lived off the great power of the engines below it. Once it had been alive, but now there was nothing-or so it was until now, for the blanket of darkness was suddenly pierced by the appearance of five glowing green dots. Like the luminous eyes of the pack surrounding its unseen prey, they gleamed in the darkness. These were no animals.

Slowly things changed. An orange light eased in like a mock dawn, dimly revealing a small, stark room with a domed ceiling and six rectangular shapes lined in rows of three against its two longest walls. The boxes, like the room that contained them, were almost featureless, and the sterile functionality of the whole place was made only somewhat less severe by the faint orange glow that now bathed it.

The appearance of the boxes, the hushed quiet, the drab surroundings, all of this might have been interpreted as some quiet mausoleum where the bones of loved ones rested. Yet the warmth of the now brightening orange light jarred against this impression. This was not death; a life and vitality rested here, dormant, but not dead.

The lighting in the room gradually altered. From the panels of five boxes the glowing green dots seemed to grow, spreading their light over the whole shape until each was engulfed in their lively glow. The orange of the room had now melted away into a warming sunlight yellow and, as if in response, the light from the boxes, transformed, slowly at first, almost imperceptibly, from green to light green, to light blue, to dark blue. The lights flashed with ever increasing speed. Green, blue, red, orange- the colors blurred, finally stopping at brilliant white, and five boxes hissed as their lids slowly rose. Then silence returned. A shower of white light cascaded over the containers, like a cleansing stream, until it flickered, winked dimly, and died. Steam rose from the newly opened lids and condensed on the ceiling. A distant pulsar beep began to sound and was met by faint wheezing, gasping breaths. A hacking cough pierced the stillness, as though someone had almost drowned and had fought their way back.

Moments passed. The steam dispersed on the ceiling. Nothing moved. Finally a man's hands grasped the sides of one box from the inside and, with effort that turned the fingers white, pulled himself into a sitting position. He blinked, looking groggily at his surroundings with uncomprehending eyes. He rubbed his fingers through his graying black hair and over his worn face. He had the look of a man waking up from a short sleep after a long day.

In fact, Thomas Birch would have been glad to feel that bad; he felt much worse. At once he was acutely aware of his own body and its pain. His head ached, his body ached; even his soul seemed to ache as a great feeling of despair washed over him like the icy embrace of deep waters. His mind struggled for focus, to understand what he was doing and where he was. He felt cold; this was reality.

"Made it", he managed to mumble inaudibly. His mind was beginning to clear. He knew where he was, and why he was here, though even in his confused state he wondered about the wisdom of it all. He knew the time for those questions had gone. He had work to do, and as his thoughts turned from the past to the present his dark mood began to lift.

His despair had been natural enough; it was all expected. There were scientific explanations. You didn't spend long periods of time in cryogenic sleep without becoming dependent on the dark, warm security it provided to your subconscious. The shock of reality after this existence was hard to deal with, and no better than it must be for the newborn babe, pushed from the womb, turned upside-down and given a swift slap by the doctor to start respiration. Birch would get over it. He had done it before.

Again he rubbed his face in his hands, then tore at the I.V. tube attaching his arm to the unit. As it came free a drop of blood trickled down his arm, like a tear for the things that were lost. Ignoring it Birch pulled himself to his feet and gingerly tested his weight against the floor.

Before the mission they had been assured that great progress had been made in cryogenics. The problems with earlier long-term hibernation experiments had been overcome and there was little risk that they would suffer any ill effects. It wasn't that reassuring. The earliest experiments had left the subjects in a permanent vegetative state, and there was always that risk. Improved techniques of neural stimulation were supposed to keep all the mental and physical functions at their peak condition, but there was still that hidden fear that everyone had to swallow when they signed up for one of these missions- the realization that things did go wrong.

If he had felt any better Birch might have been grateful for his throbbing limbs and aching brain which indicated that he had survived another trip, but the pain was too real to be ignored. The promise of the experts had been that you would wake up as refreshed as from a night's sleep. Having already experienced the reality Birch knew it would be a long time before he felt nearly that good. Cryogenics would keep you alive, but it was always a long time before you could ever believe that it had actually been worth it.

The pulsar beep suddenly intensified, becoming louder and more urgent. Birch straightened himself and saw that his four crewmates were all wearily pulling themselves from their chambers and making their way to their stations. He knew the drill, they were approaching Base Two. Now it was time to find out what had really happened. "This'll be good," he muttered to himself as he followed the others through a narrow doorway. He hoped he was right.

The adjoining room was the only other habitable space on the tiny craft. The cramped compartment served as the ship's control center and was only used on the rare occasions that human input was preferred to automation. The bulk of the flying was the mindless monotony of deep space. The computers could handle this, but when it came to the more significant parts of the mission humanity again wrestled control to itself.

As he entered the room Birch quickly sensed the change of atmosphere. He had felt it before, and now he saw that even a lifetime of sleep had failed to erase the indelible marks on their former friendships. Karla's expression, as always, had been the easiest to read. The others just became cold and motionless, refusing to acknowledge him, but Karla stole a glance at Birch, then back to the empty doorway behind him. Tears filled her eyes before she too looked away to stare blankly at the instrument panel before her. That was going to be it then, the furtive glances and sudden hush. Things weren't going to change. What had he expected, that cold hearts would melt while cryogenically frozen, or that inactive minds would be changed? None of this was possible and now, even though a hundred thousand yesterdays might have passed, the long dead conflicts of their own time were resurrected within their own breasts. So be it, he thought to himself as he marched over and sat in the pilot's seat.

"Let's get to it," Birch barked as he began punching keys in the panel before him. He was mad. Mad at everything. The mission had tested them all. Nothing had been textbook, but then he had learned that truth could rarely be found in any set text; it was just too hard. The cold, hard reality they had found wasn't anything that they had trained or prepared for. Now all they could do is live it the best they could and see what happened.

"Ten minutes to radio range of Base Two," the woman to Birch's left announced. This was Major Jane Gray, his co-pilot and something like a friend. His most recent experiences had led him to dread the word. Turning his attention to the terminal he brought up a heads-up display to follow their progress. Yes, they were approaching Mars, sight of Base Two. This would tell them a lot.

Everyone stared at the screen, willing the ship on to the communication point. The flashing green of the icon marking the ships position on the display cast a sickly glow over the crew's perspiring faces and increased the sense of numbing tension. Time passed slowly as the moment approached. No one ever leaves home for any time without some anxiety at the absence. Whether it's an irrational fear that you left a door unlocked, or a concern that some natural disaster might strike in your absence, there is nothing like the relief of that point in the return journey when you turn the corner on your road and see that your own house is still there. Birch and the others were straining to see around that corner now.

There shouldn't have been any cause for concern, after all hadn't humanity finally begun to reach for its highest ideals? This was to be the golden age. For years they had been making great strides in scientific understanding, but finally there had come a change in the social perspective. Old idioms had died away and a peaceful self-awareness had replaced the discordant voices of history. Their own mission, the Hypnos missions, had been a small part in this grander scheme of human progress. Like the old expositions of the nineteenth century, theirs was a grand display of what people could do.

And yet the voice of doubt persisted. Birch understood too much to somehow find it in himself to believe in peace. There were always those who brought discord and conflict. He had fought against it many times in his own life, even in his own head, so how could he expect anything good. For some the hope remained that one day the old enemies would be thrown down in the dust and trampled underfoot, but it seemed unlikely to him that anyone would ever rise far enough above the dust to trample anything but themselves, and so Birch wondered.

They were about to knock on humanity's door after a long absence. Would anyone answer?

# TWO

"Hypnos III to Base Two, Hypnos III to Base Two. Respond please." The almost mechanical repetition of Lieutenant DeSante`s voice had an edgy quality to it. He fingered a button on his console, turned two knobs nervously and tried again. "Base Two this is Hypnos III, code 4-1-9-9-3 Alpha Phase, please respond." A faint hiss was the only answer as DeSante paused. He started again.

"Wait!" Birch's interruption was unexpected and the young Lieutenant turned in his seat to look at his commanding officer. After half an hour of fruitless attempts at communication the words were stabbing into Birch's brain like daggers and the last thing he wanted was to hear them repeated again. "It's obvious that we're going to get no response here," he continued. "Gray, send out a probe, let's see what's going on down there." She hesitated for a moment, turned to speak but seemed to change her mind and turned again to her console.

"Probe launched," she announced flatly, "transmitting within normal parameters. We should hear something in the next ten minutes." Birch nodded and left his position to look at her screen.

"Good, that should give us a good sweep of the main control area. Let's see if we can find out what they're up to down there that's keeping them from answering. Dawson," he turned now to address Karla, the young blonde lieutenant to his right, "keep close track of that probe. I want to know as soon as anything happens. The rest of you need to finish the status evaluation of the ship and see what shape this old bucket's in. We don't want the bottom to drop out of it while we're sat here pondering the fate of our universe. Let's get to it."

Silence again returned to the room, save for the electronic hum and buzz of the ship. Glancing up from his panel Birch caught sight of the rusty orb of Mars through the cockpit window. The mute planet seemed to offer a glint of understanding to some unknown mystery, but these were secrets it was unwilling to share.

Mars had been the beginning of it all. The belief that humanity could conquer its own limitations, that it could tame the untamable and that perhaps our living might finally equal our dreaming. And they had done it. They had created a paradise on the crimson soil of cold, cold Mars. But now it was silent.

"I'm starting to get some preliminary feedback from the probe, Major," Karla's voice cracked. "Atmosphere reports at thirty-two percent off recommended levels, breathable, but only just. Something's gone really wrong here." Birch winced; the great achievement of Mars, and all other projects that had followed, had been built upon the super-science of terraforming. If this cornerstone had crumbled and failed then a whole generation of plans would be doomed.

"Keep me updated. As soon as anything comes in let me know," he turned his attention to Jane. "How does the ship status look, are we in a position to do much here?"

She shook her head and frowned. Tapping a few more keys she turned to Birch. "It doesn't look good. Take a look for yourself." He moved closer to the screen as she pointed to the scrolling display. "Fuel is low, as you'd expect, but the worse news is that the ship's hull is pretty badly damaged and the internal structure's been weakened too; I'm not sure how long it'll last. This ship has been made to do things it was never designed to do and we're all paying the price right now.

Worst of all it looks like the heat shield on the command module has been damaged. If you remember our last launch was a mess; that seems to have torn a hole right through the shield." Jane sighed and looked pointedly up at Birch, "Basically we're stuck unless someone comes up and gets us down."

"Hmm," Birch stood staring at the monitor, as though willing the information on it to change. "It's starting to look like we'll need a better plan than that though. I'd like you and Lieutenant DeSante to see what you can do about fixing the structure and hull damage. Are the auto-repair systems operative?"

Jane nodded. "Somewhat, some systems are down though and I'm not sure there's much material left for them to work with after all this time. The self-repair mechanisms should have kicked in already if there was."

"Improvise." Birch pointed to Jane's monitor, "It doesn't look like all of this is going to fix itself, and I wouldn't count on some angel of mercy coming to take us home, so we better get to work if we hope to survive."

Jane sighed and moved to DeSante's station. As they began their work Birch looked questioningly at Karla, she shook her head; no news yet from the surface. After an eternity of waiting these few moments should have seemed as nothing, and yet they appeared to be everything. The future- their future- hung on the events to come and the waiting seemed to make them weigh heavier still.

"I've got something!" Karla's voice shattered the silence and all faces turned to her. "Reports coming in show large developed areas, significant industrial development and infrastructure. Intact, but no sign of life," Birch moved quickly to Karla's monitor, "just buildings."

"Can you get a visual on that?" Birch barked. "Let's see what it looks like."

Karla nodded and punched in the code to enable the probe's visual display. The screen flickered and the tawny glow of the Martian sky merged with the dusty red of its rock and soil. As the probe shifted position structures and buildings came into view. All were covered with the same red coating, like rust eating away the very memory of human aspirations. It was lifeless. The buildings were dilapidated with holes that gaped like open wounds that would never heal; debris lay in the street, and a harsh wind blew the lifeless orange soil hard against the cowering buildings that would eventually succumb to its bullying.

This was the perfect picture of a ghost town of the old west, but it was a planet- a ghost planet. Something had gone terribly wrong here and, for the first time since this had all begun, Birch was scared. "Is it all like this?" Birch looked at Karla desperately. Her face was blanched; even in the light of the screen it was obvious.

She nodded, "It's all the same. There's nothing there." She paused for a moment, took a deep breath and tapped again at her console. The display flickered and changed. It was conclusive, this was a dead planet. For a moment everyone stood silent, looking at the screen, then desperately away. Birch's breath hissed through his lips as he hit the console. Whatever lives had been built on the rocky surface below were gone now and there was nothing left for them here.

"We're going on to Base One," Birch announced. The others looked dumbly at their commander; no one moved. In the stillness of the moment each face showed varying expressions of shock and grief. There seemed no room for hope.

Gray laughed bitterly. Her face was drained bloodless but her eyes were fiery. Birch recognized the signs: a storm was brewing. Jane Gray served as his co-pilot and had been as close to a friend as he had found for some years, but that was a long time ago and the strains of command had built barriers between them. They were adversaries now. Her soft, long black hair and dancing blue-grey eyes belied a bitter streak that ran deep into her soul. Birch had recognized that only recently, but it must have always been a part of her. Now he could feel her animosity rising toward him again.

"In a hurry to go, Major?" Jane's voice grew shrill as her seething rage let loose. "Well, hell can wait! I'm through with running! I'm through with doing everything wrong! We've got to stay!" The words were hurled like spears and their echo was left quivering in the wall. "That breaks all protocol," she rasped, "we can't go on until we find out what went wrong here first. If we do we risk getting there and finding ourselves in a worse position!"

"A worse position?" Birch spat the words back at her. "What exactly could be worse than this? If Base One is finished then we're all finished, so we may as well get over there and find out if it's our own funeral we mourn here today. I don't care what regulations you want to quote at me. We're not staying! Those old ideas are gone, they're dead, the people who wrote them are dead, but I'm alive and I'm here and since I command this mission then this is what we're going to do! If you still want to follow your rotting regulations then I'll be glad to leave you a space suit and an hours' worth of oxygen and you can stay here. Otherwise you better get used to the idea that you're going back to Earth, because that's where this ship is going."

Jane looked to her crewmates for support. DeSante shrugged in resignation, Lauren and Karla looked away. Jane rolled her eyes and moved back to her seat. "You're wrong," she hissed, "you've been wrong all along and now you're going to get us all killed for it."

"Maybe," Birch replied bitterly, "but who knows what's right. We've taken on a lot with this mission and in space you get a real perspective for what we really are. Look around, it's big out here, big and mean and looking to crush any puny attempt we might make to try and tame it. Maybe this is a punishment for our arrogance, for feeling that we could control this. Maybe we're already dead- we just don't know it yet. When we get to Earth, then we'll know if we're dead or not. Then we'll know the answer." He looked at Jane and the others. Soon they would all know.

# THREE

From silent solitude the ship returned. The offspring, battered by its experience, come home for comfort and healing. The familiar blue and green of water and earth glinted a welcome to the weary traveler as its engines slowly decelerated. The craft paused for a moment, as though reacquainting itself with family, before slipping into orbit and maintaining a position above its mother world.

The graceful movement of the ship belied the activity within, where each crew member was busy at their own task. Birch knew he had made the right decision, this was their chance to live and even now he could see in the faces of his crew that they, too, saw the truth in this. Now everyone busily worked at their stations to overcome whatever fate or providence might have planned for them. Despair had settled over them at Mars, but now being here and seeing home so close had made hope real again. Mars had looked dead with its barren, lifeless rock. Earth looked alive. From here nothing had changed.

Lieutenant DeSante again began the ritual he had performed at Mars. This was it, the first attempt to communicate with their last hope. An uneasy stillness fell on the room as everyone remained engaged in their own work, and yet distracted and listening for any response.

"Base One this is Hypnos III, code 4-1-9-9-3 Alpha Phase, respond, over." A faint hiss was the only answer. Birch shifted uneasily in his chair and, trying to ignore DeSante's droning voice, squinted at the screen before him. The readouts for the ship were pretty bad. Jane had been right about one thing, it looked like the only thing that could save them would be some kind of outside response. The heat shield was pretty badly compromised. It didn't look like it was even close to being able to sustain a reentry attempt; they would burn up in seconds. They needed an answer from earth or an answer to prayer, if there was any difference between the two.

"Hypnos III calling Base One, code 4-1-9-3-3 Alpha Phase, respond please." The hiss of dead radio waves remained the only answer. DeSante shrugged dejectedly, adjusted a few knobs and began again. The others had now stopped all pretense of work and watched intently as the process continued. The tension in the command module weighed like ballast as their hope sank. "Base One, respond please." DeSante pleaded. His voice had more than a hint of desperation. He turned to his commander.

"Have you tried all possible frequencies?" Birch barked. He knew the answer before the young man nodded his assent.

"Jane," he turned to her and was met with the scornful look he had expected, but there was also something deeper, more striking; a look of blind dejection and despair. It was plain that Jane knew she was right, that she had finally been proven in her view of him, but even she had realized that this one victory had only come at the final and utter defeat of everything, even their own lives.

"Jane," he repeated, "send out another probe. We need some idea of what we're working with down there. I want you and Lauren both to monitor it, pay particular attention to life sustainability. We may need Lauren's expertise yet. See what's happened to atmospheric and bio support systems. I want a contingency plan for whatever situation you find. Who knows what they've done to themselves."

He turned his attention again to DeSante, "Suit up. We've got some work to do outside."

Birch and the Lieutenant walked toward the airlock as the sound of the launching probe echoed through the ship. These were all desperation measures. Birch wasn't really sure how much of it was intelligent thought put to finding a solution, and how much was just keeping them all busy until the inevitable end. It wasn't a thought he liked to contemplate. He had always believed there were answers, however impossible they were. Whatever happened he couldn't imagine himself sitting on the deck listening to hymns while the ship went down. He was going to fight this, kicking, and screaming, and clawing all the way to the very bottom.

Birch and DeSante had reached the airlock. Silently they went through the routine of putting on their suits. They stood for a moment, pausing before pushing the button, raising the door to the icy chill of space. The door slowly ascended. The sunlight from without streamed through, rising with the level of the door like a tide of hope flooding the gray compartment. The only sound was that of their own breathing, confirming their tenuous existence. Finally the door was open. Birch squinted as he looked out and then back to DeSante, gesturing for him to follow as he left the ship.

For the next few minutes the two men struggled awkwardly with their own weightless bodies to reach their objective. Even the advantages of propulsion packs and hours of training hadn't made this more than a tolerable experience, and by the time they had reached the underside of the ship both Birch and DeSante's faces were wet with perspiration. Birch struggled to see through stinging eyes.

DeSante let out a low whistle, breaking the silence. "That's not good," he murmured.

Birch blinked his eyes clear and saw that DeSante had understated it. It was terrible. The heat shield was a mess! Some parts were missing in great clumps, other areas had perhaps only fractions of tiles missing here and there but even these smallest of breeches represented certain disaster.

"What can we do?" The young Lieutenant's voice cracked, almost pleading for hope.

Birch sighed as he surveyed the damage. "So farewell hope, and with hope farewell fear," he muttered softly before turning again to DeSante. "Pass me a spot joiner and some chewing gum. We've got to make this the mother of all fix up jobs. It's not going to be easy but there's still a chance we can do it. We'll have to fix and rearrange any tiles we can and then coat the rest in an emittance wash and see if that'll be enough to hold it together. From there it'll all be down to the flying, if I can take us in a perfect trajectory and hit that sweet spot just right, then we might make it."

DeSante looked dubiously at his commander, "That doesn't sound much of a chance. That wash was never made for this kind of repair. It's too big! Even if we can piece together some kind of shield I doubt it'll hold. There wouldn't be any room for error on the reentry either, it would take a perfect flight to even have any hope at all, and even then it probably still won't work."

Birch nodded. He was right. "I didn't say it was much of a chance," he muttered, "just a chance. I like that a whole lot better than no chance at all. Pass me that spot joiner and let's see what we can do."

The two men began their painstaking task, searching for flaws, repairing some, moving the remnants of some tiles to other locations, and coating everything in a thin layer of heat resistant wash. It seemed a hopeless task, seeking to withstand the fiery judgment of reentry with such a flimsy layer of protection. It was suicide. Any faults would be exposed and punished in the final destruction of them all. And so they worked, aware that no mistake could be made.

"Major," Jane's voice crackled through Birch's headset, "we have something to report on the probe."

"Good," Birch continued to inspect the tiles, "go ahead."

"Initial reports came back to indicate improved atmospheric content from when we left." Birch paused, lifting his head in surprise. "Air quality at low levels for foreign agents and good reports on water vapor purity. That's all we got though, the probe cut off suddenly with some kind of malfunction. Do we send out another one?"

"Yes," Birch started looking at the tiles again, "try another location though. We need to get a good idea of what the surface conditions are. That can help us pick a good area to land. It sounds good so far but we need to know more. Keep me informed."

"Okay," Jane's radio clicked off. Birch thought for a moment about what he had heard. The news was good but he tried not to hope again. He knew the return of hope meant the return of fear and as all of this was built on an impossible reentry it was a poor exchange. There was no real reason for hope. Earth might still be habitable, but if they couldn't get there it all meant nothing. Better to work in reality, there was a chance and that was what he worked toward, but there was no hope.

Their task continued tediously for a time until finally Birch looked at his oxygen gage. "We're a little on the low side, DeSante, let's head back. It'll take a few days to finish this and I want to run some simulations on what we're working with here." DeSante nodded and the two men started back to the airlock. As they were returning Jane's voice crackled again in Birch's headset.

"We've lost the second probe Major, same cause. We sent it to another area, but we got pretty much the same information as last time. It cut out at the same point as the last one. Do we send another?"

Birch grunted, "No, you don't just lose two probes like that. It looks like there's more to this planet than we first thought."

# FOUR

The work had been slow, but then they had to be sure. After checks and rechecks Birch was confident that the heat shield was as secure as it could ever be. He was far less confident that it was as secure as it needed to be. In continued simulations he had been unable to complete a single successful reentry; it was just too small a target to get it right. If he had thought it would make any difference he would have stayed longer to try and get at least one successful run-through, but somehow he didn't think that it would change the outcome. After so many practices he just wanted to do it. Perhaps the true chance of reality would outweigh the calculations of a computer. Anything could happen in reality and it was time to find out.

For a moment the command center was still, sitting in quiet reflection. Birch took one last look at Earth in its distant beauty; soon it would either embrace and accept them, or fling them away as a spurned child to burn up in its atmosphere.

Birch shifted in his seat and looked around. They were ready.

"Good, let's go. Okay everybody prepare for landing procedure, we're going home!" Birch strapped himself into his seat; the others hurriedly followed his example, reaching for their own belts and strapping themselves in. Jane hesitated for a moment, looking pointedly at Birch before snapping her own belt together. She turned and stared intently at the screen in front of her.

This part of the reentry process wasn't easy. Years of space exploration and satellite technology had left the Earth surrounded by a floating junkyard of metal fragments that posed a significant danger to any returning spacecraft. This legacy of early technologies had been a significant factor in the early development of Base Two on Mars as a launch pad for deep space missions before it became a fully-fledged colony. Now Jane was plotting a course through this dangerous hazard.

"We have a window of opportunity in seven minutes Major", she announced, "though it will be tight".

Birch punched a button in front of him and brought Jane's display up on his own screen. The red course line through the debris confirmed her conclusion. It would be tight, very tight, but then in his experience that had always been the case with Earth landings. Whatever had caused the improvement in the quality of Earth's atmosphere clearly hadn't gotten out this far since this was just as bad as he remembered it, maybe worse. Now he sighed quietly, steeling himself for the task ahead.

"Course confirmed", he announced, "begin command module separation sequence." Karla nodded and began tapping at the keyboard in front of her.

"Separation sequence begun", Karla stated evenly, "final separation in six seconds… five… four… three…" Birch could feel the sweat beading on his forehead, "two… one…" The sound of grinding metal and a sudden lurch to the left announced their separation. Karla confirmed it; "We're free of all moorings, separation complete".

The small ship, freed now from the burden of its fuel cells, arced gracefully under Birch's guidance and came into position, preparing for re-entry. He wiped the sweat from his eyes and glanced at the screen in front of him. Two minutes. He would have to hold position here until the window opened.

He balanced the controls effortlessly as the ship hovered expectantly. Birch looked hopefully down at his screen again, one minute forty. He tried not to think too much, this procedure always depended much more on instinct than thought. Too much thought could get you killed. His mind wasn't cooperating though. As he tried to empty his mind of all distracting thoughts, images of Earth and his hopes for it crowded in on him. This wasn't a good way to approach an Earth landing. Hope always gave birth to fear and fear to failure. He had to concentrate.

He looked at the screen again, fifty-three seconds. Glancing at the others he could see the strain in their faces, DeSante smiled nervously at him. Birch scowled and looked down at his screen again, twenty seconds. This wasn't working, he wasn't focused enough. Opening and closing his hands rhythmically Birch grabbed the control stick and stared unblinkingly at the screen before him. He had to be one with the ship, instinctive control. He watched the numbers change, eleven… ten…, concentrate, nine… eight…, think, seven… six…, he was ready now. Thoughts of failure or success were gone, all that remained was the task ahead, two… one… there it was. Their chance was here.

# FIVE

The tiny ship wove deftly through the debris, barely missing at times. Birch knew that size wasn't the issue, the small fragments could prove equally as fatal as any of those huge monoliths. In fact it was the small ones you really had to worry about. Anyone could dodge the big ones, they were slow, cumbersome mountains that were easy to see and avoid. No, it was the small ones you had to watch out for. They could tear a hole through your vital systems and leave you dead at the critical point of reentry, like a twig drifting aimlessly in the currents atop mighty Niagara Falls.

Computers and sensors helped. They laid out courses and planned trajectories, but they were only a part of the event, a small part. It still had a lot to do with instinct; you had to feel your way through. Now the display on Birch's console plotted the independent course of thousands of objects in Earth's orbit and displayed a safe path through them, but the task of navigating that course lay with Birch. Computers could deal with the theory; humanity had to deal with the reality.

Jane closely watched his progress on her own screen. As the co-pilot she had to be ready to take over instantly if, for any reason, the pilot should be incapacitated. She had to be as much involved in their progress as the pilot and the strain was showing on her face as she winced at another near miss. Birch's face showed no emotion. He stared unblinkingly at the screen, his only movement the sudden twist of his hand at the controls and the thoughtful chewing of his lower lip.

Another near miss, Jane flinched instinctively. The others sat stiffly, watching their own panels for any signs of damage, all the time hoping against it. Karla, her eyes closed and fists tightly clenched, sat rigidly in her seat. DeSante swallowed nervously and gripped the sides of his chair.

"We're almost through," Jane announced, the relief evident in her voice. Birch blinked twice and his head snapped back from the console. He glanced angrily at Jane and then back at his screen, trying to regain his concentration. His faced paled suddenly and he pulled wildly at the controls. The ship plunged instantly, just missing a fragment but moving into the path of another. Birch desperately wrestled with the controls and the ship veered away, but the crash and sudden lurching of the ship made it clear that it had not been a successful maneuver.

Karla screamed as smoke poured into the cockpit. Birch looked down at his display. They were clear of the debris field but now they had the atmosphere to deal with. Lights flashing on his screen pointed to a damaged wing, one fuel line ruptured, and a weakened hull. Miraculously what was left of their heat shield was untouched, but that was already critical enough. They were falling apart.

Birch glared at Jane. What he saw startled him. He had never seen her like that before. Her face was pale and her eyes were wide with fear. She had the look of death. "Jane," he shouted above the sound of alarms and the sputtering engines, "if we're going to do this I'll need your help. I've had to close one fuel line and I'm going to need you to balance the fuel flow to the engines and try to baby them enough to get us down, I'll have my hands full just trying to get us back into the atmosphere with this damaged wing, the ships responding pretty sluggishly now." Jane nodded mutely and began typing at her keyboard.

Birch looked again at his screen. The heat shield was already problem enough, but now he had to calculate in this new damage and hope it all held together long enough to get them down. His display panel was lit like a city skyline indicating the necessary repairs that they didn't have the time or material to effect; he ignored it. At best this was going to be a very uncomfortable ride; at worst it was going to be death.

If this had been a fairground roller-coaster this would have been the point at which the chain would have clicked you to the very brow of the hill and your eyes strained forward to glimpse what you both wanted and feared at the same time. The same mixture met Birch now, but with a far greater sense of calamity. This was the moment he had worked toward but it had a bitter taste. He ran his fingers through his graying black hair and, adjusting his position in his seat. He pulled the controls toward himself. "Here we go," he muttered and pushed the stick forward.

The ship dove steeply toward Earth, hurtling down, down. Birch twisted the controls, trying to adjust position for entry, but they were slow to respond. With so much damage to the ship it was hard to say that he had control at all. It was little better than a controlled freefall, suicide would have been a more accurate description. He glanced up for a brief last look at the others, and wished he hadn't. Karla was crying openly now, the others had a wretched look of despair. They knew their chances. Even Jane seemed limp, lifeless. Was she losing her battle to keep the engines running? If she was they were dead anyway. He turned to look at his own screen again; they had reached Earth's upper atmosphere.

A deafening noise engulfed the cabin and a red light seared Birch's eyes as he rigidly held the controls in position. For three minutes he sweated, prayed, and hoped as the ship passed into the atmosphere. His monitor flashed red as the temperature climbed critically on the ship's exterior. His arms throbbed painfully but held firm, protecting them from the searching heat.

Finally, like the birth of a new dawn, natural sunlight poured through the window and Birch's arms went limp in relief. They had made it, now all they had to do was crawl slowly home.

"Bad news Major," Jane's words hit him hard, "the strain of reentry was too much, we're losing the engines!" Birch struggled to recover, to overcome his exhaustion and the simple desire to just give up. He was crushed by the sudden rational belief that no matter how hard he tried he would lose. But he couldn't accept that. He hadn't done all of this for a pointless death. If life and existence meant anything they had to survive.

Birch forced his eyes to focus again on the screen before him. Jane was right, the engines were almost finished, and there wasn't much he could do about it. He could transfer power from non-critical functions. That wouldn't help much, still even that little might make a difference, he barked out the order.

DeSante and Lauren quickly moved to power down their consoles. Jane looked questioningly at Birch, he nodded and she too switched off her display. Karla was unconscious; there wasn't anything he could do about that. It would have to do.

"I'd better head for water," Birch announced to no one in particular, "we may need to use it for an emergency landing."

The engines sputtered, but continued. Their descent was steady, until moments later when they finally coughed and died. The sound of the wind whistling over the hull of the ship sounded like cruel laughter to Birch as they began a steep, sharp dive toward the surface. Someone screamed. It might have been Jane; it might even have been him. He struggled with the engine start-up sequence, it wasn't any good. He pulled back on the controls; they didn't function. The quiet blue waters were approaching. He braced for impact; maybe there wasn't any purpose to life after all, Birch thought to himself as black mists engulfed his mind.

# SIX

It was his favorite spot and in the peace of the moment Chief Keeper James Edwards contemplated the day ahead. It was early and only a few people had arrived to gape at his animals. He loved this place, this time of the day. A small hillock overlooking the ocean at the back of the compound, untouched by the commercial grasp of the financial backers with their plastic animals, souvenir stands, and food kiosks, this was where he sought reality. The people who came to the zoo only saw through a glass darkly. They saw the animals. They saw some approximation of their life poured into the smallest of containers for their personal enjoyment, but what they saw was no more real than the distorted plastic animals that leered at them along the concourse. Certainly those that were within the cages were animated, unlike their plastic counterparts, but they were not alive. They still breathed. They hungered. They ate, and the simple fulfillment of that basic desire remained a joy, but they did not live.

Technology had changed the face of zoos many years ago. No longer were they the high security prisons they once were. Cells and bars were replaced by the envirodome that used virtual reality to simulate their natural habitat so well that the animals weren't even aware of their captivity. They might be born, live, and die within the confines of their hundred-foot enclosure, constantly observed by the zoo's patrons, but never know it. To them life seemed to continue just as it should, but really it didn't continue at all. Every event, every experience, everything was an illusion, and so they lived a life of blissful non-existence. They were safe, protected, but nothing really happened. Born and raised in captivity from generation to generation it seemed that the essence of what it had been to be themselves had subtly dissolved under the unobservant eyes of their masters. Edwards knew he was the only one who could see it, but it was happening. There was no need to dream, enfeebled by their surroundings the animals had withered away until all that remained was what could be seen. It went no deeper. But that was fine, that's all that anyone wanted anyway, no one ever paid to see an animal's soul, and so the half-maddened pacing of the deranged beasts registered as little more to the observers than as an excellent photo-opportunity.

The peace he felt on this hilltop, with his back to a tree and his face toward the boundless ocean was always a precious, but short-lived, experience. Here fresh opportunities for life seemed to fill his lungs, but soon he would be amongst them again, another dot like so many others, all seemingly different, and yet fundamentally the same. He had watched the crowds watching the animals and wondered if there was really anything that separated them beyond the reinforced glass that protected the domes.

He looked at his watch, another five minutes he told himself as he settled back against the tree. Looking to the sky he watched the clouds drift silently past and caught a glimpse of birds, effortlessly floating on a stiff sea breeze. Birds were beautiful when they were free. They were meant to fly. There were birds at the zoo, beautiful and astonishing in their variety and colors, but none seemed to match the appearance of those scavenging gulls supported by the invisible force of air.

Closing his eyes for a moment he allowed his ears to enjoy the sound of the ocean and the cry of the gulls overhead. A breeze passed through the leaves and they rustled quietly.

A sudden harsh beeping noise jolted Edwards back from his reverie. He glared down at his watch, it was a signal from the office; he was needed there. Probably another parent complaining that the elephants were no longer on display because of the breeding program, he thought to himself. How many complaints had he had from parents who seemed to value their child's entertainment above the future of an endangered species? All they seemed to think about was that little Johnny would suffer some deep psychological damage if he didn't get to throw a peanut to Jumbo. Edwards sighed, got up, and slowly walked down the hill.

Passing the zoo's main entrance he continued beyond the enclosures to his office. The crowd was beginning to file through the turnstiles and the peaceful emptiness of early morning was being replaced with the crowded excitement of day.

Edwards walked into the small one-level building that housed his office. His secretary smiled nervously up at him from her desk as he entered. She looked worried. "You have an important visitor Mr. Edwards", she stated flatly. "A man from the DA, I sent him into your office".

Edwards sighed, Durus Authority men usually meant trouble one way or another. He wondered what form his trouble would take.

"Thank-you, Mrs. Grange", Edwards replied, moving toward the office door. He had played the DA game all his life. Most people did. You had to if you wanted to get anywhere. College entrance had required it, and so he had buried his doubts and taken the bitter pill. Against his worst fears it had seemed to work. His Faustian deal had only given him a good position in life, and had required nothing of him in exchange, until now at least. Every DA member knew how it worked. Once you made the deal it was a lifelong commitment, and if at any time the Authority should find a use for you they could make you do it, whatever it entailed. There was no room for questions, no room for excuses. You had signed your life over to them and it was theirs to take up and leave off whenever it was required.

Forcing an insincere smile Edwards opened the door and walked in to face a well-dressed, kindly looking older man. He was a little less than Edwards had expected. His actual contact with the DA in college had been minimal, and since then he had certainly not sought any opportunity to deal with them. From his limited experience most active DA men tended to be those who filled their jackets with muscle and their head with very little beyond rudimentary dogma. This must be the acceptable public face, he thought to himself as he greeted the man.

"Good morning sir, what can I do for you?" Edwards asked a little too jovially as he extended his hand toward the visitor. The man looked through him, a distant, distracted look in his eyes. He smiled thinly and finally glanced down at Edwards' outstretched hand, but did not shake it. For a moment Edwards stood dumbly, his hand frozen in a futile gesture of friendship, until the rejection registered. His face flushed and he hurried to sit behind his desk. Not so friendly after all, he mused bitterly, as he sat quietly waiting for the agent to speak.

For some time they both sat in silence, the old man smiling quietly to himself while Edwards squirmed nervously in his seat, this was not what he had expected from the DA at all.

"So", Edwards finally began, struggling for something to say to break the uncomfortable silence, "what brings you to our zoo today, I don't suppose you're here to see the monkeys, are you?" The man's smile remained constant.

"Mr. Edwards", he began evenly, "I am here to return you to the active agent list."

Edwards shuddered. This was it, what every inactive agent feared most, The Call. Edwards shrank instinctively behind his desk. "As of this moment," the man continued, "you are a fully authorized DA agent with all of the privileges and responsibilities that entails. Do you understand?"

Edwards sighed. He did. All too well he did. He had made the deal and now it was time to repay the debt. Edwards knew he would never have been Head Keeper without his DA background, it was that kind of job, but he had always hoped the nature of his work would have made a recall unlikely. The DA weren't exactly the zoological type, but now something about his work was useful to them. He couldn't imagine why they needed him, but he knew he was stuck. The DA had made his work possible and now, because of them, it didn't look like he would get the chance to do it for some time now.

"What's my assignment to be?" Edwards asked. His mind had been racing, trying to think of a way out; he knew there wasn't one. He didn't waste any effort arguing with the man. He didn't want the assignment, but he was wise enough to know that all DA decisions were non-negotiable. He might as well appear willing, even if he wasn't.

"Very good", the man responded in the same impassive tone. "This is a Code One mission. I have sealed orders for you direct from the governor; you are not to open these until you arrive at the location indicated on the datamaps which I have here for you. You will tell no one about any of this. You will leave tomorrow morning, details of the arrangements are in the datamaps. Do you have any questions?"

"Yes, I do." Edwards was sweating now. Code One missions were big. They were reserved for the most important assignments, global stuff, and so now one question thundered through his mind.

"Why me?" The question almost sounded accusatory, as though it must be a mistake, some clerical error. "Code One is a little out of my league you know. Have you seen my record? I've never handled anything like this."

"The Authority is aware of your record, Mr. Edwards, and everything else about you." For the first time a sharp steely edge crept into the old man's silky voice, seeming to threaten something else. The agent stared at him, his glassy eyes were coming into sharp focus, as though only now noticing him for the first time. Edwards shivered.

“You will understand,” he continued, “that our decision to assign you to this mission has been made with all of these issues being taken into consideration. It has been decided that you are the one for this assignment. We have every confidence in your ability." Edwards nodded doubtfully as the man stood up to leave, placing two hand sized metal boxes on the desk. "Many would envy you Agent Edwards," he continued, "this is history you are involved in, few get that chance."

Without further comment the old man left and Edwards was left to slump further down into his desk. For some time he just sat there, staring at the rectangle of sunlight that shone down from his slit of an office window. He thought wearily about the task ahead.

He looked at the datamap and felt a measure of relief as he noted that the destination indicated there wasn't more than three days travel down the coast. Even so he couldn't shake the feeling that somehow this was only going to be the beginning; Code One missions didn't usually consist of gentle rides down the coast. There was something more to this. He knew that. He wished he was on his hilltop again.

# SEVEN

Birch opened his eyes; at least he thought he did. All he could see was the darkness. There was nothing else. Where was he? More importantly, why was he alive? As the ship came down he had expected nothing but death; maybe this was death. No, it hurt too much. His whole body hurt and in the darkness the only thing that was truly real to him, the only thing he could even remotely comprehend was this throbbing, pounding reality. Somehow he was alive.

He closed his eyes to the darkness. He had to rest. If he was dead then it didn't matter anyway. He would rest.

His mind wandered. For a time he felt himself drifting, floating, but it didn't last long. Gravity was pulling against him. He was falling. For one moment he felt himself back on the ship, his feet pressed hard against the deck plates and his hands pulling at the controls to stop his momentum. He couldn't stop. Even now the bitter taste of despair was in his mouth. He should have died.

His eyes opened again, and Birch found himself lying on a grassy ridge beside a clear, blue ocean. A cloudless sky, a beaming, yellow sun, and a golden beach spread itself in harmonious panorama before him. Briefly he was lulled into the peace of the setting until he remembered the reality of his situation.

Sitting up he looked to see if any of the others had made it; he couldn't see them. In fact he couldn't see any sign of the ship at all. Squinting against the sun he scanned the horizon in all directions. The beach was beautiful, but behind him lay a large, wild looking wooded area, more of a jungle than woods. He was alone.

Struggling against the pain he rose to his feet but immediately doubled over again gasping. His hands rested on his knees until he could pull himself slowly again into a standing position. After a few minutes of this he finally took his first faltering steps. The movement seemed to help and his pain slowly subsided to a tolerable level. He was able to walk, but where should he go? To the ship, if he could figure out where it was. As his mind cleared this single fact troubled him most. Where was the ship? There should at least have been some wreckage or something. How did he end up here without any of the others and no ship? It made no sense.

Dutifully he searched the beach, but his first impression had been right. There was no sign of anything. Pain marked every step and now hunger and fatigue had brought him to a standstill. He was thirsty too, and the necessity of attending to these most basic bodily requirements overcame his need for answers. He would look again later, but for now his own survival had to take priority.

Food would be fairly plentiful in an area like this, he reasoned, but fresh water might be more of a problem. No source was immediately apparent. No rivers, no streams, no pools, no drinking water of any kind, just the vast expanse of undrinkable sea water splashing mockingly on the sand before him.

As he looked about only the dark, uninviting woods to his back seemed to offer any prospect of providing for this most urgent need. Finding it in there would be difficult though, he imagined. Judging by the climate and vegetation Birch knew that he was in a tropical environment and he shuddered at the thought of the dangers he would face there. He was no woodsman or jungle explorer. There was little choice though. He could skirt around the outside of the wooded area, hoping to find a river coming out to the ocean, but that could be hundreds of miles away, so he might as well face up to the task ahead.

Birch sighed and started toward the dark mass of trees. None of this made any sense to him. The last readings on the ship had indicated that they were coming down in the eastern Pacific, somewhere near the California coast. This place didn't fit that at all. Everything was wrong and it irritated him.

Birch reached the edge of the trees and paused for a final look back at the beach. There was still no trace of the others or the ship; he knew there wouldn't be. Suddenly, for the first time since he had awoken in this place, he felt truly alone. Turning again to face the dense foliage before him he limped forward, passing warily under the first branches and moving unsteadily into the dim light under the canopy of the tall trees.

The humidity hit Birch like a wall, making it hard for him to breathe. This was going to be difficult. The sound of unknown animals and the nauseating stench of strange plants increased his unease as he trudged further into the darkness. Somehow this was worse than he had expected. Dense foliage surrounded him. There was no path to follow and he had to tear at the thick leaves with his hands to make any progress at all. Soon his fingers were cut and bleeding. Ignoring the pain he continued pushing blindly forward, leaving a trail of bloody marks on the leaves as he passed.

Hours passed and desperation began to set in. He could find no water. He had lost his bearings and was no longer sure that he was continuing in the same direction. There had been a compass in the emergency kit on the ship, but with the ship somehow lost what good was that? The thought angered him and he pulled more wildly at the leaves ahead. Finally, overcome by exhaustion, he sat with his hands pressed against his pant legs, trying to stem the steady trickle of blood that oozed from his shaking palms.

Birch panted hard, his efforts had nearly exhausted him, and he was sure he couldn't go much further without sleep. He thought gloomily about his situation. It wasn't good. It was dumb, he had been foolish to think he could handle this alone and now he was lost. Still, it had been his only chance, what else could he do? Now he was thirstier and weaker than ever and he wondered if he would be able to carry on at all.

The branches high above him blocked the sun, but he was aware that the gloomy light they permitted was now dimming. Nightfall was approaching. If he was going to have to spend the night here he had better at least find a safe spot in a tree somewhere to sleep.

He found a suitable place nearby and climbed slowly above the jungle floor. The bark bit into his raw hands and Birch chewed at his lower lip to dull the pain. Finally he settled on a branch and prepared to sleep.

In his exhausted state the strange animal sounds that had once seemed so alarming now almost lulled him to sleep. He felt his eyes slowly closing. Despite it all he was at peace as he drowsily listened to the unfamiliar world that surrounded him. Drifting pleasantly in his thoughts he gradually became aware that there was something familiar, something important in what he heard. Mixed among the animal calls was the distant but distinct sound of flowing water!

Instantly Birch sat up, fully awake now. He strained to listen for the sound; yes he could hear it somewhere in the distance. He had been right. There was water here! A deep feeling of gratitude and relief filled him as he leaned once more against the tree. He would have to wait until morning to taste it (he would end up lost or eaten if he tried to find it in the dark) but he had found water! He was going to make it after all!

Birch settled against his tree again and tried to sleep. His throat was dry. The sound of water, that had been so welcome to him just moments ago, tormented him now. When sleep finally did come it was uneasy, fitful, and troubled by dark, formless dreams. His dreams seemed real, more real than anything yet, and so when in sleep he felt a strange sensation, a crawling, creeping along his arm, he had instinctively pulled back.

He awoke. Sweat dripped from his face. Naturally he looked where his arm had been lying, trying to see what was there. He could see nothing; it was too dark to see much.

He leaned warily against the tree again; perhaps he had dreamed it after all, but it had seemed so real and the touch still seemed to linger on his skin. He glanced again where his arm had been resting, then, turning to look over his other shoulder, flinched as a pair of green, slitted eyes glared back at him. It was a large constrictor snake at a distance of less than two feet. Unthinkingly he lunged backwards and lost his balance. For a moment he felt himself frozen in time, teetering between security and falling. Then he toppled over and crashed to the jungle floor.

As he landed Birch felt his leg crack. He knew he had broken it. The pain left him gasping and he doubled over, but somehow after a moment's writhing agony his mind cleared enough to warn him of his danger. He had to act quickly. Inspecting his wounds he saw that his legs, arms and hands were all now bleeding. His hands had been bleeding all day, and as he thought about it he recognized that he had been leaving a bloody trail through the trees for hours. Probably even now something was smelling him out, and this fresh blood letting would just add to his danger. Unless he did something soon he was meat, he was sure of that.

If he could get to the water he might have a chance. He could wash off the blood and lose the scent. The only problem, of course, was finding his way in this darkness with a broken leg that dangled uselessly beneath him. "No problem. This'll be easy," he muttered sarcastically to himself as he searched for a branch to support his weight.

Finally, finding a suitable stick, Birch turned his attention again to the sound of the water. It seemed to be coming from somewhere behind him. He turned and began to hobble toward it. His progress was painfully slow. His hands, cut and bleeding, couldn't hold his makeshift crutch well enough to support his body, and he was constantly forced to stop and rest. Even so, after an hour the sound of the water was much louder. He was getting close.

Sweat poured down Birch's face. His muscles felt as though they had given their last fragment of energy, but by force of will he carried on.

Then suddenly he stopped. Had he heard a noise? Yes, and it sounded big as it moved through the undergrowth. Birch feared the worst, a tiger perhaps. Whatever it was it was about a hundred yards behind him and closing in.

Birch looked ahead desperately, hoping to see the water. He was disappointed. He could tell by the sound that the river was close now, but still he couldn't see it. How could he escape? He couldn't climb a tree in his condition, and it probably wouldn't do any good anyway. He had one chance. Maybe he could still lose the beast in the water if only he could get there.

Birch struggled forward. He could only see a few feet ahead but he limped blindly on, hoping to find the river. It sounded very loud now. The shape behind was coming closer though, and he kept glancing back desperately, dreading what he might see.

Then he saw them, two glowing, yellow eyes- big, round, and hungry. Birch turned to face them, still edging all the while toward the sound of the flowing water. He knew enough about wild animals to believe that facing one head-on would be better than running. He couldn't run anyway so he hoped that was true.

The dark mass padded toward him, and then stopped. What was it doing, sizing him up? Waiting to pounce? Birch hesitated, what should he do? The animal was less than thirty feet away; he could almost smell its fetid breath. He did the only thing that came to his desperate mind in that moment of panic. Balancing on one leg he lifted his stick into the air and threw it as hard as he could between its eyes. It hit! The beast yelped and turned away. Birch took his chance and tried to run, but his leg buckled beneath his own weight and he screamed at the pain as he lunged forward. Glancing over his shoulder he saw the glowing eyes facing him again. They were coming fast!

At that instant Birch stumbled through the dense foliage to find himself standing atop a muddy bank that plunged steeply into darkness. The river roared somewhere below. Without a moment's pause Birch hurled himself down, sliding recklessly toward the water.

Above, the dark shadow emerged, paused, blinked for a moment and leaped down after him.

Birch careered down the slope, scraping and gouging his flesh as he spun and tossed over the rough ground. Finally he slammed into a rock at the bottom of the bank and, shaking his head groggily, looked up to see the beast bounding after him. Birch groaned wearily and clawed his way through the shallows toward what he hoped would be the safety of deeper waters.

The dark shape still wasn't clearly visible, but he could see it pawing at the bank, waiting, perhaps thinking about its next move. Birch didn't wait. He spread his arms out wide to embrace the safety of the water and swam for the bank at the other side.

The current in the river was strong but he eventually made it to the other shore. Pulling at the grass on the bank he heaved himself out and lay panting there. Exhaustion overcame him. His mind was blank and he stared vacantly into the river. Finally, remembering his thirst, he reached down and brought the water up to his mouth in his cupped hands. It tasted strange but it was fresh and he wasn't in the mood for asking too many questions. If he didn't drink he was going to die anyway, so he might as well take the risk. He drank greedily then collapsed, lying motionless save for the uneasy rhythm of his panting breath.

He lay like this for some time, his energy spent, just staring at his reflection as it moved in the water. There was something strange about it though. It didn't seem quite in sync with him. It moved with him, but not quite with him. Like when an old movie got messed up and the talking didn't quite match the lip movement. He shook his head; it was just another thing to make his aching head hurt. He was surrounded by questions. The ship, his crew, this whole place with its Californian jungle, and now a reflection that couldn't quite keep up with him- it all made his head hurt. This was the future, he had expected change, but what he had seen left him feeling as though he had fallen through time and into his own unique hell.

The sound of a branch snapping behind him brought Birch back from his brooding thoughts. Turning quickly he caught his breath. The tiger had found him. It stalked toward him, its teeth bared and its yellow eyes burning. It was only ten feet away now.

Birch had been on his stomach looking down into the water, but he quickly flipped over to face the approaching beast. Grabbing a stone from the bank he flung it between its eyes. The tiger flinched but did not turn away this time. Instead the blow only seemed to make it angrier and more ferocious. It growled fiercely and Birch slid slowly backwards on his arms. He knew this was it. The tiger only had to pounce. He couldn't get away this time.

It didn't pounce. Perhaps the big cat wanted to play with its food, like an alley cat with a tiny, tormented mouse. For whatever reason, the tiger simply drew closer. So close that its breath was in Birch's face. He flinched involuntarily and crawled back. His eyes closed. He expected nothing now but a flash of teeth and the sudden pain of death.

It didn't happen. The warm breath stopped and when Birch dared to open his eyes again he saw the animal stood stock still, completely motionless before him. Birch stared. The tiger's yellow eyes had lost their fiery hue and now just stared emptily back at him. What had happened? All sound had stopped. The birds, the animals, even the river were all silent now. Moving carefully away from the motionless tiger he looked down at the water. It was perfectly still, frozen in mid-flow, like on a hard winter's day.

In this silent stillness the sudden hissing and the plume of billowing smoke that accompanied it sounded like thunder and smelled like sulfur. Birch stared, perplexed, as a door formed in the cloud of smoke.

He had found his way out, perhaps to greater dangers, or perhaps to paradise. He didn't know, but he figured either way he was going to get some answers, and that was all he really wanted. He walked through the door.

# EIGHT

Birch had escaped, but the flash of pure, white light that engulfed him seared his eyes and blinded him. The world was spinning. In that instant he felt his consciousness flung away, hurled from his body across the room in a disjointed out-of-body experience. Through lidless eyes he seemed to see himself far below, prostrate on an operating table, the object of fevered activity. The impression lasted only a moment and seemed more like a jarring of his senses than reality.

Just as suddenly he was a part of his own body again. He struggled to move his arms. They were sluggish and heavy. Strong hands quickly pinned them in place. Distantly he heard voices, but what they said was indistinct and meant nothing to him. He did feel danger. He wanted to escape but he couldn't move. It wasn't only those iron hands that held him in place. Within his own mind there was a struggle that he couldn't seem to win. He tried, but he couldn't succeed. Now he was rooted in place as unknown fears rushed upon him. They engulfed him. He was drowning as he slipped below the surface of his consciousness.

***

Edwards squinted as he looked up to the sun and again at his directional finder. He had made good progress so far, but by his calculations it would still take him another couple of hours to get there. Before sundown he hoped. He had to make it before sundown. He needed to hurry.

His little vehicle sputtered across the imposing wooded landscape, little more than a tiny mechanical germ infecting these natural surroundings. The sense of awe was inevitable and fear was its natural companion. This should have been a convoy expedition. Nobody came out here alone, but the secret had been too great to share. He didn't like it at all. He had been instructed to leave without telling anyone, and now he was forced to make the treacherous trip south alone. It might have been easier if he at least had known the secret himself.

The trees swayed silently around him, moved by an unseen wind. Edwards glanced anxiously about. Only the trees were moving, nothing else. The lush green of the forest oppressed him. It should have been beautiful, but it wasn't. Long ago it might have been different, but now all of this only seemed to mask a deeper malignancy. Fear lived here with the common understanding that good had not thrived. Edwards, for all his experience and knowledge, was wary and watchful. He was equipped and ready to respond if he had to, but on a single vehicle mission like this the best thing to do was run. Speed was his best defense.

The shadowy forest swept quickly by. Edwards pushed down on the accelerator and sent his vehicle crashing and bumping faster along the rutted forest trail.

Through the reinforced glass windows he watched the miles pass by. Seeing the wild country set him thinking about his zoo and the animals in it. This was where they belonged, out here in reality, not caged in their perfectly protected non-existent environment. Could they ever adapt though? Would they survive? Probably not. Real life was hard. That was something you had to learn one slap at a time, from birth to death, and no crash course could ever teach you that. Send them out here and reality would come to them in one brief, life-ending moment of education. That's how life deals with the weak and the different. They would die, but perhaps they would still be better off anyway.

Edwards stooped again to consult his datamap. He was getting close now. Another half an hour or so and he would be there. He didn't look forward to what he would find when he arrived. If it hadn't been for the nearly setting sun he might have even slowed his pace to at least delay the inevitable. Instead he pushed on, certain in the knowledge that things would never be the same. It hadn't been much of a life up to now, but it was his and it was all that he had known. Though he had hated the past his mind now clung to it as an evaporating security. Things were definitely going to change.

***

Birch lay uncomfortably on a hard pallet on the concrete floor. For a time all he could do was gaze weakly up at the ceiling. The slightest movement of his breath and the occasional blinking of his eyes were the only visible signs of life he could manage. He had expected pain but there was none. He felt weak, but he felt well.

Raising his head slightly he surveyed his surroundings. It was a stark gray room. No windows and no furniture, save for the hard pallet he lay upon. He was alone. For some time he lay passively, trying to pull his thoughts together in the shattered remnants of his mind. Somehow he had survived his jungle experience, but he couldn't make any sense of it.

Earth obviously was not dead, as they had feared, but everything in it seemed like a mad jumble to him. It all raised more questions than it answered. Why hadn't anyone answered their approach messages? What had the probe's strange readings on earth's condition meant, and why had those probes all been destroyed before any final transmission could get through? Were they hiding something? If so what? His head ached.

At least they were back. They had made it. Birch wondered

what sort of reception they would get. He wondered if anyone remembered them. Had people forgotten their mission, their place in history? He wondered if they would remember what they had done, or attempted to do, for them. It seemed unlikely to him that anyone would remember anything. After all, time changes everything. The grandest plans and the greatest achievements, or even the darkest failures, all become the driest history that would eventually shrivel up and blow away on the winds of change. Every generation would forget the past a little more until nothing was left. He was glad. Most things were better forgotten anyway.

His mind cleared. He had to find the others, get back with his crew and figure out what to do. Slowly he climbed to his feet. His legs were weak and shaky, but, despite everything, unhurt. This surprised him. His jungle exploring had seemed too real to be a dream but too dreamlike to be real. Whatever had happened didn't last.

On unsteady legs he explored his limited surroundings. There wasn't much. In the gloomy light his fingers felt along the smooth, featureless walls for anything that might tell him more, but there was nothing. Not the slightest crack was to be found. Larger, more necessary features were strangely absent. Windows, and even doors, were missing. As he stared at the blank walls he wondered how he had gotten in here or how he would ever get out. Perhaps he wasn't meant to. After the vast infinity of space his existence had been reduced to this one tiny room. It seemed a fitting comment on what their greatest plans had come to. He couldn't let it rest at that though, so he kept searching, feeling for a way out. There had to be something. He kept looking.

# NINE

The hollow hiss of a door opening and the thud of heavy boots on concrete awoke Birch from a fitful sleep. It seemed only a moment ago that his fruitless search for escape had ended. Exhaustion had overcome him and he had fallen into a troubled sleep, but now the sudden realization that something was happening had him quickly crawling to his feet. Before he could stand strong hands had grabbed him and were pushing him through the door. He marveled for a moment that such an opening could exist in the formerly featureless walls of his cell.

He was pushed down a long, gray corridor as bleak and empty as the room he had left. His mind raced. What were they doing? Where were they going? What would happen to him now? The guards' expressionless faces gave no clue as to what was in store. He knew human nature well enough to be worried. The history books were filled with examples of how these things were done. People were not convenient. They were an embarrassment, a threat, or perhaps just an annoyance, and so they were removed. Were they now an embarrassment or a threat? It was hard to know what this new world would make of them.

The image of Russia's last Tsar came to mind, a living relic of a bygone age, an anachronism with no purpose, pulled from his bed in the middle of the night and shot. His family had gone with him. All murdered against a blank stone wall. Progress was brutal. Was it to be the same for them?

Birch shuddered. He dragged his feet and tried to look back to see if his crew were following behind, but the guards pushed him forward and he almost fell. Finally they stopped before a blank wall, as plain as all the others, but with a click a door appeared, just as it had in his cell. He was marched through.

The room they entered was large and warmly furnished. The echo of their footsteps immediately died, smothered in the thick carpeting that covered the floor. The papered walls were covered with beautifully framed artwork depicting classically dull pastoral scenes. Vases of colorful flowers gave off a fresh perfumed scent that contrasted sharply with the sterile air that Birch had grown so accustomed to. A fire in a polished brass fireplace glowed dully. It was all too normal.

Five plush chairs were arranged before a long, impressive mahogany table. The three uniformed men sitting behind the table looked up as Birch was thrust into the room and roughly shoved into one of the chairs. A moment later the door hissed again as Jane and the others were dragged in and deposited in their seats. Birch might have smiled despite himself, his crew had survived the crash too, but his anger wouldn't let him.

He rose to his feet. He should have been afraid. He needed to be cautious, but here finally was something real, something he could deal with, a physical manifestation of all their troubles over all those years in the form of these three uniformed bureaucrats sitting behind their fancy wooden table. All his pent up rage let loose. All his seething anger at the injustices since their return and the whole sordid mission that had led them here boiled over.

"I don't know how you normally do things around here," Birch spat, waving his finger in the face of the central of the three uniformed figures, "but torture and forced imprisonment are not accepted practice where we come from! I demand that we be released and that we meet with people from your civilian government, not a trumped up little military tribunal like this." Birch had more to say but a burly guard had grabbed him by the shoulders and was pulling him back to his seat. Birch's anger burned hotter and he lashed out at the man.

"You're not pushing me around again," he hissed and lunged at him, pushing him into the wall. The guard was surprised and caught off balance, but quickly recovered and pushed back. Birch's tired legs buckled and, as he fell backward, the guard landed a thundering punch on his shoulder that sent him reeling.

In an instant DeSante and Jane were up, ready to assist, but the other guards were prepared for that and pushed them forcefully back into their chairs. Birch meanwhile was pinned to the wall, held up by his shoulders like a butterfly on a specimen board.

"Let him down," sighed the man at the center of the table. He shook his head in disgust, "We don't want to see our guest damaged in any way, even though his conduct might seem to warrant it." Birch was thrust back into his chair and left gasping.

"Now," the man continued, "perhaps we can continue in a more civilized manner. I'm sure that you have many questions, and that is only natural. We also have questions for you, and I'm sure that you would agree that this too is natural.

"Let us first get the formalities out of the way. I am Area Commander Gibbs, to my right is Unit Commander Konik and on my left is Special Operative Edwards." Both men nodded curtly. "We are here to help you. Now, from the remains of your ship we understand that you were part of the Hypnos program, Hypnos III to be exact. Our records are rather incomplete on those missions. They are little more than ancient history to us now and all that we have left are old dusty records. From those reports I would conclude that you are the commanding officer; Lt. Colonel Ratliff." He was looking at Birch.

Birch shook his head, "No, I'm not. He didn't make it."

Jane shot a sharp glance in his direction and he ran his

fingers nervously through his hair.

"Oh. Then you must be Major Thomas Birch acting as Commander of the mission I presume." Birch nodded, but he didn't like the way he had emphasized the word 'acting'. "That is disappointing," Commander Gibbs continued, "I dislike having to deal with inferiors." Birch's eyes narrowed. He glared angrily at the man. "I mean nothing personal by that, Major," he continued, "so do not be offended. I merely meant that to us a ship like yours is like an exciting time capsule and we had hoped to have a full compliment of crewmembers in order to learn more from you. Your commanding officer would have been of particular interest to us, but we are also interested in learning from all of you."

"You mention that our ship is like a time capsule," Jane interrupted, "but what I can't understand is how we actually managed to survive reentry at all. No offense to our pilot," she shot a meaningful glance at Birch, "but the position we were in seemed like one that no one could survive, yet here we are. It's like a miracle."

"I'm afraid it is not nearly as spectacular as that, just a matter of technology. We have inherited a good deal of this type of thing and we put it to any beneficial use we can find for it. What you experienced was merely a device once used in the airline industry when that form of transportation was so popular. I believe the system was developed in response to the high levels of fatality and accidents involved in that means of travel. The concept is quite simple really; a protective cocoon of energy surrounded your ship until it could safely land, and here you are, ready to be born into a new life in our modern world. We are very glad that you made it."

"Yeah, nice sounding words," Birch barked, "but I haven't seen any evidence of those 'good feelings' you talk about. We've seen nothing but bad treatment since we've been here so why should we believe you want to help us now?" Jane shot another sharp glance over to Birch but he was too busy glaring at Gibbs to notice.

Gibbs's smile was unaffected. "Let me first stress that we recognize that our first meeting has indeed been far from ideal," his voice was smooth and apologetic. "We can understand any resentment you might feel at your treatment; it was not our intention that you should have to spend time under confinement, but circumstances made it necessary. With a more typical subject the process would have been better, perhaps even enjoyable. You see, we thought it best to allow you to serve your time for adjustment and stage-one quarantine in the envirodome. The protection of that safe environment would have allowed you to recover while enjoying whatever dreams your heart could imagine- like a holiday for the mind."

Birch snorted.

"We are aware of the problems that developed with one of you in there," Gibbs continued, "but some of you, apparently, are not ready for paradise." He was looking at Birch. "As a precaution we had to remove you all from the domes and place you in more conventional confinement. Technical difficulties aside, I think you will find that we have been looking out for your best interests."

"Those technical difficulties, as you describe them, almost killed me," Birch remarked sourly.

"Perhaps," the man replied, "but I hardly need to point out that you were in fact brought out alive. We saved you from yourself, Major. You might even say that you now owe your life to us twice. You should be thankful and enjoy our hospitality."

Birch scowled moodily and rubbed his arms where he had been pinned to the wall. "You've got a lot to learn about hospitality," he remarked bitterly.

Gibbs raised an eyebrow and shook his head. "Look," he announced tersely, "we're all military personnel here. Orders are orders. Everything has been done for your good. Deal with it, Major."

Birch fumed and stared unblinkingly at Gibbs. Jane shifted uneasily in her chair, looked at the others and then back at Gibbs. "I think," she started, "that we all understand your reasoning. We accept that you did what you thought was best, what we really want to know now, though, is what happens next. What does the future hold for us?"

The tension broke. The commander's clouded expression cleared as he looked over to Jane. "Yes of course," he smiled. His well-oiled voice regained its easy tone. "You want to know what will happen to you and that is why we have brought you here. We have wonderful things in store for you; yes, wonderful things!"

Birch eyed Gibbs suspiciously. Something in his manner reminded him of a third-rate salesman looking to close the deal. Birch wasn't buying, only he doubted whether he really had any choice. All he could do was listen and hope that things really were as wonderful as Gibbs wanted them to believe.

# TEN

Birch walked into the comfortable lounge and sat down. He was alone. Through the glass of the skylight he could see stray clouds drifting across a brilliant blue sky and he leaned back to watch. This was what he had missed; the sky, the sun; his sun. He wanted to be out there, to feel the heat and smell the breeze, but he knew it was impossible, at least for now. The vaccination program they had been forced to endure was finally complete but another week had been scheduled for observation to watch for any complications. All they could do now was wait.

As he watched the sky his thoughts turned again to their situation and things ahead. There were still a lot of unanswered questions. They had only been told so much at that first meeting all those weeks ago, and since then no further explanations had been offered. They had been promised wonderful things in their future, but they still knew nothing about it. Birch guessed that Gibbs' idea of a wonderful future wasn't the same as his. At least their living conditions had improved. Since their removal from containment they at least were allowed to wander through their part of the base with relative freedom.

Birch's attempts at exploring had proven the limits of this freedom. In their part of the compound they could go anywhere, but the doors out were guarded, ostensibly for their own protection. Whether from viral infections or a more obvious physical threat was never made clear, but they were safe. That was the important thing. They were safe.

The locked doors didn't surprise Birch, but it did irritate him. They still knew so little and he was aware that the answers to everything were behind those guarded doors. For now all he could do was wait for the scheduled meeting tonight to find out what information their hosts decided to impart. He doubted somehow that it would be much.

His thoughts were interrupted with a jolt as Karla touched his shoulder lightly. He hadn't seen her come in. She smiled and sat in the space next to him. Pushing her hair behind her ears she curled her feet under her and looked over at Birch, then, following his gaze, through the glass ceiling.

"It is beautiful isn't it, sir," she murmured softly, "it's hard to believe from here that it can be so hard up there." Birch nodded. "I guess," she continued, "it's often that way. Things look beautiful and inviting until you see them up close."

"You're not regretting it, are you?" Birch asked. Karla was the youngest member of the crew, at twenty-two he thought too young for a mission like theirs, but then he never had any say over that.

"No," she replied airily, "life is about experiences and I'm glad I experienced this. It's amazing to be here now, and I can hardly wait to get out there in it all. It'll be like walking in the world for the first time, and the first thing I'll do is to take off my shoes and run through the grass. Just feeling that grass on my feet will be amazing."

Birch smiled ironically, "I'm sure we've all got things we're looking forward to," he added dryly, "though I don't think that shoe thing would conform to the usual standards of dress for NASA personnel."

She smiled back coyly. Despite her apparent good mood he somehow wasn't convinced that Karla was as happy as she wanted him to believe. Why should she be? He felt the same way himself. He was less worried about their immediate future now, but he still had no idea about what lay ahead. He knew that these people had some plans for them, but they weren't telling them what they were.

Karla started to get up. "It's almost lunchtime, sir," she announced, "are you coming down to the dining hall?" Birch grimaced; the memory of breakfast was fresh in his mind, but he was hungry enough to try again.

"I guess I'll risk it," he smiled wanly as he rose to his feet, "I'm not convinced though that this food isn't some kind of cruel torture designed to break us down. I'm sure there must be something in the Geneva Convention about this kind of thing." Karla's smile was her only response.

Birch munched his way mechanically through another insipid meal. Of course there was a reason for it. Part of the process of acclimatizing them to their new surroundings was to introduce foodstuffs gradually. They were being cautious. According to Edwards the modern diet could be injurious to their system if it was adopted suddenly. Time might have changed things in subtle, but important ways, and so the food they had been given was basic, safe, and quite disgusting.

The others ate quietly. No one seemed in the mood for conversation. They had spent the past few weeks speculating on their future and there seemed to be nothing left to say. Jane wasn't there; presumably she had made the wisest choice and missed the meal altogether. Birch pushed his half-empty plate to one side and got up, muttering a good-bye to the others, he left the dining hall and headed for his room.

He spent the rest of the day in his quarters. Time passed slowly and his mind continued to race through all the possibilities and what he could do about them. He hated being manipulated like this, not knowing what was happening, and having no choice in it anyway. He felt like a monkey on a chain. There wasn't much he could do just now, but he was determined to find out as much as he could and be prepared for a time when he could take control of his own life again. Whatever those wonderful things were that Gibbs had spoken of, Birch was sure it was for their benefit rather than his. For now though all he could do was just wait and see.

The slow afternoon gave way to evening and finally the time for the meeting arrived. Birch made his way to the lounge again. The others were already there, except for Karla. Birch sat down and looked across at Jane. She raised an eyebrow in recognition.

"Well," Birch began, "I guess today we find out what all this is about. At least we can hope so. It seems like they enjoy keeping us in the dark about what they plan to do with us. I've got a bad feeling about it."

"It's just traditional military secrecy, Major," Jane responded coolly. "There's nothing sinister or mysterious about that. It's no different to anything we've done during our own service. People who don't need to know things aren't told. Obviously whatever they have in mind for us they don't think we need to know, at least not yet. I can't say I blame them, after all, on your orders we haven't told them anything about our own mission. If we can't trust them why should they trust us?"

"Shut-up, Jane," Birch snapped. He bit his lip hard. Sometimes Jane's eternal desire to contradict him on all points went too far. This was important and all she could think of was her petty little point scoring system. He was sure there was more to this than military secrecy, and he was certain Jane felt that too. They had all seen the way important questions had been evaded in that first meeting. They had been told the absolute minimum. They still didn't know exactly where they were, they had been told very little about how life had changed in the world during their absence, they hadn't even been told exactly what year it was, and, most worrying of all, was their unwillingness to speak about their future. This went far beyond military secrets and Jane knew it too. This was a clear attempt to keep them in the dark; the question was, why.

Karla waved to the others as she took a seat, soon after the uniformed figures of Konik and Edwards appeared. Commander Konik moved brusquely to the podium at the far end of the room and the lights dimmed. Through the skylight Birch could see the silent stars in the darkened sky above.

"I'm sure you've all been interested to know what the next stage of your return to Earth will be," Konik intoned. Quite an understatement, Birch thought to himself. "I have the duty of telling you what this next stage will be and to guide you on it," Konik's voice was gruff, that of a military commander rather than the smooth, reassuring tones of Gibbs. "Special Operative Edwards and I have been assigned to assist you and see that you complete this task successfully.

"You are in a privileged position. When Area Commander Gibbs promised you wonderful things in your future he didn't exaggerate. The orders which came through for you are exceptional. You asked to see a representative of our civilian government at the last meeting. Well, you'll get that and more. You've been called back east for a personal conference with the head of the government. I don't expect you realize how rare an opportunity this is, but President Michaels is a very private man and rarely receives personal visitors."

"I take it he hasn't had much trouble with re-election then," Birch remarked sourly. Konik ignored the comment and continued.

"It will be Special Operative Edwards' and my duty to make sure that you get to that meeting safely. I'm not going to lie to you, there will be some obstacles on our way, but you are all military personnel and you'll be able to handle it. We will be accompanied by twenty of my best men, and S.O. Edwards is an expert on the terrain and wildlife in the area so you will be well protected."

Birch looked over at the others; even Jane looked worried by this revelation. "Wait a minute," Birch interrupted, "I've heard you say what we're going to be doing, but I haven't heard anyone asking what we think about all this. You can't expect us to go on some mission with you into some unknown danger without us having any say in it."

Konik smiled coolly. "That is exactly what is expected of

you, Major Birch. Orders are to be obeyed, not questioned. You are all still registered on the active personnel list, even after all these years. I believe that was the standard policy with all the Hypnos missions since it was known that cryogenic storage would greatly increase your lifespan. That means that President Michaels, as the commander of the military, does have the power to give you orders. I'm sure things haven't changed that much since your time."

Birch glowered at Commander Konik but said nothing. He was right. What could he say?

"Now, I need to show you some of the mission details," Konik continued. A map appeared on the wall next to him. Birch recognized it as North America. So he had been right, he was sure they had come down somewhere off the west-coast of America, but the people in this place had always been evasive about their location. "We are in this area," Konik was gesturing toward the north-western part of the country but was not being specific, "and we need to reach Washington in the next couple of months before the weather breaks. It's late August now so it should be easily achieved if we keep to schedule."

Jane leaned forward in her chair, "A couple of months?" her voice was incredulous. "How were you planning to get there, walking?"

“Maybe we're following the Oregon Trail,” Birch added. “Haven't you guys ever heard of flying? It's a lot quicker and you get free peanuts!”

Konik shrugged, "Flight is not permitted, nor is it safe. Our world today is a different place to the one you once knew. There are those who want to bring change, disorder, and chaos, through their violent actions. Their success has been significant. Many flights have been shot down and you are far too important for us to risk in that way. We've got a better chance getting through on land. Maybe then you can help change all this.”

“Doesn't sound like much has changed,” Birch muttered.

"Same old world and same old hopes that maybe tomorrow we'll all change and make things better. We never will. We tried to do our bit in our own time. It doesn't seem like it helped much."

"Why don't you use that device you used to save us when we landed?" DeSante asked. "Wouldn't that work?" He had sat quietly through the meeting to this point, but like the others he wanted an easier option.

"That won't work at all," Konik's voice was growing impatient, as though he was explaining the obvious to group of dim children. "The field would guide the ship, but it can't protect it from everything they could shoot at it. If we were shot to pieces the wreckage would be guided safely to where we wanted to go, but since we all would be dead it would hardly help, would it?"

"Why not by sea?" Birch suggested.

Konik sighed. "Mines. We might get through, but again it's a high risk. We don't want to lose you."

"That doesn't sound very encouraging," Jane commented. "Just how much control do you actually have? It sounds like you're pretty badly pinned down if you can't even run flights or ships without fear of losing them. How did things get this bad?"

"I'm sure it all seems very confusing to you at this point," Konik continued with deliberate evenness, "but you should understand that we are fighting to make this world a better place, and it's working too. Our air, our water, our soil are all cleaner. We have eliminated hunger and ignorance in our domain. We are more content than your grasping generation ever was. We don't see the need to run across this earth like ants on a hill seeking happiness in things we might gain. We are at war, but it's as much a war of the mind as the body, and in both causes we will win."

"A soldier and a philosopher," Birch remarked ironically, "quite a combination."

"Maybe that sounds stupid to you, Major Birch," Konik

snapped, "but we're working to try and make a perfect world here, which is a lot more than anyone of your generation tried to do. But then I wouldn't expect any of you to understand something like that."

"I guess it all depends on your interpretation of perfection doesn't it," Birch responded. "Who decides?"

Konik shook his head silently and glared at Birch menacingly. "I see I'm not the only philosopher here," his voice was angry now. "Don't criticize what you don't understand, Major Birch." The map behind him dissolved and Commander Konik turned to face the others.

"We need to begin our journey as soon as possible and so we'll be leaving in two days at 0600 hours. That will give you one day to prepare yourself in any way you see fit. Special Operative Edwards and I will see you then." Konik nodded to Edwards and they both left without further comment.

# ELEVEN

The long night had finally passed. The light of morning came as a relief to Birch. Sleep had not come, but he was ready for the day. He pulled himself out of bed and moved toward the shower. Turning the faucet he stepped under the scalding water and tried to stretch away the aches from a night of sleepless thought.

This was the day. Finally, after so many countless years he was going to be back out there, back in the world. He might almost have been happy if it wasn't for his worries about those unspecified dangers Commander Konik had spoken of at the meeting two days ago. As it was Birch had a strange sense of dread about the future. He and the others had placed so much hope in the future. It had been their only hope. Would it all end in disappointment, as their mission had?

Birch's thoughts drifted back to those glory days when he had been selected as the second-in-command on the mission, a Hypnos mission. They had been the great hope for the next stage of human development, and they had all been treated accordingly. In the year before the launch they had been global celebrities with television appearances, autograph signings, even action figures. It had all gotten out of control. NASA had encouraged it all because of funding issues. Lt. Colonel Ratliff, the mission's commanding officer, had lapped it all up. He was a natural at it, but Birch had hated every minute of it, the way important events had been trivialized. Ratliff had done it all with gusto, even appearing on game shows. "The celebrity-guest-panelist-from-the-stars" they had termed him. The thought of it even now brought an involuntary snigger from Birch. For some time now it had been impossible for him to think of Ratliff with anything more than feelings of anger and sadness, but the memory of his proud commander on those shows provoked quite a different response.

Despite it all Birch had loved being a Hypnos astronaut. The Hypnos missions were all about the future of mankind, and while he had never counted himself a true believer in any such cause, he at least had the feeling that he was doing something significant.

Their mission had been a simple one, but filled with danger. It had also called for the greatest personal sacrifice. They were the exploration vanguard, sent out to probe the distant parts of space and find suitable locations to colonize. No longer was humanity content to await the exhaustion of mother-world's resources. What had happened for Mars would be taken to the wider stage and humanity would spread its influence across the stars.

The crew of the Hypnos III had been just one of many scattered through space. They all had the same goal, to seek out suitable locations, to begin the process of terraforming and building across the galaxy. They were the pioneers, the beginning. Engineers and colonists would come after them to finish the work. Then the people would come and benefit from the seed they had planted. This alone was enough to make the Hypnos missions heroic, but it was the personal cost of the missions that gave them their status.

The Hypnos crews all signed up with the certain knowledge that, because of the distances involved and the time it would take, they would never see any of their friends or loved-ones again. When they awoke from cryogenic sleep their former lives would be dead. Everything they had known would be dead. That was the irony and heroism of the Hypnos missions, that, while they were working for the future of humanity, they lost their own. It was a high price and it had made them legends.

Birch had always known that it was worth it. There hadn't been much for him to regret leaving behind anyway. But more than that; he saw it as a chance to do something. There was so little left to do anymore. Everything on earth had already been categorized, pasteurized, and sanitized by the time he had been born, and so the only thing left to do was sleep, eat, and breathe. The only way to escape it was to escape earth altogether. He had snatched at the chance. This was history. Going out to find hospitable planets suitable for colonization, they were the Lewis and Clark of their generation. They would discover and prepare for all that would follow.

The funny thing was that things hadn't turned out like that. For all the hopes of freedom and achievement, they found instead that their mission led only to failure. Orders were orders, but circumstances had had him by the throat from the very beginning. Things hadn't gone to plan. Now here he was back on earth feeling much less than the historical hero.

Whatever had happened here in their absence, he had the feeling that the Hypnos missions hadn't made any difference at all. From what he could tell it seemed like nobody even remembered them. This came as both a disappointment and a relief to Birch.

The hot water continued to pour from the showerhead and Birch held his neck under the scalding stream. Today was the future and he knew that once he stepped out from here his life would take on a new and unknown course, a course that he, again, seemed to have little control over. He hesitated, wanting to stay at this point a moment longer before he stepped out into the new beginning. Finally Birch sighed and turned the faucet off. He was ready.

Stepping out of the shower, Birch dried himself and walked into the other room. He took his new uniform out of the closet. They were all now officially members of the new Earth Armed Forces, all because they had continued to be listed as active service personnel during their years of cryogenic storage. That made them answerable to whatever head of government there was now. Birch looked again at his crisp new uniform, then at his old NASA flight suit in all its tattered glory. It was old now, but it had represented something he had believed in. The new uniform meant nothing to him; even the American flag had gone, replaced by some world emblem. Carefully he folded the old uniform and placed it at the bottom of his backpack; he wasn't ready to lose that small part of his history yet. He put his new uniform on and walked out the door.

Breakfast was a quiet, hurried affair. The food was up to its usual low standard, but everyone was too engrossed in their own thoughts to pass comment. Birch's hands were sweating and his stomach was churning, even before he had taken a bite of food.

Having forced himself to eat as much as he could stomach he got up and went back to his room to pick up his bag before heading toward the lounge to wait for Konik and Edwards. He was the first one there. He sat in a nearby chair and leaned back to look up at the sky. It was peaceful.

Jane and DeSante entered together; they had been talking but fell silent at the sight of Birch. Jane frowned for a moment and moved to sit on the other side of the room. DeSante followed and sat beside her, waiting in uncomfortable silence. Karla and Lauren entered next; their conversation was loud and filled with hope for the future. Their excited voices broke the tension of the room. Soon the others joined in and were talking about their favorite earth memories and their own dreams of a golden promise ahead. Birch listened thoughtfully, but his own thoughts were less optimistic.

The room fell silent again a few minutes later as Konik and Edwards entered. Konik glanced around at each of them, fixing his piercing eyes briefly on each person there. "Well," here we are," he observed abruptly. "I see you're ready so let's go." He motioned to the door and turned to leave. Birch and the others rose slowly to their feet and followed him.

Commander Konik strode through the doorway. His heavy footsteps echoed as he lead the group down a gray corridor much like the one Birch had been dragged through weeks ago. The memory of that early treatment was still raw in his mind and it had left Birch unwilling to trust anyone in this place. Things had gotten better since then, but all their smooth explanations had done nothing to dull his anger. In Birch's mind they had all been treated no better than animals and he resented that. That simple fact had made him question all of their claims. He could see that the others were more placated by the explanations, but he wasn't.

They came to a large set of windowless double doors. Konik pushed a few buttons on a number-pad and they slid open. The sudden humidity of the outside air made Birch gasp. He felt the heat hit him like a wall. Natural sunlight streamed across his face as he moved through the doorway. He covered his eyes against the glare. The warmth on his skin felt strange, but good.

As his eyes adjusted to the light Birch was struck by the greenness of the grass, of the trees, and of everything that surrounded him. It had been so long since he had seen it in its natural setting that it came as a startling revelation, like a visual 1492 that shocked his senses and shook his assumptions. He hadn't really thought about it before, but now it seemed that green was the color of life. He was surrounded by life, no longer on that cold, dead, gray rock of a planet, or encased in a sterile steel ship in space. He was back. He had missed it, and now he stood among it all and breathed in the humid air hungrily. It smelled good to him. It seemed as though he had had a lifetime of filtered, purified, artificial air and now the taste of reality was delicious.

He looked across to the others, they all were as glad as he was to be here. For a time all any of them could do was simply gaze at the world around them. Karla was carrying her shoes and walking barefoot through the grass. He should have been angry with her, but all he could do was laugh and shake his head. She smiled back coyly, "Sorry sir," she apologized, "I couldn't help myself." Birch raised his eyebrows in mock disgust.

"Consider yourself on report, Lieutenant," Birch replied with a wry smile. Somehow her action seemed to fit the moment, but he could never admit that. "There's something about this place," he murmured. "Just walking out here can make you feel something different."

Karla nodded. "It's home," she whispered.

Commander Konik glared impatiently back at the group. "Let's move it," he barked. "We are working under a tight schedule here and we need to make it to our first base camp by nightfall." He turned and strode on. Birch and the others hurried to catch up, following him around the corner and into a large fenced compound.

The compound housed a number of strange looking, rust-spotted vehicles and various other odd devices that Birch didn't recognize. He couldn't tell if they were elaborate weapons or tools of some kind. Other items were more clearly for military purpose. One vehicle that caught Birch's attention had a powerful looking missile launch system housed behind its cabin. Others had strange looking devices that Birch couldn't even begin to guess at their function. It certainly appeared that this base was well equipped and was prepared for either assault or defense. If this world was working toward perfection, as Commander Konik had suggested, this stockpile of weapons was an indication of just how far they had to go. You didn't need guns like this in paradise.

Konik was making his way toward a line of six ugly looking vehicles. Most of them had the appearance of squat boxes on fat-tired wheels. Painted in camouflage colors, they were obviously troop carriers and it didn't look to Birch like they had been built for comfort or speed. Each was topped with an impressive looking gun turret and had other, strange looking weapons systems built into their bodywork. These were foll-owed by one of the missile launching vehicles.

As impressive as all of this seemed, instead of making Birch and the others feel more secure it increased their worry. What was out there that warranted these elaborate defense systems? Whatever it was, they were going out to face it on a three thousand mile journey under unknown conditions. The thought was not a comforting one.

A group of soldiers standing next to the vehicles came to attention as the Commander approached. Konik signaled to the sergeant, who came to his side and saluted. "All vehicles are prepared according to your orders, sir," the sergeant announced. Konik nodded curtly.

"Very good, Sergeant," he snapped. "Let's get moving!" He turned to them and gestured sharply toward the line of trucks. Birch and the others clambered into their assigned vehicles. He noted that, like the proverbial eggs, they were not being carried in one basket. This was a natural enough precaution, he supposed, but it also seemed like another unsettling indic-ation that the threat of a successful attack must have been very real. Birch himself was assigned to the second vehicle with Lauren and, like the others, they shared the transport with some of the soldiers who were protecting them. Konik and Edwards were in the lead vehicle, the third held Jane, and the fourth DeSante and Karla, the missile launcher was behind them, and the sergeant and more troops were in the final carrier at the rear.

Six engines sputtered to life. The convoy slowly trundled through the rusted iron gates that opened to allow them through. As Birch looked at the sparse walls of the truck and felt the hard seat beneath him he thought of the three thousand miles ahead and sighed. This was what he had been waiting for.

# TWELVE

Birch watched as the base slowly disappeared behind them. He was glad to see it go, they had been caged there, but now as he looked back he felt an odd twinge of regret. It wasn't the secure walls they were leaving or the uncertain future they were facing that troubled him so much as the feeling that he was leaving something behind. He had hated the past and all that it had represented, and yet he still knew that he was losing something valuable. While he was still in his cell the past had been alive, now it was truly dead. This was the future. He should have been glad, he tried to convince himself that he was, and yet as they drove on he strained to look back.

Soon the trucks had turned onto a dirt road. The dust from their tires flew up and he lost sight of the distant buildings in the hazy cloud that streamed behind them. Birch turned to look forward.

For many miles the terrain was flat and featureless. A few scattered buildings and sparse settlements were the only evidence of human habitation, apart from the road itself. All was green and lush. It was pleasant, but somehow sterile, like the manufactured vista of a well-groomed golf course.

Green plains eventually gave way to tree covered hills. The manicured grasses slowly grew more ragged at the edges as nature took a firmer hold on their surroundings. Tall pines, stripped of all their lower foliage, surrounded the road and the late afternoon sunlight cast their long shadows across the convoy. The change in scenery did not change the impression. Still he marveled at the beauty, but he also recognized the practical purpose here. The cleared trees provided no cover for any assailant, and so increased the security of the road. This was a society that had adapted to war. The form of the land had been altered for their own protection, he was sure of that.

It was early evening when they arrived at the compound of the first base camp. The structure was similar to the one they had left earlier that day, though on a much smaller scale. Birch estimated it to be manned by a troop of maybe twenty or thirty soldiers, and their demeanor was calm enough to convince him that they were still some distance from any imminent danger. He also learned that this was just one of a network of bases dotted across the country. On the surface this seemed another sign of strength, but Birch found it troubling. Clearly there was a potent opposition out there to warrant this level of security, despite Konik's explanations.

That first night of their journey was a peaceful one. The rooms of the outpost were small and had to be shared, but as Birch lay on his bunk listening to the deeper breathing of his sleeping comrades he couldn't help but be thankful that so far things had been better than he had expected. Their progress had been slow, but unimpeded by any obvious danger. If they could maintain that sort of speed for the rest of the journey their travel would be finished long before the two month timeframe Konik had spoken of. It was this fact, though, more than anything that warned him of the future. For Konik's estimated travel time to be correct, Birch imagined, tough times must lie ahead.

Their experience over the next few days was less encouraging. There were no obvious threats to the convoy, but their speed slowed further and their caution grew. Birch also noted from the position of the sun that they were not travelling directly eastward, but often veered off to the south, the north, or even back west for hours at a time. "One step forward, two steps backwards," Birch mused bitterly. "At this rate we'll be lucky to get there in two months!"

As the days passed their creeping progress became marked by perceptible changes around them. Gradually the woods had grown thicker and wilder, while the bases they stopped at became ever more tightly secured. Each day Birch expected some more visible sign of fighting, but found none. It seemed to him that they must have been getting closer to danger, but all the indications were subtle.

He particularly noted that the attitude of the troops at each base became progressively harder and less open as they traveled eastward. That first night the troops had warmly welcomed their convoy. Some of them clearly knew the soldiers serving in their compliment, and the atmosphere had almost seemed jovial as they had greeted one another. But now the greetings were terse and guarded. They eyed their arrival suspiciously, before finally admitting them to the compound. In spite of all this there was still no visible sign of fighting and Birch began to wonder about the nature of the conflict. Konik and the other soldiers, when asked, remained obstinately silent on the subject.

By the fifteenth day the trees had begun to thin out, and they could see a range of mountains rising in the distance. As they progressed so the mountain's grandeur grew to fill the horizon; they were approaching the Rockies. Their escorts had been careful to say nothing about their location and he wondered where exactly they were, probably somewhere between Colorado and Canada judging by the climate, but that wasn't very helpful.

Their gradual approach slowly revealed a structure at the base of the mountain range. Small at first against the imposing rock-face backdrop, it seemed to increase to impressive proportions as they drew nearer. This was the largest base they had visited yet, greater even than the one they had been held at initially.

As gun turrets, thick walls, and missile placements came into focus Birch let out a low whistle. The sight alone of the firepower on display here should have been enough to deter any attack.

It was dusk when they finally reached the foot of the mountains. A glowing array of lights had begun appearing in the windows of the base. This was not a fearful little outpost hidden away from enemy eyes; rather it was a City on a Hill that proudly made its presence known.

The process of gaining entry was more stringent than ever. Even Commander Konik's input seemed to have little effect in speeding things up this time.

Once inside Birch was struck again by the sheer size of it all. It was a small town surrounded by high walls. Like the castles of old it was self-sufficient, but unlike those castles, it could bring deadly force to bear against any who dared to attack it. Soldiers and gleaming weapons were visible everywhere as patrols were formed and dispersed into the gathering gloom of night. It was in strange contrast to the peaceful countryside about them. Outside there had been a tranquil beauty that seemed hard to explain. Despite himself Birch had been affected by it. Inside, the industry of destruction seemed hard at work preparing for some unknown task. It was a stark difference. They were getting close to the danger now, he was sure of that. He had observed everything but there was still no way to tell what they were fighting.

For the next few days they waited in solitude. No explanation was provided; they merely waited. They were confined to their quarters and saw nothing of the life happening around them. They were back in that same bubble they had lived in before their pilgrimage to Washington had begun. Obviously they were being shielded, but it was unclear if they were being kept safe from potential dangers or just isolated from outside information.

Birch chafed at the confinement. He paced and seethed, but, as so often in the past, seemed powerless to do anything other than follow the stronger currents that life had set out for him. He tried to learn what he could by probing the guards who brought food, but they offered nothing. They were in the dark save for the one piece of information Konik saw fit to divulge to them, that this base was the last bastion of civilization they would see for a while. The "base hopping" that had gotten them this far was coming to an end. The outposts beyond this point were scattered and scarce staging posts in a wild country. They would be on their own.

"You should enjoy your beds, and your food, and your life while you're here!" Konik had snapped after Birch's hounding questions about their confinement and delay at the base. "It may be the last chance you get to enjoy any of them!" he added menacingly.

# THIRTEEN

Finally on the fifth night they were ready to leave. Birch and the others had been warned not to go to bed, but to be dressed and ready to go, because they would be driving out with one of the night patrols.

By midnight the guards had brought them down to the courtyard where the convoy was forming. Their original six vehicles were joined by two of the lighter, sleeker transports used by the troops of the base in their night excursions to the surrounding area. These were to be their escort on the first part of the journey over the mountains.

Birch was anxious for the opportunity to see what was happening out there. He was tired of all this creeping and dodging. No more running. His whole life seemed to be running and he was done with it. If they were heading into danger he just wanted get on with it now and face it down, or fall trying.

The line of trucks slipped through the fortress gates and moved cautiously toward the mountain range. If Birch had hoped for any immediate evidence of the nature of the conflict or the enemy they faced he was disappointed as they traveled in complete darkness. He hadn't noticed before, all of their travelling had been by daylight, but there were no headlights on any of their trucks. The drivers appeared to rely on a night-vision screen in the cab. All other illumination was extinguished. It was a perfect cover for a night patrol, but unhelpful for Birch's purpose. For a time he strained for any sight of what they were doing, but eventually he gave up in frustration and went to sleep.

When he awoke sunlight from the early dawn was streaming through the windows of the truck. They were traveling on the memory of a mountain road that was neither smooth, nor well maintained. The winding line of decaying asphalt seemed to cling to the side of the mountain by little more than force of habit; crumbling bits of road came free and slid into the valley below as they passed over it.

The still mountain forest hardly seemed to notice their presence as they trundled through it. The scene was beautiful as tall pines stretched up into an unblemished blue sky. Occasionally, as they turned a corner on the road, a clearing would open up before them, presenting a panoramic view of the countryside below. All the while Birch was struck by the greenness and the strong impression that there was something good about it all.

The convoy slowed almost to a crawl. Looking ahead Birch saw that the night patrol was still leading them; they had not returned to the base. He wasn't sure if that had any special significance, but he thought it likely to indicate that there was some danger here that might require their extra protection. Their slowing speed heightened his suspicions, perhaps they had observed the enemy nearby. He stared out of the window, straining for any sign of them, but there seemed to be nothing. The road ahead looked as clear as ever. The only discernable difference was their speed. They were hardly moving.

For the next few hours they crawled along the mountain road. Birch grew more impatient and irritable. Their speed alone would have been maddening to him, but his greater concern was with the cause. He suspected they were at a dangerous point, but no one was telling them anything. He had tried to speak with the troops in his truck, but as always he found them reserved and unwilling to answer.

"Maybe I should get out and push," he suggested sourly.

No one answered. His words meant nothing to them. All Birch could do was turn to his window again and watch as each mile crept slowly by.

He strummed his fingers against the arm of his seat in quiet irritation as the truck weaved and bounced along the rutted trail. The road seemed to be getting worse. Birch's mood darkened as they hit another deep hole that sent him bouncing against the wall. He couldn't imagine travelling much further like this. He sighed as he looked over at Lauren. She was sitting serenely, apparently unaffected by the bumpy terrain.

Konik's decision to put Lauren in Birch's truck had only added to his annoyance at the situation. There was something cold and distant about Lauren and his time riding with her had been awkward. She was an outsider, not NASA personnel, but a contractor brought in for research purposes and because of her knowledge of the terraforming process. She still functioned as a regular crewmember, but Birch was always aware that she was working from a different agenda to the rest of them. He never quite trusted her for that reason. He and the others were all NASA. That meant that they embraced the ideals that the organization stood for, basically human expansion and self-improvement through the space program. Lauren was Industry, and that meant basically that she was working for money.

Birch personally knew of instances where Industry crewmembers had cut across NASA orders to achieve their own individual goals. You didn't hear about it in the press, of course, their coexistent relationship was too important to air their grievances publically, but NASA had complained bitterly in private about these occurrences. Their money had been too vital to do much more than that. Instead of removing all Industry crewmembers, as Birch thought they should, NASA instead placed more safeguards on their training and left the system largely unchanged. To Birch this was just tinkering at the edges of the problem and he knew that the decision was an economic one, not a smart one. He had decided to watch any Industry crewmember he ever worked with very closely.

Lauren hadn't done much to disprove Birch's fears since he had known her, but then she hadn't done much to prove them either. She was a strangely neutral person. There wasn't anything specific he could say against her, but she was always so quiet and observant, like she was watching for something to use against you later. Apart from Karla, Lauren rarely had anything to say to anyone on any subject except work related issues. Even Karla, for all their talks together, didn't really know her well. Lauren was that type of person. Birch felt it was because there was something she wanted to hide, something that might have an important bearing on their mission.

Birch grimaced as the truck plunged into another massive pothole that lifted him more than a foot above his seat and left him grabbing wildly to save himself the indignity of falling to the floor. It was a rough patch of road and as they lurched from hole to hole he was irritated to see the unaltered, calm expressions on the faces of his fellow passengers. They didn't seem to care. Lauren had that same even look she always wore, and the three soldiers who shared the compartment were all staring out of the window, as though this was part of the blandest of routines. A fine set they'd make, Birch thought to himself; maybe I should make them into a set of bookends or something.

Sighing he turned to watch the countryside rolling slowly past his window. He guessed there must have been at least another three hours of daylight left and that meant another three hours of this type of travel. Birch rubbed his face in his hands; this inactivity was going to kill him. Lifting his head his eyes caught Lauren looking at him; she smiled and turned again to her own window. Birch followed her gaze. Outside, the green of the vegetation was still as fresh and surprising as ever, but its beauty, he knew, only masked the danger.

The truck came to a sudden stop a moment later and Birch moved to the front to see what was happening. Finally something was happening. The driver growled and ordered him to his seat, but Birch could see through the windshield that Konik and Edwards had gotten out and were talking with some of the soldiers from the lead truck. They were staring intently down at the road in front of their vehicle. Commander Konik stooped to look more closely before casting anxious glances in all directions. Edwards and another soldier both had binoculars out and were scanning the horizon in all directions. All of them were deep in discussion.

Birch moved to the door at the back of the truck, but one of the soldiers rose quickly from his seat and blocked his way. "You can't leave without permission," the soldier droned dutifully, but Birch had already pushed past the man's outstretched arm, turned the handle, and jumped through the open door before he could react. The guard grabbed at his shirt, but Birch was too quick and was already striding toward Konik and Edwards.

Konik frowned as Birch approached, but before the angry Major could reach them the guard from the truck had caught him again and was grabbing at his arm. Birch pushed back against his attacker, and in the struggle they both fell to the ground. Konik watched with distaste as the two men struggled and rolled in the dirt. He signaled for the soldier to release Birch and to return to the truck. Konik's frown deepened as Birch advanced again toward them.

"What is it with you, Konik?" Birch snapped as he reached the men. "We haven't had a second of freedom since we've been here and now you won’t even let us out of the truck without permission. Are we travelling as your President's guests or prisoners?"

Konik smiled humorlessly, "You're not our prisoners," he replied, "it's all for your protection. Would you let a two year old child walk the city streets alone? Of course not! You protect the innocent and the foolish. We’re doing the same for you. You're not used to life in our world and you don't know the dangers that exist here. There are a lot of things you don't understand and we can't have you getting yourselves killed through ignorance. Let me demonstrate." He pointed to the spot in front of the lead truck that they had been examining a moment before. "What do you see here Major?"

Birch looked closely, but could see nothing but an unremarkable looking section of the dirt and rock trail that could only loosely be described as a road. He shrugged.

"You see, Major," Konik continued, "while you see nothing here, we see death and destruction." He bent down at the spot and gently scooped away some of the dirt, revealing a small wire just below the surface. "Death, Major Birch," Konik added dramatically, "that is what you would face in this world without our help, and it is all those precautions that you seem to hate so much that are keeping you alive."

"So you've got landmines, or something like them," Birch replied sourly. I've dealt with things like that before. Why don't you just let us help? You yourself said that we were still on the active service list; it's time you started treating us like it rather than just as cargo. We want to know the truth. If we're your prisoners then just lock us up and stop pretending, but if we really are your fellow soldiers then treat us like it and give us something to do."

Birch had had enough and decided to play a risky game with Konik. So far they hadn't been told much about anything in this world, so he was going to poke at the stiff Commander a bit and see how he reacted. Maybe he would let something slip. Maybe things would change. Birch was perfectly aware that the result could be bad, like goading an attack dog. He saw that tendency in Konik and knew that both he and his crew could find their position significantly worse if he played this badly. They were, after all, totally under Konik's guidance here, and Birch keenly felt their vulnerability. Even so, Birch instinctively believed that they were not in any real danger from Konik and his men, at least for yet. At the moment it seemed that they were a valued commodity, and so long as that lasted he would be able to keep the pressure on Konik and see if they could find the truth behind all of this. It might even be true that Konik was being honest, that they really were just trying to protect them, but Birch wasn't ready to accept that. He trusted no one.

It seemed as though Birch's plan might already be working. Konik's face registered surprise and disgust before quickly turning red. A vein on his temple stood out noticeably and his jaw clenched tightly as he seemed to struggle with his rage. He looked ready to lash out at Birch when Special Operative Edwards' calm voice quietly interrupted.

"I think the Major has a point," Edwards' tone was soft and cool, in stark contrast to the hard expression of both Birch and Konik. At these words Konik's head snapped back and he turned and glared at his own man. Edwards seemed to falter for a moment under the wilting frown of his commander. "What I mean is," Edwards' voice wavered slightly but he stood firm, "I mean that we should tell them more. How can we expect them to trust us if we don't trust them? Put yourself in their position, would you trust us after we left you in the dark about everything?"

"You know our orders," Konik replied in a hard unyielding voice. "You've been out of the service for a while but even you must know that 'no' means no, especially when authorized by the President himself. You'd do well to keep that in mind, Operative Edwards. These are matters of global security."

"I'm not talking about matters of global security Commander, and you know it," Edwards' voice was gaining strength. "All I'm talking about is letting these people know about the world they now live in. It's a matter of their own personal security."

"He's right!" Birch interrupted angrily. "It's about time you told us something. I'm not some puppet to be dangled on a string for whatever you've got in mind. You've got to tell us what's going on."

"Will you shut up, Birch!" Edwards' words erupted like bursting, hot lava and stunned Birch into silence. "This isn't your decision, Major and you have no say here."

Edwards turned his attention again to Konik. "It's my professional opinion that it's important for us to tell these people about certain changes in life since their time on Earth. We're taking them out here into the wilderness and, as you say, they have no idea about the dangers that face them here. How can you expect them to survive without any knowledge of what they face? Just looking at this mine here, this close to the base, that must tell you that they're active and bold right now. This isn't going to be easy and we'll need every member of the team to get us through this."

Konik nodded thoughtfully, his face had cooled, but his jaw was still clenched, and his features had the look of flint. "Maybe you have a point Edwards," he snapped, "but let me remind you that security is a primary concern here and there is a procedure for you to bring up such points. There is a time and a place for these things," he looked pointedly at Birch and then back at Edwards. "This is not it! The mere fact that you are a member of the Durus Authority and that you are the Special Operative on this mission does not give you some special immunity. Let me spell it out to you early on; if I think you're not working with the team then I can make your life very unpleasant, both now and when we get back. I rank you Edwards and I can pull a lot of strings in Washington, don't you forget that! You DA men seem to think a lot of yourselves, but out here in the wilds it's all up to the regular military, we're the ones who do it out here every day."

Birch watched to see Edwards' reaction. He had already learned more in the last five minutes than he had in the whole time since their return to earth. To his surprise Edwards seemed unfazed by his commander's words. In fact there seemed to be something in them which strengthened him. He visibly straightened as he calmly looked Konik in the eye.

"You're right about us DA men," Edwards replied in an icy voice. A wicked smile played across his face. "We do think a lot of ourselves. We have good reason to. You might be the military commander on this mission, Konik, but in matters relating to the mission I hold superiority, this is one of those times. I will say it again more clearly so that you can understand. It is my conclusion that the mission will be served best if the Major, and his crew, are made more aware of their situation, so long as it doesn't cut across areas of global security. There is no need for discussion, I am the ranking officer on this issue and if you disagree then I suggest that you take it up with the DA when we arrive in Washington."

Konik's face paled for a moment, then blushed an even deeper crimson than before. Edwards had pushed the Commander much further than Birch had thought wise, and he watched now for the result. Konik didn't explode, as Birch had expected, but instead he glared powerlessly at the Special Operative for a moment with violent eyes, his great hands clasping and unclasping at air.

"Great," Konik's voice was stiff with rage, "but your little seminar on the state of the world will have to wait, unless you plan to camp on this bomb to do it. I personally don't want to stick around to thank the people that left this little gift, so let's move it. Get back in your truck, Birch, it's time to go." He stormed away into his own vehicle and Edwards followed after him. Birch guessed that Special Operative Edwards had made a new enemy that day.

# FOURTEEN

Streams of golden light flowed from the setting sun. Birch covered his eyes to take in his surroundings. To the west the delicate ribbons of cloud had changed to a fiery red and he remembered the old saying about a red sky at night bringing delight. That was supposed to promise a good day to follow, weather-wise anyway. He wasn't sure he could count on that, but this moment was worth it without any guarantees for the future.

Despite the beauty something troubled him. He couldn't explain it, but at that moment he felt an uneasiness that had nothing to do with all the uncertainties they faced. Somehow looking at that sky, the same sky he had remembered, he felt a continuity stretching out from his own time to this. Perhaps, after all, some things would never change and could never be escaped, no matter how long you ran.

It had been over two hours since they had stopped to examine the booby-trapped road and the sunlight was quickly turning to gloom. The line of trucks cast long shadows as they moved slowly off the dirt trail. They pulled into a circular formation and rattled to a halt. The hiss of brakes was quickly followed by the sound of doors banging open and hurried footsteps. The soldiers in Birch's own truck had already leapt out and were busily removing equipment from the roof. All of this was done in perfect silence, as though all their training had made communication unnecessary. It was obviously a routine and they performed it expertly.

As Birch and Lauren clambered out the back of the truck their silent work continued. It seemed as though they were erecting some sort of equipment all around the little circle of vehicles. Birch reasoned that it must have been some sort of protection device or monitoring equipment. The question still remained unanswered though, protection from what? Whatever it was it clearly had the power to motivate these men to action, for they were working at a manic pace thrusting what looked like small sticks into the ground at short intervals in a ring around the trucks. Others were working on the weapons or taking more equipment out of the back of the vehicles. Even Konik and Edwards had joined in the work. Birch and the others could only watch awkwardly, unsure of what they should do.

"I don't like this," DeSante muttered. "What do you think they're trying to keep out with all that stuff?"

Birch shrugged, "I don't know, but I'd like to find out. Maybe they're trying to keep us in, or something out, either way I don't think we'll be told anything about it unless they think it's really necessary. My guess though is that there's something out there that these men and their President can't quite control. I don't know why, but I have the feeling we're being marched right through the lion's den here; you only have to look at these soldiers to see it." He gestured toward the men who were still frantically working on the perimeter. "This is the first time I've seen any of the guards here register any emotion, and it looks a lot like fear to me. I think we'd better watch out for ourselves here. We are in danger."

Karla shuddered visibly at his words.

Jane shook her head, "You can't be sure of that," her voice was smooth and piercing, like sharpened steel. "We can only go on what we've seen, and right now that isn't much. This may just be a routine procedure."

"No," Birch replied evenly, trying to control his rising temper, "we haven't seen everything, but we've seen enough. Look at those men; that's not efficiency driving them. It's fear. This is a bad place, and if you'd open your eyes and shut your mouth maybe you could see it too."

"Great, Major," Jane snorted scornfully back at him. Her voice sounded as shrill as a scream and Birch wished like anything he could stop it. "You've got your theories. Well, we've all had to listen to your ideas. You want to hear mine?" Birch wanted to say no, but before the word could reach his lips she continued.

"I don't think this has anything to do with them or what they're doing. It has everything to do with you!" Jane's eyes flashed as she warmed to her subject. "You're afraid to lose the only thing that means anything to you, the command you worked so hard to get. That's what this is all about. Now that we're back you know the only way you can keep any sense of authority is to keep us dependant on you, so you try and scare us. You try and tell us that these guys don't know what they are doing, and that we still really need you. Well, we don't!"

"Just shut up, Jane," Birch snapped "you have no idea what this is about."

"I know more than you'd like me to," she retorted. "You're always trying to scare everyone with some wild idea, it was that way on the mission and it's the same here! You just want control, you got it then and you want to keep it now! Well, I'm not playing along with your little scare game any more. You don't know what you're talking about!"

"That's the whole point!" Birch spoke the words through clenched teeth. His eyes burned into Jane's skin. She had been chomping at the chance to defy his authority and it seemed she had found it. She had jumped the reservation and it was his job to bring her back. "None of us know what we're talking about," he thundered. "We don't know the facts and I'm not willing to wait around until we're spoon-fed them before we start thinking about our future!" Birch moved closer to Jane and thrust his index finger inches away from her nose. "You better start thinking about your own future, Jane," he hissed, "I'm still commanding this mission and if you don't remember that I'll break you, whatever it takes."

Birch spat the words into Jane's face, but rather than cowing her, she seemed to gather strength from them. Her stormy features cleared and she smiled defiantly back at him.

"You're nothing, Major Birch," her voice was cool and crisp, "you never have been anything. Since you took Colonel Ratliff's place I've known it and you've known it. You don't deserve to command anything, and now you don't. You see you don't rank me, Major, and there is no mission now, we're back, so you have no authority to order me to do anything. NASA doesn't even exist anymore, so you may as well forget any idea of ever telling me what to do again."

Birch stood silent for a moment, anger raged within him and he began clenching and unclenching his fists instinctively. "Jane, if you talk to me like that again..." he began.

"What? Why don't you show us all what you can do," Jane taunted. "Why don't you just show us all what a great commanding officer you are by proving your strength? That's how it went on the mission. You were the strongest then, but that's not going to work now. It's your answer to everything isn't it, brute force, not brainpower. You blunder from one problem to another, muscling your way through and learning nothing. Go on then, hit me! You've wanted to do it for a long time. Do it, and prove that you're better than me while everyone's watching."

In fact they were. The soldiers had finished their work on the perimeter and had gathered nearby to watch. Jane, only inches away from Birch, was mockingly gesturing for him to hit her. Birch's arms were rigid at his side and his fists were so tightly clenched that the knuckles had turned white. He looked away from her.

"If you're no longer a part of NASA then I accept that, Jane. I'll leave you under the protection of this government. You are no longer a concern of mine. As for the rest of you," he turned to look at the remainder of his crew, "this mission isn't over until we report to the president and find out what's really going on. Then we can break up this happy little band. Until then our mission is not over."

Jane stared angrily at Birch for a moment, his sudden dismissal of her from the crew seemed to catch her off guard and she had no reply to offer before she stormed silently back to her truck. No one else moved. Birch shrugged. "Keep your eyes open," he ordered, "let me know if you see anything noteworthy." They nodded and moved quietly back to the trucks to get their gear for the night.

Birch walked thoughtfully toward the perimeter. He had finally had it out with Jane and that was the end of it. If she wanted to go her own way then he would let her, and if NASA didn't exist for her then she didn't exist for him. She had been right about one thing though, this had started with Ratliff. That's when it had started for all of them, but there was nothing he could do about that now.

As he neared the boundary his mind turned again to their surroundings and the equipment the men had been assembling moments ago. He wanted a closer look. It clearly was intended to protect them in some way, but their flimsy construction didn't seem to offer much reassurance. Edwards approached as he bent down over one of the insignificant little sticks that marked the area around their camp.

"I wouldn't go out there," Edwards warned, "it's getting dark and you wouldn't like what you were looking for, or more to the point, what's looking for you."

"Thanks for the advice," Birch replied sharply, "but I can look after myself. So, what's out there that scares you so much anyway? You seem to do a lot of running and hiding from these guys. Why don't you just face them down and flush them out?"

"That's just it," Edwards was looking over his shoulder to where Konik stood talking to the sergeant. "They won't face us. They'll size us up, and if they're certain they can win they will attack. If they don't like the odds then they'll bite at our heels all the way to the Mississippi and melt into the ground any time we try to turn and fight. They'll resort to any method that will bring them success. It's barbaric the things they've done, so if the soldiers seem a little nervous you'll have to forgive them. If you knew what you were in the middle of here you'd be more than a little nervous yourself, Major. Ignorance can be a blessed thing."

"You might think so," Birch replied, "but then you're the one who knows everything. You said earlier that we needed to know more, so what are you going to tell me?"

At that moment the sticks gave an electrical buzz and sprang to life with a display of green light crisscrossing the sky to form a glowing grid arcing above the camp. The grid was quickly filled by a shimmering, reflective surface. It had almost a liquid look to it, like mercury flowing above their heads in rippling tides. The canopy blotted out the entire sky, making it impossible to see anything beyond it.

Edwards sighed, "I see you're determined to gain knowledge of what's good and evil in the world. Okay then. This little technical display you just witnessed is just one part of the game we play with the Ares. It sets up a barrier of illusion around us, makes us blend in with the surroundings, and protects us from attack. They could still get in if they could find us. All this screen can do is hide us, but that's important. If they could see us at night we'd be in deadly danger; that's when they're at their fiercest. It's their way, to attack when their advantage is greatest, and no one knows the night like the Ares. They live for the night."

"Who are the Ares?" Birch asked.

"They're the enemy, dangerous and violent. They live out here in the wilds. They are wild. This is their home. Wherever there is wilderness and isolation there is danger. They're all over the world, but this is their stronghold. They wander mostly in small groups but have been known to band together for a common goal, when the need arises. In recent years they have been growing bolder. They have begun to attack where we once felt safe. Our society is under threat and so we have responded."

Birch nodded. "So, what's the difference between you and them? What started it all?" he asked.

"What you're seeing here is the difference; they attack and we defend. Individually there is humanity in them, but as a pack they're wild, and so we've been forced to defend ourselves." Edwards sighed and kicked moodily at the dirt.

"Maybe one day they'll change," he added wistfully. "All we can do is work to make that happen. Maybe one day it'll happen."

"Sounds like the same old story to me," Birch muttered. "People don't change, no matter how long you give them. The faces may change, the banners they march under will be different, but people always stay the same."

"I hope you're wrong," Edwards responded gloomily. "I really hope you're wrong." His manner implied the suspicion that he was right.

"So, this is what all the dreams have come to." Birch smiled mirthlessly. "Peace can never grow where the wounds of hate have pierced so deep! It's embedded, it's in our DNA, but how did you let it get to this level? If they're just a wandering band of savages why have they got you on the run like this?"

"It's hard to give you an easy answer to that. You can't put the events of hundreds of years into a simple frame. It's been gradual; they've grown strong as we've become weaker. Maybe it has something to do with their indomitable will or just their stupidity. No matter how many times you defeat them, they never know when they're beaten. They keep fighting, keep dying, and keep coming back for more. How can you beat that? You can't, except now maybe things are finally changing.

Something in his manner and the way he looked at him gave Birch the impression that this change had something to do with them.

Birch shook his head, "I hope you're not thinking we can help you with that. There isn't much we can do. My crew aren't exactly fighters, and we're no diplomats you know."

Edwards laughed, "We know that! But maybe you can do something. We understand that the Hypnos missions were all about trying to help humanity, to unite us all. Many feel that you represent what we should have been. Perhaps with you here we can finally bring us together. We're lucky to have you. That's why we have to get to Washington."

Birch looked doubtful.

"Well," Edwards continued, "there isn't much you or I can do about it right now. In fact about all we can do at this point is get some sleep and hope the Ares don't find us." He turned to leave. "The guards will be keeping close watch for them tonight," had added reassuringly as he trudged back toward the camp. "They'll keep us safe."

Birch cast a thoughtful glance at the shimmering arc above them before turning to walk back to the truck for his gear. His mind raced with strange thoughts of what Edwards had told him. He had learned a lot more about what was going on, but it had still left him feeling powerless, perhaps even more so than before. This world was a dangerous place. He still didn't understand it all, and yet somehow they were supposed to be some kind of example to everyone else about how things could change. It was too much to expect after all they had been through. He had tried to escape all that, but even after all this time he still owed humanity something and he would have to pay.

As he settled down into his sleeping bag he noted with satisfaction that the guards on duty were vigilantly watching the shimmering field. They couldn't see out any more than their enemies could see in, but they were ready. They had to be. There would only be a split second between alert and attack. The first and only warning would be when an enemy breeched the field and entered the camp. They would have to act in an instant, and so they glared blindly at the reflective surface, guns ready. It was as close to comfort as the wilderness would allow them. Birch wished he could do something more, but for now all any of them could do was wait, watch, and hope not to be discovered.

# FIFTEEN

The night had passed without incident and Birch stretched stiffly as he was prodded awake by one of the soldiers. It was barely dawn, but the routine of preparing to leave was already well underway. They were almost as quick at packing away as they had been at setting up the night before, and soon they were traveling again as the morning sunlight came streaking low across the clearing.

Breakfast was a military ration eaten as the convoy traveled, there was no time for unnecessary delay on the mountain, he was told. There would be time enough for proper eating when they reached the other side, but for now they had to hurry. The mountain passes were already known as dangerous, treacherous places where an ambush was likely, the narrow roads were ideal for that, but the presence of that mine on the western side of the mountain spoke of a greater danger than usual. The Ares were active here and might already be watching them, waiting for a chance to attack. They had to hurry. Once they were in the open country on the other side they would be safer. Their firepower would give them the advantage on the plains.

It was a hard, slow, day's travel toward the evening. More stops were made than the previous day as mines were discovered and disposed of. Birch could see Edwards shaking his head by the fifth stop, and Konik's face seemed to glow red with frustration. As the day progressed Birch lost count of the number of times they had stopped. They came at ever shorter intervals. Finally, as the sun was drawing low in the west, the trucks pulled off the road and came to a halt. The routine of setting up their protective shield immediately began, and, if it were possible, the process seemed even swifter than before. The day's evidence of the insurgent's activity seemed to provide even greater motivation for speed, and the blanket of shimmering light soon covered the camp in its protective glow.

For a time Birch stood at the boundary, watching the display of the reflective field. It was a beautiful view of fractured rainbows glistening on a liquid canvas, but the effect was lost on him. He was straining to glimpse anything beyond it, seeking any sign of what might be there. He looked up as Edwards approached.

"I don't like it," Edwards muttered as he came near. "This has been the worst day I've ever seen for mines. The army clears them regularly, a patrol swept through here only about a week ago, so these are all part of a new batch, probably put in very recently I'd guess. I think we could be in the middle of something here."

"Like what?" Birch asked.

"Like something big, they really slowed us down today and I think that was the plan. They may know we're here." The words hung ominously in the silence that followed.

"What does that mean?" Birch asked eventually. He was straining to see through the shield again. "Do you think they just know we're on the mountain or our exact location?"

"I think they know exactly where we are. We were slowed down so much that we've been kept in this one small area all day, and I think there's a reason for that." Edwards sighed, "It looks like something's going to happen here tonight. You better be ready for it."

Birch nodded thoughtfully, "Isn't there anything we can do? We can't just sit here and wait to be attacked."

"You're right," Edwards smiled grimly. "That's my job. I

get to go out there and see what we're facing and let Commander Konik know. We're blind in here so I have to find out if they have our location yet and, if they're there, how strong a force they're bringing. If they know we're here we may have to drop the shield and fight it out. It'll be brutal, but it's a better chance than sitting here blind. On the other hand, if they don't know we're here, it would be foolish to drop the field and expose ourselves to attack."

"Sounds tough, need any help?" Birch looked expectantly at Edwards.

Edwards shrugged. "We're supposed to protect you. You really would be safer if you stayed here, but I get the feeling you've had enough of being safe. Anyway, it looks like we're all going to have to protect ourselves by the time this night is through, so you might as well get a feel for this thing now. So, yeah, I could use the help, but keep your head down and watch your back. Here, take these," he handed Birch a pistol and another device he didn't recognize, "only use the gun in absolute necessity because it'll bring everything down on our heads once it goes off. The other thing is a heat sensor, just press that big button and it'll register and display any human body heat in the area. It's not going to tell you exactly where they are but it does give a good general reading we can follow. It's our best chance of picking them up. Ready?" Birch nodded. "Good, let's go."

Edwards took a step forward and disappeared through the silvery barrier of light. Birch followed. It was a strange sensation as he passed through a reflection of himself and reemerged on the other side of the glowing shield. For an instant he was blinded by its intensity as he passed through, and then it took him another moment to see anything in the darkness beyond. As his eyes adjusted he was just able to make out the dark shadow of Edwards standing a few feet away. The camp was now invisible, though they were still standing adjacent to it. It was an odd sensation to know that it was there, but not see it.

A moment later Edwards signaled to Birch and they cautiously made their way across the dirt track and through the tall grass toward the woods. The still of the night seemed peaceful and the cool air refreshed Birch in a way he hadn't felt for a long time. He was careful to keep close to Edwards as they moved for the trees. They stopped frequently, either to observe something on the ground or in the air. Edwards almost seemed to be sniffing for danger, as an animal might. Birch couldn't distinguish any possible threats, but he knew that this man would see things he couldn't.

Their progress seemed painfully slow, but it was really only a few moments later that they reached the edge of the woods. The last embers of dusk were a distant memory in the west and Birch couldn't see much under the canopy of trees, Edwards however seemed unhindered by the darkness as he busily scanned the area. "I thought so," his voice seemed hollow. "It looks like we're really into it here." Even in the dim light Birch could see that Edwards' face had transformed suddenly. There was a strange, wild look to him.

"What?" Birch whispered hoarsely. Edwards looked alarmed, and yet looking about him he could see nothing. The night was as still and peaceful as it had been before.

"This," Edwards hissed, pointing to a mark about twelve feet up the nearest tree. It wasn't anything Birch recognized or could distinguish, just some scratchings on a tree. But it had a powerful effect on Edwards and the gravity of his words indicated a significance he didn't yet understand.

"What is it?" Birch asked, "Is it something to do with the Ares?"

Edwards laughed bitterly, "You could say that. This is probably the worst thing you could hope to find out here. The Ares are both a primitive and advanced people and they like to play their little games with us. To them it's some kind of honor to announce what they will do to us before they do it, even if it is only to a tree in carved form. What you see up there is their personal favorite, the 'hail to death.' Essentially it's a greeting to us: 'welcome to your destruction' would be a rough translation. It's fresh too, it's meant for us in fact, that's pretty clear by this marking, 'your goods are ours.' They know we've got something important here."

"Goods?" Birch wondered aloud.

"We're a pretty big convoy, they must expect us to be taking something important, but I'm surprised they got onto us so quickly, especially in force. That third stripe at the base of the marking means 'certain destruction' for us. The Ares aren't given to empty bragging in these carvings, it's some kind of honor code, so that means they must have amassed quite a force to show that kind of confidence. It doesn't make sense though, they usually stay in small cells of maybe three or four, so how could they have the kind of numbers they would need to do that? They usually wouldn't have the time to draw together before we got through, but it looks like they were waiting for us."

"A trap," Birch muttered.

"Exactly," Edwards agreed, "but let's see if we can get back some of the advantage. See if you can pick up any body readings in the area on that device. Let's see what we're up against." Birch pressed the button; two flashing red dots appeared on the black screen.

"What does this mean?" Birch held up the display. Edwards shook his head.

"It means trouble. Those two dots are us, the camp is shielded so the heat from them can't escape, so the only thing we're seeing there is ourselves."

"That's good though isn't it?" Birch was puzzled.

"No," Edwards voice was hard, "you can bet they're here. They don't leave these kind of marks and go away. This is a marking of territory and a statement of intent, so if we're not seeing them it's not because they're not here."

"So what is it then?" Birch shot the words at Edwards. He was growing weary of his own ignorance and wanted to get some sense of what he could do.

"I've heard of this kind of thing before," Edwards looked around cautiously, "but only from the northern tribes. Usually these guys rely on speed and tough terrain to keep ahead of us. They hide underground during the day and fight in small bands with surprise attacks at night. They're vermin, but in the north they have grown very bold. Somehow they've come across some way to avoid detection by our equipment; they leave no heat trace. That's not something that I would expect them to share with the tribes outside of their own area though. They're not exactly a collaborative bunch. It doesn't make sense.

"You were right, Major," Edwards continued, "this is a trap, but one of the best I've seen. I'm sure we were herded right here, this marking proves it, so our camp is an easy target. We better get back and get ready for a fight." Edwards' words were punctuated by the screeching sound of an owl nearby. Both men froze.

"More games!" Edwards spat the words. "It looks like it's about to begin. At least I haven't heard a reply yet so we may just be dealing with an advanced scout at this point, though that's dangerous enough. Okay, Major this is important, we need to get back to the camp. I've radioed back a warning about the attack but you can't expect them to come out and get us now, it's up to us. I don't think the Ares know our exact location yet so keep it quiet and stay out of sight. Keep your head down and follow me, and whatever you do don't look back, it'll just slow you down and there's nothing back there you want to see anyway. Let's go!" Edwards crouched down and crawled slowly through the tall grass they had walked through just moments ago. Birch followed.

The few hundred yards that they had walked from the camp now seemed like miles as they moved slowly through the damp undergrowth. Birch's arms and knees were sore and wet and his back was beginning to ache from the exertion. Still they edged slowly back toward the others. Birch was aware they were approaching the camp, but he still could see no sign of it. There was no light. They must have been keeping the shield up in some hope of avoiding detection, but it made their return difficult. In the dim light of the sliver of a moon he couldn't even be sure they were going in the right direction. He hoped Edwards had a better idea of where they were going.

As they crawled Birch's mind raced over what they had discussed. It all projected a pretty bleak outlook for their mission. He wondered how bad it really was. More immediately they had to make it back to camp. That noise had been close-by and if they had been seen then whatever it was would be after them. Its shadow seemed even now to stretch across them, perhaps it was only inches away, about to strike; he couldn't be sure. He shivered, partly from the cold that was seeping in with the water through his damp pants, partly in anxious anticipation of what might be following them.

A screeching sound pierced the air again, much closer this time, and was met almost instantly by another from the other end of the clearing. Edwards froze for a moment and looked over his shoulder to Birch. "This isn't working," he muttered angrily, "there's more than one and I think they're trying to get our range. If we hang around too long they'll pick us up so never mind secrecy, speed is the issue now. We're going to have to run for it. Are you ready?"

"Run? Where's the camp?" Birch looked wildly around but could see no sign of where it could be. It was still hidden.

"Just follow me," Edwards hissed as he lifted himself up and ran into the darkness.

# SIXTEEN

Birch struggled to his feet and ran after the distant form of Edwards fleeing into the empty darkness. His knees were wet and his legs ached from the crawling, but he knew that if he lost Edwards here he would never find his way back. No light was showing anywhere, save for that cast by a thin moon, and Birch couldn't see where the camp was. He had the impression of tall dark trees towering all around him, but that was all. The others had left the shield up, but it looked like that thin protection wasn't going to last long now. It was going to be a fight to survive.

He didn't look back. Edwards' warning rang ominously in his ears; he wouldn't like what he saw if he did, but somehow running from an unseen and unknown enemy made his fears grow. His nerves tensed. His whole body was prepared at any moment for the impact, to be brought down from behind and destroyed. It was hard, running wasn't in Birch's nature, but somehow his life had demanded it. Every day demanded it, if only to give himself the chance to fight again later. Still, he hated himself for it.

He was catching up with Edwards again, but there was still no sign of the camp. The encompassing darkness made it difficult to see anything, and a moment later he had fallen behind again as he stumbled on the uneven ground. It was in that instant Birch heard it again, the sound of an owl screeching, but much louder and closer this time. He knew that it was no owl, but a human predator, swooping in to attack its prey. He glanced instinctively behind him and, while he saw nothing, he was sure he could feel something back there swiftly approaching. He shivered, turned again, and ran madly, wildly after Edwards.

His legs pumped hard. His feet thudded swiftly through the soft grass beneath him. He was catching up to Edwards again, but before he could reach him the night air seemed to engulf the man, and he disappeared from sight. Birch froze instantly, unsure for a moment what had happened. He suddenly realized. The shield, he had found it and had run through to the other side. Birch lunged toward the point Edwards had disappeared, but as he ran a sudden "whoop" sounded right behind him. As he turned to defend himself he felt two large hands with claw-like nails grabbing at his throat. He struggled, tearing at the talons, but they were unrelenting. They were squeezing the breath out of him. The fingers gouged deep into his flesh, choking him. He felt his strength and his life waning as his hands fell limply from the struggle. His vision darkened and in final desperation he mustered his remaining strength to kick out behind him, landing a powerful blow on his assailant. That was enough; the man cried out and loosened his grip.

His attacker staggered in pain. Birch stumbled back on his heels, released from the powerful grip he almost fell. His breath was coming in rasping gasps and the pain almost gagged him. He tried to clear his head as he turned quickly to run for the camp. Before he had taken another step he caught the brief impression of burning eyes and matted hair as the man leapt at him again. He felt those hands again at his throat as he fell backwards with his attacker on top of him. In that instant a strange impression of jumbled light and fractured reflections fell through his mind. It might have been the last images before slipping into unconsciousness, but as he landed Birch blinked. They had fallen through the shield. They were in the camp.

The face of his attacker was now clearly visible in the light. It was wild and dirty and the teeth were bared in a snarling grimace contorted with the effort of crushing his windpipe. All of this was a blur to Birch, who was struggling for his life, and yet at the same time his mind was beset by thoughts and images. Not of his struggle, but of the past. His past. If this was the end what had it been worth? He had to live, to do more, yet the agony in his throat was real. In the grip of those hands his future wavered and he seemed powerless to resist it. Still he tried. He struggled.

Somewhere beyond his fight he heard shouting, confusion, and then a sudden blast above him, followed by the sickening crackle and smell of burning flesh. Smoke poured from the back of his enemy. He screamed wildly, tearing more viciously into Birch's neck before being pulled off by one of the soldiers. Birch blinked and watched mutely as the wild man pushed the soldier aside, ran a few steps, and disappeared through the barrier and into the night air.

"Get him!" Birch heard Konik's voice barking sharply at two soldiers who quickly ran and disappeared after the man. The other soldiers were grabbing weapons, ready for any further breaches of their defenses. All of this was very distant to Birch. He was fighting for breath, gagging and choking for air through his swollen throat.

Birch struggled to his feet. Again he had caught the flavor of death and the taste was bitter in his mouth. He shuddered as the feeling crashed over him like mighty waves; he felt as though he was drowning in his emotions.

He coughed violently through his burning throat. Birch tasted the blood flowing freely from the side of his mouth and wiped at it with the back of his hand. By this time DeSante and Karla had reached his side and were trying to help him into a nearby truck, but Birch waved them away with a scowl and limped slowly over to where Konik and Edwards were talking.

It was obvious that the Commander was extremely agitated and that Edwards was receiving the brunt of his anger. "Stupid," Konik's enraged tone rang out, "totally stupid! You're supposed to be the expert, so how did you land us in this situation? I don't even know why they choose people like you for missions, you're type have no experience. All you have is theory. It's men like me who've been out here doing it that know what to do, not you research people. Well, it seems like those eight years as a zoo monkey hasn't prepared you for this, and now we're all going to pay for it!"

Edwards frowned angrily. "Don't lecture me, Commander. I didn't see any better suggestions from you, despite all of your 'field knowledge'. This is something different to anything either you or I have faced before. It's not like anything I've even heard of. It looks like we're up against a combined assault and it really looks like they were expecting us. That's the only way they could have been this prepared."

"What are you saying?" Konik thundered, "That they knew we were coming? That's impossible. This is a Code One mission. It's utterly impossible."

"Nothing is impossible, Commander," Edwards replied coolly, "perhaps if you spent more time studying than fighting you might have understood that. Don't underestimate them. They've done more today than I ever expected them to do, and I've seen them do a lot. We shouldn't be surprised at their ingenuity. Right now they're massing for an attack out there. You better get that shield down so we can see what we're fighting against, or they'll massacre us before we even get a chance to see them."

Konik chewed on his lower lip thoughtfully, "You may be right, about the danger," he replied in a muted tone, "but my men will catch that Ares before he gets back to report to his friends. There's no need to expose ourselves by lowering the barrier. That would just open us up to attack."

"Under normal circumstances you might have a point. A single scout could be stopped," Edwards' voice was steely calm. "These are not normal circumstances. The markings out there make it clear, they've been watching us, they know where we are, and they're coming at us right now with deadly force."

Konik shook his head, "That's just not plausible, I've fought these guys for twenty years and that's just not going to happen. They prefer to attack in small numbers, terror cells that take out one or two before disappearing or dying. What you're saying just makes no sense."

"It makes no sense only because you are unwilling to open your eyes to something new." A sharp edge to Edwards' voice glistened through his words. "I don't know how it happened, but we better do something about it now. Either you give the order to lower that shield and set up a defensive cordon or I'll override you with DA authority and do it myself. I'll leave the choice to you. Either way that barrier is coming down."

Konik glowered at Edwards. The man looked ready to kill both his allies and his enemies.

"Sergeant," Konik finally bellowed, "lower the field and set up a defensive cordon around the trucks. Prepare for battle!" The sergeant saluted and passed the order along to the troops. A flurry of activity followed through the camp. The lights were suddenly doused as the shield flickered and disappeared. Their defensive bubble had burst. Amidst the noise and bustle of clattering guns and thumping boots Konik stared angrily at the dark outline of the Special Operative, "You better be right about this," he snarled, "or you may never make it back to see your beloved DA again."

Edwards laughed bitterly, "I better be wrong, Commander, or none of us will make it back to see anything again."

The soldiers took up their stations, staring out into the inky blackness that surrounded them. Like the wagon trains of old, the circle of trucks stood resolute, awaiting the onslaught that would decide their fate. Good against bad, savagery against civilization, winners and losers, the living and the dead. In the pages of the history books, or more usually in the glare of the celluloid film, the scene was a romantic one that stirred you with a fine yearning to have lived in those glorious days of expansion and exploration. From the perspective of reality it was bloody terror.

Now they waited. An hour passed without incident. Konik frowned, "Those men should be back by now. It shouldn't be taking them this long to track down a wounded subject like that."

Edwards shook his head. "They must have run into whatever's out there. You shouldn't have sent them out. There's nothing we can do for them now. All we can do is wait for the Ares to try and come in and get us. That's our best chance."

Birch glared out into the dark clearing. Sometimes he imagined he could see something out there. Shapes moving, something was running hunched over, but he couldn't be sure. His finger, frozen on the trigger of his rifle, grew stiff, and his mind wearied into fatigue as another hour passed. Finally it came, the sound they had anticipated and dreaded, the screech of an owl swooping for attack. It echoed and reechoed in the trees around them. This was it, war.

# SEVENTEEN

The sound echoed and reechoed around them, growing stronger with every passing moment. Konik shouted orders, his voice struggling to be heard above the screams, while sweaty soldiers stared unblinkingly from their positions behind the trucks. Their fingers rubbed methodically against the triggers of their rifles, urging for any viable target. "Only shoot when you're sure you can hit them," Konik bellowed, but his voice, usually a striking symbol of his power and authority, was faint against the battle cries engulfing it. "Don't waste ammunition shooting at shadows!"

There were plenty of shadows to shoot at, and they all were moving. It was impossible to tell where their enemies were. Numerous human or natural forms seemed to be scurrying and dancing amidst the darkened forest, like the old fears of Salem brought to life. It seemed to Birch that the greater number of those shadows must be little more than just branches of trees, blown upon a stray breeze and creating the impression of life and movement in the dim light. The thought was a fleeting hope that hardly had time to settle into his mind before it was dashed, for the shadows were now moving more purposefully toward the camp. These were not the shadows of branches, but rather hundreds of human forms in a great dark mass, like the waters of an angry ocean, swirling up to destroy them.

Edwards gasped, "It's worse than I thought!" His voice was hard and clear, even through the screeching cries that surrounded them.

Konik nodded grimly. "Get ready for it," he shouted. "It looks like they're trying a frontal assault and we'll make them pay for it. On my orders, rapid fire at will. Do not let them pass. Let's see if they have the stomach for what we're going to give them."

Birch's shoulders tensed as he prepared to fire. He paused to wipe the sweat from his eyes. He caught sight of Karla a few feet from him. She held her gun rigidly toward the advancing enemy. Fear was etched into her features, but as she stared into the darkness he also saw a calm determination he hadn't expected. Lauren and DeSante, too, were nearby. Instinctively they all had been drawn together at this moment. Perhaps there was more to bind them in these circumstances than could ever have divided them in the lifetime of their past. Jane wasn't in sight.

The mass of shadows swelled and surged, as with the release of a swollen river through the dam gates. They were getting close enough for Birch to make out the individual forms among the crowd rushing at them. Edwards had been right, this was bad. It looked like a lot more than they could handle. Still they waited for the order. The hard features of the enemy's faces could just be made out when the command was finally given.

"Fire!" Konik's words cut through the shrill screams around them and was instantly met with the thundering blast of repeated arms fire into the mob before them. Birch thought he had downed at least five in the fist volley, but it hardly seemed to slow their progress. The shapes neither slowed nor flinched in the slightest, but seemed to hurl themselves all the more recklessly at them. It surprised him that none of them seemed to be returning fire. It was as though their single aim was to reach them and squeeze the life out of their enemies with their bare hands, just as they had tried with him earlier.

What primitive impulse they were following in this war plan he couldn't imagine, but the effect was disastrous to them in terms of life lost.

Relentlessly they fired into the rushing throng. The crashing gunfire, and the glow and smoke from their discharging weapons cast a strange effect over the scene, like an old smelting plant, an industrial setting in which destruction was the only product. The firing continued and their faces were illuminated in the effect, but the shadows cast distorted them to ugly caricatures in deep red hues.

"Keep firing!" Konik was shouting, but there was no stopping them. As one enemy was shot another would trample their fallen friend, alive or dead, underfoot. It was a crazed rush; more like a mindless stampede than any planned strategy, and Birch shuddered at the maddened frenzy of it all. If they treated their own with such contempt then it gave him little doubt that capture was not an option. This was a fight to the death.

"Shore up the west side!" Konik's futile shouts grew faint. His words were almost indistinguishable through the deafening screams of the advancing enemy. Rather than muting the screeching, their heavy casualties seemed to increase the Ares' volume and intensity. Here was a rebel yell to set fear into the heart, and the more they died, the louder and more piercing it became. A real primordial scream of anger, anguish, hatred, and malice, all compressed into a shrill plaintive screech that numbed the mind and made it hard to think. Birch would have done anything to stop that dismal howling.

They were close now and an unholy rage seemed to possess them, so that they ran toward the barrier with even greater velocity. Finally they hit, like a great breaker against a sea wall, and the splash of the human tide was no less spectacular. A great swarm of arms and legs clawing to climb up the trucks, met by soldiers desperately firing down into the mass. The trucks shook under the barrage and one soldier lost his footing and disappeared, screaming, into the heaving throng below. The other soldiers fell back in horror as arms and hands reached out to grab them. The Ares clawed their way up the truck. Still the troops kept firing, but they were swiftly overwhelmed by the sheer numbers clambering up at them.

"The west side, reinforce the west side!" Konik was literally screaming to be heard, but it was too late. The west side was being overrun and the defenses were collapsing. The Ares had reached the top of the truck and from this position finally let loose with their own weapons in a deadly spray of gunfire. A soldier fell beside him and Birch turned to see a torrent of bodies jumping down into the enclosure. He fired into the advancing horde, but it was only a moment later that his own truck was shaking under the press of the bodies hurling themselves against it. It swayed on its wheels drunkenly for a moment before toppling over on its side with an enormous crash and explosion that sent orange flames licking up into the night sky.

Birch had managed to jump clear as his vehicle had fallen, but he was thrown to the ground by the momentum and, in the confusion, was lost between the trampling feet. For a moment all he could do was crouch with his hands covering his head from the blows; a fetal throwback in unaccustomed danger. As he tried to fight his way to his feet hands grabbed and pulled at his face, his hair, and his clothes. He fought them; he still had his rifle and used the butt end of it to smash anything that touched him. His attackers drew back from his frenzied blows and, as they did, he used the space to turn the gun and start firing again.

Somehow for the first time the Ares had a human response. After their insane drive into the camp they showed the first sign of hesitation. Birch was berserk, firing and re-firing rapidly into the attacking mass, at anything that approached him. At close range the damage was considerable and the gun grew hot in his hands, but still he kept shooting. His opponents were mesmerized in his destructive path, and in that one instant confusion seemed to grip the heart of their attackers.

Seeing the advantage shift a few of the remaining soldiers rallied to Birch and together they began to consolidate a fierce counterattack that pushed the Ares back and quickly saw their force dissolved into a rabble.

They ran. As recklessly as they had charged their camp, so the Ares fled, without any thought of defense or safety. Like wild animals in stark fear they bolted for the cover of the trees, but not alone. Birch saw that a group of them had caught DeSante and were dragging him toward the woods; they were taking hostages. Quickly Birch tried to fight his way through the crowd to get to him. He met with little actual resistance, but the sheer press of the retreating Ares was enough to make it hard for him to reach them.

For a time he lost sight of the abductors. In the amber glow of their burning vehicles he scanned the mud smeared faces of the retreating horde, but he couldn't see them. He ran deeper into the throng, and for a time he allowed himself to be carried along in the crush of bodies toward the last place he had seen DeSante disappear. Still he couldn't see him.

Panic had now seized their attackers entirely. Every individual seemed engrossed only in their own immediate survival and the instinct to run. No other thought entered their mind as they fled into the darkness, and so Birch ran among them unnoticed. It was amazing for him to think that such a ragged group could ever prove a threat to men like Konik and Edwards. Their route was so complete, and their organization so poor that he couldn't imagine them ever fighting effectively. Yet the fear he had seen from Edwards, and even Konik, was real, and told him that there was much more to these people than what he was seeing in this fearful flight. It wasn't easy to understand, but perhaps it had something to do with the type of battle they had chosen this time. Edwards had spoken of the Ares as a crafty people, working in groups of three or four in sneak attacks. Perhaps a front on fight against a determined foe was more than they were prepared for. It was the only thing he could think of to explain the discrepancy with their reputation and the reality of this night.

Whatever the answer it was clear that at least some of the Ares had retained enough of their natural instincts of war to recognize the advantage of hostages and had seized DeSante. He wasn't going to let him go, but among all those people it seemed a hopeless task. Still he continued his anxious search.

It was some moments later that he saw the group dragging the young lieutenant into the woods. There were three of them. They were now some distance from the camp and in the dim light it was difficult to see much more than the shadowy outline of the men. Their load had slowed their progress and Birch quickly reached them as the thinning crowd dispersed among the trees. Without warning he smashed the butt of his rifle into the unsuspecting back of the rearmost man and sent him crashing to the ground. One of the others had quickly leveled his weapon at Birch, but too late, for with one swift motion Birch had drawn his own rifle up and fired into the man's legs, sending him reeling backwards in a crumpled heap.

The third man lunged at him as he fired and hit him with such force that the gun was knocked from his hands. Before he could recover the man was on him, sending a flurry of fists to his head and face. Birch struck angrily back, but his opponent continued, unrelenting. The fear he had seen in the others was still there, he could see it in the snarling face, but there was something else, some kind of crazed protective instinct of his prize, the savage determination to keep and guard his possession with all of his fury. Birch's desire, however, was greater. DeSante was his man and this was still their mission. He was not going to let him go.

In a burst of raging energy Birch had flipped the man and sent him hard against the ground. Unlike the other Ares in the camp, though, there still seemed to be plenty of fight in him, and it was only as Birch's fist connected hard with his jaw in a striking blow that the man fell to the ground, unconscious. Birch fell beside him, exhausted. It was only after a few moments rest that he could find the energy to check on DeSante.

The young lieutenant physically was unharmed, though his face was gaunt and worn from the experience. Birch loosed his bonds and the two men stood shakily at the edge of the woods. The dying fires of destruction from the camp could be seen dimly in the distance and, apart from the fallen forms of Ares and allies, they were alone. It was strangely quiet again and viewing the destruction and his own blood-spattered uniform Birch shook his head. "Let's hope this was for a good cause," he muttered, "if anything good could ever be served by this."

DeSante shook his head and leaned heavily on Birch's shoulder, struggling to speak. Finally the words came through in heaving breaths, "They've got Karla!"

# EIGHTEEN

DeSante's words hit Birch like a fist and almost knocked him back to the ground. His high elation at the successful rescue of his young lieutenant was met by a double despair at the news that Karla was gone. Worse still was the realization that he had no way of finding her in this dark, engulfing forest. He wouldn't know where to start, but still he had to try. He had to find some way to help her.

"Did you see where they took her?" Birch looked intently into the exhausted lieutenant's face. "Which way were they going? At least give me some idea where we can start."

DeSante shook his head, "It was too quick," he gasped. "I couldn't really tell you. It was only a minute later that they grabbed me and dragged me away, so I couldn't tell what direction anything was myself. I just don't know."

Birch turned angrily away, enraged at life. Somehow no victory could ever be free from the bitter gall of reality. He never expected a 'happily ever after', but too often the fruit of any good thing had not even passed his lips before the bitter core at the center was revealed. Just once he wanted to see something wholly good happen. He doubted he ever would.

"Let's look around this way some more. They were taking you this direction, so maybe they were going to put you both to the same place. That seems our best chance."

It wasn't much of a chance. Birch suggested it less in hope of success than in angry defiance of the events. Like the kid beaten by the class bully, stubbornly coming back for another pounding. He wasn't going to let this one go. Whether he was beaten or not- he wasn't giving up.

DeSante nodded, but as they took their first steps toward the woods the lieutenant stumbled on unsteady legs and almost fell headlong to the ground. Birch caught him. "Are you okay?" he growled. His concern was overruled by a natural impatience with the delay. "You could head back to the camp if you need to rest. I can't wait for you. If they get too big a jump on us we'll lose any hope of getting her back."

DeSante shook his head. "I want to come, just give me a minute," he pleaded. "My head's still spinning. If I can just clear my head for a minute then I'll be ready to help, then we can both get Karla back."

Birch nodded, he knew he might need DeSante if he did catch up with the Ares, besides, secretly the excuse for a moments rest was a welcome one. He was exhausted, but had been unwilling to acknowledge it. His own guilt made it impossible for him to stop while he knew Karla was out there, but DeSante's need gave him a reason to rest without blaming himself. The only problem might be getting started again after stopping.

Both men moved wearily for the deeper cover of the trees. They weren't up to any fighting, so they hid away from the last straggling Areas running through the area. Once they were safely under cover they collapsed on the dry, earthy ground. It was only as they lay there that Birch realized the depth of his exhaustion. It was all he could do to fight the urge to sleep. His eyes were heavy, and it was as his mind slipped into one of those delicious semi-sleeping states of warmth and comfort that a thought struck him that returned him to a sudden state of wakefulness. He still had the heat sensor. This was no revelation. He had been vaguely aware of it before. It was in his pocket. What was new was its significance. He could use it to find Karla! It would be useless on the Ares, of course, because they had some kind of defense against it, but maybe that didn't matter. He had to hope they had made a mistake. The battle had been a bloody route for their side and perhaps in the kidnapping, their one limited success, they might have made a simple error that could help him. He had to test it.

Quickly Birch pulled the sensor from his pocket and pressed the button. The display took a moment to warm up, but this time, instead of the two red blips he had seen before there were many. Birch let out a low whistle and woke DeSante from his slumbering stupor with a gentle kick to the ribs.

"What is it?" DeSante asked, starting up with fear. Birch showed him the screen. "So?" the meaning was lost on the lieutenant. "What does that mean?"

"It means we can go get Karla. Get up!" Birch hurriedly explained the discovery to DeSante as they clambered to their feet. The heat sensor would help them save Karla. The display was clear. Their two traces were in the center of the screen, another group was clustered at the camp, and a lone trace was moving in a northerly direction. He was certain that one was Karla, and if he was right then they needed to get to her as quickly as possible because, in a calmer moment, the Ares might realize their mistake and cover their trail properly.

Despite their exhaustion the two men were soon making good progress. Their renewed hope for Karla seemed to energize them as they dashed northwards. Together they ran, following the signal of their hope. Both were aware of the danger of an Ares ambush, but the desire to follow that signal outweighed their caution. It would have been the same for any member of the crew, of course, but the fact that it was Karla made it seem all the more urgent. Everyone liked her. Her youth and inexperience were still a source of annoyance to Birch, and her perky cheeriness was almost too much to bear, but somehow, like a ray of persistent sunshine, she had warmed him. She had warmed them all. Even during the worst of it out there on the mission she had been better than the rest. She had given him a chance. No one could hate Karla, unless they hated life itself.

Birch paused for a moment to look down at the device's display again. The signal was still headed north and was leading them deeper into the woods, the type of territory the Ares loved and the perfect place for an ambush. Something about it worried Birch. It was quiet now, and the tranquil hush that hung in the air was as tangible as the heavy pine scent that filled his nostrils. It seemed peaceful, but he was cautious. Something wasn't right. The Ares had given up too quickly that night, and this fact troubled him; it didn't seem to fit somehow. The kidnapping of both DeSante and Karla seemed to verify that something more was happening than he had seen. There was a logic behind their panic that worried him because he couldn't quite understand it.

Birch hesitated. The silent woods opened up before them, ready to swallow them in its darkness. It occurred to him at that moment that the noise and confusion of the battle had been too pronounced, too deliberate, and now, by contrast, the silence of the forest seemed too clear and too complete. They were walking into danger. He knew it, but still he swallowed his fears and moved forward again.

As they plunged deeper under the cover of the trees Birch took a moment for a last look back. The dying embers of the camp's burning trucks were now barely visible, little more than small points of light in the distance, like fallen stars come to ground, glimmering in the darkness. He wished there had been time to go back for help, he almost wished Jane could be with them; she'd pull through for Karla. As he turned he wondered if he would see them again. He moved on.

For a time Birch was able to convince himself that his fears had been unfounded. It was harder to see in the denser tree cover, but as his eyes adjusted things appeared as peaceful as ever. All was quiet. If their enemies were waiting they were well hidden. Birch's plan seemed to be working.

It was the heat sensor that gave him the first indication that something was wrong. Karla's signal had gone stationary and in those few moments it looked as though they were going to catch them. The next time he looked, though, he had lost the reading. Their own signal still showed at the center, and the camp was now on the edge of the display, but Karla had gone. Muttering angrily to himself, he scowled at the device and rapped at the screen, but it didn't change. Karla's trace had gone.

DeSante was looking over his shoulder at the monitor. "What now?" he whispered.

Birch shrugged angrily and gestured in the direction they had been following.

"That seems our best chance," he answered dryly and started running further into the woods toward the last sensor reading. He had tried to sound optimistic but the words had been hollow in his throat. He knew the Ares would have moved on. He was sure they wouldn't still be there, unless something bad had happened. He didn't want to think about that. He also knew that if she wasn't there then all they could do is try to find their trail as best they could. With no heat trace to follow he doubted they would ever find her.

Their speed slowed as they came to the point where Karla's signal had disappeared. He wanted to be sure he didn't stumble into a trap. The soft noise of their own feet on the forest floor seemed to Birch as a trumpet heralding their arrival in the still night air. Even his own breathing sounded inordinately loud in the quiet gloom of the woods. He found himself instinctively holding his respiration until he was left gasping for air.

When they finally arrived at the spot Birch was ready for anything, but they found nothing, at least nothing tangible. In some respects this came as a relief. Irrationally he had feared that they might find a more ominous reason for Karla's loss of body heat, though he knew that even a dead body would retain enough warmth to be traced for a while. That left only one other possibility, the Ares had discovered their mistake and covered it. That was reassuring in some ways, no harm had come to her yet, but now he and DeSante were back in the dark, with no way to track her.

"Major!" DeSante's hoarse whisper interrupted his thoughts, "something's happened here, some kind of struggle." Birch nodded, it was pretty clear. Marks in the dirt, flattened grass, and broken branches all seemed to support this conclusion. The discovery of a blood stain on one of the trees a moment later seemed to confirm it. There had been a fight here.

"Good girl," Birch muttered, "she's trying to slow them down." He hoped that was it anyway. She was certainly showing a lot more spunk than he gave her credit for.

Glaring down again at the screen of the sensor Birch scanned hopefully, looking for even the faintest trace of Karla, but like her captors she had now faded into the night. If they were going to find her it would have to be another way. There was nothing left for them to do but to fumble around in the dark and hope to find some trace of where they went, a dangerous task that probably had as great a chance of finding an enemy as Karla. He sighed and did it anyway. It was the only chance they had.

They searched in silence, looking for any sign of the direction they had taken. It was tedious, futile work and seemed fruitless until some time later when Birch's brooding thoughts were interrupted by DeSante's excited whisper.

"Here," his voice was barely audible as he waved him over. Birch was quickly at his side as he pointed to a patch of earth. "It looks like they were pretty careful to cover their tracks," he continued in a more subdued tone, "but they missed this one." It was true, a single faint footprint remained in isolation, seemingly headed in an easterly direction. This deep in the forest he knew it could only come from someone connected to

Karla's abduction. That single footprint represented the rebirth of hope in Birch's mind.

The Ares had changed direction, perhaps they knew they were being followed, or perhaps there was some other reason. Whatever it was Birch knew he would have to be cautious. If they were aware of their pursuit it would be dangerous for them and for Karla.

"Let's go," he barked, "we'll just head east from here and keep a lookout for any other signs as we go." DeSante nodded and followed silently.

As they trudged onward Birch cast frequent glances into the forest around them. He was seeking telling indicators of the Ares passing. He was watching for any movement and listening for any alien sound among the soft murmur of forest life around them. Once he thought he saw something in the trees to his right, but it was a fleeting impression and he couldn't be sure. He glanced down at the heat sensor's display again, but, as he expected, there was still nothing there. Even the camp had now dropped out of range and only the two central dots for himself and DeSante remained.

"Seen any sign of them yet?" the lieutenant whispered in his ear. Birch shrugged and kept walking. Time was moving quickly and he was aware that night would soon be melting into dawn. He worried that the Ares might have a place to hideout for the daylight hours, if so they would be impossible to find.

Twenty minutes of walking had not produced a single clue to the Ares' location. They were a lot more skilled and cautious than their attack and retreat from the camp had led him to believe. They had covered their trail well. Birch began to doubt that he would find it again. He was at that difficult point of wondering whether to go back and try to retrace their steps in case they had missed something, or go on and hope to find something ahead. For now he would go on. He would give it another five minutes.

Again there seemed to be a movement to his right. Had

DeSante seen it too? His question was answered before he asked it, as the lieutenant's rasping voice broke the silence. "Did you see that?" he hissed, "Something's up there." Birch nodded grimly, something was there and whatever it was it didn't come up on the heat sensor.

"I can't get a bead on it," Birch muttered, "it isn't showing any heat traces at all." He circled the tree, gazing upward, but saw nothing more. Nothing happened. For a time the dark embers of his hope grew dimmer. He stared habitually back down at the blank screen of the sensor, but there was still no trace. Then it happened again, a noise that echoed in the branches of the tree. Birch stepped back, glaring into the lofty boughs above.

"It's up there," he growled, "let's go find our little bird and get him to guide us back to his nest." DeSante looked dubiously at his commander for a moment, but before he could comment Birch had started toward the base of the tree.

Birch knew what his junior officer was thinking. He was right. It was a recklessness move, but it didn't matter because right now it was their only hope of finding the Ares and saving Karla. Besides, he reasoned to himself, it was no less dangerous to go after him now than to just leave him to follow them and attack at a moment of his own choosing. Perhaps he was a single scout, like the one that had attacked him at the camp. If he could stop him before he had a chance to report then that would give them the advantage. He was glad for the chance to take action. Now they could do something.

At the foot of the tree he carefully scanned the distant branches towering above him. He caught sight of something. He couldn't be sure, but yes, up there in the dark greenery something was moving! Ignoring the pain and fatigue in his limbs he launched himself at the tree and began clambering up through its lower branches. DeSante stood agog, watching his commander struggle upward. Birch didn't care. It was clear that he had treed something that didn't want to be caught. As he climbed further the topmost branches began to sway wildly as though something were trying to escape, but couldn't quite manage it. He had them.

His assent was slow. His hands, numb against the brittle bark, found it hard to grip and the pain in his body increased with the motion as he scaled ever upwards. As he neared the upper half of the tree his caution slowed him further, and he glanced about frequently, looking for his prey. Even so, he was startled when a pair of fiery eyes glared back at him as he lifted himself on to another branch. He caught the brief impression of gleaming steel coming down on him like the bared teeth of a wild beast.

# NINETEEN

Whether by instinct or by miracle, Birch swerved just enough to avoid the knife as it came flashing down at him, cutting through the air in front of his face. He caught a glimpse of the blade quickly shifting in his attacker's hand as it came at him again with frenzied stabbing motions. He hardly had time to react and, unthinkingly, Birch loosed his grip and fell crashing back to a branch a few feet below, hitting it hard in the chest. His rifle fell from his hands and went clack-clacking through the branches to the ground below.

For an instant he was winded; unable to move and only hanging loosely to the limb that preserved his life. Without looking he could feel the evil shadow descending after him.

Struggling to regain his breath he heaved himself up painfully, but before he could get his bearings he felt the slash of cold steel as the knife cut through his left arm. He heard the soft pat-pat of his blood falling, like a red rain onto the branches below. The cut wasn't deep, but it hurt and his eyes narrowed as he bit his lip angrily. Enraged, he lunged at the small, dark form, grabbing at the hand that held the knife. He struggled to force the weapon from his grasp. The fingers loosened slightly, but just as it seemed he might strip him of the blade his wiry assailant's other fist came thudding against the side of Birch's head, pounding repeatedly there like a piston. Birch lost his balance and fell back from the branch. Somehow, in spite of the thick haze that clouded his mind, he kept his hold on the hand that held the knife, and as he fell back the Ares was pulled over with him. In that moment it seemed that they would both fall, but their momentum was quickly stopped when his adversary, despite his smaller size, grabbed nimbly at the branch with his free hand and saved them both. They hung there precariously.

Birch gripped his attacker's wrist with both hands, trying to pull himself up, but now but he could feel it wrestling against him, trying to free itself of the burden and send him plunging to his death below. The sweat covering his own hands made it almost impossible to hang on, and yet he did. The knife, still clutched firmly in the fist he clung to, came again at Birch's face in short stabbing motions. His own weight was enough to restrict the knife's range of movement, though, and it couldn't reach him. It might have occurred to Birch in an abstract sort of way that it was a marvel that someone smaller than him could have the strength to hold them both up by one arm and still have the energy to attack. Of course these thoughts only came to him later, for at this point he realized that his grip was slipping and he looked wildly around for any way out. There wasn't much. All he could do was to drop to a lower branch and hope he could catch it in time.

Birch never made the decision to try it. It was made for him as his hands slipped and he instinctively swung toward another branch. He was falling.

He howled as the knife's blade passed through his hands leaving deep red trails. He didn't have time to think about it, though, as he grabbed at the branch that hurtled toward him. The pain of contact as his ribs smashed into it was almost unbearable, but still he held.

Slowly he drew himself up again. His hands were a mess of blood, but there wasn't much he could do about it except wipe them on his clothes and get ready for the next assault that he knew would be coming. Already he thought he could make out the evil little shadow, like some demon monkey, coming down from the higher branches. Would it ever give up?

His breathing came heavily and he winced with pain as he clenched his fists, ready to fight. The shadow came closer. It seemed native to the trees, holding on to the smooth surface of the trunk and jumping from branch to branch. It had reached Birch's position much more quickly than he had hoped, but he was ready. As the dark shadow leapt onto his branch Birch lashed out, landing a number of blows in its back. The pain from his own bloody fists made Birch scream, but still he attacked.

The creature fell back as Birch landed a punch to his ribs, and he heard the knife clacking against the tree as it fell to the ground below. Sensing the advantage shift Birch punched viciously at the slight form of his attacker. The pain from his own gushing hands barely registered as he struck a blizzard of blows on the retreating Ares. Relentlessly his fists thudded against his enemy until he landed a single punch that sent his enemy falling silently into the black void below.

For the first time in the dim moonlight he caught a glimpse of the face as it fell. It was young and wild, almost like that of some errant teenage boy, but harder and covered with blood. Something about that face and the look it gave as it fell choked the triumphant cheer in his throat, and he descended the tree as quickly as his painful body could manage.

Birch had expected serious injury, if not death, to result from such a fall, but upon reaching the ground a few moments later he was surprised to see DeSante, not aiding the injured youth, but preoccupied with keeping the writhing boy pinned to the ground. The Ares was not in pain, but making an angry attempt to free himself. He was a tough one, Birch mused, and he couldn't help admiring the Ares people for this diminutive example of their spirit and strength. This was much more of the character he had expected from Edwards' description. Not the frightened, fleeing foes from the battle.

DeSante, with his knee placed firmly on the young captives back, waved Birch over. The young lieutenant smiled ruefully as he approached.

"He's quite a little fireball," DeSante commented dryly. "He fell on his feet and came up fighting like a wildcat. It took all I had just to get him down again."

"Hmm," Birch mused, "let's see if we can douse his flame." He grabbed at the boy's shirt, pulled him to his feet, and pushed him hard against the trunk of a tree. For the second time he looked into the dirty face and saw a boy of sixteen, maybe fifteen, with flinty features and eyes filled with defiance. Birch smiled grimly, "It's time for us to talk," his words came cold and hard. "Where's your base? Where's your hostage?" No answer came. Birch's early sympathy had evaporated and he squeezed the boy's arms persistently. "You will talk," he rasped, "one way or another. Where is your base? Where is your hostage? Is she Okay?" He fired the questions like bullets at the boy, but he remained impassive. Only his eyes showed his silent disdain.

"Okay," Birch spat, "we can play it that way." He looked over to DeSante, "Give me the gun lieutenant." DeSante hesitated for a moment before handing him the rifle.

"Now," Birch continued, "I don't have time to waste here so let's just get to it. I've got somebody I need to rescue and I'm willing to bet your life that you know where they are." The boy's eyes bulged as the gun was pushed into his face.

"Major!" DeSante's voice came loud in the night air.

"Shut-up, lieutenant!" Birch hissed and turned back to the boy. "This is how it works," he rasped. "You'll tell me where our crew member is and we'll rescue her, ensuring that nobody gets hurt. The other option is that I'll have to dispose of you and go on the rampage through this forest until I find her. One of those things is going to happen, choose now which you want it to be because I don't want to waste my time on you. Are you going to do it, yes or no?" Birch fingered the trigger rhythmically.

The boy's face was wild and angry, but his eyes were fixed on the gun leveled at him. "Yeah," he growled, "I'll help, but don't think it'll help you. Our people are stronger than you; they will see things right."

Birch smiled coolly. "Yeah, yeah, your dad's bigger than my dad, and he'll beat us all up. We'll see," he muttered as he pulled the boy away from the tree and pushed him forward.

"Let's go," he called to DeSante, "it looks like we have a volunteer to help us out." As they moved away Birch caught the expression on DeSante's face, his disdain was clear and at another time he might have agreed with him, but this was different; they didn't have time for anything else.

"Are we the good guys here, Major?" DeSante muttered as he passed him.

Birch shrugged. "Is anybody?" he retorted.

A cold silence fell on the group as the chill of early morning came about them. It would be dawn soon and he feared that the Ares would dig in for shelter from the daylight. As long as they were moving he had a chance to catch them; hidden away they might miss them and never know it. The longer they went without finding them the worse he felt their chances were of getting Karla back alive. They had to get to her quickly, but the only thing they really had to depend on was the willingness of this unwilling Ares to get them there.

The boy proved to be an efficient guide. For the next twenty minutes he led them through the trailless woods without hesitation. Turning occasionally at unexpected places, the secrets of the earth and the undergrowth were revealed in a strange array of hidden dens, burrows, and passageways through the forest. The area seemed honeycombed with them, and the young Ares carefully maneuvered them from one to another. Birch was watching him closely, but it seemed that the boy no longer offered the same sullen resistance. He almost seemed eager in his leading. That was worrying. What was he leading them to? It could be a trap, but he still had to depend on the boy to get them to Karla. The best he could do was to try and be ready for whatever would come.

Finally they came to a stop at the edge of a wide clearing.

In the gray light of early dawn Birch surveyed the landscape. A large, imposing rock face climbed steeply up before them. "That's it," the boy announced pointing to the summit of the rocky expanse above them. "Your friend is there."

# TWENTY

An ominous shadow passed over Birch's mind as the brightness of dawn poured over the landscape. Daylight was here and should have lifted his spirits, but instead it seared his eyes and intensified the pain pounding through his skull. He failed to notice the beauty of the golden sunlight cast upon the feathery clouds above, or the glistening diamonds it generously bestowed in twinkling little points of dew on the grass and trees around them. The sweet yellow light streaming across the land seemed to offer a future of milk and honey, but he knew it lied. They stood for a moment and silently gazed upwards.

"It's beautiful," DeSante murmured softly. Birch grunted and scanned the jut of gray rock the Ares boy had pointed to a moment ago. The lower portion was a mass of fir trees; the top was a bald dome of stark stone towering above them. It was formidable. It struck Birch that this was a perfect position to defend and the worst possible one to attack. The trees lower down offered cover for the early stage of their approach, but the upper section was exposed. It wouldn't be easy to get to the top unseen. His mind was already processing the options. It was clear there wasn't any easy choice. He sighed.

"Okay kid," he pulled the boy to him. "It's time for us to get to work. Where's the place?"

The boy smiled widely. "On top of course," he answered slyly. "That's the best position to see everyone." Birch looked sharply at the youth. Something in the tone of voice, and his smug, satisfied expression made the statement alarming. They were in danger. Somehow he had turned the tables on them and led them into a trap. Probably he had found some way to signal his friends during their approach. Birch couldn't guess how, he hadn't seen anything, but he was certain that at this very moment the young man's cohorts were coming after them, and he guessed by the boy's gloating confidence that they only had a few minutes before they were captured. He had to act quickly.

"Thanks," he muttered and brought the butt of his rifle quickly down on the young Ares' head. DeSante gasped. The boy's smile withered and his eyes rolled as he crumpled to the ground, unconscious. "Don't say a word," Birch hissed in response to DeSante's incredulous look. "He was leading his friends to us and we need to act quickly here. We don't have time for the extra baggage. It'd be better if we split up; it's going to take a lot for us to make it and I think we'd have a better chance from different directions. Take this," he handed the rifle to DeSante, "you'll need it more than me."

DeSante shook his head. "That doesn't seem right, Major," he interrupted. "I can't leave you unarmed in this place."

Birch scowled, "Don't go feeling sorry for me until you've heard what I want you to do with that thing," he barked. "It's no use both of us trying to make it up there; we'd both get caught. If they are up there then nothing would get past them, especially if they had the luxury of just sitting and watching for us. What we need is a distraction. That's where you and that rifle come in. I need you to do all you can to draw their attention away from that rock face. I'm going to need you to fire that thing around like there's the mother of all battles going on down here. Keep moving though. If you can tempt them down that'll make it easier for me to storm the top, but it also means they'll be after you, so watch out."

"Storm the top?" DeSante asked dubiously. "With what? You'll have no gun and your hands are injured. It'll be hard enough for you to even make it up there in your condition. There's got to be a better way."

DeSante's words were spoken in genuine concern rather than malice, as Jane's often were. Even so, they still sounded like mutiny to Birch. They were unwelcome, and for a moment he let them hang uncomfortably in the air before he finally wrestled them down. His answer came short and sharp.

"No," his voice was calm but failed to hide his anger, "there's not a better way. I'm the only one who can do it. You've got to make the distraction; I've got to make the rescue. It's the only way it'll work."

"But how will we get back together? How can we find each other again in a place like this?" His voice trailed off. Birch detected the hint of fear that he hadn't picked up before. He understood. This wasn't a place to be alone, but it was their only chance.

"It'll be fine, DeSante," Birch's voice sounded almost soothing for once. "You've got the gun and I've got the heat sensor. When we've finished I'll use the heat sensor to find you and then all three of us will get out of here together. Now we better get going before neither of us gets anywhere. Got it?" DeSante nodded resolutely. "Good, head to the east and try and draw them off there, I'll come in from the west and maybe the shadows will give me some extra cover while I climb up the other side. I'm counting on you to make sure they're not going to be watching for me."

DeSante smiled nervously. "I'll do it," he replied.

"Good," Birch spoke evenly, "if we all get out of this alive I'll remember to thank you for it. Well, let's get going."

"Good-bye, sir."

It was the briefest of farewells and without further word the two men took their own direction without looking back.

As Birch walked back from the clearing he again felt the towering presence of the trees surround him. Their influence was a strange paradox of comfort and fear in his mind. He knew that they offered him protection and safety. It would be harder for the Ares to find him among the trees, but he was also aware that it would be harder to see anything himself, and the Ares were experts at hiding.

The morning air was still and cold under the canopy of branches, except where small gaps had allowed the warming sunlight to reach the forest floor. Birch shivered and walked silently on. The noisy chorus of birdsong had replaced the stillness of night and he found himself listening intently for something, anything that might be an Ares communication among the noise. It was hard to tell, but he thought he heard something different, something out of place, less striking than the screech of an owl in the still night air, but equally ominous.

He glanced around him. The daylight had made little difference to the gloomy impression of his surroundings. In the sunlight of the clearing the earth had seemed new and fresh, now under the dreary shade of the forest he could only smell the dank rot of old trees and an earthy mixture of vegetation and mud. Somehow he didn't feel alone. Wary watchfulness marked every step; he knew he must be cautious. The Ares, though unseen, seemed to be everywhere, if only in his mind.

The sudden sound of intense gunfire brought him to a stop. It was coming from somewhere to the east. DeSante was firing already. The sound ceased as suddenly as it had begun. There was no way of telling what had happened. It didn't sound like there was any return fire, but something must have made him shoot early. Perhaps the Ares had caught up with him. That wasn't good; he had counted on DeSante providing cover as he climbed the bare rock of the crag. If he was out already he would have to go it alone and hope he wouldn't be noticed.

For a moment Birch found himself considering going back to help, but he knew that risked everything. He had to save Karla and trust the young lieutenant to do his part. Still he couldn't help wondering at the sudden end to the gunfire, and his ears strained to hear the reassuring booming start up again. It didn't, and Birch sweated his way through the rest of the woods until the tree cover ran out and he found himself facing the bare rock leading up to the overlook some five hundred feet above.

The rock face was impressive enough, smooth and featureless in a straight vertical line to the top, but it wasn't the steep assent that worried him. It was his hands.

Birch was a climber. He loved to climb. It hadn't always been so, but in later years he had found a true passion for it. It seemed to match the purpose of his life, the solitary pleasure and the feel of the rock, solid beneath his hands and feet, with the challenged sky waiting above. It was in this pursuit, rather than in space travel, that he felt closer to life. The ground was secure, the goal was above, and only the honest bluntness of nature's obstacles lay between him and success. He could do this. At least usually he could. This time was going to be different. The pain and fear made this something else. What might have been a challenge on a gentle Sunday afternoon had become a life struggle on this cool mountain morning.

DeSante had been right; this was going to be hard. Flexing his fingers below the bloody cloths that served as bandages he bit hard against the pain just to stop himself from screaming aloud. He dared not look more closely. The condition of his hands seemed better left a mystery beneath the oozing cloth. He might cope better that way. Instead he concentrated on the task before him. He could see how it might be done. The danger of detection was great because of the exposed rock, but he imagined that he could see some natural cover from overhangs and ruts in the stone, and he knew that if he was careful to use every natural advantage he might make it.

Barely within the protective embrace of the forest, he sat plotting his path. The shadows created by the jutting rock's own form against the low morning sun created dark crevices and cracks in the smooth stone that he knew he could exploit. It was possible. It all depended where they were watching, and how carefully they were watching. Of course it also depended on how well his hands held out. There was hope, but again there was fear. Only in despair was there true fearlessness. If only DeSante hadn't been pushed out of the way so quickly, the chances would be better. Grimly he steeled himself to the task and moved into the open.

His mind was clear on the direction he would take, and without hesitation he bolted from the trees to the rock. He didn't waste any time dodging or weaving, the bare, exposed ground gave nothing to dodge or weave behind, and the extra activity would have only increased the likelihood of detection. His run was straight and fast and when he reached the bottom of the rocky cliff a few minutes later he was puffing breathlessly, confident that so far he had gone unnoticed.

He was at the bottom. Looking up the steep incline he felt the same old anticipation for the climb, despite the circumstances. It began easily enough. The incline started gently and as it increased he found generous handholds and footholds that, though they seemed natural from a distance, were clearly made for this purpose. In other circumstances it would have been easy, even as free-soloing, like traveling on a paved road with street signs and road maps, but today it wasn't. Back an eternity ago, when climbing was nothing more than an amusement, he might have even complained that it wasn't challenging enough, but today he was struggling. The pain in his hands was increasing with every heave and lift upwards. The expert placement of the holes should have made it easy. They allowed him to put much more weight on his feet when he was in the resting position, but he couldn't avoid the wrenching and tearing at his hands as he pulled himself up. He was leaving little red patches on the stones he touched, like a bloody trail of crumbs that might lead him back down if he ever made it to the top.

Exhaustion was setting in. His mind was struggling to concentrate, to overcome his pain and still focus on what he needed to do. The shadows had covered him pretty well up to that point, and he had used any crevice he could find to allow him a place to hide in his frequent stops. But at last, two hundred feet from the top, he came to a complete stop. He couldn't do it any more. The task ahead, the exhaustion from the night before, his hands, it all seemed to crash together in his brain like a blur of reality and he felt himself sway and drift, both mentally and physically. He just wanted to rest. He would do anything just to rest. It was that dangerous point where the distance above was so hard, and in the delusion of the moment it almost seemed right, that it would be easier to just fall into an everlasting rest than to have to go on.

For a time he just hung there. No thought came to him beyond the simple act of clinging to that one piece of rock and to life itself. He dangled, but he did not fall. Slowly again one arm moved, then another. With deliberate, wrenching action he started again, one hand, then another, until momentum took over and he was able to believe again that he might make it to the top.

Mechanically he climbed. As his mind slowly cleared Birch began to wonder at the lack of reaction to his assent. Either they hadn't seen him or they were waiting quietly at the top to gather him up after he got there. He knew he had made mistakes on the climb. They should have seen him. Probably they had and were just waiting for him, letting him exhaust himself before they picked him up at the top. They wouldn't take him that easily though.

He wondered about DeSante. He hadn't fired again since those first few shots. The thought nagged him that he may have rescued the young lieutenant just to get him killed a few hours later. That didn't seem right. If there was any purpose to anything they had to make it. Too much had happened for them to fail now. It was this irrational hope that fueled him now in the grueling climb toward Karla, and it was that same hope that told him that DeSante wasn't dead. They hadn't come this far for nothing; they would live and he would save them all. He would get them out of this place. Beyond that he wasn't really sure. He guessed the convoy would have continued east rather than wait for another Ares attack. He'd probably try to catch them in that direction.

Birch stopped himself. His train of thought had taken him far beyond where he was and what he was doing. He knew it was foolish to hope too much or to think too much about what they had to do. First they had to live.

Finally, by the steel of his will, he had mastered the indomitable rock. He placed his bloodied hand into the last hole and heaved himself up to eye level with the top. From here he could see what was there to meet him. He was looking for any kind of camp or settlement, but there was nothing, not even a lookout or a sentinel. It was abandoned, or perhaps no one had ever been there at all. Cautiously he waited. He suspected a trap, but he could see nothing. Finally his weariness won out and he pulled himself up with one last flash of energy that died immediately as he collapsed onto the dusty ground at the top.

If the Ares had been watching Birch would have easily been subdued. For a time all he could do was lie in the warming sunlight as he drifted into a shivering semi-consciousness. It was a few minutes before he awoke again; he was still alone. As he stumbled to his feet he cautiously looked about him, no one was there and his fears slowly melted into doubt and then finally anger. The boy had tricked him. There was no sign of any activity here and he'd wasted probably six or seven hours in the climb. Now he had lost both DeSante and Karla. He had been so caught up in the difficulties of the task that he hadn't even stopped to question if it made any sense, and now he raged angrily within at his own stupidity. It was the one thing he could never tolerate, his own mistakes.

For a time he stewed, but eventually he took advantage of the altitude to view the vista around him. He was looking for any clue that could help him. To the east there was the prairie, stretching out as a flat table, laid out for miles beneath a fierce blue sky. It was wild. The tall grasses of old western days had replaced the regimented order of fields and the geometric patterns made by irrigation machines. He had flown over it hundreds of times, but he looked on it now as he had never seen it before. The Midwest was wild again. Nature had taken back what had been wrested from her hands years ago and it seemed an ominous foretelling of a future of change.

To the West Birch saw the mountain range they had passed through. The dense forest stood in contrast to the open plains to the east. In all this panorama he saw nothing of those he was looking for. He was alone. The heat sensor provided no comfort, even DeSante wasn't showing up now and Birch's solitary flashing red speck on the display seemed to increase the impression that he was utterly alone in this world.

It was as Birch contemplated his descent down the cliff that a thought occurred to him. This lump of rock seemed useless, a diversion, but the way he had gotten up here proved the lie in that idea. That climbing path was too smooth, too perfect to be anything natural, and it had seemed to prove to him that this was some sort of Ares haunt. It was only in the disappointment at the empty top that he had flung away all hope. Perhaps there might still be more to this, it was at least worth looking more closely before he left.

The task was not a lengthy one, the rock was bare and his search seemed fruitless. There wasn't much to see but bare stone and rocks in great heaps. The thought of those stones began to trouble him. They looked natural enough in these surroundings and hadn't drawn his attention until he considered how it was they got here. He couldn't think of any natural cause for their presence, not in piles like that, but what did they mean? He had some idea, but he had to test it out. He had to move those rocks.

Birch was quickly to the task, though his screaming hands rebelled at the activity. His bandages were now little more than bloody tatters and his fingers were nearly crippled into gnarled claws, so that he could only lift the larger stones with the palms of his hands and roll them roughly aside. He kept working. It took some time, but eventually a tuft of moldy cloth and a broken rusted cage appeared amongst the rubble. He pulled at it as best he could and exposed a part of what lay underneath. He turned away heaving from the stench, it was the half rotted remains of a corpse. He had discovered a burial ground.

It seemed too much to take, but as he bitterly considered this latest defeat he noticed something about one rock pile that seemed different. Where the other stones were dry and blanched, these were dark and muddy. Some were slightly wet. They had been placed recently. Birch's heart quailed at the thought of the meaning behind this little pile, but doughtily he set to this last vestige of hope.

The stones came off easily and slid down like little tears shed for the people in this place. As he came closer to the bottom Birch noticed a wire cage, not rusted like the last one, but with a similar cloth beneath it. He pulled at the metal, wrenching it free from the stones and clumsily causing smaller ones to tumble onto the cloth swathed figure. Trembling, Birch removed them and pulled at the sticky, oozing material. It was Karla.

# TWENTY-ONE

Morning had come as an unwelcome relief to Edwards. The light of dawn meant the lifting of uncertainty. It meant a return to their world of day from the Ares' world of night. There would be no more attacks until the darkness returned, at least he believed so. What had taken place already had been so far from his expectations and experience that he couldn't feel certain of anything.

The light of daybreak had not brought its usual comfort. It brought the grim reality of what had happened. It exposed the destroyed trucks with their last wispy traces of smoke bleeding out from their burned shells. Ash and death were strewn everywhere. In the darkness of night you could almost deny the events. It had been so unreal that it wasn't unreasonable to doubt what you knew and consider it nothing more than a grave delusion. Daylight made it what it was, a slaughter. Still, he told himself that it hadn't been their choice to kill.

The choice had belonged to the Ares'. They had attacked in numbers, and it wasn't just their methods during the battle that had surprised him, but also the result. He'd known for sure they were all dead when he saw the force ranged against them. There had never been an attack on that scale before, and their own security preparations had been woefully inadequate. They had not been prepared for it. Somehow the Ares had surprised them, and if they had pressed their advantage they would have destroyed them. For some reason they didn't and Edwards marveled that he was still alive.

In the end they had won out over the Ares' overwhelming force. Something inside their attackers must have flinched or buckled at the crucial moment. That wild unthinking side of them, so formidable at other times, had been turned and changed into that other most basic animal instinct, the need to run. It was strange to Edwards though; it didn't fit with what he knew of the Ares. They had run, but he didn't know why. Some would glibly claim that it was a natural victory, superiority had won out, but he wanted a better answer. Something incredible had happened here and he wanted to understand it.

It was the age-old battle between good and evil, between reason and force. Like everyone else, he had learned it from childhood. Like everyone else, he had seen its bitter results, and like everyone else, he hoped it would end. He remembered what everyone knew, what was known from the very beginning, that when reason battles force the contest may be brutish and foul, but reason would win. They had won. Last night's events seemed to prove all of this, but as the memory tumbled through his mind the two sides merged into one bloody conflict. Two sides of the same coin. Maybe they had proved their superiority here, but at a terrible price. In that moment he hated the Ares, not for what they had done, but for what they had made him do.

To his weary eyes the smoldering ruins of the camp presented a distressing sight. The mangled wreckage of the trucks, bodies strewn about them, mud and blood everywhere. It was hard to see. Through the night they had cleared the circle of the camp, but all around them the twisted wreckage of humanity still lay, deserted like so much useless equipment. It made Edwards sick, not from the sight of it, not even the smell of it, but from the idea of it. He wasn't made for this; no one should be made for this. For a moment all he could do was stare up to the heavens, the one place unsullied by the scene.

Little wonder that people like the Hypnos crew had dreamt of an escape out there, to get away from this, from what they had made it, but if they took themselves along then what would really change? Could that big blue sky cleanse and wash them of who they were, like refreshing waters? Could anything clean them?

His eyes went to ground. They had to go. The situation was tough and they needed to get out of the mountains as quickly as possible. Another night would kill them. Already they were decimated. Six men were known dead. Nine others were missing, Commander Konik was one of them. Also missing were three of the dependants, Birch, Dawson, and DeSante. That left just two and they had to get them to safety with all speed. He was in command now. The sergeant was gone and only twelve men of the complement were left. Two of them were from their escort that had been due to return once they reached the other side of the mountain range. They would be staying with them now.

The search for survivors didn't last long. The heat sensors had shown no signs of life in the area apart from their own. There wasn't any use wasting time looking for something that wasn't there. The bodies of a number of their company, including Konik and the three passengers, had not been recovered, but that didn't mean they weren't there somewhere among the carnage. They didn't have the time to look. If they were there they were dead anyway, and if they weren't then they had been carried off somewhere out of range. There was no way to follow. It was an impossible task.

Jane had argued about it, they were her colleagues and she wanted to help, but Edwards had refused. He had almost pushed her and Lauren physically into the trucks to get them to go. They had wanted to stay, to look for their friends. It was understandable but he couldn't let them. His job was to get these two to Washington. They were in enough trouble as it was without risking the loss of these last two. They had to make it.

What was salvageable was swiftly packed away and the convoy was quickly moving again. It was a sorry reflection of its former self. Two battered troop carriers and the missile launcher were all that remained of their group; the rest were left to rust or rot where they lay. Edwards had been careful to remove or destroy anything useful to the Ares; at least they would be deprived of the spoils of their attack.

The next step was clear, get to safety. There was an outpost three or four days travel from their present location, on the eastern side of the mountains. These eastern bases were tiny, but well protected bastions against the wild excesses of the Ares. Their complement was small, but their firepower was formidable, as was their reputation. Despite their size none of the Ares ever willingly engaged them in open attack, but waited for troop changes or patrols to ambush. If they could make it there they would be safe, for a time at least, before they traveled on to Washington. They needed time to rest and repair, and to gather whatever strategy they could for what lay ahead.

Edwards' immediate concern had been with the condition of the road. They needed to be fast, another day of delays would leave them stuck in the mountains another night and he knew that another attack like the last one would destroy them. They had to get off that mountain before nightfall. In this respect the day's experience turned out better than he could have hoped. Where their travel had previously been slow and interrupted, this time it was swift and uneventful. Apparently the Ares had been confident in the success of their night raid, and had made no provision to slow their progress beyond the camp. As a result they encountered no mines and passed swiftly through the remainder of the mountain range.

Their speed was a blessed relief to Edwards. He couldn't get away from the night's scene quickly enough, but as they drew away he had seen the futility; he would never leave this place. His body might move on, but the scene would live with him forever. Maybe the others could live with it, they were trained to kill, but he was trained to protect and understand life, not destroy it. He understood death well enough, but his hands had been unbloodied until now. In theory he knew what had to be done to protect themselves, but the practice was alien to him. He was in a foreign land. He knew that they had only done what was needed to keep themselves alive, and he understood that their enemy was merciless and wild, but while his mind accepted these things his stomach could not.

These were the feelings Edwards fought with as they traveled. He took no pleasure in the victory. Unlike the soldier class, who high-fived at the defeat of another Ares attack, he was affected. It made him sick. Somehow this had to stop, and yet here he was in the middle of it all and in the sad realization that he had to do the very thing he hated to survive. He must defeat the very hopes he held or die uselessly supporting them.

***

Birch leant silently over the grave. The futility of his search dawned slowly on him as rage welled up inside him. Angrily he pulled at the iron ribs and inner cloth that embraced Karla. Metal cracked and cloth tore until a few minutes later she was free of her primitive sarcophagus and lying limply at his feet. She was peaceful now. Her face showed no sign of distress and her restful countenance only seemed to fuel Birch's fury. He shook the body mercilessly, madly seeking life in the lifeless, but instead of waking her it seemed she had the power to draw him down, even down into her own grave. His head spun. The robe she had worn was sticky, pungent, and powerful, and a putrid residue from it remained on his bandaged fingers. Something in it, or perhaps in her, seemed to grip him physically and to pull him down into a spinning darkness, he pulled away instinctively but felt the magnetic attraction irresistibly beckoning him. Karla was there, but no longer dead. She was alive and vibrant, and it was he who had died.

# TWENTY-TWO

Birch's head hurt, and the fact that someone was slapping his face wasn't helping. It took three blows before his muddled brain finally recognized what was happening enough to react. He pushed the hands away and punched back hard. A light, laughing voice responded to his heavy blows. "Hey, getting feisty aren't you?" his attacker complained. "It seemed like this was the only way to get you to wake up, but you can cut the rough stuff now! I promise not to hit you again."

It was Karla's voice and as Birch's eyes cleared he was astounded by a vision of her bending over him, not dead, but looking very much alive and vibrant after her ordeal. She was somehow better than before, better than last night before the battle, better than before everything had gone wrong on the mission, better than he had ever seen her. He guessed that she was glad to be rescued, but she seemed positively radiant, and under the circumstances it struck him as strange to be so happy.

"What happened to you?" Birch muttered, rubbing his head painfully. "Weren't you dead?" Karla laughed again, but a shadow of trouble passed across her face for an instant as she shook her head.

"I guess not," she responded, her hair bobbed and her eyes danced as she spoke, "though I don't know why I'm alive. I guess I'm just blessed."

"That and the fact that you've got crazy people who'll come and get you when you get yourself kidnapped," Birch remarked bitterly. Karla didn't notice his tone. She was too happy. She only seemed to have two modes of operation and it was hard for Birch to know which irritated him more. Most of the time she was a bouncing ball of personified happiness. It was like she was some kind of conductor of human joy, and she had to inflict others with the same condition. Birch found it maddening, but probably marginally preferable to her rare dips into despair, that could be pretty ugly. She could crack under pressure. A few times on the mission he'd worried that she might come unglued, but that was just part of the baggage of Karla.

Right now it was her exuberant joy he had to endure. It was understandable, she had come back from the dead, but still it grated against his nerves. His head throbbed and she was like one of those ever-smiling flight attendants that woke you on a redeye flight with their inane patter about good mornings and disembarking. The difference of course was that on the flight all you wanted to do was sleep, and all he wanted to do right now was curl up and die. His legs ached, his back hurt, and his hands were a pair of bloody numbed pulps at the end of his arms. He had rescued her, but her life in the face of his exhaustion was draining. The effort of the night and reaching her had left him utterly empty.

"What do you think we should do now?" Karla asked, prodding him again as if to make sure he didn't go back to sleep. He wished she would just let him alone, but somewhere within the remnant of his thoughts he knew she was right. They had to get going. That didn't make it any easier. He sat groggily up and looked around. The sun was toward the west and the shadows were getting longer, it must have been late afternoon; he had been out for a while.

"The first thing we have to do is get off this rock as quickly as we can. It would be very easy for them to trap us up here if they come back. You look around and see what looks like the easiest route down, I'm going to see if I can get any reading on DeSante again." He pulled the heat sensor from his belt and clicked it on.

Karla frowned, "You don't think they'll be watching for us in the daylight do you?" Her voice was nervous again and a shadow crossed her once carefree face.

"It's possible," Birch snapped. He was glaring down at the sensor's screen. Karla's heat was registering again; her disapp-earance from the readout must have had something to do with that foul cloth she had been wrapped in. Now DeSante was missing and he couldn't help wondering if he was now in a similar position. He turned to look at Karla.

"Trust me," his voice was calm, "I made it up here. We'll make it down. We still have some daylight left, and from what I know of these guys the night is their time. I don't know why they stuck you up here, or what their plans were, but I'm sure I don't want to be up here tonight to see if they're coming back to get you." Karla shivered in the early evening sun. "We need to get down," Birch continued, "and the sooner the better. It'll be dark soon and I want us to get somewhere safe and find some cover before night."

He staggered to his feet. Karla tried to steady him as he stepped closer to the edge. "I'm okay," he muttered gruffly and pulled his arm away. Shoving the heat sensor back onto his belt he strode to the precipice and looked down. There was no sign of the Ares, but he was sure that the longer they waited the greater their chances of bumping into one of them coming back up.

He and Karla scanned along the top for the best way down. Instinctively he was drawn to the idea of descending the same way he had climbed, he was familiar with the terrain, but now that side would now be covered in sunlight, exposing them clearly to any watching eyes below. It might not have made a difference, but he thought it could. He wouldn't go that way, besides he had noticed an easier incline on the shaded eastern side.

Looking about the cliff-face he saw more holes. The same type of holes marked out across the stone as those he had used in his assent that morning. The rock surface was covered with them in all directions, well-worn holes and grooves like the cells from a bee's hive. The impression came to him suddenly that this was somewhere important. This wasn't just any rock. It was a place that meant something to the Ares. The marks and holes in the side of the cliff gave evidence to frequent travel. Perhaps there was some deeper reason for putting Karla up here. This was more than just as a safe place to stow her while they rested in the daylight hours. As he looked around he could imagine the holes used by hundreds of wild Ares at a time, all pushing for the top from every side. This was a dangerous place. He turned quickly to Karla.

"We better get down now. I've got a bad feeling about this place, and it looks like we've probably only got a few hours of sunlight left. We won't make it to the bottom by nightfall. I'm not sure what'll happen after that, but we have to try. We need to hurry!" Karla looked doubtfully at her commander.

"I'm not that confident a climber, Major," her voice trailed off for a moment in response to his withering glance. "I don't know if I can do it." Her bright smile had disappeared. Birch sighed. There was something fragile in her voice that warned him that if he didn't handle this right she wouldn't go at all, and then, because he couldn't leave her, they'd both be stuck at the top. At least she wasn't so irritatingly cheerful anymore, he mused bitterly.

He tried to be patient.

"You'll just have to do your best, lieutenant. You can make it if you try." It was as close to sympathy as he could manage. "You better make it quick though," he added pointedly, "because if we're not down in the next few hours then we probably won't make it at all."

Secretly he wasn't so sure that he could make it himself. His hands had gone numb, and while this gave him welcome respite from the pain, it also robbed him of the climber's most important asset, the ability to feel. Without it he would be groping for handholds and cracks. His hands would grasp, but could not perceive. The potential for catastrophe was obvious.

Absolution from his pain had led them into deadly danger. He didn't share his fears with Karla. He just planned around them. He would go first on the descent. It made sense anyway; he could lay out a path and guide her over the problem areas as they came to them. It also meant that if he fell he wouldn't take her with him.

He glanced down one last time at the cliff face then turned to Karla. "Let's go," he muttered. His eyes went briefly again to his bandaged hands, the blood had dried to a crusty brown but the tattered rags were wet with perspiration. He rubbed them in the dirt and then on his pants before turning and slowly edging toward the precipice. His foot found the first hole and slowly he began the descent.

His hands were working. He could imagine the feel of the grains of dirt and flinty rock beneath them and he felt secure. His mind was absorbed in the task and he had taken a few dozen steps down before he noticed that Karla wasn't following him. He sighed. "What are you doing up there, Dawson?" he hissed as loudly as he dare. There was no answer. Grimly he retraced a few steps, resenting the lost ground, and repeated the question.

"I'm coming," Karla's voice came weakly from above, "this isn't my favorite part and it'll take me a minute to get it right. Birch sighed again, but didn't press her too hard, he was desperate to get down and even now the sky seemed to be darkening visibly, yet he knew that if he wanted her to get down at all he needed to just let her deal with it. It was always easier getting on the roof than off it, anyone who had ever climbed a ladder knew that, and though he was impatient to go he also knew that Karla would do this better alone and without his comment.

Finally he could see her. It was like watching a child fearfully pulling themselves to the edge of their grown-up bed for the first time. He doubted many children were as slow and fearful as Karla looked just then. She couldn't have looked more alarmed if the whole Ares force had suddenly appeared at the top with their weapons drawn.

Eventually her tentative legs found the first foothold and she slowly began her descent. Birch shook his head, "How did you get up here?" he asked "I can't imagine how you made it at that speed." Karla didn't answer for a moment; she was fumbling for the next foothold.

"I don't have any idea," She mumbled, "I was totally out of it. I guess they must have carried me up." She clumsily began her descent. "You wouldn't like to help me out on the return journey would you?" she added slyly, "That might speed things up you know."

Birch laughed in spite of himself. "I'll see how you go. I think the way my hands feel right now it would probably be a faster shortcut than you'd be comfortable with."

Karla smiled and shook her head. She was strange, her despair had melted away again and that irrepressible sunshine she had inside her was trying to burst out again. She would get down better that way anyway.

Birch tried to turn his attention again to the rock face. Staying still had been difficult. When he had momentum he could keep going, but now his hands bothered him again. He wiped the sweaty bandages on his pants then began his descent again. Karla was still a distraction; he was constantly aware of her hesitant movement above him. She was going at a steady speed, but it was much too slow to get them down in time. This route was easier than the one he had taken that morning, and on a good day he could have finished it in two or three hours. This wasn't a good day. Karla was holding him back. Even in his debilitated condition he could have done it more quickly alone. "Hurry Karla," He repeated, "it's getting dark!" She nodded, grunted, but continued at the same languid pace.

She was doing her best, but it didn't look like it would be good enough. The sun would be down soon and the Ares would be back.

It was impossible to see the western horizon from their side of the cliff. The rock obscured their view, but the dusky hue of the sky made it clear that the sun had set, leaving them in the cold night until it should rise again the next day. This was the Ares' time and they were on the Ares' ground.

They were still nearly a hundred feet from the ground as the last dim ray of sunlight gave way to the ebony sky of a moonless night. This was going to be hard. Now he and Karla would have to find their handholds and footholds without seeing. Karla would be slowed even more, and his own danger of falling would be greatly increased. More alarming, though, was what the darkness meant. He hadn't seen anything in the dying daylight, but Birch nervously expected the Ares to return with nightfall. The first they would know about it would be when they bumped into one of them on their way to the top. That was a real possibility. All they could really do right now was get down as fast as could and hope nothing met them on the way.

At that moment he heard it, the call of an owl from the woods beneath them. It wasn't the screeching of the night before, rather the more calm hooting sound, but it still came as an unwelcome shock.

"Did you hear that?" Karla's rasping voice came from somewhere above. "Is it one of them?"

"I heard it just fine," Birch hissed. "Just shut-up and get moving!" In the darkness He couldn't be sure where Karla was anymore, but she sounded closer than he had expected. Perhaps fear had finally inspired her to find it within herself to speed up. He began to hope. If they both hurried then they might just make it off of this rock alive. As unsettling as the birdcall had been it was the passive call, not the war-like screech of the other night. Perhaps they didn't know they were here yet. That was as much as he could have hoped for; the only thing was making sure it stayed that way. The call had sounded like it was from nearby, though, so he would have to be careful.

The last few feet passed swiftly and finally he found himself standing once again on solid earth. It felt good. He slumped silently against the rock for a moment, with his head resting between his knees.

A few minutes passed. He listened anxiously for any sound of Karla; he was still too tired to do any more than that. As he waited the owl's call sounded nearby again. It was on the cliff this time, somewhat to the left of his position, close enough to Karla to put her in real danger. If she made a noise or moved at all she would be discovered. He had been lucky. His exhaustion had left him silently sitting when he was in danger, and he had not been discovered. Now he had to hope Karla would be equally fortunate. He wanted to let her know, to warn her to stay still, but there wasn't any way he could without being detected himself.

For a time he waited breathlessly, waiting for the sound of discovery, the upheaval that would probably result in the capture of them both, but no sound came. A few moments later he made out the slight silhouette of the girl shakily stepping down onto the dusty ground. He sighed tiredly and beckoned to her with a hoarse whisper. For an instant she started, but quickly recognizing his voice she walked over to him.

"How did you escape that one?" Birch whispered.

Karla shrugged. "I heard him coming, that habit they have of whistling like a bird comes in handy you know. All I had to do was stay still for a while. He must have missed me by about two feet," she added coolly. Birch shook his head in wonder. How anyone could be so broken up over a simple thing like a climb, yet so calm over something like a near miss with a deadly enemy was a mystery to him. He still couldn't understand Karla. He probably never would.

The Ares' speed of assent was almost superhuman. To them a climb like this seemed as natural as walking or running. As a result they were reaching the top not long after Karla and Birch had reached the bottom.

From up above the calls of the Ares were growing more frequent and loud. They formed a discordant chorus of sound that grew and echoed in the air around them. Birch shuddered. They had to get out of here; if they were looking for Karla they'd find her missing pretty soon and he guessed things would get pretty uncomfortable around here once that happened. He wasn't sure what their plans had been for her up there, but he didn't want to be around to give them a second chance at it.

"Let's get going," he murmured and led the way cautiously back toward the trees. Once under their boughs he might have allowed himself a moment of relief, a brief thought of safety, but he still realized that cover in the forest worked both ways, and probably more to the Ares' advantage than his. They had to find somewhere to hide, and quickly. They couldn't run in the darkness. It was too treacherous and there might still be plenty of the enemy down there. They needed to get out of the way for a while; if they were still on the move when that mass of savages came back down he knew they wouldn't have a chance.

The sudden howling screech made Karla jump. Birch's eyes narrowed, they had gone to get her from the rock pile and had found their cupboard bare; he was sure of that. Now they would be after them. Their warlike screams came hard and long, a hundred angry voices raised in raging tempest. It didn't stop, it seemed as though the mountain was erupting with sound and Birch and Karla quaked involuntarily at the fury of it. At all costs they knew they must never fall into the hands of those howling savages!

In dreadful fear they sought any cover, any place that might hide them from the coming attack. The voices already were moving. They had not lessened in their intensity, but had grown in power and seemed to be descending the cliff. Soon a tidal wave of maddened Ares would hit them again and desperately they sought for safety.

It wasn't much, but eventually Birch found a hollow dip at the base of a huge coniferous tree. A few large, needle covered branches lay about it. It wasn't a great hope but if they passed by quickly enough it might suffice. "Over here," he whispered. "It's not great but it'll have to do. They're getting close by the sound of it." Indeed they were. Their speed down the rock was in striking contrast to the long descent of Birch and Karla. This wasn't a surprise to Birch, who remembered the Ares youth who had attacked him in that tree the night before. They could move like wildlife.

Karla looked at the rut dubiously. "That's it?" Her voice was disappointed and desperate, she'd hoped Birch had found somewhere to hide, something that might save their lives, not some dip at the foot of a tree.

"It'll work," Birch reassured her, "I'll get in first, then you. We cover it up with the branches and wait for them to pass. They'll be in a hurry to catch us. They'll probably expect us to run so they could easily miss us if we lie low here. You better hurry though. They sound like they're almost down already."

Karla nodded.

"I guess it might work," she said, picking up the branches by the tree, "but we could make it a little harder for them." She retraced their steps some twenty yards back and then, carefully ensuring that she left prints in the dirt, ran out in another direction toward a large clump of pine needles. She then returned to their original path, taking care to brush away all their other tracks with the branches. Birch shook his head. Karla was full of surprises.

"Hurry," Birch's voice was barely a whisper, "they're almost here." The screaming was deafening now. It was impossible to tell how many of them had come down on their side, but it sounded like a lot and Birch was anxious to take cover.

Coolly Karla finished erasing the final footprints.

"Get in," she responded, "I'll be right there." Birch dived in first and Karla quickly followed. The hole was inadequate. Birch could barely fit much of himself in and Karla was hanging out pretty far. Desperately he pulled her closer.

"Pull yourself into a ball. Get as close as you can!" he hissed. Finally they covered themselves, settling under the branches where they lay quietly waiting. Under their green canopy they sweated and listened for any sound. The air was stifling. The heady mix of pine, sweat, and the sweet scent of Karla's hair in his face made it hard to breathe.

They waited. In a way it was like a childhood game of hide-and-seek, except that the delicious anticipation of discovery in the game was replaced with actual fear. Under the blanket of branches the stale air became hard to breathe. In the childhood game you would finally give up and come out gasping for breath. They knew death would follow if they did, so they held on to each other and their hope in the stifling atmosphere.

The screeching voices were nearing. Quickly a few passed their spot and kept running. Birch tried to see them through the small gaps between the branch's needles, but Karla's head was in the way. It was dark anyway and there wasn't much that could be seen out there. Another form passed by a moment later letting out the same intermittent scream. The sound brought back the horrors of the night before, but this night's new terrors alone was enough to make him cold beneath the suffocating branches.

Another form passed a short time later, not so quickly or noisily as the others. It paused near them. It seemed to be sniffing the air, as if he could find the scent of their location. It was unnerving. They were helpless, like the innocents of the womb in total darkness. Safety and warmth were the illusion that surrounded them, but with adult knowledge they knew it could all end in the next instant. Karla shivered and Birch squeezed her reassuringly. He shivered too. He heard the slow, deliberate footsteps coming back toward them. At any moment he expected the branches to disappear and the snarling face of an enemy to glare down into their tiny sanctuary. That moment didn't come. Instead the footsteps continued past them, paused again as though checking something, and hurried off into the distance. Birch couldn't help but think that Karla's forethought in laying a false trail had probably saved their lives. He should have thought of it.

For a time they just lay there silently. In his mind Birch considered the possibilities. They could wait there overnight and get the rest that he knew he desperately needed. The danger of course was that the Ares would realize they had started after a false trail and trace it back to them here. The other option was to leave and set out through the woods looking for better cover. This too had its dangers though, since wandering through the darkness with a swarm of angry Ares looking for them might easily end in their capture.

It was an easy choice in the end. In his mind Birch had favored the latter solution. Instinctively he just wanted to get away from the whole area and move on. Physically though it was impossible. He needed to rest. Karla had already taken on the rhythmic, peaceful breathing of sleep in the few minutes since the footsteps had died away in the distance. She had fallen asleep, and he marveled at how quickly exhaustion had so totally transformed her fear into a peaceful dreaming. He needed it too, and so it was only a short time later that he too was drifting into an exhausted slumber. They would just have to face any dangers when they came. For now they slept in peace beneath their piney covering.

# TWENTY-THREE

When a day goes as well as this one, particularly after a night as bad as the one that had proceeded it, it is possible to feel a certain disconnection from reality. As a child you might ask for someone to pinch you, and the pain would reassure you that this was true. For Edwards the pain was already there, it had remained from the night before.

They had made it through the last of the mountains and come out on the other side into the wide open plains. They were literally out of the woods, but in a very real sense danger still surrounded them. The Ares would not let them go so easily. Ares groups were on the plains too, but they didn't have the same advantages in this terrain. They would find it more difficult to surprise them. Just a short day ago this might have been enough to allow Edwards some small feeling of confidence and comfort, but the attack that night had shaken his old beliefs and left him doubtful.

As night fell the same routine of the protective field was followed. The trucks were positioned, the sticks were set out, and the guards were placed. This time Edwards set two guards outside the perimeter to watch for any signs of attack. It increased the chances of detection, but he wanted to be ready for anything that came at them. Altogether the precautions were as thorough as could be managed, but they were greatly reduced from the night before. They just didn't have that much left to work with.

The stealth field about them sparked to life, sending a silvery shimmer across the sky. It was not as comforting as it had seemed before, that illusion was gone, but its eerily beautiful glow was calming and seemed to finally draw them into a more restful frame of mind. The day had been one long retreat, and while their fears still gnawed within them there was some respite in this pause, if only for this instant.

The weary travelers naturally congregated together at the center of the camp. Three separate elements: soldiers, DA, and passengers, all merged now into a single unit. Alone in this hostile world they craved the company and had become as a family and support. They were their solid earth to cling to in troubled times. Of course like all good families they fought. Even now under the threat of personal extinction this instinct continued as Jane and Lauren sought answers from Special Operative Edwards.

"You should have done more," Jane remarked bitterly, "it was wrong to leave them like that.  I thought it was your job to protect us."  Edwards sighed and shook his head.

"It's my job," he responded evenly, "to advise and assist the military in protecting you, not to be your guardian angel. That was Konik's job, and I think you could say he did his best for you there. He paid the price."

"You know what I mean," Jane argued. "This has nothing to do with Konik and everything to do with you. You're the one who decided to leave them all there without looking for them. You're the one who left them to die." Jane was turning crimson, but Edwards continued to look down at her coolly.

"I'm sure it looks that way to you," Edwards' voice remained calm, "but you don't know what you're dealing with. We could have gone out there chasing them, but we would have been giving the Ares exactly what they wanted, a chance to attack us on their terms. It would have been stupid to go out there, and since we didn't even have any trace to follow it would also have been useless.  We did what we had to do, and because of that you're alive at least."

Jane's head shook sullenly, Edwards knew she understood, but he also knew that she couldn't accept it. They had already had this same fight this morning. Nothing had changed. What he had said then and what he had said now hadn't altered her view. He doubted anything would. Some things were too hard to accept, and nothing was harder than the death of your friends. She would have to learn to accept it. Edwards changed the subject.

"It looks like we should reach the base in a couple of days," he continued. "I've tried radioing ahead, but the Ares must be jamming us. I can't get through. We'll be an unannounced arrival. They'll be on high alert when we get there. They don't like unannounced visitors in these parts. It'll be worth it in the end though. If we can dodge the Ares that long then we can at least get our equipment restocked and get out from the mountain clans' area of influence. They've always been a pretty divided group but last night it looked like they've overcome that problem. If they've started joining forces we had better leave them far behind as quickly as possible. The plains clans are much more dispersed."

"What do you mean, they're 'jamming us'?" Lauren asked doubtfully.

"Just what I said, I can't get a radio signal through. They're blocking us."

Jane shook her head. "How is that even possible? I can't see how that rabble could do anything more complicated than shouting and screaming or killing and running. They threw as many bodies at us as they could yesterday. It didn't look like they had a plan more intricate than that, and when they failed they ran like a bunch of whipped dogs. How could they ever do anything more than that?"

Edwards smiled knowingly. "I can see why you'd think that, but there's more to the Ares than what you saw last night. They can be pretty ingenuitive. They know how to use technology against us. Their methods seem crude, but there's a primitive cunning there that you should never underestimate. Their power, of course, is destructive. Their purpose is to thwart and hinder rather than establish or build. They could never build a city, but they could destroy it. They could never create anything, but they are experts at dismantling what already exists."

"They're just a bunch of hooligans, then," Jane concluded.

Edwards laughed.

"Most people would agree with you. After last night I'm almost ready to agree with you too, but I've seen more than that in them. I know there's more than that in them. I've seen it myself."

"Do you think you'll ever beat them?" Lauren asked.

"Yes," Edwards answered simply.

"If last night's anything to go by you've got a long way to go," Jane remarked coolly.

"Well, yes. It's true we've had a few setbacks recently, but we'll win, not because of any physical advantage or technology, no, but because of this." He gestured to his head and to his heart. "It's what's here that will win it for us."

Jane looked unconvinced, and for a moment Edwards felt ashamed. These were the words he had learned and that he had heard others repeat with confidence, but they sounded hollow in his own throat. He returned to a subject he was more comfortable with.

"Yes, communication, like travel, has been made harder by the Ares. Transmission towers can't be kept operational, and they have monkied with our satellite systems, sending reverse jamming signals and even adjusting their orbit and sending them crashing into the debris field. We've tried encryption codes and security setups of all kinds, but they always find a way through. If they're now joining forces the greatest danger won't be from attacks like the one we saw last night, but from the things they might imagine if they work together. The product of their collective thought would be far worse than anything we've seen yet."

"And you still think you're winning?" Jane asked sternly. "It sounds like you're just hanging on for your lives."

Edwards' eyes narrowed. Jane's tone was dismissive and her interpretation of their struggle stung him. Of course some of what she said had been a part of his own deepest fears: that they weren't winning, that they weren't superior, that theirs was not a manifest destiny to change the world. Perhaps in his darkest moments he had doubted, but he had never given voice to those thoughts. It had troubled him before, but hearing it from her raised his defenses and made him angry. What did she know?

"I guess you haven't been here long enough to judge that, Major," his voice was like steel, "but you'll have to make up your own mind. We saved you though, didn't we? I doubt you would have found life as easy if the Ares had gotten hold of you when you landed. I'm sure things would have been quite different."

The bitter words hung uncomfortably for a moment and Jane offered no rejoinder. Finally Lauren spoke.

"I hope that base has a bath," she commented innocently, "I really need one right now." No one answered. Hers was an obvious attempt to give the conversation a lighter tone, but the subject was so disconnected from what had gone before that it was difficult to think of an appropriate response. It was a valiant attempt and the absurdity of it in these difficult circumstances made it all the more amusing. Jane smiled involuntarily and Edwards laughed outright.

"You're right," he responded, "though looking at the rest of us you may have to run to beat the competition for it." It was true, they were a bedraggled, muddy band, but as they laughed they were strengthened and reminded of their bonds of family. They were all they had out here, and to survive they would have to work together.

# TWENTY-FOUR

For one terrible moment he thought that he was back home. His arm lay in its old accustomed position over the warm form beside him, and he lazily drew her closer to him before the thought flashed through his mind; he shouldn't be here. Icy, electric fingers stroked his spine as he sat up in fear. He was instantly relieved to see the towering trees and the wild forest around him. Karla was still sleeping peacefully among the evergreen branches that had covered them. He was glad to be here, despite the way things looked. He pulled away from Karla and got quickly to his feet.

It was morning and the cool air was refreshing after a night lying under the heavy branches. The world seemed changed, and the sound of noisy day birds gave a lively sense to the daylight hours, so different from the ominous night.

His mind swiftly turned to the task ahead. Though he was aware of the peril around them his first thought turned to food and water. He hadn't eaten or drunk at all yesterday, and in the danger of their circumstances he had thought little of it, but now it was the one thing that surpassed all other thoughts in his mind. He was gasping for water and after the exertions of the previous day he felt weak. He needed to eat and to drink.

There hadn't been any time to think of supplies when he and DeSante had chased after Karla, now he had to find his own water and seek out something edible. The prospects were not encouraging. He supposed there would be a mountain stream somewhere up here, though he would have to find it. Food was another issue. There would be wildlife, though he didn't have a gun for hunting. He could fish, if he found a stream, but again he had no equipment. That left the unappetizing prospect of berries, roots, leaves, and fungus. That wasn't something he would look forward to, assuming he could even find any of them. Still, he was hungry enough for anything.

Karla stirred. He looked down at her; she seemed so innocently helpless, lying there with her eyes closed. He was glad he found her, but the extra baggage was going to make his job harder. At least he could feel relief at his success. DeSante troubled him though. He had promised to get him back and now, even if it had meant beating at the Ares front door, he would have done it. But he didn't know where to start. Another glance at the heat sensor didn't help. It left him with the same conclusion, with no trace of anything, and with no hope at all. He couldn't help it. DeSante was lost.

Karla moved again and opened her eyes. Looking quizzically at Birch she half-smiled and sat up, stretching stiffly. Birch was still glowering at the heat sensor and didn't meet her gaze. Her smile faded.

"Still no sign of Carlos?" She murmured. Birch shook his head slowly and replaced the device on his belt.

"It doesn't look like we're going to find any," Birch's voice was flat but barely concealed his anger. "They've covered their trail better this time than they did with you. It looks like we just made a straight trade, getting you back but giving them DeSante in exchange." Karla cast a hurt glance at Birch. This reduction of DeSante and herself to a mere commodity to be won or lost was not an intentional insult, but perhaps that was more hurtful, because it seemed to indicate what he really thought of them. Birch didn't notice, he was considering their next move.

His initial intention had been to go back west to the base they had left a few days ago. It meant going the opposite direction from where they were heading, but it had the advantage of returning them to known territory. It would also allow them to team up with another military convoy before attempting the rest of their eastward journey again.

In the end he had discounted the idea. It would mean retracing their steps through the harshest part of the mountains, only this time on foot and without the same level of protection they had enjoyed before.

It might have been possible to sneak through undetected, but it was too risky. It would take them back near the scene of the last battle and open them up to the chance of another attack like the one they had already faced. With just two of them that would certainly mean death, or worse. He couldn't risk that.

The second option hadn't really seemed much better. It dealt with the unknown on the eastern side of the mountains. It was possible that this side was less dangerous than the area they had just passed through. He doubted it though.

The deciding reality, in the end, had simply been the fact that the eastern side was closer. The shorter option was appealing. He wanted to get out of the mountains. From what he had seen from the Ares' ridge above he knew that they could make it down the eastern side more quickly, maybe even by the end of the day. The west would take longer and lead them back into danger. He would risk the unknown over that.

If they could make it off the mountain by nightfall he would feel a lot better. Edwards had set great store on the importance of getting to the other side as quickly as possible, and this was now his own goal. Once they made it there it might even be possible to find the others with the heat sensor, though his experience with that device didn't fill him any great hope. He doubted they would be in range. If they were waiting for them there might be a chance, but more likely they would have gone. That left Karla and him on their own with no clear destination beyond the mountains. There was Washington, of course, but that was a long way off and the perils between them and it were a mystery to him. Without help or safe haven he doubted they could make it, still, they would have to try. For now they had to survive the mountains, and to do that they needed to eat and drink.

"We need to get food and water soon," Birch announced, "but we can't hang around here looking for it here. We have to get as far from this place as possible before nightfall, so we'll just have to keep a watch out for whatever we can find as we go. With any luck we should get out onto the prairie by nightfall, if we keep up a good pace. I'm not sure that it'll be any better out there, but at least we won't have to worry about what's hiding behind the next tree."

Karla nodded and the two were soon moving down the eastward slope under the cover of the trees.

The evil shadows of the night had changed, but the light of day had not fully transformed the scene. The murky green of shaded daylight was only rarely broken, where brief gaps in the covering branches permitted shafts of light to pour their golden rays in patches around them. The sense of danger, like the gloom, had lessened, but was still there. The daylight gave their troubles a lighter tone and made them at least seem manageable.

For the next hour they traveled in silence. There was nothing to be said. They should have been watching for any sign of the Ares, but they were preoccupied, looking instead for something to eat or drink as they hurried eastward. Finally Karla found a berry bush in one of the few sunny spots between the trees. At this stage Birch would have preferred water, but his hunger was almost equal to his thirst, and so he ravenously devoured the little black berries. He and Karla ate at great speed, unceremoniously stuffing them in, until their fingers were stained black and the bush was bare, but for a few pieces of green, unripened fruit. It took all his willpower to stop himself from even eating them, despite the knowledge that they would probably make him sick.

This meager meal did little to stem their hunger, though the juicy center of the berries did a small service in lessening their thirst somewhat. Even so, another couple hours walking without water had left them gasping.

It was late afternoon when the welcome sound of a nearby stream finally met their ears. Karla was ready to run toward it when Birch hastily signaled for her to stop.

"Wait," he hissed, "we've been lucky so far, but we better be careful. Let's take it slow and see if any Ares are around first."

Cautiously they crept down to the water's edge, looking for any sign of their enemies. They hadn't seen anything of them all day, but he wasn't really sure that meant they weren't there. He hoped right now that they were somewhere resting, dormant during the daylight hours, but he couldn't help but wonder if the woods were really as deserted as they seemed. Where did the Ares go during the day?

For now everything looked clear, and as he and Karla caught their first glimpse of the muddy, slow-moving stream it seemed like the most majestic thing they had ever seen. Its silty, brown water, that a few short days ago would have been foul and undrinkable, now became delicious ambrosia that they couldn't get to quickly enough. Forgetting their fears they both plunged into the water and hastily lapped up the murky, brown liquid.

Grabbing great handfuls of water Birch gulped them down and grabbed for more. Brown, muddy streaks flowed down from his lips and left strange tear trails of earth on either side of his mouth. Karla did the same.

It was a few minutes later before either of them stopped. Karla rubbed her mouth on her sleeve and coughed. As their desperate thirst was slacked so their concern for taste returned and left them both gagging on the earthy flavor and the glooping mud that clung to their throats.

"Maybe we should have boiled it first," gasped Karla between coughs, "though I'm not sure anything could improve that taste."

"That might have been an idea," Birch admitted through his own retching coughs.

"We better get going," he added when he was finally able to catch his breath.

They rose wearily to their feet. The stream was wide but shallow and wound like a long brown ribbon through the landscape. Its banks were bathed in sunlight as the trees stood respectfully distant from its lazily lapping current. Drinking its water had quenched their thirst, but now in a more sober light the water appeared muddier and less inviting than before. Further down a series of mossy stepping stones promised an easier crossing. They walked toward them.

Cautiously Birch stepped onto the first stone. It was slick and wobbled unsteadily under his weight. He raised his arms slightly to steady himself and determinedly pushed on to the other side.

The water's current was gentle and at its deepest point would probably have come no higher than somewhere above his knees, but he wanted to stay dry. A few steps later he slipped and almost fell headlong into the water. It was only by a great effort that he was able to regain his footing and avoid the embarrassment of a dunking. Karla laughed. She was still sitting on the bank and was removing her boots.

"Don't laugh until you've tried it," Birch barked grumpily. Karla by now had strung her boots around her neck, but instead of using the stones as a bridge she rolled up her pants and waded into the water. She moved easily through the murky stream and was soon standing beside Birch, thigh deep in water.

"This reminds me of my old fishing trips," she remarked dreamily. Birch shrugged and concentrated on his next step.

"I'd prefer a boat," he responded dryly. Karla laughed again. She was really starting to annoy him.

"You missed out on half the fun," she bubbled, "you have to be one with the river and with the fish. It's only when you know what the fish knows can you think lie the fish, and then you'll really know how to catch them. It really works."

Birch imagined that if anyone could think like a fish Karla would be the one. He kept that thought to himself. All this talk of fish wasn't helping his hunger much either.

"Maybe you'll just have to show me how you do that when we get to the other side. I could use a good fish dinner right about now, you know." For once he hoped Karla was right. She nodded brightly and they both continued in silence.

A moment later he slipped again, almost falling backwards this time. Karla smiled innocently up at him. Her bright blue eyes sparkled, and she extended a hand to steady him. Her stride had deliberately slowed to keep pace with his faltering steps, like a child walking an elderly relative home. Birch grimaced. Karla waited patiently at his side, her toes sunk easily into the stream's muddy bed. Birch sighed impatiently and stepped off of his rock, plunging with a splash, knee deep into the stream.

"You'll get your boots wet," Karla gasped.

"So what," Birch muttered and strode to the other side.

A few moments later they were both clambering out. Birch was first. Water bled from his boots. His socks were sodden and squelched uncomfortably with every step. He ignored it. Karla's bare feet were coated in a syrupy, oozing mud that she struggled to wipe off with the brittle, brown needles that covered the forest floor. She laughed at her lack of success.

"Maybe you were right," she suggested generously. "Keeping your shoes on avoided this stuff!"

"Yeah," Birch responded impatiently, "but let's hurry. We need to get going."

"Hold on a minute," Karla was up again, padding bootless over to the stream's edge. She fell to her knees, delving her arm deep into the muddy bank.

"What are you doing?" Birch asked incredulously.

"Getting bate," she responded, biting her lip in concentration as she struggled to grab at something.

"Got it," she yelped. She pulled out a long, fat worm. "These are the best. We'll catch a big one now." Birch watched, amazed, as Karla removed the rank insignia pin from her uniform and fashioned the long steel shaft into a makeshift hook. She attached it to a bootlace, then impaled the worm on the pin and dropped the line into the water.

"Rank has its privileges," she remarked lightly, and laughed at her own joke. Birch shook his head.

"Is that really going to work?" He asked doubtfully. "We don't have a lot of time to waste waiting for some fish to take a fancy to the smell of your bootlaces you know."

Karla smiled reassuringly. "Sure it'll work, you just watch."

They watched. For a time nothing happened, and Birch took the opportunity to examine his wounded hands. It was something he had tried to avoid. He shuddered now as he looked down at the bloody shreds of bandage and the crimson-stained fingers that hung numbly beneath them. The pain had receded into a numbness that he could ignore, and he was tempted to keep on ignoring it. He didn't want to see what was under there. He hesitated.

"Major," Karla's concerned voice came from behind him. Though he had tried to turn away from her she had noticed what he was doing.

"What?" Birch's voice was impatient.

"Can I help?"

"I thought you were fishing," Birch's answer came back sharply over his shoulder as he hunched over, examining his gnarled fingers.

"Well, you could hold onto the string with one hand while I fix other one. Then we could swap over and get them both fixed up." Her voice was soothing. Too soothing, like someone who cared and wanted to do something for you, like someone who would invest emotion into you and expect some return on that investment. If people cared they expected you to care back. He didn't want to care.

"I can do it," he responded gruffly. "Thanks," he added as an afterthought.

Birch moved closer to the water's edge and slowly began removing the stained brown cloths from his hands. The acrid smell of wet, putrid flesh rose up from them and almost made him swoon. His hands were still numb. In some ways this had almost seemed helpful, but now it worried him. Now, looking at the deep red grooves and the oozing watery wounds was enough to remind him of his pain and leave him shivering convulsively.

Karla hastily pulled up her makeshift fishing line and came to his side. He tried to motion her away but she ignored his gesture, gently taking his hands in her own.

"That doesn't look too bad," she murmured encouragingly. Birch gave her a doubtful look between shivers, but she carried on. "It could have been much worse. They're pretty deep, but it doesn't look like you've made it down to the bone. If we wash them and keep them bound up they should heal okay." She took his hands and gently started bathing them in the stream. Birch pulled back.

"I can do it myself! Nobody's washed my hands since I was three," his voice was gruff, "I think I can still manage." Karla shook her head.

"Not well enough, you can't," she responded, pulling his hand back. Birch flinched, it seemed that the air and water were bringing back more of the feeling to his numbed fingers, but the sensation was not a pleasant one. "I need to make sure you get all the junk out of the wounds, if you don't it'll take longer to heal. There's no way you could do that with your fingers in their condition. You told me yourself they're too numb to feel anything, so you need me to do it."

"I can feel them just fine with now," Birch remarked bitterly as she prodded painfully into his palms.

"I'm sorry," she responded flatly, noticing him wince in pain. Her tone was not sympathetic, like the school nurse who had seen plenty of tears over the years. "It'll feel better in a minute."

Surprisingly she was right. Expertly she rubbed at his hands and as the water cooled and soothed the fiery trails left by his attacker's knife, he felt his fingers finally loosening from the gnarled claw-like grip they had assumed. He couldn't move them very far, it hurt too much, but he could move them. Karla noticed the fingers twitching and smiled.

"See," she commented brightly, "I told you I could help." Birch's mouth was a hard thin line and he only grunted a response. Her voice had assumed that cheery tone again, and if she wasn't actually making him feel better he'd have gladly told her to go away. As she was helping he said nothing.

Finally she pulled his hands from the water and dried them on her own uniform. Birch found, to his surprise, that he was sorry it had stopped. In the water his wounds were cooled and seemed almost to melt away under her soothing touch. Outside, in the air, they began to sting again. At least he could move his fingers now, he thought to himself, though at the cost of considerable pain.

Karla tore at a vest she wore under her shirt and produced two strips of white cloth that she used to bandage his hands again.

"I hope your hands get better soon," she laughed, "otherwise I think I might run out of clothes."

Birch laughed in response; sometimes you couldn't help it with Karla.

A few minutes later she had caught dinner too. It was a mediocre fish, and they had eaten it raw, for fear of a fire being detected by their enemies, but it still seemed a remarkable thing. She repeated the process to catch another which she wrapped up in her jacket to save for later.

Soon they were walking again. Birch felt fresh and invigorated. True, his hands were hurting again, and the muddy residue of the water and the slime from the uncooked fish still clung to his throat, but somehow all of this hadn't seemed to matter since the first flicker of movement had returned to his fingers. Karla had made them feel again. Those bloody bandages had seemed to hide an evil secret, a truth that his hands might never do their work again. That was all changed now, and though it hurt, he knew he was alive and was going to get better.

Their speed had increased, the rest and refreshment had worked a powerful good in them, and the next few hours seemed to pass as quickly as the miles. All was calm and their journey continued uneventfully. Birch was watchful for any indication of the Ares' presence. The lively trees seemed to grow still as evening approached, expectantly awaiting the night's events. He still hoped that they might make it out from under them before the darkness had fully come. It wasn't long now. They had to hurry.

Their descent had greatly quickened in this last portion of the journey, and as evening finally gave way to dusk, they caught sight of the rich plains stretching out below them. The darkness was beginning to gather and the sun had disappeared behind the western mountains. Still, he could make out the tall grass being blown like waves across the land. Like a glimpse of freedom it beckoned them on, and with almost reckless abandon their last few steps sent them crashing through the trees and out into the free air. They had made it.

Were they safer? The question was a good one and Birch couldn't logically answer it, but it felt true. It may have been that within the forest they could have hidden more easily than in this wide expanse, but instinctively he knew they were better off out in the open prairie, or so he believed, and that was enough for now.

They were alone; at least they seemed to be. As Birch scanned with the heat sensor he already knew that no friends were nearby. Either they had made it further east, or they hadn't made it at all. Whichever it was Birch knew that he would have to make it without their help. They were friendless and alone on this wide-open range.

Quickly their minds turned to finding shelter for the night. It might have been easier, and perhaps even wiser, to spend a last night under the cover of the trees before exploring these expansive grasslands, but Birch would not consider it. Once freed from their darkness he had no desire to return. They would find somewhere on the plains to spend the night.

In the last dying embers of the day he scanned the horizon, searching for any sign of life, any sign of friends or enemies they might need to prepare for. He couldn't see much. There was no life. In the dim light he noticed a strange feature to the south, what seemed to be a gray mass, perhaps of buildings huddled together at the foot of the mountain range. It was dark. Though the light of day had now almost faded to black and the stars had begun to burst forth in the gloomy night, still the place, whatever it was, remained lifeless. Not a single point of light appeared and not a sign of movement could be seen. Karla shivered.

"What do you think it is?" she asked breathlessly.

Birch shrugged. "It was something once I guess. We'll find out what it is tomorrow. For now let's just concentrate on finding a place for tonight."

A short time later they had found a dip, or ditch, that, with tall grass surrounding it, provided excellent cover from the eyes of any who might seek them. They settled to sleep. Their circumstances were less cramped than the night before and Birch appreciated the time to rest on his own; to think about things. He was tired and as he lay in the tall, rustling grass his mind drifted between what they had done and what they still had to do. He had ideas that, if he was fully awake, would have seemed foolish. He had hopes, but at the same time those distant gray buildings seemed to lie on them, like a blight on his consciousness. It was a gray smudge, a human stain on this natural landscape. They were his first chance to find out for himself what this new earth was all about. Not to hear it from others, but to discover it for himself. Tomorrow he would see for himself what this old world had made of itself.

# TWENTY-FIVE

It was a bright dawn on the plains. The land was so flat and so empty that the sky seemed to fill the space it had left with a radiant, fierce blue that burned away even the slightest suggestion of impurity in its cloudless realm. What a contrast it made with the old, gray light of the forest. Two domains, an ocean of sky, cloudless and unsullied above, and an ocean of grass below, swaying in waves at the wind's command. Here, it seemed, you could be a king of infinite space. All of this cheered Karla and even Birch felt its influence prying its way into his darkened mind. It opened their hearts and poured the sun right in from the bounteous overflow of that big sky. This was what it was like to be free, freed from a dread danger that threatened their lives. Now, finally, it seemed to have let them go, but like all illusions it could not last.

It was the city that stole away all impression of freedom. It was yet distant, but they could see it, an indistinct gray line on the horizon. No other detail could be seen from this distance, but even from here the impression was wrong. It was a dwarfed gray mass, with no grandeur and no life. The night before it had remained black and cold in the darkness, now even in the daylight it hardly seemed warmed or lightened by the sun that brought light and life to everything else. This was where they were headed. Rather than go to the open plains, that seemed to invite them eastwards to safety, they would move south toward this monstrosity. It was their best chance to get what they needed for the next stage of their journey. It also might provide some of the answers Birch was looking for.

Their hurried breakfast of fish saved from the day before was eaten in silence. Their hunger was less pronounced than yesterday, and as a result the raw, slimy flesh was harder to stomach. Still, Birch was glad of what he had and when Karla produced a few berries she had saved from yesterday he felt it had almost been a meal worth eating. It would keep them going for a while anyway.

Soon they were walking toward the city. It took some time to cover the distance, but as the first hour passed they drew close enough to get a clear impression of where they were going. Their sense of gloom deepened, like long shadows cast over their minds. This seemed to jar against reality, for even in the low morning sun the city cast only the shortest of shadows against the mountains behind them. There were no sky-scrapers. It seemed like nothing taller even than the tenth or twentieth story remained. They were gone. Their approach revealed the ghastly effect, jagged edges of metal and exposed girders protruding from rusted bases showed a sudden, calamitous destruction of all those structures in a great swath. It was as though a giant scythe had swept across the city and destroyed its towering pride in one swoop.

Karla drew closer to Birch, and for once he didn't mind. This place was dead. It had died a long time ago and any presence of life was a comfort.

"I think I know this place," she murmured softly, "at least I did." Birch gave a start, somehow in his mind this location had been all about the future, some strange city that they had never known. As he had thought about this terrible scene it had escaped him somehow that this was their own world and that they might know it. His curious interest was instantly transformed into a dour moodiness.

"Where are we then?" He was now looking himself for any signs.

"It's the mountains and those buildings, a lot of it's gone now of course, but what's left of them is in the right place. We used to come here all the time; it was like the big day out. It took hours to get here and then even more hours to get back it always seemed, but it was so pretty with the mountains and the big glass buildings all standing so tall against them, but look at them now. How could this happen?"

"Just tell me where we are," Birch sighed impatiently.

"Denver. It's Denver. Can't you see how what's left just lays out just right?"

Birch had never been to Denver, but he could imagine she was right. He had no reason to doubt it. So a great city had been reduced to this. He shivered in the cool morning air. He was glad this wasn't a place he had known, not because he hoped that the places where he had lived had been spared this fate, but rather because he didn't want to see them, whatever had happened. Everything would be changed, and yet still somehow the same. To see it like this would have been the hardest. Better to have the past obliterated totally than to stumble upon the rusting remains of what you once knew. Even those who cherished the past so much at least wanted it buried out of sight, so they could remember what it was, not what it would become. He could see those same feelings conflicting within Karla now. She seemed both horrified and fascinated to be here. A strange fear seemed to come into her eyes as they drew closer to the city.

By late afternoon they were at the outskirts, and the first signs of the mangled mayhem of the city's destruction became evident. A great expanse of rusted vehicles lay along a packed road, weathered and beaten, like so many grave markers where the writing had disappeared with the memory of those who lie within. They had been here a long time, but the evidence of violent and sudden destruction remained. Cars and trucks lay upturned, metal fragments, and holes in the road all spoke of some final struggle here, a final hope of escape for some that had lead to nothing. Karla sighed but it sounded more like a sob.

"There's nothing we can use here," Birch remarked, "we need to go further in." Karla nodded stoically and followed close behind.

Cautiously they moved toward the center of the city. The great press of rusted out cars did not lessen, it was as though every vehicle that the city had possessed was thrown out onto the street on this one occasion, a last parade of all the city had to offer before it was finally destroyed. Looking at it now it seemed like it had all happened only a minute ago. Rusted doors still hung open from cars where panicked drivers had left them, debris and personal belongings lay scattered where they had fallen. More poignant than Pompeii, this was real to Birch. He stooped to pick up a single shoe left rotting on the roadside. What story could it tell? What had happened to its owner? He shuddered at the images that poured into his brain, and with all his effort flung it into the demolished remnants of a building nearby. He didn't want to know its story, nor its owner, nor its past. It was too painful. He would get what he could use from this place and he would find out about what happened to the city, those things would help him, but he didn't want to know about the people. Everyone else had forgotten them, why should he remember?

Karla and Birch had moved onto one of the long, wide roads that would once have been a main artery into the heart of the city. They were far enough out that it contained all of those conveniences that had moved out from the city center long ago. The malls, the restaurants, and all the other mega-stores lay in ghostly silence. Some were largely intact, others were totally demolished and left little evidence of their existence but for rubble, or perhaps a hole where a structure had once stood. The destruction seemed almost random and, where it hit, as total as the most destructive tornado, but this 'tornado' had gone through the whole city. Whatever happened here was no natural disaster though. That much was very clear.

Finally as they passed a large superstore Birch turned off from the road and walked toward its abandoned parking lot. A skeleton of faded white lines crisscrossed to show where cars would have once parked. None were there. That same familiar dread was resting in their stomachs as they drew near. It was the dread of seeing everything you once knew come to this, and wondering what new horrors you might find in these old, familiar surroundings.

The door, that once would have opened to welcome them, remained firmly shut. This wasn't surprising, there would be no power to operate it, but from habit Karla had almost walked into its smeared glass pane, expecting it to slide aside and admit her. She smiled sheepishly and her mood seemed to lighten with her own mistake. The door wasn't locked and Birch was able to pull it open so that they both could pass through.

The air inside the foyer was stale and slightly foul and grew worse as they walked further in. Natural light streamed down through the skylights, but the overall impression was not cheery; it was dank and dark. Pipes hung loosely from the ceiling and debris lay everywhere. From the condition of the floor it was evident that a number of animals had made use of this building over the years. Some of it was fresh and that didn't help the smell.

"Cleanup on aisle five," Karla quipped. Birch smiled despite himself, he was just glad she was holding together better than he had thought she would. "This is quite a mess," she added brightly, "but it looks like there's a lot of stuff left here." She was right. The produce section, naturally, had rotted to dust, but most of the other things seemed largely intact. It was strange. There was no sign of the type of looting he would have expected to see under this type of circumstance. Neither those fleeing, nor the victors here seemed to have touched a thing. It was all left as though the store might open again tomorrow. In some places the shelving had given way and spilled its contents on the floor, but mostly it was a picture of dusty, dilapidated order. Everything was left where it should be. It was like an evil Christmas, everything you could possibly want, but at a terrible price. Still Karla, and even Birch, couldn't help feeling cheered by this bounty.

"Let's get some stuff," Birch gestured to the shelves, "concentrate on canned goods. I'm not sure how good they'll be after all this time, but that's our best chance at getting something edible. And whatever you do keep your eyes open for a can opener. I don't want to get back on the plains and have to chew my way into these cans to get a meal!"

Karla laughed. "I bet you could though," she added mischievously. Birch turned sharply to look at the lieutenant but she had turned her back and was getting a cart from a long column at the front of the store. Birch looked on in disbelief.

"What are you doing?" he asked.

"Getting a cart," she answered flatly.

"You know this isn't a Sunday afternoon shopping trip, right?" Birch's words dripped irony. "We're here to grab stuff quick and get out."

"I know," Karla didn't seem phased by his words, "but I wasn't planning on carrying everything in my hands you know. I may as well use the carts while they're here."

Birch shrugged. It made sense but it didn't seem right, you didn't do doomsday shopping with a cart, you grabbed and ran. "I guess that's fine," he admitted, "but don't forget to ask for a price check if any of the price tags have fallen off. We don't want to get caught short at the checkout." Karla and Birch stuck together in the store. It was a gloomy place, which didn't bother him, but he didn't want to leave her alone. She seemed to need the company, and so they shopped together like a normal couple in normal times. He picked some things, she picked some others. They disagreed on some things, but compromised where they could. The atmosphere was heavy with the past and you could almost peel away the years like a greasy film and find them fresh and clean in the old days, shopping together and returning home to their suburban lives. This parallel did not escape Birch's attention and it made his head hurt.

Finally they had as many cans as he thought they could carry. They moved through the store looking for other useful items, Birch found the much-needed can opener and Karla stopped in clothing. She had even wanted to try something on, but Birch had insisted that either she grab what she wanted as they passed by or she got nothing. Sulkily she picked a few items and suggested that Birch might need a few things. He scoffed and continued toward the sporting goods department. Karla followed behind, but stopped in the men's department long enough to pick up a warmer jacket for him.

It was sporting goods more than anything that had held real hope for Birch, and when they arrived he found the glass display cabinet just as he had hoped he would. It was filled with weapons and ammunition. Even these had been left. Whatever happened here must have been sudden and disastrous. It seemed like all they did was run.

"This is what we're looking for," Birch muttered to himself as he grabbed a hunting jacket from a nearby hanger and wrapped it around his arm. With a quick shove he had broken the glass and was taking the rifles out of the display. "Just hunting rifles, shotguns, and a few low powered pistols," he spoke more to himself than Karla, "not anything fast or impressive, but it's better than what we've got now." Karla nodded and lifted one of the rifles, feeling it for weight.

"These aren't bad," she noted lifting a shotgun from the display case. "They can pack a punch. You'll have to watch out for the reloads though. They can be tricky under pressure. My guess is the Ares will give you even less time to load again than the deer this weapon was made for. At least the deer would run away from you rather than at you if you missed!"

Birch laughed. "I give up on figuring you out," he chuckled. "You're supposed to be the computer geek, not the all fishing, all hunting outdoorsman. What is it with you?"

Karla smiled. "I guess you don't know me as well as you thought, Major." She clicked the shotgun shut. "It's all in my personnel profile. I'm surprised you didn't look."

"Oh, I looked alright," Birch was stern again, "I didn't see anything like that." Indeed Birch had looked at Karla's records, over and over again. It was he who had objected to her inclusion, despite Colonel Ratliff's support. He had poured over those records to find anything to keep her off, but he couldn't find anything more than her age and his own personal hunch about her to support his view. That hadn't been enough and Ratliff had won. It angered him just to think of it, even now.

"All I saw," Birch continued, "was that you had the usual stellar education I would have expected. You hadn't done much else, but Colonel Ratliff didn't care. He wanted you for the mission. He wanted you all along"

Karla eyed Birch thoughtfully, as though his words had revealed something to her she hadn't thought of before. For a moment she looked hurt, but the cloud over her seemed to move quickly away. When she spoke again her voice remained upbeat.

"You have to read between the lines," she enthused. "That's where you learn the most! You can't tell about a person just from their education, you know. Sure, from that you could easily say that I'm just a 'computer geek', as you so nicely put it, but that's not all I am. I was raised out here, on a Kansas farm, and I know a lot more about plenty of things than you ever could."

Birch doubted it. He smiled wickedly. "Why you're Dorothy," he laughed, but his voice was hard and harsh. It came as no surprise to him that Karla was some corn-fed farm girl. It seemed to fit. "Perhaps if you just knock your shoes together and say 'there's no place like home' you can end all of this. Why, you could be back home in a minute with Toto and the whole family gathered around your bed, and what a story you could tell them."

Karla's skin took a grayish tint and she looked down, her eyes filling with tears. Birch didn't notice. He was working himself up in his analogy.

"I wonder who I could be," he continued. "Perhaps the Wizard as I'm the one showing you how to get home."

"Seems like you're the Tin Man and the Scarecrow," she responded angrily, "as you don't seem to have either a heart or a brain!" She turned and kicked the cart hard and sent it flying into the display, sending boxes and cans crashing to the floor. Birch watched in stunned silence. Anger welled up inside him, but before he could say anything he caught sight of her face as she turned and ran to the doors. She was hurt, and for once Birch felt bad. Something he had said had hurt her more than he had intended, and despite himself he felt guilty and wanted to make it better.

He ran after Karla. Dodging racks and displays he caught her at the doors as she was about to leave.

"Don't go out there alone," he thundered, "you don't know what's out there. You need me."

"I don't think anyone needs you, Birch," Karla snapped. "I've tried more than anyone to understand you, to help you, even when things seemed so bad. I stuck by you when Major Gray said we should've stayed, and I caught you a fish, but you don't think about anyone or anything but yourself, so no, I don't need you, Major Birch. Good-bye."

"Wait," Birch called after Karla. She was struggling to pull the door aside. "Stop, I'm sorry." The words were almost a whisper, but Karla heard them. She stopped pulling at the doors and turned to face him. Her hair was unkempt and her tear-stained face wore a wary expression.

"Do you mean that, Major?" she asked softly. Birch nodded, though he couldn't make himself repeat the words. Strangely, he found that he really did mean it.

She smiled, like a burst of sunlight through the darkened clouds. "Thanks," she said, squeezing his hand. She walked back to the overturned cart, and as she stooped down to pick up the cans Birch wondered what he had said that hurt her so much. He couldn't figure her out.

Slowly he walked back to help Karla. He felt exhausted, this whole experience, everything in this place, had been much more than he had wanted. They needed to get out of here. Even to be in the desolation outside was preferable to staying here. He would have rather faced the Ares in open combat than face another moment in this musty, rotted out memory of a building.

Soon they had picked up the supplies and packed them away in their backpacks. Birch slung his over his shoulder and helped Karla with hers; they were ready to go. They would leave this place of stale air and stale memories and step back into the real world outside.

Birch walked quickly to the door, but Karla hesitated and took a last look around her, as though drinking in this last vestige of normality. She took in the neatly stacked shelves, the dusty racks of clothes, and the happy faces of long-dead models smiling blissfully from their faded display pictures around the walls. A grim smile played across Karla's lips as she adjusted her pack and followed after Birch.

The evening air was cooling and refreshing after the dead atmosphere within. Birch scowled at the darkening sky. "Looks like we need shelter again," he said looking around. "That should do." He was pointing to a two-story motel court across the street from where they stood. Karla looked doubtful.

"I'd rather sleep outside," she was looking around for a suitable spot. "I can go into those places, but sleeping in them is something else. It's like sleeping on a grave or something. I just don't think I can do it."

Indeed the analogy wasn't a bad one. The building's cheery painted facade had fallen away and left exposed the dirty, bare-block bones beneath. A bright yellow awning, upon which the words 'Welcome Our Guests' could barely be made out, fluttered in tatters above the office door. It was not an inviting scene, but none of the buildings were. All of them had this musty, fallen look that made you want to run from them rather than enter, and yet Birch thought it was important. They had to get inside.

"Look," he sighed, "I can understand how you feel. Maybe I feel the same way, but we don't have time to waste so just get in there." She shook her head, but Birch pushed her toward the door. "Look, if you don't get in there it'll probably be your own grave that you'll be sleeping on tonight. You don't think this city has gone unnoticed by the Ares do you? It'll be dark in about twenty minutes and this place will be crawling with them. I'd like to have a chance to choose the best location in there to set up for the night, so please go in before I have to throw you in."

Karla smiled gloomily at Birch. "Okay," she looked up into his eyes but he looked away. "I only wish things could be different."

Birch shrugged. "Things don't get much more different than this," he muttered as he pulled open the rusty door and walked into the office. Just a short time ago he had decided to be easier on Karla, but she made it so hard for him. Annoying character traits were one thing, but stupid arguments about stupid things that could get them killed was too much. If she really wanted things to be different then she had to be different.

The office, like the store they had just left, was strangely intact. It was like a living time capsule or a crumbling museum display of the lives of the people of the past. Everything was orderly and in place. But for the dust and debris of an age, it might have been left only a short time ago. You almost expected to wait for the clerk to return in a moment and check you in. Of course no one came and Birch looked to the key rack behind the desk. Most of them were still in place, a few of the slots were empty and he shuddered at the sudden impression of what might lie, rotting behind those long locked doors. He would keep that idea to himself; Karla was jumpy enough already.

He reached across the desk and pulled a key from the ring. "It looks like this one's in the middle of the second floor," he said looking at the motel layout map on the wall. "That'll make it less likely they'd find us."

Karla looked doubtful. Why's that?" she asked.

"If they start searching for us they'll start at one end or the other, where the stairs go up. To get to the middle they'll have to walk past five other rooms," he indicated the location on the map. "That's our best chance right now. I don't see why they should check every room, or even know that we're here. I think we should be safe enough. It's better than being in the open anyway."

"What if they do check every room though? What if they find us? What do we do then?"

Birch sighed wearily. "Plan B," he said glibly and patted his rifle.

# TWENTY-SIX

Things had been quiet since their narrow escape in the mountains two days ago. There had been no new sightings of the Ares, and Edwards almost dared to hope they had left them behind, but he knew that wasn't true. He knew they would see them again before this journey was over.

Edwards had finally managed to get off a radio message to the base, but the news from them hadn't been good. They had warned Edwards that reports were coming in of Ares activity across the whole area. It seemed that their mountain ambush had not been an isolated incident. The attack was part of a wider pattern across the whole center of the country that had erupted about the time they had started their journey across the Rockies. The military were only now able to mobilize an effective response. An attack force was being launched from the east to quell the uprising, but it would be a long while before they could get out this far. The mountains were still seen as too dangerous and had been sealed off to all traffic.

Edwards had been stung by the news. Under the circumstances he wasn't even certain that they could continue their journey. All they could do now was hurry on to the base; it was the only safe ground nearby.

While the last two days had been uneventful, they had not

been free of fear. The open plains had made it harder for the Ares to launch a surprise attack, but if they could muster the kind of numbers they had in their previous offensive then surprise wouldn't be needed; they could just crush them. This knowledge made their travel hard. Tension had seemed to follow in their footsteps, and the news of wider uprisings only added to their fears. But now they were close to safety. They hurried with all possible speed.

It was late afternoon when they finally caught sight of it. A squat walled fortress concealed meekly among the long, waving grass that bent over in the wind. The tiny fort gave the impression of a little boat, a tug, lost on the stormy seas, riding out the waves and gales as it struggled to reach shore, though it was perfectly still.

Things were very different here. On the western side of the mountains their base had been a bold statement of confidence. The lights, the bustle and activity, and its very size all spoke of a brash certainty and assurance of power and superiority. In the west their base had seemed like arrogance, it was an affront to the Ares. There was no attempt at camouflage, it did not cower or hide, but stood proudly and said 'I am here, do your worst'. This was not the case here. This small, insignificant structure clung to the inhospitable ground, seeking as little notice and interference as possible.

The small line of trucks chugged doggedly toward the fortress, finally stopping fifty yards from its smooth featureless walls. Edwards knew the routine. If they went any closer, even in these friendly vehicles, they would have been destroyed; no questions asked. These places made no exceptions, even if they were expecting you. Edwards got out of his truck and motioned for the others to do the same. Slowly they climbed out of the vehicles and joined him at the front of the convoy.

"What's this all about," Jane asked, her voice filled with apprehension.

"It's the way we've managed to get a foothold in Ares' territory. We don't give them a chance to pull any of their tricks. If you don't stop to be scanned then you'll be shot without hesitation, whatever you are. They've tried to fool us before with stolen vehicles or bogus approaches; we've lost a few bases that way in the past, but we're ready for most of what they try now." He pointed to a gleaming square tower in the structure.

"Those are the anti-missile batteries, there's not much that gets past them. We've built around our circumstances. We've had to adapt. One day these bases will be the basis for our new beginning. Like the army forts of the olden days, these will be the heart of new towns and cities, expanding and changing this country and our world. This is just the beginning."

"You don't really believe that, do you?" Jane scoffed. "You guys seem to really like saying things that don't match what's actually happening. If this is the beginning of something, then it's a very small, microscopic start!"

Edwards laughed mirthlessly. He was too tired of doubting these things himself to put up any customary defense. "You won't let anything slip by, will you? Well, we hope it's true," he admitted. "That's what we've been told anyway. Who knows?" he dropped all pretense of assurance. "That's about the best we can do for now anyway." Edwards shook his head thoughtfully. Jane and Lauren had a part to play in that hope. He didn't understand it fully himself yet, the DA only ever told you enough to take the next step on the path they had marked out for you, but he knew they were important.

He hated this job. He would give anything to be back under his tree looking out to the ocean. Instead he was here watching waves of prairie grass blown on a stiff breeze, waiting for this fort to admit them to their tiny island of safety. He had already more than half-failed in his mission. Three of the passengers were gone. What would that mean? For him he knew it meant trouble, the DA didn't take failure well, but it was more than that. He was supposed to protect them and he had failed. Had he ever protected anyone or anything? His whole life was supposed to have been about preserving, about protecting the endangered, but what had he really done? He imprisoned them. Maybe that was life's only choice, be safe or be dead.

Edwards glared at the base's turrets. What was taking so long? They needed to get inside.

Finally things started to move. Three impressive cannons from the top of the wall were turning menacingly toward them, closely following their movements. "Just a precaution," Edwards reassured Lauren, who had glanced up at them, wide-eyed. "They're just checking that we are who we say we are. They'll let us in there in a minute, just wait."

They waited again. Inside the base they would be scanning them, checking their records, making sure. It was some time before anything more happened and they shifted uneasily in front of the trucks. Though he had been through this a number of times it was still a nervous process for Edwards. He sweated. His calm exterior hid that irrational fear that something might go wrong. The computer might malfunction, the records might be inaccurate, something you knew wasn't there might turn up on their readout and they would be blown apart, destroyed before they could say anything about it. He had heard of such cases, though it wasn't something anyone talked about openly. Just the idea that mistakes could happen was an uncomfortable thought in these circumstances.

Finally his radio crackled to life. "You may approach," the grainy voice announced tersely. "Come to the north gate. Set the computer to approach pattern nine. I don't need to remind you of the importance of getting it right." Edwards very well knew the importance of getting it right.

"Understood," he answered flatly and gestured for the others to return to the trucks. "We'll be approaching by pattern nine; out." He clicked off the radio and got back into the lead vehicle. This was the tricky part. They had to guide the trucks through a particular intricate path set out by the base's computer. The coordinates were beamed directly to his onboard computer from the base, and the slightest deviation meant destruction. It took special software and training to manage it, and so far the Ares had been unable to mimic this little trick. They had tried. So far their attempts had ended only in suicide missions that had achieved nothing but the deaths of the attackers.

The green glow of the monitor filled the cabin. Edwards was at the wheel. His training was old, but he was better equipped to do this than any of the troops he had left. He wished he wasn't. He sweated his way through the first few turns and came to a difficult maneuver that almost caused the truck to double back on itself. His timing had to be perfect in order to avoid hitting one of the two vehicles following him, and his breath came sharply through his teeth as he squeezed through the narrowest of gaps between the second and third truck in the convoy.

"This is crazy," Edwards muttered as he wrenched the wheel to the left to perform another required movement. "They've got this thing on the worst setting. I'll kill them, if I live long enough to make it in there."

Like a massive centipede the line of vehicles twisted and turned in line to a silent dance set out by their computers. Finally they approached the northern wall and came to a halt. Its smooth shiny surface was unremarkable. It contained no door, nor any other feature that indicated there could be any entrance there. For a time the trucks sat silently idle. Nothing happened, but then with a hiss the metallic center seemed to dissolve and a gate opened before them. The trucks moved in and the wall behind them quickly returned to its former state.

Once inside the base the trucks were quickly surrounded by grim looking soldiers with weapons drawn. Edwards and the others slowly climbed from their vehicles at the barked command of the troop's leader.

"Show your hands! Show your hands!" one shouted gruffly at Lauren, who had habitually reached for her pockets. She quickly raised her hands in surrender. Edwards laughed.

"You're not a prisoner, lieutenant. They're just making sure you can't pull a weapon on them while they perform this last test. You can lower your arms. Just keep your hands in sight."

Lauren smiled sheepishly and lowered her hands, almost putting them back into her pockets again before remembering and hastily letting them drop loosely to her side.

Edwards shook his head. They were all pretty jittery. The base troops still had the rifles leveled at them. They fingered the triggers of their rifles nervously, watching for any reason to shoot. The sooner they got this over with the better.

A soldier passed each of the new arrivals, confronting each of them with a little device that shone a red light deep into their eyes. "A retinal scanner," Edwards explained to Jane and Lauren. "They have records of everyone on file. They're just checking we are who we are." Jane nodded as the soldier finished his scans and led them toward the base commander's office.

"Oh yes, this is all very impressive," she commented. "I'd love to see how this will work in those towns and cities you spoke of. How long before you start building them? Next year? Next week maybe? You know, I don't think you need me to tell you, but you're not winning this war, Edwards. Open your eyes. If this is the best you can do I don't think you ever will win."

Edwards' lips compressed into a grimacing smile, but he said nothing. Jane's words were too closely related to his own suppressed doubts to resist. He couldn't immediately refute them, but at the same time he knew that he could never accept them. He *must* never accept them. It would change everything. It went to the heart of everything.

It was an old question. Were they ever going to win? They had always been told so. It was an article of faith, the sure knowledge of their superiority, but long ago this very question had been the first drip in the erosion of the old certainties. Certainties had filled his life. They had filled his mind, the belief that they were right. Whatever seemed to go wrong, he always knew that they were right. Once he had known they would win, because they deserved to win, and that would be enough. Now he wasn't so sure, and he felt like a huckster preacher, teaching a gospel he had never experienced. It wasn't that he was a hypocrite, he wanted to believe all that he said, with all his heart he did, but he was wise enough to know the difference between hope and reality.

The struggle never seemed to end and the Ares were never beaten. Battles went on, but fundamentally nothing changed. When would their superiority show? This question had dogged him at his work, in his private life, and in his dreams. He wrestled within himself to understand it, to know why what seemed right didn't seem the true shape of reality. Why did the wicked prosper, or at least why couldn't they be beaten? It troubled Edwards and so Jane's words scalded his already scorched mind.

It was a war in his mind. He couldn't agree with Jane. She had to be wrong. He had to believe it. There had been times that he had felt he had lost it all, that he couldn't see the same hopes as the others. There were days when Edwards had fallen far from the faith and everything had seemed hollow, empty, and void. This whole existence opened up before him, emptier and more desolate than the driest desert or the most frigid icecaps. He was alone. It was like looking over the steepest precipice into nothingness and he had slunk back in fear. Beyond these hopes there was chaos, he had to hang on to them or die. He knew nothing else and wanted nothing else; he was attached enough to his old thought patterns that Jane's words stung him like a personal blow.

"Don't judge what you don't understand," he snapped robotically. She had questioned conventional reality and he had vended the correct response. Privately he still feared that perhaps she understood better than he did. Her eyes were unclouded by their years of struggle and their hopes, perhaps she saw more clearly than any of them. She was an outsider and it was possible that she could see the truth because she hadn't spent a lifetime constructing it. He couldn't accept that. "There is more happening here than you know," he continued. "We will win."

"I'd like to believe that," Jane smiled thinly as she looked up at him, "but somehow it doesn't look like it. Remember, this is all new to us. It's a new world to Lauren and me and when things look like this it's a scary world too. We want to understand our world, and help if we can, even in the smallest of ways."

"You will help," Edwards answered stiffly, "but first we must get to Washington."

# TWENTY-SEVEN

As they climbed the rusty, rickety stairs to the second floor Birch used the vantage point to look for Ares positions. The city looked as dead from here as it had from the ground. The sun was beginning to disappear behind the mountains and the light played cruel tricks of movement and life in the shadows of the surrounding streets, but beneath it all the complete stillness of the city was evident. It was a museum and a mausoleum, showing the past but having no future. It felt diseased, like the rotting corpse of a city. Nothing could live here, nothing human anyway. He found himself beginning to doubt whether even the Ares would have ventured into such a place. He felt instinctively that they also shouldn't stay here long. Tomorrow they would get some answers and then get out, back onto the healthy plains.

Night was quickly approaching as they reached the door to the room. Birch and Karla shivered, even in the last remaining heat of the day. As darkness fell it was as though this gray city were drawing a cover of darkness over itself, seemingly relieved that its horrid aspect could again be hidden until another day. Its unnatural deformity could be forgotten for the night and it could rest again in peace.

With some effort he pushed the door open. They walked into a dusty, decaying example of basic motel accommodation. In its prime it might have been tolerable, and if you had watched the color TV enough you might not have noticed the dank smell, or the mold, or the mouse that ran across your floor at night to investigate your edibles while you slept. All of this might have happened in its prime. Now, with the onset of deterioration, it wasn't that good.

The room, like much of the city, was largely intact, but decayed. Some evidence of rodents remained on the carpet and on the bed. The dank smell, that once would have been a vague impression, was now an overpowering stench that was almost enough to send Birch to the windows to fling them open, but his natural caution kept him from doing it.

In addition to the thick smell of mold and decay the room had accumulated a layer of dust and dirt that showed the neglect of many years. The carpet seemed to crunch underfoot with debris and the simple bed in the center of the room was grimy. As Karla set her bag on it an explosion of dust rose up into the air and set her coughing.

"Ugh," she exclaimed, "this is horrible. I wouldn't let my dog sleep in this room." She looked about her with dismay, poking suspiciously at the covers beneath her bag.

Birch grunted. "At least it's a bed. You can have that tonight. I'll sleep in the chair. If anything tries to get in I'll be waiting for it." He moved toward a garish orange chair with plump cushions and sat heavily, putting his feet on a nearby table and slinging his rifle across his lap. "You go to sleep," he continued, "I'll stay up for a while just to see if anything happens."

Karla eyed the bed distastefully. "I'm not sure I really want it," she looked down at the filthy floor, "though I guess it's better than the alternative. Maybe you could take the bed and I could have the chair, I can wait up to see what happens as well as you."

Birch was not amused.

"Just get on the bed and get to sleep, Karla; you'll need all the rest you can get for tomorrow, so stop messing around. This may be the last chance you get to sleep in one of those in a long time you know, you better take advantage of it while you can."

"I'm not sure that's the best term for it, but I will tolerate it because it's the only thing going. I wish we could have checked in at the Ritz instead of this flea-pit, the price would have been the same you know." Karla's voice was filled with a humor that Birch missed.

"Next time I'm planning a vacation itinerary I'll keep that in mind," he remarked sourly. He slumped down in his chair and said nothing more. Karla pulled her bag from the bed and brushed at the covers gingerly. He watched her from his seat. Computer geek or not, sometimes he thought she looked more like one of those prissy girls who was probably on the cheerleading team. Now she was being confronted with the real world and real dirt for the first time she was worrying that she might get her hands dirty. Sure, she could catch a fish, and shoot a rifle, but she was still who he thought she was, someone who couldn't cope with the hardships.

A moment later she had pulled all the covers from the bed and flung them to the floor. "Finally," she muttered and curled up on the bare mattress, "this is much better."

Birch tried to watch her for a time, but in the gathering darkness it wasn't possible to see any more than her outline in the thickening gloom. It wasn't long before her breath could be heard rhythmically rising and falling in the peaceful rhythm of sleep. She had fallen asleep almost immediately. His own eyes were heavy. They stung. Still he struggled to keep them open. He was under the impression that if he waited long enough something would reveal itself to him.

For a time he stayed awake. He listened to the still night air, but there was nothing unusual in that, except perhaps the quietness itself along this once busy street. There was nothing more than that, certainly nothing to indicate that anything more sinister than dark memories remained here now. He relaxed, and as time passed and nothing happened his tiredness overcame him. It seemed like a very long time since they had started out that morning; a lifetime of discoveries had been made that day. It was more than he had ever wanted to learn, and tomorrow he had go into the heart of this dead city and learn more. He had to know what had happened here.

Overcome with fatigue he slept. He wasn't sure how much later it was when he was awakened by Karla's voice hissing at him in the darkness.

"Did you hear that, Major?" her voice trembled. "I heard something out there."

Birch shifted groggily in his chair, his back and neck ached and he was feeling very hazy about where he was. Finally he remembered. He strained to listen; there was nothing except the same unusual silence. Only the sound of insects busily doing whatever they do at night, nothing else.

"What do you think you heard?" Birch asked after a moment.

"It sounded like something passing the door outside. It was pretty faint but I'm sure it was something."

Birch moved to the window and looked out. He couldn't see much without moonlight, and the city's skeleton around them was dark and dead. He moved back to his chair and slumped down into it again.

"I couldn't see anything," he muttered, "I'll stay up to see what happens though. You can go back to sleep." Karla didn't answer but he could see her outline on the bed shift and reach for something on the floor. He couldn't tell what it was in the dim light, but from the position she seemed to take on the bed he knew she was waiting with her pistol aimed at the door.

"What are you doing?" Birch asked in the tone of an older brother catching his sibling playing around at bedtime. "You should go to sleep, I'm sure there's nothing to worry about, and if there is then I'll wake you up later."

Karla shook her head in the darkness. "I'm not sleeping, I heard something and I want to be ready." Birch grunted, but said nothing. Fine, he thought, stay awake, but stay out of my way.

He sat in deliberate silence. For a time it seemed that nothing would happen. The dreary stillness, punctuated only by the insect chorus, continued undisturbed. It reminded Birch of that old question that philosophers used to ask about a tree falling in a forest and wondering if there was any sound if no one was there to hear it. The sounds of the city were gone, with those who created them, but now a strange thought came to him. This city wasn't really dead. Now, as he listened, he could hear it. Life of some sort continued. Not human life. It was the insects. He could hear them, but it just hadn't seemed important to him, and so it had registered as silence. Was that the measure of human arrogance; that we couldn't imagine even sound existing if we weren't there to observe it? This city had existed without the observation of humanity, but it had still lived. It had carried on without us; even in the grave there was life.

That was the wonderful thing about the Earth; it was always alive. You just couldn't stop it. No matter what havoc you inflicted, life just kept coming back in one form or another. What a contrast to space, where life is so delicate. He thought of the planet on their mission, or now even to Mars, where all life was gone. Out there even the smallest error meant total destruction. Here it thrived. Even in this city, where humanity had done its worst, life continued without them.

A sound interrupted his thoughts. It was faint but distinct, a padding, like the sound of bare feet slapping on concrete. Someone was running across the balcony outside. Birch sat up in his chair, facing the door he released the safety catch on his rifle and took aim.

The footsteps rushed past their door without stopping. Birch sighed and lowered his rifle. So much for the idea that the city was deserted. He was surprised. The city had seemed dead. Perhaps these people were more resilient than he gave them credit for, but still, he would have expected more evidence of habitation. It didn't seem right that everything in the stores had remained untouched, exactly as it had been left years ago. It was hard to answer, but at least it reminded him that he still didn't know enough about life here to make any assumptions. He would learn more tomorrow.

The silence had returned, but only for a short moment. The footsteps were coming back, more slowly this time and more quietly, but he knew he could hear them. As they drew closer, so they continued to grow ever slower and stealthier. Finally they stopped at their door. It was like being sniffed out by a dog. He thought he could even hear a rasping breath from outside, and he slowly fingered the trigger of his rifle, ready to shoot.

The next moment was confusion. The metallic click of the doorknob being turned mingled in his mind with another sound he only later identified as the hammer of Karla's pistol being drawn back to fire. The locked handle rattled as the figure outside tried to gently open the door and get in. Before the rattling had stopped a cascade of loud shots echoed through the room, Karla had fired at the door. A squealing, indignant screech sounded from the other side. Birch quickly reacted and sent his own volley of shots thundering into the door that exploded in a shower of splinters.

Birch was instantly out of his chair and hurling aside the tattered remnants of the door to get outside. From there he could hear footsteps clanging down the iron steps, despite the ringing from the gunfire in his ears he could still hear that. More alarming was that distinctive Ares screech, screamed by the fleeing figure. It was one of them, and it would bring more with them if he got away.

Quickly Birch chased after the figure, but by the time he had reached the stairs it sounded like their enemy was at the bottom. Without pausing he fired blindly down into the darkness; the figure below whimpered but kept on running. By this time Karla was at his side.

"Did you get him," she shouted. Birch whirled angrily to face her.

"Shut-up!" he spat the words at her. "Just get in the room and put your head between your knees or something useful like that. You've scared him off and I've got to try and fix it before he brings his friends back!"

Birch ran recklessly down the stairs, but when he reached the bottom he could see no sign of the intruder. He had disappeared into the darkness. The sound had stopped too, the Ares screech had been replaced again by the sound of insects and nothing. That surprised Birch. There had been no answering call as there had been on the night of the battle. No mass attack followed. Was this just a small patrol, or a trick of some kind so they could lead them into something? Perhaps the answer simply lay with the reddening sky on the eastern horizon and the coming dawn that it foretold. It might be that another night would give the Ares the chance to finish this; perhaps they would wait until then. Birch knew now that they couldn't spend another night in this city. Quickly he re-climbed the stairs. Karla was waiting at the top.

"I'm sorry," she admitted quietly, "I heard the doorknob turning and I though he was going to get in so I shot at him. I was trying to protect us."

"The door was locked," Birch remarked bitterly. "You may be just great at shooting prairie dog, or whatever it is you used to hunt out on your Kansas homestead, but you've got a thing or two to learn about combat. Shooting at him with a low powered weapon like that through a door was never going to do much more than warn him that we were waiting for him. If you could have waited we could have had a clean shot at him when he opened the door. Now he's gone and is probably off warning all his friends about us. I bet this town is about to become a much less friendly place to be. Even in the daylight I guess we'll have to keep a close watch for them, now that they know we're here."

Karla nodded. "Why do you think he went after our door and not the others? Do you think he knew we were there?"

Birch stopped for a moment, looking down at Karla in the growing light of dawn. He hadn't thought of that. As he thought about it now he remembered, the footsteps had rushed by their room the first time and then seemed to come directly back to theirs after that. What did that mean? How did he know they were there? Birch couldn't figure it out. He shrugged.

"We better get out of here," Birch turned to go back to the room, "they still may come back, so let's get our stuff and get moving." Karla nodded and followed him back up the walk-way to the splintered remnant of their front door.

# TWENTY-EIGHT

The walk from the motel took them past a series of strange sights. Car lots, with rusted-out vehicles resting uncomfortably on their flattened tires, empty malls, and faded billboards from which only the gleaming smiles of the once-happy consumers could barely be made out. Everywhere that same sense of sudden abandon was evident. Life might almost have gone on as usual here if it hadn't stopped.

They were getting closer to the downtown area now. It was the TV studios Birch wanted to reach, and Karla remembered enough about the area to be able to guide him. Things in the city center seemed stranger still. Many of the smaller private buildings were left untouched, while larger commercial and political ones were decimated; there seemed a logic behind it. Karla pointed to where the U.S. mint had once stood. Only a pile of rock lay where the sturdy stone structure had once been. Further on they found the State House, its golden dome had been opened like a great can and the contents left to rot under the open sky. One wing of the impressive structure had collapsed and the great stone columns had fallen into the street. The remains of the felled church steeple lay nearby. The rest of the building was unrecognizable, reduced now to a pile of bleached orange bricks mingled among the cake-icing blocks of the State House and the shattered glass of the tallest towers.

Where the destruction further out of town had seemed almost random, this seemed more like a systematic attempt to destroy the symbols of civilization. The question still remained, what had done this? Had it been the Ares or someone else? This seemed to go far beyond the capabilities of the Ares as far as he had seen, but if it wasn't them then who could it be? He hoped the TV station would provide the answers to these questions.

It took some time to find the TV station. The scene was much changed from her time, and so it was difficult for Karla to be sure where it was. The gleaming glass-sided towers had been dwarfed and reduced to squat stumps of buildings and piles of unrecognizable rubble. When they finally did find the site it was not an encouraging one. Like the others around it, the building had been felled like a great tree of metal and glass; it was as though a giant blade had cut through the building and the top sections had fallen away. The top floors were completely gone, cut from their roots and hurled aside, leaving the stump of the bottom few floors largely intact.

Birch sighed, "I guess there's not much chance of finding anything there," he muttered. "At least the building didn't collapse on itself like some of them have. We can get in and look around anyway."

They walked toward the crumpled remains of the broadcast center for News Channel 36. He wasn't sure that this was a wise move. The last few remaining floors of the building had been left exposed to the weather and elements for so long that they were rotting in on themselves and seemed as though they might soon collapse, joining the rest of the structure sprawled out on the pavement around it. Still, he knew that this was his best hope of finding out what happened here. He needed to know what had happened. If he could understand Denver then maybe he could understand the world.

The door into the building opened stiffly and they passed

through into a rubble-filled foyer. Stone, dust, and metal fragments lay across what might once have been an impressive, polished marble floor. They could just barely make out the logo for the news station etched in bold letters across the stone. Strangely the remains of an impressive glass chandelier remained incongruously perched in the flaking ceiling, though much of the glass had fallen away and left it looking much like the dead branches of a rotten tree.

Water had gotten everywhere. Without a roof the weather had taken its toll on the building and left a moldy mess with scummy growth on everything. The impression was much the same as if you could walk now along the decks of the submerged Titanic in the depths of the sea. An eerie peace held over this scene of violent destruction, and as they walked now through this once impressive hall the sound of their feet echoed emptily around the decaying walls.

The first floor produced nothing of interest. The showy part of the building, it was filled with executive offices with rotting art and furniture. The next floor was more promising, and contained practical working equipment for the station. There was no power to work any of the terminals though, and so their dusty screens stared blankly back at them. Diligent searching provided no other evidence to what had happened here. The papers left scattered about the building were worthless, insignificant memos and letters about company policies or ratings and advertising information. Nothing remained to tell the story of this city's end.

They passed through an abandoned studio, perhaps the scene of the last reports of the city, but not an echo remained. They were still no wiser about what had happened here. Birch had expected the power problem, but he had hoped that something else might have been left, some papers or anything that could help them. They saw nothing but decay.

They continued up through the remaining floors. Dusty and empty, there was little here to help them. The seventh floor was the last one remaining and it was worse than the others, its ceiling now acted as the roof for the building since the rest of the structure had fallen away. It had taken the brunt of the weather and this was a task far beyond its original purpose. Holes had allowed water to destroy much of what had once been here and the sagging ceiling and floor left Birch unwilling to venture any further to investigate.

"I guess there's not much here for us," Birch muttered. "Maybe we should try somewhere else, perhaps a newspaper office or something. I'm not sure that would be any better though. It looks like things happened so quickly that I doubt anybody had time to write about it. Still, there must have been some warning, some indication that would have been left on record somewhere. It's just a question of getting at it." He glared angrily at the dead equipment around him. He knew they probably contained the answers he sought, but they were mute, a silent witnesses who refused to speak or share what they knew.

"What about alternative power sources?" Karla asked. "Most of these places had backup generators in the basement in case of power cuts. We could see if there's any chance of getting it running again. If we could power-up the terminals then we could see what happened, assuming we could get the other equipment working of course."

Birch scowled thoughtfully for a moment. "I guess that's possible, though I'm not sure that any generator engine left dormant this long could ever be started again. And even if we could, getting those computers working after that would be something else altogether. I'm not sure it'll work, but I guess it's worth a try. Let's see what we can do."

Together they descended the same musty stairwell they had climbed moments ago, but instead of stopping at the ground level and escaping into the wide foyer, instead of fleeing out the dank rot and stench of decay into the open daylight, they continued down deeper into the basement.

It was dark and difficult to see much beyond the bottom of the stairs. Birch took a box of matches from his backpack and lit one. In that instant of illumination they saw lines of doors along both walls. A large pair of swinging double doors at the end of the corridor was marked with a yellow diamond shaped warning sign, indicating that electrical equipment lay within.

"That looks like our generator," Birch said pointing to the sign. "Let's see what kind of shape it's in."

The match went out, burning Birch's fingers. He didn't light a new one, but instead used his memory of the corridor to feel his way to the doors in the darkness. A dim outline of the crack between the doors became clearer as he approached. A faint light was seeping through from the other side. Cautiously he pushed the doors open and peered into a workroom filled with heavy equipment for the heating and lighting of the building. At one time this would have been the noisy heart of the structure, pumping power and air to all the rooms above, now it was still and dusty. A trickle of natural light through small, muddied windows high up on the wall lit the scene. The machinery was all still there, but it was badly neglected.

"This looks like junk," Birch muttered as he examined one of the furnaces. It was rusting and decaying where it stood. Clumps of broken metal lay about it, where they had dropped off, and the instrument panel seemed to have corroded to a goopy mess.

"The generator doesn't look much better," Karla comm.-ented ruefully, as she poked at another machine in the corner of the room. "I think it might be possible to restart it, but only if we had a couple of weeks to strip it apart, clean it up, and put it back together. Then we'd need some fresh fuel of course. Even with that it might need some other replacement parts when we looked inside."

"In other words, it's junk too," Birch remarked curtly.

"This is kind of an interesting feature though," Karla added, ignoring Birch's bitter words."

"What?" Birch asked, hardly interested.

"Well, this has an external feed, some kind of solar support system that gives extra power to the generator and adds that to the grid. It's a good way to reduce building fuel consumption with free, natural energy. If we could tap into it maybe we could get some juice flowing back into this old building yet."

"How could you do that though?" Birch was interested again, but doubted that the young lieutenant had considered all of the obstacles to her plan. "The solar panels must have been destroyed when the rest of the building went down."

Karla shook her head. "That's what's so interesting about this. What you say would have been true of the old style solar panels, but this must be something new, because it looks like there's still some kind of flicker of power barely dripping into the system from somewhere."

"You mean there's power going into the system from some outside source," Birch was puzzled, "where would that be coming from?"

"I think it must be the building itself," Karla was already excitedly working on a panel of the old generator. "It's something I heard of as an idea once, the theory that these tall buildings, with all their windows and that potential for collecting solar energy, could become more efficient if a better collection panel could be developed, something transparent and thin, like a window. That must be what we have here. Because so much of the building's been destroyed it's barely a trickle now, but whatever's left of that system is still trying to collect and produce energy. It's just enough to barely register when it's spread through the system like this, but if I could direct the energy just to the right place, then there might be enough to get one of the terminals working up there."

Birch nodded. "How are you going to do that?"

Karla looked up from her panel. "This is a pretty modern building, at least it was. I'm already getting enough energy to use on the building's mainframe computer here, from that I can turn off wiring routes and direct power where I want it."

She continued tapping at the keyboard as she talked. "Things like that were useful for fire and emergency measures. This should be enough to get us into the records anyway."

"Great," Birch patted Karla's arm enthusiastically, "how long before we can get in." Karla didn't look up from her screen.

"It'll take a few minutes for me to work out a good route, a lot of the wirings out so I'm just testing for a path I can make to the terminals upstairs. Once I've done that I'll need you to go up there and test it out for me to make sure the connection works, if not we'll need to find something else."

Birch looked doubtful. "You mean I've got to leave you down here, alone? That doesn't sound a very good plan. Don't forget that Ares guy rattling at our door last night. I'm not sure it would be a good idea to leave you down here."

"I haven't forgotten anything. I haven't forgotten that we need to get out of this town as soon as we can, and that if you insist on us sticking together then we'll have to keep going up and down the stairs every few seconds to try and get this thing working. You need me to stay down here to keep this running. If you don't want to do that then this is a waste of time." Birch marveled at her words.

"It looks like I can get the internal phone system working too," she continued, "so when you're up there you can tell me what's working and what isn't. I can fix things better that way."

For a moment Birch remained silent. He didn't like the idea, and he still didn't know if he could trust Karla to take care of herself. If any Ares came across her down here, alone what would she do? She wouldn't have a chance. Still there was a logic to what she had said. He couldn't deny that. It seemed like the only chance they had to get out of the city before nightfall. When he finally spoke his words came slowly, as though he hardly wanted them to escape.

"Sure," he muttered, "that makes sense. Keep a watch out though, I've got a bad feeling about this."

Karla smiled. "Don't worry, I will." She looked down at her screen again.

"I've got a clear wiring path through to a few locations up on the second floor. Office 227 seems to be the closest to the stairwell so I'll start there. If you go up now I'll get things ready and let you know when I'm about to send the power through." Birch nodded and walked to the door. In the dim light of the basement he turned for a last look at Karla, she was engrossed in her work. Her golden hair, muddied by the dimness around it, bobbed in time to her typing fingers. Birch turned and left.

It was easier finding his way back up than it had been to find his way down. The light from the stairs seemed to guide him out and soon he was climbing to the second floor. When he reached it the same sense of desolation hit him, only harder. He wished Karla was there. He was worried about her, all alone in that dark basement, but not only that, it seemed that this place was darker without her.

Office 227 was a few doors down from the stairs. As Birch turned the knob and opened the door he almost feared what he might find inside. The evil smell that pervaded through the building might have only been the rampant mold and rotting furniture around him, but it smelt like death to Birch. Again, he had to fight to suppress his thoughts about the individuals here, about the sudden death or the terror that must have filled this very room all that time ago. It seemed now that the screams still echoed in his mind and he didn't want to hear. His hands went to his ears, but he couldn't block them until his thoughts turned towards life and what he was doing now. That wasn't much of a comfort but it snapped him out of it. He was here to find out what happened. Not what happened to the people, but to this city. This inanimate thing that could feel no pain and register no remorse or regrets; this would help him, nothing would help the others. If he could find out what happened here he was sure he could understand this new world better.

The office contained a desk, chair, and computer. Its window was still intact and Birch looked through its smeared pane out onto the surrounding destruction, and beyond it toward the majestic mountains that towered above them all. A moment later the telephone on the desk rang rustily and Birch reached over to answer it. It was a strange throwback to the normal times this building would never see again.

"Hello?" Karla's voice came muddily through the dirty receiver, "is that you, Major?"

"Yes," he answered impatiently. It wasn't as though there would be anyone else around here taking calls.

"I'm about to send power up to your office. Could you check the plugs and see everything checks out before I do." Birch grunted a response and looked at the computer and the wiring to the outlet. It looked like it had been wet at one time, but he wasn't sure he would find anything better anywhere else in this decrepit building.

"It seems okay," Birch answered, "let's give it a try."

"Okay," Karla answered brightly, "power coming up. Let me know if you have any problems and I'll switch off." Birch waited, nothing noticeable happened. Karla's voice came through the receiver. "You're getting power now, try the computer."

Birch moved back to the desk and leaned over to look at the dirty monitor's screen. With a deep breath he pushed the button on the terminal and waited. For a moment nothing happened, but then it started to hum erratically, like an old car trying to catch its ignition and start up on a cold day. Eventually it seemed to catch its rhythm and start loading up, but in that instant a shower of sparks flew from the screen and a strange, high-pitched screeching howl filled the room.

"Shut it down, shut it down!" Birch shouted into the receiver as he ran for the door. The sparks were flying up into the air and flames were licking at the screen as he dove through the doorway to escape its gleaming destruction.

"Thomas!" Karla's voice sounded distantly from the phone lying on the floor. "Are you okay? Are you alright? Talk to me, Major!" A thudding boom sounded through the phone's receiver.

Birch shook his head groggily and picked up the phone from the hall floor. "I'm here," he answered flatly, "that one didn't work." Karla laughed in nervous relief. "Okay," he continued. "What's the next office to try?"

"Are you sure that's a good idea," Karla's voice was filled with concern, "you could have died up there."

"I'll be careful, we've come this far and I'm not going to give up now."

"Try across the hall, 232," Karla's voice came back faintly through the phone, "please, be careful though."

"Sure, thanks." Birch turned and looked at the office he had just escaped. The sparks were gone, but a thick smoke billowed from the computer that had melted in on itself, leaving a dripping pool of plastic residue on the scorched desk. He used a ragged rug from the floor to smoother the last remnants of the flame before moving up the hall to the next room.

Office 232 seemed somewhat better than the previous one. Moisture hadn't reached this room to quite the same extent, and an examination of the wiring on the terminal showed a much healthier looking connection. "This looks much better," Birch said to Karla, "juice her up and let's see what she'll do."

"Okay," Karla's voice came back over the handset. "Keep your distance this time though."

"Don't worry about that, just tell me when we're ready and I'll hit the button and run for the door." A few moments passed. Birch could hear the sound of the keys as Karla tapped away at her console.

"Right, I've got it patched through now. Start it when you're ready, watch yourself though."

"Sure," Birch was starting to get irritated with her concern. If she told him to be careful one more time he would turn the phone off. He glanced down at the computer and finally pushed the startup button. Taking a few steps back he waited and watched to see what would happen.

It wasn't the smoothest of beginnings, like the last computer it made a chugging, clunking start and for a time it seemed that it wasn't going to do anything more. Finally, though, it seemed to cough and then purr as it remembered its long forgotten purpose. Its programming kicked in and it started through the opening screens.

"Great, we've got it!" Birch, casting his caution aside, quickly sat at the desk and pulled the screen closer to him.

"Is anything happening yet?" Karla's voice came faintly again through the phone. In his excitement Birch had forgotten her and put the phone on the desk. He picked it up.

"We're getting in right now; it looks like it's going to work!" The symbol for channel 36 flashed across the screen and Birch watched expectantly for what would happen next.

# TWENTY-NINE

A night's rest made everything look better. Edwards' head didn't hurt as it had before. His mind didn't ache and his eyes didn't smart with the sting of the glaring light outside. Jane's words had troubled him. His own thoughts had troubled him, but from the safety of this place he knew what was right. In his sleep Jane's words had mingled with his own doubts to oppress and haunt him, but he had awoken to certainty. In his sleep his own mind had worked it out. Freed from his conscious doubting he knew the truth. This place was secure and they were secure, all of them.

This fort was tiny, but it was safe, and from its battlements you could see the plains stretched out below. He saw the emptiness of the land. It was waiting to be reclaimed, rescued from its fallow state and brought back to its former glory. It was wild and had lost its use, someday that use would return and he was one of the few, the idealists that believed the Ares could be brought with it. The more he had known them the more he had known it to be true. It wasn't just the Ares land that was fallow, but also the Ares' mind. They had some intelligence and a remarkable cunning, but still they lacked what it really meant to exist. Someday, after their final defeat, they would learn.

The meeting, as arranged, took place after breakfast. News had come through from the east with their new instructions. It was an anxious time. These soldiers held the balance of their lives in their hands. Edwards nervously glanced from one uniformed officer to another, watching for any sign or indication of what form these orders would take. He could make nothing of any of them. Each sat, their faces cast from the same impenetrable, military, concrete mold.

The stolid base commander with the gray moustache and dark-rimmed eyes now sat at the head of the table, preparing to speak. Inwardly Edwards was groaning, he hadn't exactly been glad to see Konik lost in the battle, that would be stating it far too sharply, but he had been glad to be out from under military control. That was about to change, and it filled him with dread.

"Men," the commander spoke gruffly, "new orders have come from the east and it is my responsibility to brief you on the next steps you must make." Lauren and Jane looked at each other, it seemed that he was looking right through them and addressing only the troops. "There is considerable disappointment at your progress so far. It seems as though the entire mission is already in jeopardy, if not fatally compromised, and so drastic measures have to be taken." Edwards played with his glass on the table before him. He did not look up. This was all directed at him and he feared to see the final blow brought against him.

"Special Operative Edwards," the Commander's voice thundered, "you have been serving as Chief Officer on the mission since the loss of Commander Konik." Edwards nodded dumbly. "You are hereby relieved by my sub-Commander," he gestured to a gray, thin man next to him. "Commander Linkhorn has done a great deal of work in the east, he will guide you to where you need to go without further incident." There was reproof in those words, but Edwards knew that was only a taste of what would come later, when he had to answer to the DA. It wasn't fair, after all Konik had been the one in charge of military issues. It was his failure, but it would still be seen as a reflection on him. Things would be pretty hot for him a while, then it would all blow over eventually. He just had to hope his whole life wouldn't be blown away with it.

"We will also be sending ten of our best men with you," the Commander continued, "that's a third of our complement and is as much as we can afford to give you."

"Now to the changes to your mission," the Commander leaned forward and as he did so the lights dimmed. A map of the country was projected onto the wall behind him. "As you know, circumstances have changed since you set out from the west. The Ares have started an uprising like we've never seen before. You experienced a part of that in the mountains. Just that alone was remarkable enough, but we have seen a level of cooperation between the Ares groups across the country that is unprecedented. These are not just small tribes banding together, this is the whole rotten lot of them coming together in one great push to steal our territory, our homes, and our lives. As you might imagine we have resisted." The map zoomed in toward the area around Missouri and Kansas. Blotches of red and blue denoted the different forces. From this level they seemed almost evenly matched. Edwards knew, though, that their weaponry and training would be decisive, despite the apparent parity in numbers.

"Of course, this call to war has not gone unanswered. Perhaps this fight is even for the best. If they crawl out from their holes to attack us we will destroy them."

Edwards looked thoughtful. He raised his hand and the Commander acknowledged him. "What caused this?" He asked tentatively, his hand still in the air. "There must have been some sort of trigger or some indication that this was building up."

"Who knows," the Commander responded dismissively. "You can't figure these people out. They just act. Perhaps they saw some opportunity, or wanted to prove something among themselves. Maybe they just did it in a fit of passion. I don't know. We don't have any information on that. It doesn't really matter right now, does it? The more important thing is figuring out the way we're going to stop it!"

Edwards' eyes went back to his glass. He said nothing more. Their answer was stupid, typical military hierarchy! Looking at the extent of the uprising on the map it was clear that this was no sudden 'act of passion'. There was simply too much to it. He wondered again at how military intelligence could have missed this coming. With something this big there must have been some signs, like the seismic shifts that warned of coming eruptions. Things couldn't have blown up like this without some rumblings beforehand, and yet he had heard nothing of it. And so their mission, a vital code one mission, had been sent out into this havoc ill-equipped, and ill-prepared for what they would face. He couldn't understand it.

Glancing up at the map again he was struck by the pattern visible there. The whole central part of the country had gone up into mass confusion and it all began in the very area where they were attacked. It then spread out from there like a wave across the plains, and now stretched as far as the Mississippi. This left their route ahead a difficult and dangerous one. Washington was going to be very hard to reach from here. Something about all of this troubled Edwards, not the obvious concern for their immediate safety, but instead a sneaking inkling that this might be all about them. Someone knew what they were doing, and that someone was trying to stop them.

"As you can see from the map," the Commander droned on, "there is a lot going on between here and the safer regions to the east. For that reason we will have to delay your departure for at least a week while the situation is resolved. As a precaution we've also re-plotted your route, taking you further south, where the action has been a little less hot. The delays are difficult, but you should still get into Washington in a few weeks time. We'll restock and expand your weaponry, and you should be in good shape to make it there safely.

"Your new route will avoid the main body of Ares and any you meet should be in full retreat by then. Already we are pushing back hard from the east and early reports indicate things are going well. When you leave things should be clear out there. Everything should be straightforward from now on; Commander Linkhorn will make sure it stays that way."

"What if the Ares come after us?" Jane asked. She was determined to be recognized and, despite the base commander's disdainful look, she continued. "It looks like they have a pretty big force out there. How can you be sure you'll get them all? If those that are left come after us again like they did in the mountains we couldn't handle it, even with your ten extra men."

"That is paranoia," the Commander's tone was both reassuring and condescending- an irritating mix Edwards thought. "There's nothing to indicate that they were particularly after you in that attack, it was just part of this wider uprising that is being dealt with right now. The Ares are under heavy attack this very instant so you have nothing to worry about. In a week most of them will be dead. Worst case scenario is that you are caught up in their retreat, and even then it's unlikely that you would be captured or attacked as they will be running to get back to safety. We're sending you by the more southern route to avoid even this slight danger. Don't worry, there is no need worry about things that won't happen."

'Another stupid answer,' Edwards thought to himself. Something about the pattern of that map made him uneasy, and Jane had been right to point it out. It wouldn't make any difference though. These guys never listened.

The Commander turned again to the screen and tried to move on, but Jane wasn't satisfied. The military bluster didn't impress her and she wanted some real answers.

"I take it then," Jane continued doggedly, "that what that means is that there's no plan for what to do if we're attacked again. We just have to hope we miss them."

The Commander's weary, black-rimmed eyes looked blankly at Jane for a moment, as if trying to comprehend the incomprehensible. Finally he gave up the struggle.

"That's what the extra troops and equipment are for, Miss Gray. They will make sure that all of you get there safely. It's important that you do. The best men I have will be going with you. You will make it."

The Commander's head snapped back to the screen again, and he on plowed with the mission briefing. Jane and Lauren sat silently through it all. Edwards thought he detected more than a hint of doubt from the looks on their faces. They were wise. The mountain battle had shaken their faith in the military and now they listened with unbelieving ears to the confident projections of the mission's schedule. He couldn't blame them. They didn't know that what they had seen in the forest was unusual, not normal at all. They hadn't heard of the whole catalogue of victories against the Ares over the years, or of the progress that had been made by their society in combating and outwitting them. Edwards did know all of these things, and he was still scared. Something about all of this just wasn't right.

The commander's briefing was drawing to its terminal conclusion. As he had closed he showed pictures from the battlefront to demonstrate their progress there. The scene was grisly, like the one that they had fled days ago in the mountains. Ares' bodies lay stacked like firewood, ready for the burning. Jane and Lauren looked away. A moment later Edwards did the same; he'd seen enough of that already. Some of the soldiers about them were cheering and clapping, but his hands stayed still and his voice remained silent.

This was quite a culling the Ares had brought upon themselves by their rash actions, and Edwards still wondered at what could have caused it. It was all beyond what he could understand. It went against everything he knew about them. Perhaps it meant that they really were the unpredictable beasts that so many believed them to be. That was something he was unwilling to accept, but he had to admit that he was baffled about their actions and their motives. He knew nothing of them, and that was what troubled him most. In a few days they would be out there amongst them again, and he had no idea what they would do next.

# THIRTY

The emblem on the screen slowly faded to gray and the startup menu took its place. Finally Birch began looking for the last reports filed in the city. The records demonstrated the stark change. The transmission list showed a steady and continuous stream of stories being filed right up to the last day. Then it all stopped. Their number never significantly increased or decreased, they just stopped, dead.

It was a surprising list in many ways, and the fact that it had ended so abruptly seemed to point to a very swift and climactic end. The subject of all these reports seemed to confirm this. Nothing among the story titles indicated any sense of urgency or danger. Life had just gone on as usual until it ended. Burglaries, city tax issues, park maintenance, and school testing, all the mundane everyday issues, that was all they talked about. There was nothing about what was to come. There was nothing to indicate that they had any idea what was happening, even at the very end. The evidence from the city itself had proven that there had at least been time for people to panic, to run. Their destruction was not that instantaneous, there had been time to see it coming and be afraid. Why hadn't anyone picked up on it before that last moment?

Birch moved through the menu to play the last recorded

broadcast. The computer slowly chugged and sputtered through to the media player and started playing the final entry of the doomed city.

The screen was grainy, and the image jumped, but apart from these visible signs of age the broadcast might have been yesterday. It seemed typical of so many others he had seen in his lifetime. The grand and purposeful music and the impressive graphics told you that you were going to watch something important. This was the news. The opening faded to a formulaic desk with two cloned presenters sitting stiffly behind it. A blonde woman, pretty in a blow-dried sort of way, and a suit-wearing man with short black hair, looked blankly back into the screen. Both wore that empty news smile that somehow pervaded all second level news broadcasts. The woman was already telling viewers of all the interesting things they would be talking about later in the show. Somehow the final destruction of their city didn't make the list. They were planning on telling about tomorrow's weather later in the show, unaware that no tomorrow was coming.

A series of monotonous reports passed, interrupted occasionally by advertisements for redundant products, until at last harsh reality broke into a typical traffic report from the 'Flying Eye' Channel 36 helicopter. At one moment their concerns had been all about the congestion on the westbound section of Interstate 70, the next it was all about survival in the last mad moments of this metropolis.

"...traffic should let up beyond exit 137 in the next half hour," the reporter was announcing, shouting over the thumping of the helicopter blades. "Police have cleared two lanes but you should expect some delays at least for the next hour." A sudden boom shook the craft and a flash of green light streaked across the sky.

"What's that?" someone was shouting from behind the camera. The reporter looked over his shoulder and stared dumbly ahead, all thought of the transmission gone. He gaped down at something below. The camera swerved wildly; out of focus, showing only a blur beneath them and the same green light growing stronger and more persistent. The sound of crashing metal and explosions thundered about the craft and from within someone screamed as they were shaken again by another blast.

For the briefest of moments the camera caught its focus on a building below. That great beam of harsh, green light, like a giant blade, cut through metal, glass, and concrete. Explosions blasted to the sky and smoke filled the air with an acrid blackness. The camera lost focus again and the scene was lost. Only the sound remained. Outside destruction boomed and within the helicopter there were small voices, tiny, like a pantomime mouse. The words made them big. Their final struggle, hope and despair all played out live on TV. This was what news was all about. Yet in that instant Birch knew that these were people, not a story. For once the news seemed real to him, like he knew them, and the death of these people so many years ago was something more than the recorded images flickering across a screen. He looked away.

Finally both image and sound went dead, the craft was destroyed and a panicked technical director instinctively switched back to the studio. The blonde anchorwoman sat in shocked silence, unable to speak for a moment before that old training took over and that hollow smile lit across her face. Everything would be alright her assured expression seemed to say. You didn't really see what you just saw. The world may fall apart, but while we still have our news to condense and sanitize it everything would be just fine.

Stupidly she moved on to the next report. It was their job to report the news, and if ever there was news this was it, but it was off script and they didn't know what to do. They couldn't do anything else. Perhaps with more time they would have responded better, but for now all they could rely on was faulty instinct and the old adage that the show must go on. It had taken years of training, but now, while the city collapsed about them, her instinct was to tell the them about their new dog code ordinances and its effect on public parks. If Nero could fiddle while Rome burned then Channel 36 News could talk about dogs while their city was destroyed. Little had changed.

She droned on, tears were in her eyes and her hands were shaking, yet still she continued. Finally, halfway through this report the studio lights suddenly dimmed and the transmission cut out. That was it. There was no final call to fight whatever this was, no stirring words of encouragement, no final advice, not even any understanding, just the last word on dogs. It was pathetic. The city hadn't even gone down with a whimper, but with a bark.

"What have you found Major?" Karla's voice sounded distantly from the phone receiver on the desk. "What happened here?" Birch didn't answer. What was there to say? He was both sad and angry. He had wanted to know the story of the city, but in that last transmission he had seen the story of people, people who had died. Through his whole life he had avoided that terrible reality, the effect of death. He had even blasted himself into space, into this uncertain future to escape its vice grip, but here it was still. Some things can never be left behind.

He sat staring at the blank screen, struggling to rebuild his defenses. He tried desperately not to understand what it must have felt like to have been there, to have been *here,* when it all happened. Above all he wanted to forget, and so he walled up his heart against the reality of the events he had just witnessed. He turned his mind to the wider, less personal, less painful perspective of the city. It was a place, an inanimate object that had been destroyed.

Through the confusion and destruction in the images and sound of the video a single word had cut through into his brain like the finest laser. It had been faint, almost indistinct in the background noise aboard the helicopter as it had been gripped in the cataclysmic skies, but he had been sure of it. It was a single word, spoken as a curse and an accusation, the word was 'Ares.' This confirmed what he had almost wanted to believe. It was a nice answer, but it created more questions than it resolved. How could those savages be capable of such power, and if they were, why didn't they use it to destroy their enemies now? If they could destroy whole cities in minutes then why had they run from them in the mountains? They should be the hunters in this world, not the hunted. It troubled Birch more than ever, but the word and its meaning had been clear. The 'Ares', they were the destroyers! What all of this really meant was less clear. He had gotten the answers he had been seeking. He knew how a city like Denver could be destroyed, but not how the Ares could do it. He knew more, but he understood less.

"Major!" Karla's voice screamed through the phone, "Is everything okay?" Birch's head snapped back, he had forgotten Karla.

"We've got what we need," Birch answered evenly, "let's get out of here. I'll meet you in the foyer." He put the phone down and smiled silently as he caught himself reaching to turn off the computer. A single computer in a dead office, in a dead building, in a dead city, and still he was going to turn it off. It was funny how effectively habits enslaved you, or perhaps they just freed you from thought. Despite himself he seemed to understand in that moment why that pale newscaster was reading about dogs as the city burned; it was all she could do. It was a snapshot of humanity and how we cling to the very last form of reality in the time of evil. That was why the bow of the Titanic was full as the last railing dipped into the icy waters, that was how people kept sanity in the concentration camps, that was why she had talked about dogs, and that was why he now had the desire to turn off a computer that didn't matter. It seemed to represent everything he had wanted to get away from, his world of the past. Still, he wanted to do it.

He sighed, turned off the computer, and walked toward the door. He passed quickly through the gray halls and down the gray steps into the foyer. Karla was already there, standing in the doorway ready to leave this scene. The light streaming through the doorway seemed to promise a portal to better things. They were going to get out of this place and leave its death behind.

The two quickly escaped through the doors and out into the desolate streets. A single thought pressed into both their minds, get out. Like an ancient plague house they felt the infectious influence of this decaying city seeping into their very bones and they wanted to be free, out from its shadow. Together they moved eastwards, half running in their anxiety to leave this place behind. At times they stumbled and faltered, but they did not stop. In their desire to beat the sun they continued without rest through the remainder of the day.

The rusting remains of skyscrapers soon gave way to a long street lined with small, dingy shops. Pawn shops with old forgotten junk, clothing outlets, and greasy restaurants all stood abandoned. These in turn gave way to the out of town mega stores and finally to the scattered buildings edging on the open countryside. Everywhere the broken windows and yawning craters in the walls seemed to open wide in invitation to draw them in to investigate their contents, but their course stayed true. They would not stay here another night. They had taken everything this place could offer and now they were leaving it alone.

The walking was hard. Debris was everywhere, but they had maintained a good speed and with determined effort they had made it out into the open plains before nightfall. They didn't stop. It wasn't a fear of the Ares or any visible thing that drove them on, but just a desire to be free from this place. In Birch's mind he still seemed to hear the hollow screams of despair aboard that doomed helicopter as it had plummeted to earth. To him it had become the sound of the city dying and even now the whisper of it seemed to echo about him in its empty streets. This was why he hurried, even after they had left the last of the buildings behind them.

Finally they stopped. The sun had long set, but they had pressed on for another hour in darkness, wishing to get as far as they could before they rested. They lay wearily in the long, cooling grass. It was some time before either of them spoke. Karla had questions. Birch had said very little about what he had seen, and she understood from the look on his face that it hadn't been the time to ask. But now, in the starry darkness, under the open sky, she wanted to know.

At first Birch had been reluctant to answer, he had left it behind and didn't want to return to it. When he finally did speak it was to give only the barest of details. He explained the technical aspects of the destruction but left unsaid all of the humanity behind these events. It was history now and the only part that interested him was the technique and the meaning of these things. He told her of the Ares involvement.

"Do you think they'll do that again?" Her voice wavered in the darkness. Birch shook his head.

"That's the funny thing. I don't even see how they could have done that in the first place. Look at what they were like when they attacked us, fierce and mindless. Their attack plan was to trample their own comrades to get to us, and then use that savage force to destroy us. It doesn't make sense that they could ever have used a technology like that. Still, it seems the best answer for now."

"Maybe we're missing something," Karla's voice was thoughtful. "There may be more to them than we've seen."

"We're definitely missing something. I don't know what it is, but something's not right. I don't know where we'll find the answers, perhaps from the Ares themselves, but I think if we can find the answer to what happened here we'll really know about what's going on everywhere. That's the only way I can see us knowing everything."

Karla unpacked her sleeping bag and curled into it. "If you figure that one out let me in on it. I wouldn't mind knowing 'everything.'"

Birch snorted as he pulled himself into his own bag. "I'm

sure you wouldn't," he replied moodily. "I already feel I know too much." Karla didn't respond and Birch lay back, staring silently at the stars above. He did know too much, and he would have gladly forgotten much of it, the useless baggage you carry around in your mind, the stuff that weighed you down like ballast, but you can't seem to lose it. If he could trade it all like baseball cards on the playground for the truth of what was going on here he would have done it. If he could have given it away for nothing he would have done that too, gladly.

"Major," Birch had just been drifting into sleep when Karla's voice brought him back to the grim night. He grunted a response and turned over. Karla went on undeterred. "I want to go home." It was a plea, like a little lost child wanting to reunite with her family. Birch turned to her.

"We all do," he lied, "but we can never go home again."

"I can." Karla's voice came still in the night air. "We're almost there now. It's just another few days' travel from here. It wouldn't take us out of our way to go through it, toward the east. Could we go there?"

Birch sighed. The last thing he wanted was to reminisce with Karla about her old times, to be taken to some weathered, rotting buildings that meant something to her but were really just old abandoned junk, like the rest of the places out here. He wasn't even sure it would be the best thing for her either.

"I'm not sure that would be a good idea," he answered. "You seemed to take it pretty hard in the city. Think what it would be like to see your own town like that." They had both taken the city pretty hard, and he wasn't sure that he felt capable of handling that sort of thing again himself, much less Karla in her own home town. "I think we'd better avoid it."

"No," Karla's voice came back with perfect clarity. "I need to go back. If I'm this close then I can't just walk by without looking. I know it will hurt, and that I'd rather remember it the way it was, but still I want to see it again and know what happened there. It's a part of me and I need to see it this one last time."

Birch was irritated by her words and by her request, but he couldn't find it within himself to refuse her. Finally he agreed. Karla was going home.

# THIRTY-ONE

The days that followed had been ones of anxious anticipation. Karla always awoke first and was impatient to get going. In the darkness before dawn she would noisily pack up and prepare to go. Birch wasn't sure, but he guessed she was trying to wake him up so they could start earlier. It's like Christmas to her, he thought to himself, though he didn't think she was going to like what she found under the tree this year.

Finally the last day's travel to her home arrived. After a quick breakfast of canned food they started toward the east. Karla's town wouldn't be hard to find, it was straight off old I70, just over the boarder into Kansas. As they walked she told him all about the place. It was called Goodland, apparently the settlers had been impressed with the farming there and had taken root, literally. She described it in glowing terms as an example of the great American tradition of small towns. Friendly, hopeful and, above all, quiet. It was the kind of place unaffected by the changes of the years, except that farmers drove better tractors and the TV's got bigger.

Like many small towns, it was insular. The outside world was an alarming place, lying somewhere down their arterial road, Interstate 70. Some people left, youngsters seeking adventure, or displaced families looking for work. Most stayed. The rest of the world could go on without them. They had made a deal. They would feed the earth with their grain, soy, and seed, and in return the world would leave them alone, its exposure left to be filtered down to them for the price of a cable package or a glossy magazine from the local drugstore.

There was certainty; their way of life was best, and those outside were missing something in their fast-paced, overpopulated existence. Their world did not center around Washington DC, New York, or any other major metropolis. They were the center themselves, and the fact that their preferred world map placed the United States at the very center of the earth seemed to confirm this, for right in the center of the country, and therefore in the center of the whole world, lay Goodland, Kansas. To the locals this was a truth they already knew. They produced the bread; they kept America true to what it had once been. They felt as though they were truly the custodians of an important truth that would be needed again some day. When that day came they would still be there, or so they had believed.

Birch had listened patiently. To his ambitious mind Goodland sounded small and constricting. The simple fact that Karla had left seemed to indicate that she had felt the same way, not that you could tell it from her words now. He indulged her for a time, taking in her descriptions of the calming summers of nature and sunshine, or the crisp winters with the cloudless sunny sky lighting up the pure white fields beneath. Karla was in a whirl of nostalgia. Soon harsh reality would jar her back from her dreams. He decided to bring her down more gently before they arrived.

"So, if it was so good why did you leave?" Birch's words hadn't been harsh. At least he hadn't intended them to be. He had judged that a reminder of what had inspired her to leave might bring her back from the idealized version of her past and make the grim reality they were about to face a little easier to bear. From the look on her face he could see that she had taken his words as an attack. She stopped walking. For a moment she fell silent. When she finally spoke again the words seemed to come through pain.

"I had to go," she almost whispered, "I had no choice."

"There are always choices," Birch muttered. Secretly he still wished that the farm girl had stayed here, only now it wasn't anything to do with the mission. It was all about Karla. From her words he felt he knew her. Perhaps she would have been happier with a simpler life and death out here on the plains. This new world was nothing like the old one that she had cherished so much.

"There are always choices," Karla repeated, "but, you know, as much as we complicate things and imagine a world full of total free will, our options are pretty limited. Life has a way of often giving you two simple alternatives, two ways, the right one and the wrong one. I could have stayed here, but it would have been the wrong choice. I chose the right one."

"That's a pretty stark way to see the world. Two ways?" Birch shrugged dismissively. "Who knows what's right anyway? And what's so right about the choice you made? You don't seem any happier for it."

"What's right doesn't always make you happy," Karla responded doggedly. "It's about more than just what you want. I didn't say I did what I wanted. I just did the best thing. I loved this place and the people in it, but I had to go." She looked wistfully out to the long, wind-blown grass on the open plain.

"Have you ever felt like you didn't belong, like you were out of sync with everything around you, even with yourself?" She paused for his answer.

Birch shook his head.

"That's what it was like for me here. I don't think I ever felt like I really belonged anywhere. Once you get that habit the whole world seems like an alien place. Maybe that's where my thoughts of the Hypnos missions began, the idea that I was an alien already in my own world. If I joined a mission to another planet for once I'd have company. We'd all be aliens together. It didn't work though. It only made it harder because I found I still loved a lot of what was here."

Birch nodded, that was the hardest thing about the Hypnos missions. This, in fact, had been the very reason he had used to oppose Karla's placement on the crew. He had argued that someone so young couldn't cope with that kind of pressure, with the loss of family and future. It gave him no pleasure to discover that for once he had been right.

They started walking again.

"So what was wrong?" Birch asked absently as they trudged through the swaying grass. He wasn't looking at her but toward the distant eastern horizon. It was empty. Nothing was coming into view and it almost seemed that they were stationary as they walked under the expanse of open sky.

"I just didn't fit. I never did. I could have put on the cowboy boots and listened to the country music, or I could have worn the pretty prom dress and joined the cheerleading team, it didn't make any difference. I was tagged as different as a young girl and once you get a label like that it's hard to rub it off. It seemed to show through, no matter what clothes you wear over it."

"Sounds like typical teenage angst to me," Birch remarked sourly. Her conversation seemed trite, he thought, like so many other girls before her. She was young enough that some of the adolescence hadn't rubbed off yet. Given another five years he might have liked her. For now all he could do was endure her.

"So you were different," he concluded scornfully. "What's the big deal? Everybody's different one way or another, so what does it matter?" He was regretting opening the floodgates on the subject.

Karla shook her head. "It matters a lot more than most of us want to admit. The way we play up to everyone's expectations. A lot of what we do is just to fit in with what they want from us. How many of your choices in life do you think you based on wanting to look good to others? More than you would ever admit, or even recognize I bet.

"That was me. I was stuck. I was labeled as 'gifted' or 'different'. In a small town a tag like that kills, but I found out later that it's no different anywhere else. In a small town there's just fewer people, so it's harder to hide our feelings from each other. People everywhere hate difference. Because I was smarter than others they ignored me, tried to avoid me, I was a threat somehow, and so I didn't belong. Even my own family couldn't relate to me.

"We were on a farm on the eastern side of town and my younger brother took to it like he'd been born in that barn. From the age of five he was wearing the boots, talking crops, and trying to drive the tractor. He was born a native in this land, and I didn't belong. I tried, I fished, hunted, and did whatever seemed right, but I never could break through. They loved us both, but they understood him and felt comfortable with him. I knew I had to leave.

"I could tell you about all the petty snubs, all the times people unintentionally let me see their true feelings with their actions, but what would be the point? I loved this place, but it didn't love me, so like anyone who has been rejected I looked elsewhere.

"You've seen my records. You know that I was in college by thirteen. I thought it would be better there, among the best and the brightest, but it wasn't. I was younger than any of them, and again I made them uncomfortable. It's always the same, people look through you. It had been better back home. At least there people smiled at you. In the city they pretended you weren't there at all."

"I'm sure it wasn't that bad," Birch suggested hollowly. "So you went to college early and some of the geeks were intimidated by your age. It's not like people would look at you on the street and start shouting, 'unclean', or anything."

"It feels that way sometimes, Major. What did you think of me when I was first signed up for the mission?"

Birch kept his eyes firmly directed to the horizon. "I thought you were young," he admitted, "but that had nothing to do with your education or how smart you are. I was just worried the mission wouldn't be good for you at your age. Leaving everything behind is a hard thing to do, no matter how old you are. But as young as you are, you have a whole life ahead of you. Why waste it?"

This was largely true, though if he allowed himself to think about it he recognized some of himself in what Karla had said. Her reputation had made him uncomfortable, but he had told himself that this wasn't the true reason for his opposition to her.

"I'm glad about that," Karla smiled at his words, "on this mission above all I need to feel a part of the team, a part of a family."

"A pretty dysfunctional one," Birch mused bitterly.

"Oh I know," Karla stopped and Birch turned to wait for her, "but we still felt things. It wasn't like anything I'd ever had before. I was a part that mattered, not something that didn't fit in anymore. I loved my family, but at the time I never thought that I belonged. That's why I left. When I finally joined the Hypnos mission it seemed the perfect answer. I wouldn't be around to make anyone uncomfortable again, and my income would be transferred to them for the next thirty years. The farm would be safe. They would all be secure for life. I could finally do something for them."

"It sounds like the perfect answer, so what are you so wrung up about? They all lived happily ever after, right?"

"That's the problem," Karla's voice faltered and she began walking again to cover her emotion. "It did seem like the perfect answer, but it wasn't. A week before I was supposed to leave my mom finally phoned. We hadn't talked for years, it wasn't like we were mad or anything, we just never had that much to say to each other; it was uncomfortable. She told me that she missed me. It shocked me, she told me I was her special girl and she didn't want to lose me, she asked me to come off the mission." Karla pulled in a sob. She turned her head so Birch couldn't see the tears welling up in her eyes.

"I said I couldn't, it was too late and I was locked into the contract. She cried and said I would always be in their hearts. That was it, I never heard from them again. They couldn't take it, the emotion of it all, so they missed the launch and everything. That was the worst day ever. Sitting there on the launch pad about to be blasted from what I had sought all those years. It seemed as though the fire of those engines was burning my own heart to cinders."

Birch remembered that day. With shame he also remembered that he had seen her tears at the launch and had pointed it out to Ratliff with a knowing wink. He had taken it as a sign of her weakness and proof that he was right, now it seemed to tell him more about himself than he really wanted to know.

"You want to know the funny thing," Karla continued. "I don't think my mom would ever have told me all of that if I had stayed. It was only at the very end that she could tell me, and then only when it was too late to do anything about it. Why do you think we do that to each other?" Birch shrugged uncomfortably and looked at the ground.

"I don't know," he muttered after an uneasy silence. She was expecting an answer and he knew he didn't have one. "We do whatever seems best at the time I suppose."

"But it's usually wrong. We go through life like ghosts, never touching the world around us or being touched by it in turn. We're all apparitions of ourselves. Life could be so much more if only we would reach out and grasp it. We don't. We're satisfied with ourselves until the very end. Only then do we wake up to our mistakes, but by then it's too late. That's why this mission and our crew mean so much to me now. I've seen the mistake in my life before the end, while I can make a difference. This is my life, my only chance. It's important for me to hang on to this last family now," Karla looked into Birch's eyes, "you are all that I have."

Birch looked away.

"I hope the others are okay." Her voice wavered. "I want to see them again."

"We will soon enough," Birch concluded confidently. "We're all headed for Washington, so I'm sure we'll see them again soon." Karla nodded and smiled.

They continued in silence for a time. Karla seemed spent, exhausted by their conversation.

Birch kept his eyes on the horizon. No evidence of civilization presented itself to them as they walked. He wished for some break from the monotony and from the privacy of his own thoughts. Karla's pain was a little to close to his own for comfort, and any distraction would have been welcome.

His mind turned again to the Ares threat. In the daylight he hadn't given them much thought, but as the day turned to afternoon he found himself wondering about their strengths out here on the plains. There hadn't been any sign of them yet, but he knew they were around.

He had no idea how many of them there were so it was very difficult to know just how much danger they were really in. It was strange to him that the city had been so empty, that the Ares hadn't taken possession of it. He might have thought it totally abandoned, but for the incident at the motel. One Ares on his own, that didn't seem to fit with what Edwards had told him about their way of working, but then it didn't seem like much that he had seen had fit into that pattern anyway.

"Over there," Karla's voice broke in on Birch's thoughts. She was pointing toward the horizon where a clump of trees could be seen, dwarfed against the wide, open sky. "That's a sure sign of a settlement out here," Karla shouted. "I think that's it, so we should be there in a couple of hours." Birch nodded but wasn't cheered by the news. This was going to be tough for Karla, and for him.

# THIRTY-TWO

This was safety. As tenuous as it was: this tiny courtyard, in this insignificant base, on these wide plains was a haven. It was all he had, and he clung to it. It was enough, for now.

He was alone in this small courtyard at the center of the base. It was lush with abundant vegetation, but it was a wild, overgrown abundance, the result of neglect rather than care and cultivation. Wild vines climbed the grimy, grey walls. They crept along the crumbling cobbled terrace. They choked a solitary tree struggling for life and light in a dreary corner of the enclosure.

This was meant to be the heart of the oasis. It should have been the hub, a center of hope where a generous garden of trees and plants alien to this harsh land would take root. It was part of their plan to change the world. Towns would grow up around them. It would spread from here and from all the other bases like it, until they had transformed this grassy desert. But it wasn't happening. The walls were still here. The flaming sword of their military still guarded this garden from the savage hands and feet that would trample and destroy it, but what was inside had turned rank and rotten. They were defeated before the Ares had even gotten in.

Edwards sat on one of the rusty, metal chairs scattered randomly about the place. He had placed himself in the slender sliver of warming sunlight and was gazing up into an unblemished sky. A bird floated high above and he watched it, dreaming of more peaceful times. He knew in just a few short moments things would be very different and he wanted to take this last chance to rest.

They were almost prepared. The trucks were loaded, weapons were restocked, and food supplies were replenished. After a few final adjustments every physical measure would have been taken to be ready for the journey ahead. Mentally Edwards felt less ready. That was why he was here. He was finding some sense of peace in the madness before they left.

The pallid leaves of the clinging vines rustled, and the bare branches of the tree clacked against the stone as it creaked and swayed in the wind. There was no peace here, only empty desolation. He sighed. Already Jane and Lauren were making their way toward him and their faces told him that his moment was over.

"Hiding out under the tree?" Jane asked ironically. "I can't say I blame you. This seems like the only place around here not humming with tension over our little trip. Of course no one ever talks to us about it. We're just the ones going, so whenever we're around things get very quiet. You can tell it's all about us though by the looks on their faces. It's like they're saying 'good luck, you'll need it,' with their eyes."

"That may be true," Edwards responded. "We will need it. We'll all need it. There are big things happening out there right now and I think a little luck wouldn't hurt."

"So what are our chances?" Jane asked directly. She seemed to feel she could trust Edwards enough to get a straight answer to a straight question. "I'm not sure I believe what those guys told us in the meeting. It doesn't seem right. I think it must be a lot harder than they're telling us, and the way everyone's been acting here only seems to confirm it."

Edwards laughed. "You're starting to sound like Major Birch. I thought you trusted us."

Jane frowned at the mention of that name.

"Things change," Jane fixed her penetrating gaze on Edwards. He almost looked away. "I don't like the way they talked to us in that meeting. More to the point I didn't like the way they *didn't* talk to us. It seemed like we weren't even important, like we didn't even exist. Why won't they talk to us?"

"They're military. They don't talk to anybody. You might have noticed that they didn't have a lot of time for me either," Edwards confided. "And you'll also notice that it didn't take them very long to relieve me of the command, or to place the blame for their past mistakes on me. We're outsiders here so they won't say anything they don't need to."

Jane looked puzzled. "So what's the difference between you and the others? You all work for the same people don't you?"

Edwards laughed bitterly. "I doubt that things were really that different in your day. You know how it is, one agency against another, friendly competitors can quickly become bitter rivals and eventually enemies. The army and the DA are like that. We're not exactly enemies, but I guess we're not exactly friends either. If you look back I'm sure you'll see the same in yourselves."

"I do." It was Lauren's voice that answered. "I know exactly what you mean." Edwards was startled. To him it seemed that the young woman had come to life for the first time. She appeared ready to say more, a look something like anger crossed her face, but an instant later the calm had returned and she thought better of it. She had descended back into the shell that protected her. Her eyes dulled and she was quiet again. Edwards wondered about her. She almost seemed like a shadow of the rest of the crew. She was always there, but somehow she was never there, the silent, invisible element that would eventually go unnoticed once you got used to her. Edwards wanted to notice her, to say something kind or helpful, but Jane was already speaking.

"Do you really think their plan will work? Is their alternate route south any safer?"

Edwards shrugged. "It could be. The maps seem to show a clear path down there for now, but it all depends on what happens. If the attack goes well then there won't be much to worry about. That's a big 'if'! If anything goes wrong then there could be plenty to worry about."

"I knew it! I knew those guys were glossing it!" Jane barked. "It's stupid to hope we could just outrun them. What do you think our chances really are?"

"Well, that's hard to say. Even a partial success for the army could still mean trouble for us," Edwards' voice had descended to a hush, as though he were divulging a great secret. "If the enemy force isn't totally destroyed in the north it's likely they'll splinter off into smaller groups. I would expect some of them to go to the south. It'll be a natural corridor of escape. Depending on the size of group, we could be in a lot of trouble if we run into any of them."

"And didn't the army think of that?" Jane's voice was incredulous.

"Of course," Edwards answered smoothly. "They think of everything. They don't always know what to do about it, but they do think of everything! I'm sure they don't like it, but they seem to believe that this is the best choice. We just have to hope that the troops to the north can route them, or if not that we at least can avoid any of the run-off."

"Then wouldn't it just be safer to just stay here? We could wait behind the walls until it's all finished and then walk out safely."

"No," Edwards' voice was barely audible now, "that's the other issue you raised at the meeting." Jane looked blankly at Edwards. "When you talked about the attack in the mountains you suggested that maybe we were the focus of the attack, that we were the start of all this uprising. I think you've struck on something important there."

"But that was the one thing they were most sure of, that it was all part of a wider plot and not directed at us at all."

Edwards laughed again, perhaps more bitterly this time. "I'd thought you were beginning to learn how things worked. It was their very adamancy on that issue that made it most convincing! They know more than they want to tell. I sensed that myself in the meeting. It all really confirms what I've felt for quite a while, even before we were attacked on the mountain. Little signs that something big was brewing and we were right in the middle of it."

"I still don't see why we don't wait here," Jane complained again. "Why are they pushing us out from the one safe place in this dangerous time?"

"Yes, you obviously don't see, Major." Edwards' words came harshly. "This isn't a safe place and the reason we have to get out of here today is that they know it's only a matter of time before they're overrun."

"But you said these places were safe," Jane's voice was exasperated, like a child promised something she couldn't keep.

"*Were* safe is the best way to put it. When this place is hit with the kind of mass attack the Ares have been launching across the plains, then it will not stand. The soldiers here know that. They're sending us away early. We were supposed to be here at least another three or four days to let things blow over. They've heard something. They're not telling you, and they haven't even said anything to me, but the Ares are coming. I'm sure of it. This base will fall. They're doomed. The commander has just left himself enough men to make a stand at the end and give us enough time to get away."

"That's fatalistic. There must be something we can do."

"Run, that's about it. There isn't any help nearby."

"So why don't we all run then? Why should they stay and defend a base that they know they can't hold? We would be stronger if we ran together."

Edwards paused for a minute and looked around. Finally he gestured to their withered surroundings. "This is what it's all about," he murmured. "They will defend it. If you weren't here we all would stay to defend it, but we have to get you to Washington."

"This? You all want to die for a bunch of dead plants and some walls?" Jane's voice was angry. "No wonder you can't win this war. What a waste! It's stupid."

Edwards glared angrily back at her, his lips compressed into a thin line. He said nothing for some time. When he finally spoke his words were cool and rational.

"Remember the Alamo. Maybe you've never understood those words. Maybe you've heard them but they only echoed in your mind, reaching no deeper than some superficial history lesson in high school! Well, we once knew what they meant, and what they told us about the men who fought there. More importantly, we knew what it told us about ourselves. That we were proud of those who fought for what they believed.

"What was the Alamo? The place itself meant nothing. It was just an old mission that was hardly worth defending. When you travel to see it you wonder that anyone would care what happened to a place like that. In the cost of bricks and mortar what really was its worth? Not much. It was hardly a thing worth dying for. You could easily replace it, build another one just like it, or even better than it, but still men fought for it. Not because they loved that structure, or even the ground upon which it was built, but because they loved the idea of it. No thing is worth dying for. People die for ideas, not the pitiful things and objects that represent them. This fort might not seem to be worth anything to you, but the idea is worth everything. Don't question those brave enough to defend it."

Jane shook her head. "It sounds like boys and their games to me. You and your army can play fort then, and chase, and whatever else you want to get up to with the Ares. You can even drag me into it with you because I have no choice, but don't expect me to applaud you or support you in any of this.

"You know, your ideas sound a lot grander than the grim

reality of death and destruction that will happen because of them. Some day it might actually be nice to see if people could live for  ideas instead of die for them, or better still listen to ideas instead of kill for them."

Edwards rose to his feet. He glowered down at Jane. She knew nothing. He wanted peace more than anyone. Edwards had tried to understand the Ares more than anyone, but what Jane expected was unrealistic and stupid. Her way would open them up to destruction. One day they would understand the Ares, but from a position of power and strength. That was the only way to deal with them.

"I think," Edwards hissed icily, "we'll see what happens when you meet up with the Ares again. You'll get your chance soon enough, I expect. I'll be interested to see what you think of their 'ideas' then."

# THIRTY-THREE

Only the trees remained as a testament to what had once been a town. The destruction was complete, much more so than in the city. Where Denver's buildings had been attacked in an almost haphazard way, leaving some standing and others destroyed, Goodland had been razed to the ground. Nothing was left.

The sight of each new street and their flattened structures seemed to plunge Karla deeper into depression. She glanced around her helplessly. Occasionally she stopped, as though trying to fix things in her mind. It wasn't good for her. She seemed to be crumbling physically in these surroundings, to be collapsing into a pile of human rubble. Birch kept trying to hurry her along, to get her out before she totally fell apart.

"That's the museum, the ball park's down there, I played tennis sometimes over there." Karla pointed to identical patches of bare earth and broken fragments of buildings. "That's the school, the drug store, the church, the library." All of these barely distinguishable sites came to mean something this one last time. Karla was the only one who knew them, whose memories had the power to bring them back to life. For this one instant these places were something more than what they had become, because someone remembered. They were home, but once Karla left Goodland would slump again back into its anonymity, eventually to succumb to the creeping prairie grasses nibbling away at its very existence. Karla seemed to sense this and lingered. It was her life that fueled the town now, and Birch urged her on before she was completely consumed by it.

As he watched Birch imagined that he could see a change, like she was draining away. Her skin had turned a pale, salty white. Her eyes were dreamy and glazed. She was living in the memories of this place and Birch feared she might never want to leave if he didn't get her out soon. He almost pushed her through the final few yards toward the open country on the other side. He felt some relief at that point, until he remembered that Karla had said that her old home was on the eastern side of town. The greatest hurdle still remained and he was worried about how she would take it.

Her house was a couple of miles from town and that at least gave them time to digest what they had already seen before the next specter presented itself. Karla led the way and strode silently ahead. She seemed unwilling to talk, but Birch thought it would be better for her if she did, the only problem was what could he say? In the end there wasn't anything he could say and so they remained silent. Finally Karla herself spoke.

"Why did they do it?" She flung the words at Birch like an accusation.

He shrugged.

"It looks like they took out this whole area. I don't know why."

"That's not what I mean," Karla's voice was unusually cold. "Why did they destroy everything? It was like they wanted to even wipe the memories from this place. Why would they do that?" Karla stopped walking and looked tearfully back at the greenery of the town. "They didn't destroy the trees anyway."

Birch sighed heavily. "It looks like a scorched earth policy to me, except they only destroyed the shelter rather than the earth itself. Perhaps they just wanted to make it as hard as they could for anyone to come back here. Probably if you went to all the other towns around here you'd find the same thing. It seems like they were pretty systematic."

"So why didn't they do the same in Denver, that's a much bigger danger isn't it?"

Birch shook his head. "I'm not sure I really understand that either, maybe all these small towns would be harder to keep and protect from enemies. They may have just been trying to make sure none of them could be taken back and used as bases against them later. That would be my guess, though I suppose only the Ares themselves really know. It may all be less logical than any of that. It may just be another sign of their savagery."

Karla was silent again. Birch's answers seemed to calm her somewhat. Perhaps the thought that her town was not alone in the destruction gave her some strange sense of relief, a perspective that lessened her sense of victimization. This wasn't just about her and the place she knew, it was hundreds of towns and millions of lives across this land that had been destroyed. To grieve only for herself and what she knew was selfish.

Birch himself was finally getting the scope of it all. Strangely, in the city he had felt it, but he had been able to blank it out. It was a big, impersonal place, but now, seeing Karla's town through her eyes he couldn't escape the pain of understanding what all of this meant. It almost sent his mind back to his own pain, but he struggled to avoid that. Karla wasn't the only one to have lost, but he was far more capable of acknowledging her loss than his own.

For a time they followed an old paved road, cracked and worn into a thousand pieces, like sun-baked dirt in a drought stricken land. Grass grew high through the gaps as nature struggled to overcome the bonds of civilization, soon it would win. Eventually they turned onto what he guessed must have once been a dirt road. There was little left to indicate what it once was, but by the way Karla walked it seemed that she was following some unseen highway. This was a road she knew from memory, for it was only there in her mind now.

"Is it much farther?" Birch asked, trying to break the silence again. He wanted this ordeal over, partly because of his concern for Karla. This was a living horror to her, and if he hadn't thought it would make things even worse, he would have snatched her away from these moldering memories already.

His primary concern, though, was with his own horrors. They seemed to grow greater with every step. He was still fighting to master them. Most of all he wanted to leave these dead cities and towns behind, to get out of the past and finally live in the future. It seemed that the longer he stayed here the more real it all became and the more his mood darkened. He could almost slip back into the former life and exist, not now, but then. This was not what he had come back for. He had wanted a new life, not the old one.

"Not long," Karla answered hopefully. "It's just a little farther along here."

Silently they walked on the featureless landscape. Birch couldn't see anything to indicate that anybody had ever lived here. All that was there was the flat grassland with occasional undulations too small to be called hills, more like wrinkles on a great flat tablecloth that spread out for miles. The crumbs of civilization had all been shaken off years ago and left this uncluttered land. It might have been beautiful, but while the sun was still bright, the sky still blue, and the grass and wild-flowers as active and lively as ever, it didn't seem to make any difference to the gloomily empty scene. Finally Karla stopped. She glanced about in all directions before looking helplessly to Birch.

"I can't find it," she stuttered through a sob. "I don't know where it is." She slumped over and fell listlessly onto the long grass. Birch cast an uncomfortable glance where she sat but said nothing. He looked away. "You'd think I wouldn't forget something like that," Karla continued. "It's my family, how could I forget? What kind of evil person forgets their family?"

Birch sighed. "Everything's forgotten," he remarked bitterly, "you just have to wait long enough." Karla looked up at Birch, but her bleary eyes couldn't meet his. His gaze was fixed into the distance.

"Think of all those worn tombstones in the graveyards," he continued, "'To the loving memory of my husband, wife, parent, or child... whoever. We will always remember.' That's a lie, it's a promise they can't even keep because they'll die too, and when they've gone so has the memory. It doesn't even take that long anymore because nobody cares. So this is our fate, to be forgotten, leaving nothing behind but a pile of meaningless photographs that no one wants, or our impressive stone marker that will only wear away until the writing becomes as faint and meaningless as the feelings they were supposed to represent. We all disappear in the end!

"Nothing lasts. This place, above all, should make it clear. We'd be better off if we could leave it all behind anyway. I can tell you now that there will be no happy ending here. There never is when you go searching through the rubbish of the past. Even if you did find your precious home, what would you find? Rubble and dust that have decayed to nothing and won't even leave a memory once you're gone. That's all that any of this is, so I don't even know what you're looking for because there's nothing here except what is in your own head. Leave it behind!"

Karla's face had crumpled into an angry frown.

"Why do you do that?" she spat the words at him. Birch couldn't see the pain etched deep on her features. He was still looking to the horizon ahead as she wiped her eyes on her sleeve.

"Every time it seems like you're going to be different, like you're going to be human, you come back worse than ever." Birch still did not answer. "You don't understand things nearly as well as you think you do. People do live forever.

There are more memories alive than you could ever know! A lot of things will never turn to dust; they will live forever. You may never understand it, but you're a part of it. What you've said and done will live after you, Major, whether you think it will or not. You can't change that. You're living your legacy!"

"Oh spare me your simple Midwestern philosophy, Lieutenant," Birch snapped angrily. "I don't need your home-spun country goodness wrapped up for me. I don't need your Sunday-School-happily-ever-after stories to make me feel good before I go to bed at night because I'm not buying it. This is a hard world, it's hard to be born, it's hard to live, and it's hard to die. Nothing is easy, and you haven't experienced enough life if you think anything different. We are nothing, and then we die"

"I've experienced plenty," Karla responded, her face reddening. "What about you? What have you experienced? Sure, I bet you've done stuff, but have you experienced it? Maybe you just never cared enough about anyone else in your life to want to know that there's something more you could do!

"We are everything, and we have to live it! It's our world and it's all about what we do. The good or the bad will live on in the lives of those we leave behind. You will be immortal in the lives you affected and the lives they will affect after them. You don't need my Sunday-School-philosophy to understand that, just a heart and a brain!"

Birch glared furiously down at the young lieutenant. His eyes blazed and the muscles at the side of his face tightened as his jaw clenched.

"I understand fine," he hissed through gritted teeth. "Now get up! We're getting out of here!" He pulled Karla to her feet so violently that she almost fell forward into the grass. She regained her balance with her face just inches from Birch's. Their eyes met. Her still, blue pools gazed deeply into him, as though trying to cool his fiery emotions. He almost felt it happen, but he released her hand and turned away.

"We'd better get going," he barked gruffly, "we haven't got much daylight left and I want to get as far from this town as we can before dark."

Karla nodded mutely and followed him toward the horizon.

# THIRTY-FOUR

The departure was simpler than their approach had been. Instead of the contorted twists and turns of their entry they moved away from the base in a swift, straight dash to the south. Their line of vehicles ploughed through the tall grass, flattening it beneath them. Soon they had reached top speed and were thrashing through the blowing weeds toward safety. As they pulled away Edwards stole a last glance at the little base behind them. Soon it would be gone, like so much before it. The Ares were coming. When they got there they would destroy everything, but their victory would be brief. They would pay this time, and the revenge would be swift. The army coming from the east would repay in kind.

There wasn't anything they could do about it- nothing, except run. From what he could gather Edwards figured that the retreating Ares were fleeing from the advancing armies to the east, while another horde of Ares attackers was rushing in from the west to help them. They were in the middle and had to squirt away to the south as quickly as possible to avoid getting caught in the fight. Above all, they had been told, get to Washington safely. No more losses.

And so they would flee, running from the danger as fast as they could, hoping that in the confusion they might escape alive.

Edwards couldn't shake the impression that they had a more central part to play in this drama than anyone was willing to admit. Perhaps the Ares had some idea about their mission and its deeper meaning. If they did then this convoy was in terrible danger. Their flight needed to be swift, for he knew the Ares would give chase with all of their rage and might. No base, no army, nothing other than their complete destruction would stop them. And so they had to run.

Their flight continued without pause through the rest of the day. The emptiness of the countryside engulfed them. They were alone, but Edwards kept his eyes on the horizon, watching for any sign of pursuit. There was none, and he felt some sense of relief as they entered the last few hours of daylight with no visible sign of danger. That quickly changed.

The peril came from an unexpected source. He had been watching for any sign of attack, but it was not a human foe they had to contend with, but nature's destructive power that now approached at speed. It was one of those summer storms, a mighty squall that the plains could suddenly bring up on even the brightest of days. A huge thunderhead cloud was moving from the southwest and, like a great black blanket, was draw-ing itself over the blue sky.

Darkness spread like an incoming tide across the land as the clouds covered the sun. The tiny line of trucks kept moving swiftly, but was soon caught up in the storm. From his window Edwards could see a great curtain of hail approaching. It hit a moment later with the sound of a thousand thud-thuds against the bodywork of the trucks. They were big, and heavy, and there were a lot of them. Even with their armor it seemed that the trucks must suffer some damage from the barrage.

More worrying was the visibility. Edwards, in the second truck, had already lost sight of the lead vehicle ahead of them. The radio cracked to life, it was Linkhorn from the truck ahead. "This doesn't look too good," His voice hissed through the speaker. “I can't see any of you back there. We better stop here for a while until this storm blows over. We can start up again as soon as this clears.” The radio went silent and their truck came to a halt.

Edwards watched the hail fall. The windows fogged and the wipers screeched against the glass. He could see nothing. It was strange how a storm made the world seem so small.

Nature's fury gusted about them. A gale howled and rocked the truck on its wheels. The hail beat down on them harder than ever. It seemed to Edwards that the dormant power of the earth had been awakened and was seeking them out, just as the Ares were. Perhaps this was a global conspiracy against their advances. So be it then. If this was the worst they could do then they would overcome both the world and the Ares if necessary to make their mission a success. They would win.

As if in response to his thoughts a sudden burst of brilliant lightning illuminated the whole scene in an unearthly glow. It was instantly followed by an explosion of thunder that rolled ominously around the plain. In that one moment of light he saw the mass of hail hurled down at them like a solid sheet of ice. He laughed nervously to himself. He had better watch what he thought. That lightning was close.

***

Birch had seen the storm coming first. It was one of those fast moving ones that wasn't going to give them much time to find cover. There wasn't much to be found out here anyway. They had to improvise, and as he saw the curtain of hail drawing toward them he pulled a blanket out of his backpack and shouted to Karla. She looked gloomily back at him but didn't move.

“Move it Karla,” Birch growled, “this looks like a real heavy storm coming in and the more cover we can get from it the better. I don't think you'll want to take too many hits from those hailstones, they look pretty big."

She shrugged, "What are you going to do, push me down if I don't?"

"I won't have to; the hail will do that for me. It's your choice."

Karla moved sulkily toward Birch, pulling her own blanket from her pack. They both quickly combined their bedding to provide the thickest possible cover from the storm, and as the dark clouds rolled over them they both ducked beneath the blankets.

It was hot, stifling, and awkward under the makeshift shelter. Their animosity, already present before this inconvenience, seemed to be magnified under the confining blankets. A great gulf of empty space opened up between them as they struggled to stay as far from each other as possible, while still remaining protected from the hail. And so they wrestled between them for the covers, like an old married couple on a cold night. It might almost have seemed comical if they hadn't been so angry.

For a time Birch just watched the storm. A heavy torrent of hail was now dropping on them, but the protection provided by the blankets kept them safe. The hailstones were impressive, big balls of ice, the type that would put some serious damage on anyone, or anything, struck by them. From under the cover it was almost peaceful to watch them striking the ground around them. In pleasant silence the two watched the fury of nature and listened to the thunder rolling above their heads.

Birch and Karla's anger cooled and their hearts warmed beneath the blankets as they watched the scene around them. It was strange the calming effect a storm could have on the mind when you felt warm and protected from it. Even the lightning that flashed and danced across the sky in powerful bursts somehow seemed distant; it couldn't touch them. Their thin blanket covering, in their minds, became a substantial barrier against harm. Like the old blanket tents of childhood, it was almost a magically safe place as they hid silently beneath it.

Finally Karla spoke. Her words were soft and quiet amidst the blasts of the storm, but they were more clear and penetrating than any of the noise outside.

"So why did you sign up for this mission?" Her voice was warm and kindly, with no hint of the bitterness of before, but still it jolted him like an electric shock. "Everyone has a reason. You don't volunteer for this kind of thing without having something pushing you to it. You know my reason, so what's yours?"

Birch was silent. The only sound was that of the thudding hailstones against the ground and the rolling thunder above. He wished it could stay that way, but he knew it couldn't last. She was waiting for an answer.

"Nothing," he finally muttered, "nothing but duty." Karla had turned to face him. The blankets made it dark, but not dark enough for him to avoid seeing her expression. She didn't believe him. A knowing smile played across her lips and her deep blue eyes fixed upon him, as though to penetrate through his skin to prize out his inmost secrets. It made him angry. What were his secrets to her, and why should he tell her when he couldn't even tell himself? So what if she had told him all about herself, he hadn't asked for it. It wasn't as though he was interested, or really cared to know about her. She had forced the information on him, so why should she think that she had the right to know about him and his life. It was like some grown-up version of truth-or-dare. He wasn't going to play. Karla's smile remained and she seemed to change the subject.

"That was a brave thing you did for me," she gushed, "coming to get me off that mountain. I don't think I'll ever forget that moment I came around and saw you there. It was like you were my guardian angel or something, except that you'd passed out from the fumes on the cloth!" She giggled lightly at the memory. "You saved me. It takes a special person to do that."

"That was duty too," Birch remarked sourly, he wanted to hurt Karla. She was hurting him, bringing him back to where he didn't want to be, and now he wanted to strike back, to make her feel it too. "Everything's a duty in life. On a mission it's just easier to know what that duty is. In life it's not so easy. I had to save you if I could. I'm your commander." He watched for her reaction, but to his surprise the smile remained fixed to her face. She seemed to understand more than he had hoped.

"Not everything," she responded quietly. "I've seen more than that."

She was right, of course, but he hated to think of it. He hated to think of anything because it just hurt too much. Somehow, in spite of his efforts, he had felt himself opening up to Karla. She seemed to care and that had made a difference. It brought down his defenses. It was like she was some great emotional can-opener, and he was the helpless can caught in her grip, and, no matter how hard he tried to hang on, the lid was going to come off.

It was her cheerful goodness that had done it. He had hated her for it, but she wouldn't give up. That persistent sunshine had broken through into his dank soul and let all the light in. Even now, if she would just say the right words, he knew he would be helpless. She would know everything.

"Why can't you accept my thanks? You and Carlos both saved my life. I would be dead without you. I only wish he could be here too; you both were so brave."

"DeSante was brave," Birch muttered stiffly, "he did what he didn't have to do. He should have stayed with the others. I'm your commanding officer; I did what I had to do. I am sorry he was lost. He is the one you should admire."

"You're right, I do admire him, but I admire you too. I can't understand why you always seem so unwilling to accept the good in yourself. You like to blame every good thing you've done on duty or honor. Why can't you just accept that you are good and that you have been brave?"

Karla was a wily one, Birch thought to himself. She appeared to have found his one weak spot and even now seemed to be prizing at the lid of his innermost thoughts. It was that word again, 'brave', 'brave', 'brave'. She kept hammering it into his head like nails and he couldn't stand to hear it again.

"Oh, shut-up," he stormed. "Just shut-up you stupid little girl! I'm not brave. If I was I wouldn't even be here. And I don't even know the first thing about duty or honor. I just do the same as everybody else, whatever it takes to survive.

"I saved you because I could. At least I thought I could. I could handle that, but I can't handle you. Get out of my head! Get out of my business! Get out of my past! It's all dead. They're all dead. Never again, I don't want to go there again! Leave it alone. Leave me alone." He flung the covers aside and walked out into the storm. After a moment's silence she followed him.

"What's the matter?" Karla's voice was soft. "How can I help?" Birch's back was to her. He said nothing, but stood looking into the tempest. The hail had thinned and the smaller pellets stung his skin as they fell onto his face. Finally he turned to her.

"Nothing can help anymore," he responded sadly. She hardly recognized his voice, stripped as it was of its customary authority. "The past," he mumbled, "is a place you can never visit. Oh, you can imagine you're there. You can even go back to the places, but you can never go back to it. You should know that. Your precious town was gone wasn't it? It was a broken shell of itself, and nothing you could do would put it back together again.

"Sometimes," he growled, "the past is just like a useless weight hanging around your neck. It drowns you."

"That's true," Karla put a hand on his stiff back, "if you let it. Sometimes you just have to let go of the weight or it will drag you down. I've had to do it. I'm still fighting it now, but the fact that I could walk through Goodland proved that I can make it. I was sad, but I accepted the way things are. I have made peace with my own memories. You have to do the same."

"Well, that's just fine," Birch snapped, "but maybe your memories are a lot easier to make peace with. What have you got to be sorry about? That your parents didn't understand you? That's hardly a lot to feel guilty about, you didn't do anything wrong, so what's the problem? My memories are a lot harder to deal with than anything you've got."

"Then let them go."

Birch turned to look at Karla. "I want too. I've let everything else go, but that's my one punishment, the memories remain. You call me brave, but my memories call me coward. They live to remind me in every waking moment of what I really am.

"If ever I do anything right or good, my memories are there to remind me that I am a fake- a sham- a non-hero! If I stand up today I know that if only things got hard enough I would run tomorrow. Perhaps the mission has proved that true. I've run back to earth and see what it's gotten us."

"No," Karla's voice was firm, even indignant. "You did what was best for all of us, despite what the others said. It was a brave decision you made, to stand up and do what was right, despite orders. You saved our lives."

Birch's hands went to his head. "There you go with that word again. Stop it! It's going through my head like electricity! I'm not brave. Let me tell you how brave I am, I came on this mission because of fear. I was a coward. I was far less brave walking onto that ship and being blasted out into the universe than I would have been if I had just stayed home and loved my wife."

"You left a wife behind? That's hard."

"No, it was easy. You don't know all of it.

"When I was a teenager my uncle died. He had one of those wasting cancers that took months to kill him. We would go up and visit him every week or two. For months we'd go, and he'd be weaker and thinner every time. It was like I could see the life being sucked out of him. The last time we went before he died my mom took some pictures, the last memories of her brother. You want to know the stupid thing? Something went wrong with the camera. The battery died or something and she fiddled with it, trying to get it working, but she couldn't.

"When we got home she looked through the pictures, and there it was. The last picture on the card, what was supposed to be his last picture, was messed up because she'd pushed the button on the couch, trying to fix it. Instead of his last picture she took a picture of the cushions. It might almost be funny but there were times when I caught her looking at that picture of cushions and crying over it. Sorrow makes us fools."

"I knew then that I couldn't handle that kind of thing. I could see my uncle's family pulling together for the last hard moments, and in the end they were all gathered about his bed as he breathed his last. But I was glad to leave. Every week it was like stepping into a living mausoleum. The place was cold and dead. We spoke in hushed voices and thought of delicate things to say to him, things that didn't mention the future. Every week I was so glad that I was the one leaving that place, not staying behind, not dabbing his forehead, not helping.

"Maybe you suspect what I'm going to tell you next, but it did happen to me. I faced that situation again with Sarah, but this time it was my own family, my wife. I was to be the one at the bedside. Others would come and visit, others would sympathize, and above all, others would be glad when they could leave my house. Looking down that dark, narrow tunnel I couldn't take it. I left."

"You left?"

"I left. I didn't even pack or anything. I went out the front door, and I never came back. I can remember almost every step I took to the car. It seemed that they should have been marked in blood, for it felt like murder I did that day. I would erase them if I could, but they have left an indelible mark.

Everywhere I go they follow me. I've been half way across the universe and still they follow me.

"And here we are, back on earth again, but I can never go back home."

"You see now, lieutenant, that I wasn't brave to join this mission; it was just what I needed, a chance to run. I signed up the very next day. By the time the Agency found out the situation, the condition of my wife, the publicity for Hypnos III was in full swing and they didn't want to look bad. They covered it up, and so I got my chance to run, to run as far as our technology could allow. Funny thing though, I've found you can run from a lot of things, but you never can outrun yourself. Now, no matter how busy I am, or what I do, or where I go, those footsteps follow me. Sometimes, in my mind, I can hear them still, echoing the truth of what I really am. So, lieutenant, don't call me 'brave'. But of course you won't, now that you know what I really am."

He sighed wearily. "It's strange. It hurts more now than if I'd just stayed. I ran to escape the pain, but now it's worse! Now there's nothing I can do about it. She's dead; they're all dead, aren't they? But I can't mourn them. I don't deserve that because I ran away. I've never been able to cry for Sarah, and I think that hurts the most. It's a pain right in here that no surgeon could ever remove." He gestured to his chest before letting his hands fall limply to his side.

Karla was silent. The hail had turned to a rain that was drenching them both, but neither of them moved. Raindrops streamed down their damp faces, but still they didn't move. Finally Karla raised a hand and wiped the water away from Birch's eyes.

"We better get out of the wet," she whispered softly. Birch nodded.

# THIRTY-FIVE

They heard them coming before they saw them. The splashing clump of horse's hooves on the muddy ground sounded distantly. Karla and Birch turned suddenly and in the darkness of the night could just make out a large band of riders urging their horses on at great speed. Instinctively Birch knew that these were no friends.

"Get down," he hissed as he dropped to the ground. Karla did the same and they lay there, hoping they hadn't been seen. No other hope remained. They couldn't defend them-selves against such a great number. All they could do was rely on this single wish as they hid among the tall grass.

The ground was wet. A steady drizzle still fell from the sky and their already wet clothes seemed to soak up the moisture as they lay, clinging to the earth. They had given up on their blanket tent. It had deteriorated to a sodden lump, and they had started walking eastward again. They had wrung their coverings as best they could and slung them over the top of their backpacks. Their heavy weight and dripping dampness was no comfort now, but they would need them again later.

Fearfully they watched the riders, looking for any indication that they had been seen, any change of direction or sudden movement that would show that they were now their new target. Nothing happened. For now, at least, it seemed they had escaped detection.

Birch moved slowly through the long grass, trying to get a better look at the men as they passed. His gun was drawn, ready for conflict, but he went unnoticed as the horses whipped through the weeds and on toward the south. There was a long line of them, a huge column of wild eyed, wide nostrilled beasts, both man and animal. The Ares and their horses were like one wild entity, thrashing and flailing with all their might to reach their goal. The horses' mouths foamed and their skin was wet with perspiration. Their riders, grim faced and snarling, were whipping their mounts mercilessly. They thundered by at an incredible gallop, with hooves thudding hard against the soft mud and sending up little clumps of grass and dirt behind them as they scuffed through the countryside. The tall grass hid Birch and Karla well, but these riders seemed too preoccupied with their journey to have noticed much around them anyway.

"I'd hate to be where they're going," Birch muttered thoughtfully. "I wonder what they're after in such a hurry."

"Here come some more," Karla pointed to a second group riding up over the horizon. Their band seemed wilder and more furious than the last. Birch shook his head.

"Something big must be happening and it looks like it has to be close by or those horses will never make it at the pace they're running. Once they pass we better make a dash for the east and see if we can escape the net. I have a feeling it's going to get pretty hot around here very quickly."

***

The trucks started up again. They had spent some hours waiting, but now, finally, the weather had cleared enough for them to continue. As he looked out the window Edwards could see the rain falling still from the dark, leaden sky. It was dark, but they wouldn't be making camp tonight. Their orders were clear: run! Don't stop for anything, just run!

As Edwards watched the raindrops made little streams and chased each other down the window to the bottom. Identical droplets, all fighting, pushing, merging against the glass, until they had all rolled off and disappeared. They would all be gone until the next rain, and then they would do it all over again. Sometimes nature could amaze you.

From near to distant, Edwards' eyes changed focus as he tried to look into darkness. He saw something on the horizon that stopped the breath in his mouth. A movement! A great, dark mass rising and falling in the distance, like some mighty leviathan with thousands of writhing limbs. It was swarming toward them. Quickly he picked up his radio.

"Linkhorn," he shouted into the transmitter, "attack coming in from the north!"

***

Birch had been waiting for the steady stream of gray riders and horses to dry up. It almost seemed that they never would, for they continued by in hundreds, perhaps even thousands by the time the last stragglers had passed. It was going to be a mighty battle, wherever they were going. He hoped that whoever they were after would be able to defend themselves. He doubted it; he remembered what Edwards had said about them only taking on enemies they knew they could defeat.

Finally, after the last of them had disappeared to the south, they prepared to go. Both he and Karla were exhausted but neither trusted this gloomy landscape. They wanted to move on.

It was as they were starting to move away that Birch saw it, a single rider, a straggler no doubt trying to catch up with the others.

"Look," Birch whispered to Karla as he pointed to the horseman approaching in the distance. "We'd get back east a lot quicker if we had a horse. It would sure beat walking."

"Great idea," Karla answered, "how are you going to get it though."

"Watch," he pulled his rifle from the side of his backpack.

"No," Karla held his arm, "you can't do that. You can't shoot a man as he rides by. Defending yourself is one thing, but that's cold blood."

"Cold blood?" Birch pulled his arm from Karla and clicked the safety off the rifle.

"What do you think they're all riding over there for, a church picnic perhaps? No, they're sending out a huge force to swamp and destroy some poor outnumber souls, you can be sure of that. Well I'm about to even the odds, at least by one. It's just the same as they'd do for me."

"No," Karla persisted, "don't sell your standards for theirs. It's always a bad trade. Keep your own or you've kept nothing at all. Haven't you already got enough blood on your conscience?"

Birch spun violently around and shoved Karla down to the ground, leveling the gun at her for a moment before his flaming eyes cooled and he turned to look again at the approaching rider.

"Don't ever use what I said against me," he spat. "You should know how cold I can be. I'm lost. Didn't I tell you I couldn't even cry for those I loved, I'm not going to cry for this guy who I don't even know. He is my enemy and I will do what I need to win here."

"I doubt you'll ever win," Karla's voice was faint and Birch's attention was focused on the approaching rider, "because I don't think you know who your enemy really is."

'Crack, crack', the rifle shot twice in quick succession. The rider fell to the ground, but the horse was spooked by the sound and reared up before galloping on toward the south. Birch threw down the rifle and chased after the animal. It stopped a few hundred yards away and lay down, but when he approached it his heart sank. Blood. Somehow he must have hit the dumb beast at the same time as its Ares rider.

Now it was useless, dead. He started back toward Karla. She was bending over the fallen Ares.

"Good shot," she commented dryly, "you got them both."

Birch shrugged. "Just lucky I guess. Let's move on."

# THIRTY-SIX

When the order came through it astonished Edwards. He asked for confirmation, and as Linkhorn's voice crackled again over the speaker it was clear that things were going to be very different from his expectations. They were going to break rank. Usual practice was to stick together and form whatever barricade they could against the Ares, pioneer fashion. Sometimes it worked. It was usually most effective in the small scale attacks of the past. Even with larger offensives, it seemed to Edwards to be the best option. It had helped to save them in the mountains. Not this time though. They had been told to flee, scatter as quickly as they could in all directions.

Perhaps it was the scale of the attack that had inspired this decision, the fear that they were dead either way, and that at least running would make them a moving target. Whatever the reason, the convoy split apart as a great, dark mass of horses and riders hurtled toward them, swarming over the land in full battle array like black beetles. No barricade could have stopped them. These were not the groundlings of the mountain battle. These were the Death Riders, the scourge of the plains and as fearless as they were frenzied. They would not scare so easily. Perhaps running was their only option.

What was incredible, again, was their numbers. Like all Ares groups they had always fought on the small scale, little bands of riders picking off small convoys and using their speed to escape across the plains. Now, like the rest of the world, they had gone mad. Their numbers were incredible, Edwards had never even suspected that this many could exist, but here they were, and all ranged against them. Indeed, they must run, run fast.

Still they came. They seemed to fill the horizon like a dark cloud that swiftly covered the earth around them. Edwards swerved his truck toward the east and accelerated as quickly as he could. Behind them red lights flashed and boomed as the missile launcher shot a barrage into the advancing throng. Fierce explosions blistered up sending clumps of Ares and their horses into the air in a shower of dirt and debris. It didn't make any difference. The hole that they left was quickly filled with more riders chasing after them. The missiles shot again and again, but with the same result. Whatever breaches they made quickly disappeared as more and more attackers poured through.

The missile launcher moved slowly away. The other trucks scattered more quickly in as many directions as they could. There were two choices, use the truck's weaponry to attack the advancing enemy, or run and hide in the darkness. Then, perhaps, in the gloom of night they might yet escape, if only they ran quickly enough. He knew it was hopeless; the Ares lived in the dark, but it seemed a better chance than standing up to fight against such numbers. They would run silently with their tail between their legs, giving themselves the faint hope of fighting another day.

He wasn't certain they would make it, but it was the only chance he could imagine, and in those last moments he would grab at anything. He barked the order to hold fire and gunned the engine, their wheels spun on the muddy ground for an instant, but quickly they bit against the soft turf and the truck lurched away toward safety.

The attackers pursued. Lauren, who was looking through the back window, shouted that the missile battery had been overrun. A moment later a loud explosion and orange glow across the inky sky confirmed it. Edwards gripped the wheel and pressed hard at the accelerator. The light from the explosion had lit up the plains and left them exposed again to their pursuers. The sooner that truck burned itself up the better, he thought callously to himself. They needed the darkness to cover their escape.

As if to mock his hopes another explosion went up from the launcher's fuel tank and sent a great pillar of crimson flame up into the sky. Like a beacon it guided the Ares to them as they fled further to the east. The predators harried their prey. Edwards kept the best speed he could, if he could only get far enough away they might still be lost in the dark, but the terrain was tough and ruts and bumps made swift progress difficult.

Incredibly, the horsemen were catching them. They seemed to glide over the difficulties that had slowed the truck, and Lauren saw through the rear window that they would soon be overtaken. The glow from the missile carrier's fire had dimmed, but the riders hardly seemed to need it as they chased after them. Under the cloudy night sky Lauren could see very little of their approaching enemies except their dark forms. It seemed to her that there was something else, a certain phosphorescence about them in the dim light. There were little specks of light shining, like a thousand glowing eyes. It only served to increase Lauren's impression that they were hunted and that these were wild animals that chased them now.

The truck fled on into the darkness. Edwards was driving using night-vision and the sickly green glow from the screen threw ghostly shadows on his face, strangely mirroring the effect of the lights Lauren saw on their pursuers.

They would be overcome at any moment. The soldiers manning the weapons stations waited for the order to fire. They knew it would be their last order.

Still Edwards clung to the hope of escape, and they sped on with all their might, fleeing mindlessly for even a second more of life before the end.

Suddenly from ahead an advancing column came into view. Edwards shouted his rage to the air, somehow they had been surrounded and the net was closing around them. He screamed the order to fire, fire weapons and take as many of them out as they could before they went down too.

A pulse of red fire leapt from the truck's cannon and lit a beautiful explosion into the throng behind them. Again they fired with small arms and cannon into the crowded prairie, but it seemed to make no noticeable difference, still they came and soon it would be over.

Edwards knew they were dead, but obstinately he pushed on, ready to smash into the enemy before him, but something about this advancing group seemed odd. It was their equipment and trucks. Suddenly he knew, these weren't the Ares, this was the promised reinforcements from the east. They had arrived in time. The explosions must have alerted them to their location and they were here to save them.

Instantly Edwards pushed hard on the brakes, bringing the truck to a sliding halt on the muddy ground. They spun sideways as he pulled at the wheel, but he managed to stop before they plowed into their rescuers. The riders pursuing them were not so fortunate. They had whipped their horses into such a frenzy that they had almost caught them, but now they were so close that they had no time to react, and they slammed into the side of the truck at full force. With a sickening thud one horse smashed into the vehicle, sending its rider flying over the roof and rocking their transport back on its wheels. An instant later another five had crashed into them and sent the truck tottering over onto its side.

From inside the truck all of this had come as a quick succession of confusing events that seemed to hit in a single moment. Before they could do much they had found themselves upside-down and swamped by the Ares horsemen that had been pursuing them. Some managed to jump over the downed vehicle. Others clambered over it with the heavy thud of horse's hooves on the armor plating. Most were too stunned to do much, but as one of the soldiers groggily opened a door to escape he was shot by a waiting Ares and slumped back down and on top of Lauren. She screamed and Edwards and a soldier pulled her out.

Through a broken window Edwards returned fire into the night. Another soldier poked his weapon cautiously around the opened door, sending a volley of fire in the direction of the attack. The drizzling rain splashed through the cracked glass and into Edwards face as he shot repeatedly at an enemy he couldn't see. After a time no return fire came and the sound of horses grunting and clumping through the muddy soil was replaced by the thunder of heavy engines and heavy fire being turned against the fleeing Ares. Edwards gingerly crept toward the door and looked out.

The advancing trucks had their searchlights on and were sweeping the countryside for any sign of movement. This time it was the Ares who sought the cover of darkness to save themselves from the dreadful onslaught. Great masses of horses and riders could still be seen scurrying across the landscape, but when a beam of light found them a multitude of missiles shot colorfully from the launchers and bathed them all in the brilliant glow of their explosive power.

The battle had moved on and they were left alone among the wreckage. To the north they could see the brilliant flashes of explosions as the Ares were pushed fearfully back. They were in full flight now as they slunk into the night. Their overwhelming force had been overwhelmed, and now they ran for their lives. He hoped Jane had escaped too. If things kept up like this there wouldn't be anybody to take back east and, explanations or not, Edwards knew things would be very bad for him then. He had to hope that Jane was okay.

As he watched the last cleanup operations of the battle

Edwards sighed. They were safe, at least for now. A large number of the Ares had escaped. They could evaporate like a mist in the night. At least their convoy was going to be that much larger now, and with this military escort it seemed unlikely that anything would try to stop them from here on. Still, he wasn't ready to celebrate yet. He didn't feel he could be sure of anything right now. Their enemy was just too unpredictable for that. That was the horror of all of this- the Ares, who he thought he knew so well, were not behaving in any way he could understand. It made the world an alarming place. What would they do next?

# THIRTY-SEVEN

The flash to the south, like an explosive dawn in the dark sky, had been enough to tell them that the battle had been joined. Birch wondered who those horsemen were fighting and, more importantly who was winning. The explosion looked distant, but powerful. The red glow lingered on the horizon. Someone had taken a big hit. He was almost tempted to go to the south and see for himself, but he knew that would be a foolish risk to take. He might find the others down there, but if they were defeated he would be caught in the middle of their problems. It was wiser to keep going east and see if they could make it on their own.

They continued to the east. Karla had been quiet since the shooting incident and he was glad at least that it was dark so he couldn't see her face. If she had only been angry then that would have been tolerable, he had expected that, but instead she had been disappointed in him. That was much worse. Even after all he had told her she still had the capacity for belief in him, and he hated it. Her face had taken on that hurt look that seemed to say that she was expecting something else, that she had believed something better of him. That was the worst feeling of all, the way some people could look at you with new eyes when they disagreed with something you did.

Approval was something he hadn't sought for years. He was good at what he did, and that was enough. People tried to tie you up in their strings of approval and respect. They held them out as a prize, something to be earned, and once you fell short it would be snatched away.

He didn't care. That was what it had felt like before he had gone on the mission. His family and friends had taken Sarah's side, why wouldn't they, she was in the right. They had all with-drawn. They would still talk to him and smile if they saw him, but he knew it was false. They would talk to him while he was there, and talk about him when he was gone.

He thought there was nothing left to miss on earth, so the Hypnos missions had seemed the perfect escape. But here he was now facing the same thing. You couldn't escape it unless you escaped from people. He had faced the very same thing since his tough decision to bring them all back to earth and to abandon their settlement. They had hated him for it. They had all withdrawn their approval and friendship, but he did what needed to be done. Now Karla was withholding her approval, like it was supposed to hurt him or something. She obviously didn't know the kind of callus that had formed over his soul. Nothing she could do could touch him. Nothing anyone could do would ever touch him again.

They walked silently for a time, neither was willing to speak first, and so nothing was said. Birch could see her form in the moonlight and hear the swishing of the grass as she passed through it. He wanted to speak to her but he couldn't. They would remain silent.

Finally Birch halted. They needed to rest. The glow to the south had died away and there were no further signs of the battle, so perhaps they were safe. They would rest and start again in the morning. Without a word he removed his pack and began taking things out he would need for the night. His blanket was a soggy mess, and there wasn't much else he could use to sleep in except the jacket Karla had picked out for him in Denver. That at least would keep him warm as the night air turned to chill and made him shiver.

At first he thought that Karla was going to keep going. She took a number of steps beyond him and then lay down on the ground. Her backpack served as a pillow and she curled up for warmth beneath her own coat. Neither of them said anything. She was going to hold it against him and they weren't going to be friends for a while. Fine. He deliberately turned to face the other way.

The night was unremarkable and still. It was strange, too, that only a few miles away some great battle had taken place while here everything seemed at peace. He dozed quietly beneath the stars, but he looked to the ground. It was there that he caught the first impression of something- something out of place that might have alarmed him, if he had only been more awake. As it was he distantly felt that there was more to this dark shape than his drowsy brain could comprehend and he thought in a distracted way that he should do something about it, but it wasn't until the crack of gunfire and the orange glow of discharged powder that he really understood and reacted.

Instantly Birch was on his feet, grabbing for his rifle he ran into the tall grass. He quickly fired at the place the shot had come from, before stopping to reload again. In that moment he heard a sound that stopped him cold, a whimpering sob from where Karla was lying. He turned to look back, but was quickly aware of another movement to his left. More distantly now he could see the fleeing figure of an Ares running in the moonlight. He took two shots that missed as the shadow ducked low to the earth. He was already fifty yards away and running at great speed. He would be gone soon. Birch took a few running steps in pursuit but was halted again by the cries coming from Karla's direction.

Birch trembled in the moonlight, took a last futile shot at the now distant assailant, and turned to where Karla lay. She hadn't gotten up and Birch dreaded to see her, to learn what had happened to her. He still wanted to run, to chase the one who had done this and to wreak a bloody revenge, but his legs walked mechanically toward that small, wet patch of earth. Step by step he approached.

Karla was alive, but only just. Birch looked desperately for any sign of the wound as he neared. The shot had gone into her stomach and she lay there bleeding beneath her practical coat. She smiled inexplicably when he approached, a red, bloody smile that tore at Birch's hopes. She was in bad shape. She coughed weakly, bringing up more blood, but she weakly held a crimson hand out to Birch.

For a time he couldn't move. He watched the hand, like some ghostly apparition, the writing on the wall, but he couldn't translate. He didn't want to go, to find out what it all meant. Still he did, and as her hand clasped his it seemed to warm him after the cool night air.

"Thomas…" she began, but started coughing again with convulsions that wracked her small frame. She didn't speak again. Her breathing became erratic and she coughed so violently that Birch believed she might almost fall apart in his hands. He put her head on his lap and stroked soothingly at her hair. Her eyes closed. She was drifting away, and as Birch looked down at her face he saw how natural she looked. He wiped the blood from her mouth and she almost looked as she had every other day, every day he had known her. He hadn't noticed how many days it was, but suddenly it seemed like there must be so many ahead without her, stretching like a barren road toward eternity.

A single tear escaped before he could blink it away and rolled down his nose before dropping onto Karla's face. Her eyes opened. She hardly moved now, her breath was so faint he couldn't detect it, yet in those eyes there was life. She looked at him. Nothing moved, her mouth was still, her hands lay limply at her side, and the convulsing coughs had stopped. Only her eyes showed life and they showed it all. They spoke with a deeper meaning than any of the words they had spoken in any of the days, months, or years that he had known her and it felled Birch, as though her bullet had passed through him too.

In that moment he knew about her and he knew about himself. For once he understood. He knew what it all meant and he wanted it now. He wouldn't turn away if only she could hang on. He pulled Karla up into his arms and clung to her desperately. An age seemed to pass as he held her in his embrace. Finally as he drew back he could see her eyes staring vacantly into nothing. She was gone. He sobbed.

He stayed like that through the night, and as the light of dawn came across the prairie it seemed to make things more real. It was a long time before he could think clearly enough to decide to do anything but sit there with Karla's head resting against his shoulder. Finally his mind began to work and he decided to bury her. He wouldn't leave her out for the animals and the elements. She deserved better than that. She deserved better than anything she ever got. She deserved better than anything he could do, but he would do this for her.

With whatever tools he had he dug down until he could lay her into the earth and cover her lonely form with soil and rocks. There would be no marker, he felt as though he would be her living monument. Still he wanted to remember this place. He looked about him, as though to forever fix this scene into his memory. Finally he was ready to go and one single thought burned through his mind like a fever.

Someone was going to die for this.

# THIRTY-EIGHT

The battle had ended well. Edwards was jubilant and buoyed by what he had seen. It seemed to confirm the impossible, that they could win this war and change the world. The night had proven that the Ares were a dangerous enemy, but for the second time it had also demonstrated that they could be beaten in battle. It was impossible to tell exactly how many of them had fallen, but it was a great number and that seemed, again, to prove their vulnerability.

These massive attacks had worried him, but now they seemed their greatest chance for victory over them. Whatever had inspired them to open warfare was uncertain, but it was clear that it was exposing them to great danger, and eventually great loss. If the battles to the east had taken the same course as those he had witnessed then this war might finally end in victory. The rebuilding could begin.

Jane and Lauren were both safe, that was important, and for the first time since they had reached the Rockies it looked as though things were finally under control again. With a large military escort to guide them and a defeated Ares force in full retreat it seemed as though the path to the east was opening up before them.

To ensure their safety the military had set up camp here

and had sent search and destroy missions out in all directions to mop up any remaining Ares resistance. When they were done with them it would be a long time before the Ares would be a problem around here again. That would certainly buy them a little time and a few miles free from attack. They just had to wait to find out if the Ares had anything more to throw against them before they could make it to the relative safety of the Mississippi.

It was strange, this feeling of security. He had spent so long running and hiding, dodging and escaping, that he hardly knew how to comprehend safety. But here he was, in a convoy of nearly a hundred vehicles, with six hundred well-armed, well-trained troops, mopping up the remainder of the Ares. As he looked out onto the plains they seemed a very different place.

***

As Birch looked out onto the dreary landscape he sought for any sign of the killer. He didn't expect to find anything, and he didn't. The figure had run to the south, but that had been hours ago. All he could do now was go after him and hope for some luck. If it was a matter of determination or persistence then he would get him. But he knew his chances were slim. If only there was something more.

His distracted mind tried to think of a way he could get any advantage in these circumstances, but none came. His only asset was his resolve, the promise that everything he ate and drank would be fuel for this single purpose, that every thought and action would be put to this end, to repay in kind for what was done to him.

He would get him.

Birch clenched his teeth angrily, shouldered his backpack and rifle, and started running hard to the south. His progress was swift, but his eyes were watching, hawk-like, for any sign of his prey as he ran. He missed nothing. He was hungry with such a desire for revenge that all that he saw seemed to be bathed in a red hue that stung his watery eyes.

Not once did he look back. He would remember that place well enough for the rest of his life. It was forever fixed in his memory. It was a part of him now and it seemed that the only way to make the pain go away was to make a good end to this, to give a sense of justice, and to wash the page clean with this man's blood. Then at least he would look back and know that something had been done. He wanted Karla, but if he couldn't have her then her killer wouldn't have life. This was the essence of revenge, and if there was any flaw in his logic his mind was too clouded with it to see anything else. He would get this man in the name of true justice and make him pay for what had done, then Karla would be at rest, and so would he.

He knew all the time that his chances were slim, but somehow luck did seem to be with him, for as he ran he caught sight of a trail of trampled grass. It was the path the horsemen had beaten down the previous day in their rush to the battle. It was left now as a muddy highway that Birch could easily follow. In his mind it seemed right that whoever had attacked him would be seeking to join again with their colleagues, and for this reason it appeared to be his best chance of catching him. He would follow the trail.

This was the only chance he needed. He would pursue this killer until he was in his hand, and then he would make him feel some of what he was feeling right now. Birch was aware of the danger, that he might meet up with the riders he had avoided yesterday, but he didn't care. His mind was filled with passionate rage, and he would die if that was what was required to set this record straight.

He ran along the muddy track, but as he ran he watched for his quarry or any sign that would lead to him. He had expected a long chase. His hours with Karla had cost him time and surely given his enemy ample chance for escape. Therefore it was a surprise moments later when Birch saw a body lying beside the track, not dead, but shivering in the cool morning sun. His back was to him and he seemed oblivious to his presence, or to anything else around. He just lay there and shivered in the mud with no precaution for concealment or thought for safety. This was going to be easy.

Birch strode furiously toward the prostrate form, curled as it was into a fetal ball, so sad and alone. It was only a matter of a few steps before he had reached the figure, and with one swift kick of his foot he had lifted him over to see him. The face he saw surprised him. It was the boy from the mountains, the one who he had fought in the tree and who had led them into the trap. It was a sad, bitter, mud-streaked face. Those piercing eyes bore into Birch's flesh. There was something in that look that seemed to warrant pity, though they certainly did not ask for it, for though the face was pitiful, it was also proud.

As he looked into the eyes Birch's heart almost changed. They looked nothing like Karla's, hers were blue and his were brown, but something was the same. Perhaps it was just because her memory was so fresh, he could see her in everything, but still it struck him that these hurt, angry eyes had a look he'd seen in Karla before she died, but then he saw the gun. The rifle had been lying next to the boy all the time, but it had only just caught Birch's attention now. The boy followed his gaze and instinctively reached for it. In that moment all thought was gone.

Birch snatched at the gun and quickly leveled it at the Ares youth. The boy's face blanched but he remained uncowed. His bravery only served to fuel Birch's rage. He looked down at the gun. It was *the* gun; he knew it by the feel of it. He knew it by the sullen, guilty look on the boy's face, and it was all he could do to resist pulling the trigger there and make the circle of death complete. Instead he brought the heavy butt of the rifle down in the youth's stomach. The boy writhed but Birch was merciless. Again he did it. Again and again, he brought the wooden end of the rifle down until it was stained red and the Ares boy had stopped moving, but Birch couldn't stop.

This wasn't a boy any more. He wasn't a man anymore.

This was something primitive, something within himself that, once he had let it out, all the will in the world couldn't put it back in. But then, he didn't want to put it back. He had every right to this rage and so he pummeled the limp figure until he too collapsed in exhausted rage.

When he finally stopped he fell to the ground beside his bloody victim. He looked down at his own hands and the scarlet butt of the rifle and shuddered. It seemed that the weapon had grown hot in his hands, it almost scalded them now with its power, and as he lay there he felt its weight pushing against his chest, burning into him. With great effort he stood and hurled it beyond him, out into the open fields where it could harm no other soul again.

The boy next to him moved weakly and with the fire of his rage extinguished he looked down at what he had done. Like a blast of rancid air his face was met with what he had truly done, and with a sudden impulse towards mercy he stooped to cradle the young man. His blood mingled with the stains already present as a part of Birch's garment. He tried to bandage him as best he could, but the blood continued to seep through, whatever he placed over it. All he could do was sit with him, and that is what he did. Perhaps it was for an hour. Perhaps it was longer, but he sat with him as a second life now slipped from him.

Birch had no thought of the future now. It had all been destroyed in a matter of a day, and now all he did was sit with this boy and live in this moment. He was watching him die and he knew that he had killed him. His hands were red. He couldn't think of anything but that, and as a line of four vehicles approached him he didn't notice. They existed in another world, a world with a future, he existed only in this point in time, and so even the bang of doors, the shout of voices, and the stamp of heavy feet registered as nothing to him as he gazed down at what he had done.

"Get him up," a voice was saying as rough hands grabbed at Birch. He didn't resist, he had nothing left to resist with. He didn't deserve to resist.

"This one's wounded," another voice was saying, "pretty bad. Get medical quick." Birch and the boy were separated and for the first time he resisted, but he was weak and was swiftly pulled into a separate vehicle.

The line of trucks quickly started off again toward the south. As they rode on Birch's mind began to clear. This was a military car, like the ones they had ridden in at the beginning of their journey. He had been rescued. One day too late they had been rescued. Wearily he slumped against the window and watched the distance speeding by.

It seemed very little time before they were stopping again among a larger group of vehicles and equipment. Soon Birch was being pulled out. His tired eyes looked about him. He strained for any sight of the Ares youth, but he couldn't see him. All he could see were military personnel and trucks, and guns, lots of guns. Everywhere there were guns and cannons and missiles and their launchers. This was their version of security. If you had more firepower than anyone else then you were safe. Birch was pretty sure they were safe.

Birch trudged through the camp on the guiding arm of a medical orderly. As they passed one truck Jane and Lauren rushed to his side, but stopped short as they caught sight of his bloodstained face, uniform, and hands. His dirty disheveled form limped past them without acknowledgement.

"Major," Jane's voice called after him. He turned to face her. "Karla? Carlos?" Single word questions that carried such weight, such a heavy weight. Slowly he shook his head.

Jane blinked away her emotion and cast her eyes downwards. Birch thought she would cry, but when she looked up again he saw instead a fiery anger that had evaporated any tears she might have had for them. Instead she had anger, and all of it was directed at him.

"You've done it again," she spat furiously, "first the Colonel, now Karla and Carlos. You just seem to get better every time. How did you manage to lose them this time? You know, the amazing thing is, you always make it back safe-and-sound. How do you do that? How is it that you lose everyone who depends on you, but you always manage to make it back safe-and-sound?"

Birch took two limping steps toward Jane and looked into her face before punching her hard in the mouth. She rocked on her heels and fell backward, sitting on the dirt with a thump. Her mouth was bleeding and she snarled at Birch as she struggled to get up.

Birch shook his head. "Nobody made it back safely this time, Gray," he muttered and followed the orderly toward the medical tent.

# THIRTY-NINE

The next week seemed to prove Edwards' prediction that things would be easier now. The entire convoy, when the patrols had all returned, numbered over a hundred vehicles including troop carriers, missile launch systems, and other armored transports. It was an impressive display and would have inspired Birch with greater confidence if it hadn't made him wonder all the more about their mission and what it meant for them. Something important was happening here. He just wished he could figure out what it was..

Obviously recent events had caused their protectors to reevaluate their tactics. The former method of a lightly protected, but speedier convoy was gone. They had abandoned stealth in favor of overwhelming and obvious force to dissuade any further attacks. Indeed, it was assured that they would make it now. They were safe. The army had told them they would make it. He only hoped they were taking them somewhere they really wanted to go.

These had been lonely days for Birch. His thoughts were dark and narrow as memories played and replayed in his unwilling mind. Snippets of conversation or things they had done. Butterfly moments flitted through his mind. He would suppress them, bury them, but, light as air, Karla's spirit, her words, her face would rise again. The memories hurt. Like something dead, he wished he could bury them. He wanted to leave the pain out here, but at the same time he knew that he had finally been caught. He hadn't run fast enough, and they had become a part of him. He could never leave her behind.

In those few days Birch hadn't seen much of Jane or Lauren. Jane was probably off nursing her broken lip, and Lauren was just being Lauren. It wasn't much of a crew anymore. The thought of it filled him with a great emptiness. He had lost the best and now he was left with this. It was a thought that included himself. He knew enough to be honest in that. Karla had gone, DeSante had gone, even the loss of Ratliff seemed to take on a greater resonance in his mind as he looked back at all they had suffered. Now they three alone were all that was left and he couldn't have imagined a less united, less hopeful band than theirs. Whatever was ahead they weren't ready for it.

As the days passed Birch saw the countryside around them gradually changing from the barren prairie to the wooded hills and lush green of the eastern states. The Mississippi seemed to mark this change most notably. It was the mighty dividing line between a bitter past and the hopeful future. Its heavily fortified, imposing bridges were a gateway that returned them to the tranquility and safety of civilization.

The feeling washed over him even as they reached the eastern side of the river. It was the work of an instant and seemed to transform the world around them. It wasn't anything he could explain, but it was something like walking out of the cold air and into the balmy atmosphere of the greenhouse. Once again Birch was bathed in a feeling of order and peaceful beauty that he had tried to understand in his time in the west. Here, in the eastern half of the country it seemed even stronger, as though it had taken deeper root and had become more truly ingrained into the landscape. It reminded him again of what people like Edwards, and Konik, and Gibbs had talked about, this idea of changing the earth, and making it into a paradise. It almost felt real here.

The fortifications that met them as they traveled were similar to what they had seen in the west. The bases nearest to the river were formidable, but as they moved farther east, so their scale diminished. Yet, as with the western region, Birch noticed that the bases continued to exist deep into their own territory. Apparently they also had been unable to free themselves entirely of the Ares threat, even this close to their own capital. Despite this he noticed no visible sign of the battles that had raged across the country recently. If they had fought here then the Ares hadn't even made a dent in the defenses. Birch guessed that there could be more to it than this though. If there had been fighting on this side of the river, their convoy could simply be avoiding the sites of the devastation. Birch knew that he really had no way of knowing what truly happened here.

This was certainly the down side of being back under the protective power of the military. He felt helpless. He wasn't in control anymore and, as usual, he wasn't being told anything. Sometimes it was hard to imagine that they were supposed to be the center of this whole rescue operation, because they were ignored. He hadn't seen Edwards or Linkhorn, and his requests to see the Ares boy were flatly denied. The boy was alive, he was told that much, but they wouldn't let him near him. Perhaps that was wise.

The convoy hardly stopped in that week, except at night. Even then it was only for a scant six hours rest before they moved on. Unlike before there were no attempts at hiding or disguise as they camped. The reflective shield was not used. Instead the cordon of vehicles was encircled by stony faced guards and smaller search vehicles that zoomed about seeking for any sign of an enemy to destroy. The mood was much more aggressive and seemed to demonstrate the greater power and security of these forces in the east compared to those in the west. On this ground the Ares were the hunted again.

Finally his frustrating week came to an end. It was then

that Birch had seen it. The first sign had been the glimmering tower shining in the sun. It had seemed like a good sign, climbing loftily over the landscape. These were not the dwarfed structures of Denver, the maimed remains of a proud past. This was a vibrant present and a hopeful future. Whatever had the power to destroy the cities of the plains had not been able to achieve the same result here. Perhaps here, he hoped, the nobler aspirations of humanity had stood proudly and had not been bowed or destroyed.

Finally they arrived. This was Washington, and as he looked on its beautiful form he was taken by its appearance. It was not like the cities he had known, the dirty places where the jumble of life had thrown the pieces together in a confusion of rich and poor, stylish and ugly, happy and sad, good and bad. The place seemed like a single unit, like one voice calling out in harmonious melody to the surrounding land to say that all was well. It was mesmerizing.

Birch still had his doubts. He knew they were still in there somewhere, in his mind, but they were strangely distant to him now as they drew closer to the city. All he could see was the great contrast between the empty plains they had left far behind and the fullness of the land about him now. This was a place to live.

"I guess we're not in Kansas anymore," Birch muttered ironically as they approached the city gate.

# FORTY

Little evidence remained of the Washington Birch had once known. It was as though some great galactic eraser had swept over the land and obliterated even the memory of what had once been there. Things that had seemed so permanent, like a tribute to the good things in humanity, were gone. The natural features were still there, the Potomac still glugged wearily through the city, but this single thread of continuity was hard to grasp and gave him little comfort. He felt much as an ancient Greek, Roman, or Babylonian might have if they could have seen the modern outcome of their great cultures. Everything he had believed was gone, washed away by time and the natural course of human events. Nothing lasted forever, however well you tried to build it. Every eternal flame must eventually be snuffed out. Most, however, were fortunate enough never to see that truth laid out on this scale. Their tired little lives, their four-score-years-and-ten, were never forced to see beyond that pitiful little range, and so their reality was only the comfortable normalities that had built up around them. They never had to see below that thin veneer. Birch envied them.

It was beautiful, Birch had to admit that. Before they had entered the city he had been struck by the way everything just seemed 'right'. Now, though, he mourned for the loss of those great stone monuments and the history they represented.

They had been replaced by an almost Eden-like natural grandeur that was both alluring and alarming. So beautiful it stung your eyes. This was like the center of goodness that radiated out into the surrounding country. It was an epicenter of the order and peace that seemed to fill the eastern half of the nation. He had felt it gradually increasing as they had crossed the Mississippi, like ripples that became more pronounced the closer you got to the disturbance. The western outposts were a pale reflection of what had happened here and the rugged prairies had somehow escaped the effect altogether, but here it was clear to see what their final goal for the world was. It was hard to escape the desire to see this fulfilled every-where. Now he knew what they fought for.

The city was gardenlike. Where dead stone had once existed life had replaced it with greenery of amazing variety. The buildings were no longer imposing masters of the landscape, but blended features, living as a part of the place. The single tower in center of city was its only structure above the level of the nature that surrounded it. Concrete and asphalt no longer smothered the earth, as the usual infrastructure of the city seemed to have melted away into something more natural. It all made Birch wonder. How could a metropolis like this exist without the roads and buildings that had once been such an integral part of it?

It seemed likely that population levels must have decreased significantly for this to work at all, but that left him with more questions about what happened to everyone else. As he looked now he could see very few people. The city was incredible, but almost empty, like a beautiful ghost town for their own personal enjoyment.

It wasn't just the buildings that were different, but the whole way of life. People walked, people smiled, people lived. He wondered how it had happened and what had made this change. Was it the war? Was it just in this place? He knew enough not to expect any answers from those that guarded him. If he could get to Edwards he might find out more, but even he had seemed unwilling to say much to him about their mission since he had returned. A new wall of secrecy had developed between them as they had drawn closer to Washington. No, Edwards had withdrawn into himself again and Birch knew he would find no answers there.

Finally the convoy stopped, not at another military compound as Birch had expected, but at a small cottage nestled among the greenery. Four of the vehicles broke off from the long line and pulled up to the quaint building. Birch's truck was one of them. The rest of the line started up again and veered away from the city center toward the west, driving off in a cloud of dust.

Soon they were alone with only their few soldiers left to guard them. Edwards had gotten out of the lead truck and was walking toward the cottage. Wearily Birch watched him through the dirt smeared window before he opened the truck door and stepped out into the sunshine. He winced in the light as he looked around him. It was good, the land and the buildings all were good. Through the tinted windows of the truck he had seen darkly, now in its true aspect he was able to believe what he could only imagine that he had understood before. Something marvelous had happened here. The colors, and the taste, and the smell of it all engulfed his mind, but it was almost too much.

His thoughts strayed back to that muddy prairie and how such a small, meaningless patch of rock and earth could come to mean so much, while all the beauty around him could mean so little. Kansas was home. He wished himself back there now.

"Come on," Edwards was calling to him. Jane and Lauren were already at his side and he was opening the door to the little home. Birch moved slowly toward them.

"We've got the best place for you here," Edwards continued cheerily. "You'll find all the comforts of home and the freedom to come and go as you like while you wait for your audience with the president."

"Sounds great after that long journey," Jane enthused.

"Hmm," Birch grunted. "Kind of a change for you guys isn't it? Where's all the guards, and the fences, and the off limit zones? Where are we supposed to stay away from in order to make you happy? How are you going to protect us from ourselves here if we can do whatever we want? Why do you trust us now?"

"So many questions," Edwards smiled thinly at Birch, "but just one answer. You were in danger before, but here you will be safe. Nothing can touch you here, so you are free to see whatever you want. We have nothing to hide here, so go ahead, look anywhere you want. You'll see what we are really working for in this place." Birch nodded doubtfully but followed the others in without further comment.

"These places really are wonderfully designed," Edwards was sounding more like an anxious realtor trying to close the deal with every moment. "It should be a few days before the president can see you, so enjoy it. This is your home while you're here."

"What about you," Birch questioned, "where will you be?"

"I've got reports to fill out and debriefing to go through. You'll see me soon enough. I'll be back in time for your meeting in a few days time." Edwards turned to the door. "Just relax and take time for yourselves, you don't have anything else to worry about now that you're here. You're safe. I'll see you in a few days." With that he turned and left the three standing uncomfortably in their small lounge.

"I guess we should get settled in," Jane picked her gear up from the floor where one of the men had left it. "I just wish they could have found a bigger place for us," she added looking pointedly at Birch. "I think it could get quite crowded here."

"I'm sure it will," Birch muttered sullenly as he picked up his own things and headed to the door of one of the bedrooms. "Just stay out of my way." He flung the door open and hurled his things onto the bed. "It would be a lot better for you if you just left me alone."

"Yeah, that's the way you work best, isn't it?" Jane snapped back. "After all, we know you're *so* anxious to be alone that you'll lose everyone you ever team up with."

Birch's eyes narrowed and his teeth clenched. He was moving menacingly toward her now, but Lauren had nimbly stepped between them.

"You know," she began vacantly, "Karla used to joke about what a cute couple you two would make if you could ever stop yelling at each other long enough. I never thought she was serious, but I don't know. You two certainly have something."

Birch stopped and looked down at Lauren. She had probably said the only thing that could have stopped him. "What did Karla say?" He asked. His hands were numb and fell limply at his side. "Tell me what she said."

"She said a lot," she answered evenly.

"Like what?" Birch's voice was probing.

Lauren looked thoughtful. "She admired you," her eyes met Birch's. She was surprised to see how quickly the fire within them had cooled, dissolving into a liquid mistiness.

"I think she thought more than you could ever know," Lauren continued quickly, seeing that her intervention was working. "We all felt bad about what happened on the mission, but she seemed to see your side more than any of us could. She was sad for Ratliffe, of course, but more for you. She hated the way you and Major Gray fought after that, and she used to joke that you'd make a fine married couple. I don't think she ever meant anything by it, though. It always seemed like she'd have done anything for you if you'd have just asked."

A distant smile played across Birch's face before he turned to look at Lauren. His expression changed, but deeper than that, his features changed, and perhaps a few of the lines on his brow were smoothed away.

"Thanks," he muttered thoughtfully before turning again to Jane, "I think she did, even without my asking"

"I'm sorry," Birch's soft voice spoke to Jane more from memory than anything else. "We've both lost a lot. Maybe you blame me, maybe I blame myself. I can't change it. If I could do anything I would change it all, but that can't be, so we just have to live with it. Let's just deal with today and be a team again. Can we be a crew, a family one last time?"

Jane nodded dumbly but couldn't respond. The 'family' crew: that had all been Karla's idea. She'd always gushed about them being a new family, all they had for each other now. Birch had never bought into that before. She couldn't comprehend why he had now, at the very end of their mission.

"Okay," she responded cautiously, "at least until we see what this president has in store for us."

Birch smiled silently to himself. He had heard many words in his lifetime, but now he had finally begun to listen.

# FORTY-ONE

This was a nice place. They had taken Edwards' advice and explored the city. All that they had found, and all that they had seen was as remarkable as had been claimed. The beauty of nature seemed to have been blended with human composition, until it had become an almost symbiotic relationship. Buildings were interwoven with breathtaking flowering plants, all bearing blazes of color that could only have been contrived with human assistance. Everywhere the assembling of natural beauty could be seen in the presence of perfectly placed foliage and glassy-still lakes and ponds. It was almost too good to imagine.

The thing that was missing was people. Birch had been the first notice it. It had struck him even as they had arrived, but it had grown into an obsession for him. Where was everyone? This was a city, the capital city, but it seemed to have the population of a village. It was ideal, but it didn't seem right. Those few people he had seen had been friendly, but unhelpful. They were happy and vacuous. Birch had been unable to get anything more from them than felicitous smiles and cheerful nods of acknowledgment. He couldn't seem to break through the pretty surface of either the people or the place.

The preservation of this environment within a city was an incredible thing. The smaller population no doubt helped, but even then it would still have been impossible without the innovations in transportation. This was all built on the back of the old subway system. The Metro system wasn't anything new, but it had been so greatly extended that eventually all above ground transportation had been phased out. The impact on the city had been incredible as many roads had been replaced by greenery. Only military vehicles now traveled above ground, and even these were rarely permitted.

It was all very impressive, like a step back into the deepest desires at the heart of humanity, but still Birch wasn't happy. He had dreams. He might have enjoyed this place except for those dreams and the vivid impression they left in his wakeful mind. They were perhaps the most real thing to him now as the phantoms from his past haunted him. Karla was there now, and for the first time he realized that the past was the one place he really wanted to be. But you can never go back.

As each day passed the dreams grew more real and reality became more dreamlike. Something wasn't right here. It had started with the dreams, but it seeped into the world about him. His mind was cluttered and he couldn't clear it. He was plagued by a dizziness, like vertigo, that always kept him on the edge of falling. He was weak. Doubts came buzzing in his ears. Yes, something wasn't right, and if his muddy mind wasn't so clogged right now he was sure that it all would have meant something to him.

The mental dam finally broke as he sat silently reflecting on the idyllic scene on the banks of the Potomac. He had been sitting watching the perfect sunshine, the perfect sky, the perfect people, the perfect everything, when he finally saw what he had been looking for. Imperfection.

In the rippling flow of the river he saw what he should have seen all along, what he should have known all along. His reflection- it didn't fit. His face was right, his body was right, and at first glance everything was right, but a closer observation showed that everything was wrong. It wasn't in sync. It was better than he had seen before, less obvious, but he'd been looking for it this time and there it was. It was very subtle. You had to almost look out of the corner of your eye to see it, sneak up on it as it were, to catch it, but it was there.

He sat for a moment, drinking this all in. He knew what it meant. They were in trouble. They were in the envirodome. This had all happened before, when they had first landed, and everything had seemed so real, and yet it wasn't. Nothing had been real and he had been nowhere. And that's exactly where they were now. How long had they been here? That was the troubling question. Had they ever really left?

Was anything real? Was this all a game, one big rat's maze that he was running? He almost hoped it was. Then maybe he could reset the game and try again. There was a lot he would change if he had a second chance. Life wasn't like that though. You got one chance, and somehow things seemed too permanent for anything else but that. He doubted there would ever be a second chance.

The others seemed to notice nothing. He had tried to subtly raise the issue, but it was clear from his gentle probing that neither of them had been aware of anything unusual. He found himself considering the possibility that they also might be a part of the illusion. He wasn't sure he could trust them, and so he kept his fears to himself. Even so his concerns grew, even as his awareness of the unreality around him increased.

He noticed other things. He had become aware of a slight, almost imperceptible electrical hum and buzz that followed everywhere he went. It masked itself behind everyday sounds. He could hear it in the murmur of friendly voices, in the ripples across a still pond. He could hear it in the tinkle of the bell on a child's bicycle, even in the splash of the water as he shaved in the morning. It seemed to mock him, to seek to provoke a response, yet he continued to ignore it. If anyone was watching he wasn't going to let them know that he was aware of it, at least not yet. He wanted to see what would happen first, and then react to any opportunity that came along. He had gotten out before, he could do it again.

The opportunity seemed to come on the third day, when Edwards returned. Birch knew better than to say anything of his suspicions to him. He trusted him less than Lauren or Jane. Birch knew that if he really was trapped inside an illusion, then Edwards, if he really existed, was more likely to be one of the keepers than one of the good guys. He would just have to watch for now and see what developed.

Edwards had brought news from the president; he was ready to see them and had granted an immediate audience. Edwards had been sent to collect them, and a military escort was provided to get them there. A line of ten vehicles now waited outside their idyllic cottage, ready to carry them into an uncertain future. The stark appearance of the military trucks and the men assigned to them seemed in striking contrast to the soft tones of everything around them. A touch of reality in this fake world, Birch imagined. He was happy for that. He felt he needed a dose of truth after the sugar-coated existence they had lived over the last few days, even if it did come in the form of guns and troop carriers

They were hurried into a truck. As they settled back in their seats Birch noticed that even the tinted windows couldn't completely filter out the bright joy of their temporary home. It was just too radiant. Birch nodded thoughtfully to himself.

The trucks pulled through empty streets toward the one building that towered above the landscape, the great stone tower. It reminded Birch more of Washington's past than of its future. It filled him with an odd sense of nostalgia as he saw it looming ever larger in the window. Alone, of all the things in this new city, this seemed almost to be a monument and a tribute to the history that had happened here. It was more than that though. It was a final surpassing of all those things, for it was larger and grander than any of the simple monuments it had been built to replace. It was a statement of power. This was a final statement that had eclipsed all previous statements and made a new reality for itself. Like all new innovations this structure had striven to better anything before it. The new dynasty had wanted to outdo the old one, and in stature and grandeur it had succeeded.

Soon they arrived. Birch and the others were quickly pulled from their truck as the line of vehicles came to a halt in front of the massive stone tower. A few minutes later Edwards was guiding them through a plush foyer and onto a shining, chrome elevator that sent them, bullet-like, up into the highest parts of the building. An instant later their dizzying assent had stopped with a hiss as the doors opened to place them on the topmost floor. They had arrived at the presidential suite.

# FORTY-TWO

The elevator doors hissed shut behind them. They were led into an expansive hall filled with light and wonder. Even Edwards seemed awed by what he saw. The floor shimmered, polished to a glossy sheen that reflected with a greater purity or clarity than any mere mirror could. The furniture and fittings were made of oak with a burnished gold trim that seemed to come alive as light streamed through the great glass windows high up on the four walls. These windows were arched and made from colorful, cut glass, like a cathedral's, and the light they permitted was awash with color and life.

This was opulence. The best that wealth could afford had been poured into this place, and nothing here was ordinary. Like the tower itself this room seemed to purposefully eclipse all previous human achievements in both scale and beauty.

It was like the great hall of a castle or an ancient place of worship with a gothic ceiling arching loftily above them. There was a golden sheen to everything that seemed to lend it a cold, hard quality. The place was beautiful, but not comfortable. Stiff furniture and hard, bare surroundings gave a crisp, angular feel to everything. This was a place to be impressed, or to impress others. It spoke of wealth and power, but it was impossible to tell anything else about the occupant here. Birch saw all of this as no more than an impersonal statement of authority, it didn't seem to go any deeper than that.

At the far end of this room stood a great golden portal with two guards positioned attentively at either side. This was the center of it all. Lauren shivered. The hall was cold and silent and as they walked toward the grand doorway the sound of their feet clacking against the glassy polished floor was the only thing to disturb the hushed atmosphere.

The two golden doors were incredible, huge, heavy things with intricately detailed carvings of symbols and writing that Birch felt he should recognize, but he couldn't. One in particular drew his attention. It depicted a battle; one side had the better of it and was inexorably pushing the enemy toward a cliff. Some had already fallen, others fought wildly to avoid it, but soon they all would be in the abyss. Above it all a bird flew. It should have been an eagle, or perhaps a hawk, or maybe even a vulture judging by the subject, but it was a dove. He wondered what the bird-of-peace had to do with a battle.

The doors slowly, noiselessly swung open to admit them. For a time the way stood empty and open, like a gaping black maw. No one came to greet them. Finally Birch impatiently strode toward the entrance, but was blocked by the rough hands of a burly soldier guarding it.

"Wait," the one grabbing him announced tersely as he pushed Birch away, "you are not permitted to go." As he spoke a smiling, oily young man appeared in the doorway; his expression changed as he caught sight of the scuffle.

"Be careful," he chastised the guard. "He's been through a lot to get here and he is our guest; we don't want to hurt him." The soldier nodded mutely and released Birch. "I'm sorry for that," the man's smile had returned, "but that's what they're trained to do so you can't really blame them." Birch frowned angrily.

"Please follow me," the young man intoned, "the president is waiting." He turned to speak to Birch. "You, on the other hand, must wait here. We will return shortly."

Birch was at him in a second. "What do you mean, 'wait here'? I'm the commander of this mission and if anybody gets to see the president today, it's me!"

"But you are not required," the oily assistant replied tonelessly. It was a simple matter of procedure to him; he was following orders. He merely responded to the authority of those above him. Birch was about to suggest some new orders based on the authority of his fists, but Edwards saw his intent and shook his head. He moved between Birch and the young man.

"Let me handle this my way. I'll get you in, Major, without resorting to punching anyone."

He smiled vaguely and pulled the man aside to speak with him. From where he stood Birch could see that they were engaged in an animated conversation, but he couldn't hear any of what was being said. Obviously Edwards wasn't getting the better of things; he was gesturing back to where they stood and a look of exasperation had taken hold of his face. He kept shaking his head, but after a while the man barely seemed to notice him. Like a stone he would not be moved for all the breath in the world. Finally Edwards gave up and came back.

"It's no good," he muttered as he reached them. "I can't figure out why they'll let everyone else in to see him, even me, but not you. Nothing I said could convince him otherwise. He has his orders"

Birch growled and took a step toward the young assistant. Edwards restrained him.

"I wouldn't bother. You'll just get a beating and still not make it in. They've made up their mind. It's no good. Just sit down and cool it. There's nothing else you can do."

Birch fumed.

Lauren shot a worried look at Birch. "You don't think there's some plot here to separate us or something?"

Birch shrugged.

"Don't worry," Edwards added hastily. "It's not surprising

that he wants it this way. Hardly anyone, apart from his immediate staff, ever get to see him. He's very busy, very private. I'm sure he has a good reason for wanting it like this.

"Hurry now," the young man was speaking again. "He is waiting for you. Don't make him wait."

Birch turned with deliberate pause and watched unblinkingly as Edwards and the others approached the portal. This was the moment he had wanted: to finally draw his wearisome journey to an end, but he was left here. Left alone.

They passed through the golden doors into the darkness and disappeared. The doors shut behind them and Birch was left alone, gazing again at the golden carving of the dove presiding over the battlefield.

For a time he stood there, perfectly still and stared at the doors, as if hoping they would open to admit him just on the basis of his will. His eyes bore into the door. He glared at the soldiers guarding it. He waited impatiently. None of this had any effect. His effort was wasted. The door and the soldiers guarding it remained unaltered, perfectly unaware of his insignificant presence.

Finally he gave up and sat uncomfortably on one of the angular chairs arranged tastefully along the edge of the room. Nothing happened. He sat and fidgeted morosely as time passed slowly, tick-by-imperceptible-tick.

He got up. He looked around the room, studied each feature, each item, anything to gain some knowledge of who he was dealing with, but it all told him nothing. Beautiful, sterile functionality was all he could make of this room and all of its contents.

He sat down again. He waited, and still nothing happened. But then he heard a click. Metallic. Not loud, but distinct and noticeable in the silence of the room. He looked at the guards. They seemed not to have noticed. They stared straight ahead, unaware of anything but their duty and their door.

He got up again. He searched the room again, looking for any perceptible change. At first he couldn't see anything, until he noticed the smallest of cracks in the icing-cake walls. That was new. It was right over a large air vent. The vent, like the rest of the walls, was perfectly white and, until this moment, had been almost undetectable because of its tasteful concealment. Birch pulled at it and, with some effort, it moved slightly.

He straightened up, pretending to look at a clear crystal vase sitting on a side table nearby. He picked it up, whistled in mock appreciation, and turned the item reverently over in his hands.

He had to find out how attentive these soldiers were. With no one else here they seemed as wooden as the rest of the furniture. They reminded him of those guards you used to see in London, the ones people would poke and prod and stick ice cream up their nose just to see if you could get them to move. They never would. Their duty was to that gate. Nothing must pass through their gate. The world could go up in flames, but as long as that gate was secure, they would not move. He wondered if these men were the same.

He dropped the vase. It smashed into hundreds of pieces, sending shards of glass skidding across the floor, but Birch wasn't watching it. He was watching the guards, and they didn't move. Not a bit. Even their eyes didn't move. Their attention was still focused straight ahead. They were guarding their door. That was their duty and that was all they were doing. It was almost as if they were turned off until you challenged them. He had other ideas now.

It was worth a try. The vent was in the same wall as the doors, but far enough down to be out of the line of vision of the guards, if they didn't turn their heads, which obviously was something they weren't going to do.

He waited for a while before starting. He wandered the room randomly, observing the guards as he went. Their eyes never followed him. Certain now he walked directly to the vent, pulled firmly and yanked it open. A narrow black passage opened up behind it. He had found his way in.

It was a tight fit, but without hesitation he swiftly pulled himself in. He couldn't close the covering behind him; he didn't have the space to turn and do it. It would just have to stay open. If anyone was looking for him they would know where he went, but he didn't care. He wasn't trying to hide. He wanted to get somewhere and get some answers. That was all.

He crawled along, worm-fashion, for a few minutes when, sooner than he expected, he came out into the open again. It was dark. Only the thinnest trickle of light showed through from the vent shaft, illuminating little more than a few feet of floor before him. He could see nothing else.

For a moment he stood, waiting for his eyes to adjust to the darkness. It made no difference. It was impenetrable. All was still and Birch looked impatiently about for any sign of anyone or anything he could identify. There was nothing and all he could do was grope in the dark for the way.

It was a world of ebony emptiness that greeted him. Like the cosmos that he had explored, it was a place of alien mystery, both lonely and bleak. It was a smaller space than the room he had just left. Something about the echo of his footsteps and the feel of the air told him that this place did not have the high ceilings or grandeur of the great hall. His senses could detect nothing more, and yet he imagined he could feel eyes watching him through the darkness, studying, scrutinizing, evaluating, making decisions about his life and his future while he was here, blind and helpless.

Something else was strange. On the surface this place gave the impression of stillness and peace, but Birch could feel energy, like the electric hum of a power station. You couldn't see it, but you could feel the energy coursing through the air. It crept on his skin and buzzed in his ears. It irritated him.

This was the center of things, he felt that too, but that was the oddest thing of all. From what they had seen of this world he knew they were working for a bright and beautiful future, but here at its very center was darkness and a deep sense of foreboding that brewed in Birch's stomach.

From the far end of the room a faint light flickered, like the striking of a match. A tiny yellow flame glowed meagerly. It wasn't much, but a little light was more than nothing. He walked toward it.

# FORTY-THREE

"Modern Icarus has fallen to earth." A feeble voice rasped in the darkness. "The sun has burned your wings," the voice laughed. "You came back."

Birch was walking toward the sound. In the dim light of a single candle he could just make out the face that the voice belonged to. It was ancient, an old man with a halo of wispy, white hair floating above his balding head. The candlelight darkened the shadows and deepened the lines on his face, accentuating his age. He attempted a smile, but seemed exhausted by the effort and gave it up half way through.

Birch was tempted to dismiss the old man as a crank or a decrepit member of the janitorial staff that no one had the heart to fire, but something about his manner suggested more. He listened.

"You don't disappoint, Major Birch," the man continued. "Again, you have seen what others have failed to see. You are a perceptive man, Major Birch. Indeed, an impetuous, obstinate, bumbling fool of a man, but perceptive for all that."

"What?" Birch growled. "Who do you think you are, talking to me like that?"

"I think I am the president," the old man responded evenly. "And you think you're the commander of the Hypnos III mission, but only one of us is right. Isn't that true?"

. Birch blinked dumbly at the question. The directness of it had caught him off guard and left him with no ready answer. Finally, when words did come, they were half strangled with restrained emotion.

"I am the commander," he rasped. "And since the others were taken in to see the president, and are still there now, you must be the liar."

"Ha," the old man laughed weakly. He lifted the candle to observe Birch's face more closely. In the wafting light Birch could get a better look at this old specimen. He was certainly old, except for the eyes. His eyes didn't exactly look young either, just different. They were a piercing green, clear and sharp. They didn't miss much and they were looking deeply into Birch now, sizing him up, appraising him, and weighing his value.

It wasn't the fierce, probing, green irises that were the most striking feature though. It was the sclera, or the whites of his eyes as they should have been, but they weren't. They were red. Not the bloodshot red of a sleepless night, but the crimson hue of a thousand sleepless nights and of a thousand more burdened days. They were troubled eyes, wise, knowing, and sad. If they cried, and Birch didn't doubt that they did, you would wonder if salty-clear tears would fall, or if two bloody trails would stain those withered old cheeks.

"Who said anything of lying," the old man chuckled wearily. "You do have a habit of getting right to the point, but let's not be so blunt. Besides, if we tell ourselves something, and we know it to be true, who can call us a liar for believing it?

"You're not a very good liar, Major Birch," his eyes never left him. "You've tried, as everyone has, but you just can't make yourself believe it, can you? That's why I couldn't let you in to see me with the others. You never would have believed."

"What do you mean?" Birch felt on an instinctive level he already knew exactly what he meant, but for some reason he couldn't quite force it to the surface, into his conscious mind.

"You have an inkling of it," he responded. "You've always had an inkling, even before your mission. Sometimes you are a blind fool, but that doesn't alter the fact that you can see, when you choose to."

"What can I see?"

"Everything."

"Yes!" Birch thundered. He had been planning to keep his knowledge of their captivity in the envirodome to himself, to bide his time and wait to see how that information might serve him later. It didn't work out that way. Something about the way this man so coolly analyzed his life, and in a matter of seconds reached conclusions about him that he had been struggling a lifetime to achieve brought all his customary anger bursting to the surface. In his frustration he let loose on the old man.

"Yes, I do know everything! I know you've got us locked up in your pretty cage. You've penned us in, but we're not your animals. I won't be your performing pet to dance on your chain! Release us now, or you'll get no cooperation from us. Not on a single thing! Whatever you want from us, under these circumstances you can forget it!"

The president seemed neither shocked nor dismayed by this outburst. He managed his half smile and simply dismissed it with a wave of his hand.

"These are personal matters. They are of little consequence. We will discuss them later. We have more important issues to consider first. That will inform our discussion of these trivial matters."

"I don't see what could be more important than 'personal matters' like freedom and choice!"

"You will."

"Maybe if they were your 'personal matters' you might see it differently," Birch muttered.

"No," the old man responded with calm certainty. "The price I pay is greater than yours, but that is not your concern."

"Since you have made yourself a guest in my personal chambers, Major Birch," he continued, "I suggest you take a seat. Make yourself comfortable." He gestured to a uncompromisingly hard, high-backed wooden chair next to his. "We have much to talk about."

Birch sat stiffly in his seat.

"For a president, you have pretty poor accommodation," Birch mused aloud as he sat upright in his chair.

"You still doubt me, Major?" The green eyes were probing again.

"Well, let's just say that in a palace like this your dark little hole here hardly seems like the presidential suite, maybe more like the janitor's closet! I think you could do better for yourself, Mr. President." Birch's tone was mocking.

"Yes, I see," he replied. "You assume as the head of state I would want the best for myself. That is how you expect governments to work?"

"That is how I *know* life to work!"

"Yes, I suppose it does, or a least it did for many, but you shouldn't be surprised at my choice. Remember your history, Major. The same church that raised the towering cathedrals and built the Papal palaces also provided the humble monastic cell. Is it so strange that I should choose the lower, lesser path? What I do, I do for others, not myself.

"I am pleased you made it here, Major. You need to see a little behind the curtain. You are already where no one is permitted. You have seen more than is ever allowed. You have seen me.

"People expect a great deal of their leaders. I am President Malum Michaels. The great, the powerful..." he paused, "...the weary," he sighed. "I have dedicated my life to this work, to building something out of this world. To transforming it. It is a long journey, and yet even after all these years I have only just begun."

"Yeah, sounds like a tough job," Birch was still skeptical.

"You expect something more, but I have no desire for those

trappings of state and power. This does not interest me. This tower, its great halls and opulence are all for the benefit of others. It meets their expectations. So does President Michaels. Not me, the public version of me- the one the world gets to see. The imposter your colleagues are meeting now. They are still with him, and no doubt are very impressed with his appearance and his tone and his voice. He is impressive, but he is an empty vessel, as they all are. I could not risk such an encounter with you. You would have seen through him, spoiled it for the rest of them. You see too much, question too much, and fight too much. That's why I kept you out.

"Still, I wanted to see you personally, to talk with you. You are different from the rest, you see more, and so I gave you the smallest of clues, opened my door just a crack, and let you in, if you could find the way. And here you are. You really do have remarkable perception. It will get you into trouble one of these days, I have no doubt."

"Well then? Why did you open your door 'a crack' for me? What do you want from me?"

"Yes," the president responded with satisfaction. "This is just the sort of question I expect from you. You really are remarkable"

"Well then, how about an answer!" Birch snapped, exasperated.

"You are very direct, Major. Very well, I shall be direct with you. We need you. We need all of you. It was most unfortunate that two of you were lost in transit. That could be a mortal wound to our hopes."

"Yes, most unfortunate," Birch echoed bitterly.

The old man looked up sharply. He recognized something in Birch's tone, something distantly familiar that he knew he should have remembered. He nodded silently and placed a gnarled hand on Birch's shoulder.

"Yes, of course" he patted his shoulder in a way Birch assumed was supposed to be comforting, but was somehow more mechanical than affectionate. His voice, when he spoke, had that same quality, like a paid caregiver who gives just the right amount of support and compassion, but is always thinking about the paycheck.

"I know it's been hard for you, Major. You've lost half of your crew. I understand your losses since your return. What I really can't understand though is how you became acting commander. Where is Colonel Ratliff?"

Birch choked on the question.

"He didn't make it," he finally answered.

"Obviously," Michaels responded eagerly. "Why?"

"What's it to you?" Birch snapped back angrily.

"Everything." Those green eyes were on him again, sifting, searching, looking deeper into his thoughts than even he wanted to look himself. The question had cut deep into Birch's brain, penetrating to the heart of what he didn't want to know. He couldn't escape it. He would have to face the truth someday, but not today. He could delay it. That's what he did now.

"Things went wrong," he answered more coolly. President Michaels was his Commander and Chief. He had to answer him. He knew that. He would do that because it was his duty, but then he could evade. Answers didn't have to be clear.

"We had trouble from the start," Birch continued cagily. "The terrain wasn't good. The conditions were harsh. Probes that we sent out on approach suggested a manageable atmosphere, only mild terraforming required, but there were difficulties. Projects went wrong, machinery broke down. One thing after another. And then Colonel Ratliffe disappeared."

"Disappeared?" Michaels leaned forward with interest.

"Yes," Birch lied, "and we looked for him everywhere we could, the base, the ship, the planet surface. There wasn't a trace." Well, at least part of that was true. He hoped that was enough to convince him.

"The mission was a wreck. The equipment was junked. We had lost our commander, and there was no chance of success, so we left."

"You gave up."

"No!" Birch barked. "We had to leave. There was no reason to stay. Our supplies were gone, our equipment was shot. There was nothing to do but go! Where could we go? This was our only chance, so we came back to earth. We sent back the message: 'Mission abort. No life sustainability. Send no one. Mission abort.'"

"And yet they did send someone." Michaels' voice was cold and hard.

Birch looked up, daring to meet the gaze of those searching green eyes.

"They sent someone? Who?" he managed to stammer.

"Not a someone, but many someones. A whole colony."

"But the message…"

"It never got through."

"But that's not possible," Birch gulped. "We sent the message before we left. A colony up there without any preparation, without bases, and terraforming, and irrigation, they couldn't survive! They'd all be dead!"

"And yet they weren't." Michaels answered evenly. "Reports from the colony were most promising at the start. Homes were built. Society began to take root. And then nothing."

"Nothing? What happened?"

"We don't know. All communication stopped. We hoped you would have some answers for us. Instead you seem to have raised more questions."

Birch sat brooding for a moment. It made no sense to him. So many questions, and yet one came to the fore in his mind.

"So, how do you know so much about us, about our mission? When we first got back nobody knew us. No one had even heard of the Hypnos missions except as some historical oddity they didn't really understand. It's been a long time since we left. How come you remember?"

"Many people have short memories." Michaels tried his half smile again. "I do not."

"I suppose I really should give credit," he continued, "to a certain historical artifact in this very city. It lies concealed beneath us, in the old Metro system. Station twenty-three. I really must take you there sometime. Very educational. You see in the later years of one of the former governments things were very fraught. Doom and gloom were everywhere and they trusted no one, and so they brought the Hypnos mission to Washington, to keep it directly under their noses, as it were. They put it underground, like the old missile defense silos, cleared whole sections of the city to do it too. A monumental task, all to keep their dream, their Hypnos dream, alive! They might lose their country, but they would gain the stars. A noble aspiration!

"Those were violent times, and when the government came to a violent end, so did Hypnos. And for many years it was forgotten, abandoned in its subterranean tomb. I discovered it. I have since explored its secrets. What wonders there are! Equipment left, just as we found it, just as it was left all those years ago. Why, the end came so suddenly, we even found a Hypnos rocket left on the launch pad, fully fueled and ready to go! What a sad testimony to the lost dreams of a generation.

"That is how I know so much, Major. Your records are, quite literally, an open book to me. Of course, as you noted, few people today know much of that past, but I always feel we must remember our past to understand our future."

"Yeah," Birch muttered uncomfortably. He changed the subject.

"So how was that last government defeated? Was that something to do with the Ares?"

"Ah yes, the Ares." The president's eyes narrowed. "Our little problem. Yes I suppose you would want to know about them. Well then, let me tell you about the Ares."

# FORTY-FOUR

"Where there is light, there is darkness. Where there is love, there is hate. Where there is warmth, there is cold. Where there is victory, there is defeat. It cannot be escaped. Where one exists, so must the other. To understand one, you must know the other. Has there ever been a time without this knowledge? Will there ever be a time without it?" President Michaels sighed heavily. His bloodstained eyes glanced upward, as if seeking solace. Then his head fell forward, as though resigned to the answer.

"Not in our time, Major Birch. Not in our time. You and I are old enough to know that things don't really change. The faces change, the names change, all the superficials change, but the fight goes on. You either have to accept that or go crazy. I have accepted it.

"The Ares are the shadow to our light. As we have progresssed, so they have regressed. Where we have sought change and improvement, so they have sought stagnation and deterioration. We are the builders and they are the destroyers. In the last hundred years the Ares have built nothing except maybe those subterranean rat-holes they use to harass and attack us wherever we go."

"Yeah," Birch interrupted, "but when did all this start, and why are they trying to destroy everything you've built?" He was growing weary of the president's philosophizing and wanted some cold-hard-facts on the subject.

"The when isn't important, it was the work of many years, the gradual separation of a people both geographically and ideologically. There is no single date I could give you. The 'why', on the other hand, is far more significant.

"As I told you, the Ares are a regressive culture. They seek to move backwards. They love the past, but not the past of reality, of course, instead they venerate some mythical time that never truly existed. They think the past is a beautiful place and they wish to go back to it, even with all of its dangers for destruction. That's why they find you so fascinating, Major."

"Me? They find me fascinating?"

"Well, not you alone, of course, but all of you, all of you Hypnos astronauts, that is. That's also why you were such a target for them. They were after you from the very start."

"They *were* after us then." Birch felt as if he were beginning to understand something he should have known all along.

"Somehow they found out that you were coming," Michaels continued. "They arranged the ambush in the mountains, and then all that followed after that. We are still dealing with the aftermath of their attacks. It was all coordinated as a plan to try and stop you from making it to us. We kept that fact from you during the journey because we didn't want to alarm you."

The admission angered Birch. He knew the reason behind it, but he hated to be lied to. You never could trust a liar; you never could trust anyone. For now he swallowed his anger and tried to get answers to his questions.

"So why did they want to stop us, what's so important about us?" Birch growled. He was beginning to feel like a very small piece in a big game he didn't yet understand.

Michaels nodded quietly. "You are everything to them," he continued. "You are from the past. That alone would mark you out as special to them, but it goes deeper than that. You are astronauts. You represent the future they had hoped for, a future based on the grasping ideals of space exploration. You represent all that they wanted. And so the Ares have sought you out, but I wouldn't let them have you. You are almost messianic figures to them, fulfilling a promise that your missions made to them long ago."

"What promise?" Birch's voice was doubtful. "We made no promises."

"But you did," the president's voice didn't seem to fluctuate at all from its reassuring monotone. "You promised a future they wanted; a future of exploration and conquest. A future that our society has rejected today, we don't waste our time on such expensive, impractical dreams. But the Ares have resisted the changes, the advances toward the common good here on earth, by glorying in the excesses of the past and demanding that they continue. You represent the last hope to them; your missions are a part of their mythology. Over time your legend has grown. You all came to be deified, the colonies you were sent out to establish were the promised lands, and your heroism and goodness grew to ridiculous proportions. Now you are like gods to them."

"So why did they attack us then," Birch asked bitterly, "and why is Karla dead? What you say makes no sense."

"They didn't attack you, Major, they attacked us. They thought they were rescuing you from our evil influence. Didn't you wonder why they waited to fire on your camp in the mountains? It was because they were waiting to get a clear shot at our men; they didn't want to risk hitting any of you."

"That's why they tried to grab Karla and DeSante!" Birch exclaimed. His mind was trying to adjust to this seismic shift. It was as though the whole universe had been turned inside-out and he wasn't sure what it meant or who his friends or enemies were any more.

"That is correct," the president continued. "It seems that you must have discovered Lieutenant Dawson in storage in one of those sacred ancestor sites they seem to cherish so much. You were lucky to find her, but I think your performance earlier that night might have rattled them a little. You rocked their world."

Birch shook his head, as though doubting his words.

"Don't underestimate your influence, Major, remember what you are to them. I wish I could have seen that moment. From the reports you caused quite a stir; you started shooting and when they saw who it was fighting against them they ran in panic. Imagine that, their very savior come down to earth to destroy them. No wonder they ran. Nothing is to be feared more than an angry god, eh Major Birch?" The old man laughed weakly at his own joke. Birch wearily put his head in his hands.

For a time neither said anything. When Birch finally spoke the words came in choking half-breaths.

"So that's why they killed Karla." He muttered. "I turned them against us!"

"Not exactly," the president shook his head. "The events of that night had nothing to do with why they killed Karla. In fact, strictly speaking, they didn't kill Karla. It was that young boy you tangled with in the mountains. He was acting on his own. He's staying not far from your little home right now; perhaps you'll see him soon." Michaels' eyes took on a meaningful look that Birch couldn't interpret.

"He's a sullen, surly little fellow, but we managed to prize the main gist of the events out of him. He's not a part of any Ares tribe, though, but one of those orphan kids that roam around out there. They have no status or support in their culture, so they have to make their own lives.

"It seems he lead you, Major, to the burial ground, believing he would be throwing you straight into the hornet's nest. He was hoping to see some fun, I guess, but then instead of being caught you survived and rescued Lieutenant Dawson. He was surprised and impressed. He took an interest in you after that. He followed you."

"Does he know what happened to DeSante?" Birch interrupted.

"No," was Michaels' monosyllabic answer. He continued.

"Your little encounter had quite an effect on him, and so he began keeping an eye on you through the mountains, in the city, and then later on the plains.

"Despite what you had done to him it seems he liked you, and then, through overheard conversations, he learned who you really were. All those old Ares superstitions and hopes came to mind. He remembered the legends, the tales of the noble astronauts who had gone to build a future, who would return one day to save them all. He became your disciple, your protector, and your shadow. Even though he dared not approach you, he followed you wherever you went. To his devoted mind your every action showed all the fortitude and the nobility he had expected to find in his heroes. But then it changed.

All of that changed the day before your young lieutenant was shot. He saw you kill a man in cold blood; it killed the hope in him. It changed everything. Before that event he had seen how you and Lieutenant Dawson had helped each other; it had shown him a different life to that of a wilderness orphan. It had shown him that the legends were true, that the past had been a better time. He knew the future would be too.

From what I gather you gave him a hope of better things, far more than he had ever experienced in his life. It awakened the thought in him that there were good people in the world and that he could be a part of that, but your murder of that Ares rider shattered his illusions and strangled his newborn hopes. You were as bad as everybody else. His savage little mind reverted to the only course it knew. He was angry and disappointed. You had let him down, so he took his revenge. He killed her first; you were to be next. When you chased after him he would ambush you, but you never came. He snuck back to find you sitting there with her. You stayed all night. He is a little confused about what happened next, but obviously what he saw stole away his desire to kill, and so he ran. You know what happened after that. Rather a sad story, don't you think?"

Birch said nothing. He was perfectly still. Not seeing. Not breathing. Not thinking. When finally his lungs rebelled his breath came in gasping sobs. Tears filled his eyes, but he would not let them fall. Not here, not now. The gnarled hand reached out to comfort him again, but he shoved it aside. The president's blood rimmed eyes widened in surprise.

Alone he might have punched walls, kicked the floor, or tried to tear the flesh from his own blighted bones. His anger raged so hard that it seemed to consume him, and he didn't care because it was himself that he hated. He had blundered through life up to this point, and only now could he really see how much of his pain was of his own making. He wondered how many times he had been hurt before without knowing that he himself was the cause. Worse still, how many others had he hurt?

For a time they both sat silently. There was nothing to say. Finally Michaels spoke again.

"This orphan boy has learned the same truth that all of the Ares have discovered: that the golden past is only gilded by their own faulty imagination. All of them know now what you are. It will be interesting to see how they cope with that. Sadly, I believe they will not abandon their love for the past, just their love for you.

"The Ares are blinded by their desires. They think they know what they want. They think they know the past, but they don't know it as well as you or I, Major; if they did they wouldn't crave those things, would they?"

"I would," Birch confessed gloomily. "Maybe you're the one who doesn't know as much as you think."

President Michaels seemed unfazed by his outburst.

"I know enough, Major. Oh, I haven't been asleep for hundreds of years like you, and I haven't been blasted out to some distant planet, but I'm old enough, and wise enough, and I've seen enough to know that people don't change.

"We're all so limited. We try to understand from our own experiences. We fail. Sometimes we try to learn from others, but usually we learn the wrong thing. Mostly though, we have to fall down ourselves before we recognize the danger. That is the advantage of age. With age we gain experience and wisdom through our failures. Eventually we might know it all because we have seen it all. But then we die and it starts all over again with the next generation. What a waste.

"You, Major Birch, are old, but you have slept through the ages. You have gained nothing, have learned nothing, and achieved nothing through all that time. You slept. You have awoken as stupid as you were when you closed your eyes all those years ago. You haven't grown. What use are you? You are nothing more than an oddity, a historical aberration.

"But fortune smiles on us. You're differences are a blessing. You are a glorious anachronism and..."

Birch had been sitting numbly, letting the words wash over him. He felt sick to his stomach. He was lost. His mind drifted out over the lonely plains, out to that mound of dirt and stone. The wind blew the grass there. His actions had put her there. He wished he could be the one to die. Just once he wanted to be the one to die. He was tired.

"...which will render you useful. More useful than even the Ares imagined." The aged President droned on earnestly.

Birch's mind came into sharp focus. He had missed something here, something about them, something important.

"What do you mean useful?" Birch didn't like the connotation of that word.

"Your purpose," the president sought for a better word, a smoother way to describe the matter. "It's your way to help your fellow man."

"No."

"No?" Michaels blinked dumbly, as if the word had never occurred to him, and now that it had been uttered he wasn't sure how to respond. "But you don't even know what we're asking of you!" he spluttered incredulously.

"I haven't heard you ask me anything at all. I've heard you *tell* me plenty! You tell me that nobody can understand the world. We're all the stupid ones and you're the one with the plan. You tell me we're useful. What you don't do is ask if we want to be useful."

Michaels paused. Those green eyes were probing him again, trying to prize out his inmost thoughts. He sighed. The reddened sclera seemed to liquefy. He was about to cry and Birch would learn if he wept tears of water or of blood, but he blinked them away. The eyes quickly hardened.

"I was right about you," the old man rasped sadly and shook his head. "You see too much for me to offer you a false choice. I could tell you that you could choose, and hope that you would do what we needed, what is right, but I couldn't fool you. You would know. We can't let you choose. It's just too important for that."

"Life has a way of often giving you two simple alternatives," Birch remembered, "two ways, the right one and the wrong one." He mulled this over in his mind for a moment before continuing. "I *will* choose. My answer is no."

President Michaels seemed unfazed by his refusal.

"You are an optimist, Major Birch," he purred. "You believe in the myth of the open road and the old American road trip with a whole country of choices opening up before you. But I ask you, who built those roads? Who decided where those roads should go? Who decided where those roads should not go? The motorist? No, the planners. Some towns died, others thrived, all on the decisions of those planners. They knew what was needed. They shaped your 'freedom' on the road. You go where their roads tell you.

"Every choice that you think you have has been engineered. Whether by parents, or experience, or employers, or fear, or religion, or politics, or lust, or love, or duty, it doesn't matter. You make no free choices. Instead these conflicting influences lead you into a whole cascade of contradictory, purposeless decisions that will lead you nowhere. No wonder so many lives end worthlessly.

Imagine a better way. Imagine lives being planned. Imagine if someone had gone ahead of you who knew all the dead ends, all the sorrows, and all the hazards that lay before you, and they closed those roads. Only the best way remains. You know that in the ancient world all roads led to Rome. In our modern times, all roads lead to happiness. Isn't that a better way?"

"No."

"Why not?"

"Because even God put a tree in the garden."

"What does that mean?"

"It means that life without freedom is no life at all. We were not made for safety. We were made to be free."

"Freedom?" Michaels rolled the word on his tongue, as though tasting it. "The beautiful illusion. Many have fought for it, some have even died for it. Few have experienced it.

"If you are fortunate you may live in a country where the illusion of freedom is more potent. The powerful will let you imagine you are free until your rights conflict with their interests. The strip mall could destroy your home; the power company could fell your trees; a road could be built through your living room. All of these things happened to the little people, and the law allowed it. The freedom of the individual meant nothing and power meant everything. This was acceptable, but this was not freedom. Yours was a government of the powerful, for the powerful, by the powerful. It was not free. It was expensive, and those who could afford it bought it.

"All they needed to finish the job was a crisis. Real or invented, it didn't matter so long as people panicked, so long as they learned that they needed the powerful to protect them.

"In their panic they would grant that government greater freedom to snoop and pry, to take away even some of those illusions of personal freedom. In protecting they would endanger. In fighting tyranny, tyranny was accepted. People wanted safety, and so they accepted it. They wanted security, and so they applauded it.

"They thought they were safer behind the walls that were erected around them, the very walls that imprisoned them. It was a vain hope. The days of safety behind the castle battlements were long over, that era went with gunpowder. Still the people hoped, but no wall could ever be built high enough to keep all the dangers out. It was far easier to build a wall to keep them in, and that is what their government did.

"If you love freedom, Major, you should love me. I have restored freedom, the freedom to be happy. I do not seek my own benefit. I have done what all governments have claimed, but few have ever done. I have put my own interests aside. I live and breathe in this darkened tower for the good of others. I have sought the common good."

Michaels opened his arms wide, spreading out his open hands, palms up, in a gesture of pitiful supplication. Thomas Birch was probably the only person in the whole world who knew Michaels' heart, who knew his plan for the world. In a strange way Michaels needed the approval of this one man, this one pitiful example of human flesh, to know that it had all been worth it, that his sacrifice had not been in vain.

"I helped. I did it all for the common good." Michaels murmured again.

"Through manipulation!" Birch thundered. "Through taking away our chance to know anything else! You think you are different, but you're like every other petty little dictator that ever lived. You may be able to kid yourself, but it's all the same old lies! You're on a power kick and want to control everyone else! Well, whatever you're trying to do here will fail in the end."

The words stung Michaels. He shook his head dolefully. "The sad thing is I think you're right. I've seen it. All human endeavors are doomed to fail. Whatever noble and good thing we try to do, we will not achieve it, because everything has our fingerprints all over it. Our imperfections show through in everything we do. We can't help it. Everything we build, whether it's as complex as an empire or as simple as a toy, it will be destroyed because of the mistakes we make when we build it.

"The greatest example of this truth is this country's own Liberty Bell. Like the democracy it represented it was imperfect from the very beginning. The problems weren't obvious; no one could see them, but they were there from the start, when the metal was poured into the mould, and so the bell cracked. It became a useless ornament that couldn't serve the purpose it was made for, and this is what we all do. We try to do good, but we never achieve our purpose, and the only enemy we can blame is ourselves."

"If you know that everything fails then why try?" Birch remarked sourly. "Why all these big plans?"

"Yes," the president sighed, "I see your point. I once was close to that conclusion myself, but we must hope. Perhaps I have finally found the balance, the perpetual motion that will keep my plans in place. We will see. Time will tell."

"I hope you're wrong. I hope you fail. I want no part of this," Birch snapped.

"I'm sorry you see it that way, but it is unimportant. I don't need to convince you. What I am doing is for the good of everyone. Like the Ares, you disagree, but like them you do not possess the power to do anything about it."

"You watch me," Birch thundered as he rose from his chair, moving menacingly toward the president."

"Ah, yes, brute force. That is your only recourse. Sit down, Major Birch. You can't win. Whatever you do to me can't stop this. You have no choice. We need you, but your cooperation is not necessary."

Birch paused. "What do you mean?" he asked. Something in the old man's voice was alarming, more threatening than any more obvious intimidation.

"We are all in trouble, Major. Humanity's history is filled with mistakes, and the more power we get the more dangerous these mistakes have become. Genetic experiments and all manner of scientific tomfoolery has led us here. They blundered into it without understanding the repercussions, and it has worked a powerful evil that has been hard to fight. The very things that were supposed to improve our lives have put them in peril.

"Power and money spoke. They allowed their own people to become their experimental lab for genetic alterations and modifications in the food chain. Why? Because it was cheap, because they could, and because some faceless committee somewhere decided it was a good idea. And for that the world went down. They did it because the people were not their constituency and because they didn't care. But they hadn't foreseen the long term effect, and once it had gone wrong it was hard to put right. No one was spared. They got their cheap food, but now we all pay the price.

"We've fixed the food, but the human genetic material we're dealing with today is degraded. The producers of this food, no doubt, would have described this as an 'unforeseen circumstance' in the annual financial reports. I describe it as what it truly is; the murder of a generation. It is not general knowledge, but all that we have worked for is in jeopardy. Within the next five to six hundred years humanity will be extinct. We've killed so much on this planet with our reckless attitude, now we've finally done it to ourselves. Nature must be laughing."

"Okay," Birch snapped angrily, "so you guys have ruined the world. I expected that. I don't see what that's got to do with us."

"It has everything to do with you. You left before the worst experiments took place; your bodies did not absorb the destructive elements that our ancestors did. You are our reset button, the chance to restart the biological clock, back to a time before we undid ourselves. The material you three can produce will save us all."

"And what if we say no," Birch fixed a hard stare on the man. His expression didn't alter.

"I wish you wouldn't," his half smile was back. Suddenly it looked like a smirk. "It won't make a difference either way, of course. You understand. There is too much at stake."

Birch did understand. They were about to be torn down to put up a strip mall. Now he raged at himself. All of his instincts had been right. From the very beginning he hadn't trusted these people, but still, like a lamb, he had allowed himself to be led here to this.

Thomas Birch understood their position perfectly. Clearly President Michaels had the best of intentions; he was nobly motivated, and he was completely evil.

The most dangerous predator wasn't the wolf disguised as a sheep. It was the wolf that believed they were a sheep. There was no limit to what they would do in the name of righteousness.

# FORTY-FIVE

Birch was brought back into the great hall by the two guards from the golden doorway. They placed him in one of the angular chairs and resumed their former position by the entryway, as stolid and resolute as before.

For a time Birch sat brooding silently. The others still hadn't returned and he was left alone with his thoughts. They had no choice about what was going to happen to them, Michaels had made that clear. The only single freedom he had been permitted was the choice of what to do about Jane and Lauren. That was a freedom that couldn't be avoided. Even President Michaels couldn't withhold that.

Birch was the only one that knew. Jane and Lauren had been presented with the beautiful illusion of what this world was supposed to be. He had seen the truth. The question was, should he tell them? Should he steal away the security and peace they felt in this place, even if it was only a fantasy. His natural answer would have been yes. He would always take truth over falsehood, but Michaels had made him doubt his instincts.

"You are free." Michaels had informed him. "You are free to tell them what you know, or free to conceal the truth from them. Which do you think will make them happier?" The elderly president had been clear about his thoughts on the matter. Birch was the kind of person, he imagined, who could endure the truth, but why burden the others with it? Let them have their dream. Let them enjoy the life they imagined they had. Then they could live their lives in contentment, knowing that they were truly happy.

It could all be done with subtlety. Birch would know they were in the envirodome. The constant buzzing in his ears would remind him. This was the side effect of the extra ampage needed on the settings to make the illusion stick in his disbelieving mind, so Michaels had said. He would know that everything around him was a lie, but the others would be free. In their mind they would be free.

Sometimes the technical crews would come. At night they would pump the dome with gas, knock them out and collect what they needed from them. They would never know. They would wake the next morning, stiff but unknowing. Their lives would be full, happy, and false. This was how Michaels had put it. Why steal away their happiness?

The idea made sense to him, but it also repulsed him. Why would he plunge these two into the same despair he was experiencing now, and yet how could he lie to them? He hated lies. And yet this was the one freedom that Michaels had left him- the freedom to lie.

Birch sighed and folded his arms in angry futility. He knew what he would do. He didn't like it.

The great golden doors opened and the others walked in. Their voices were buzzing with hope and optimism. They liked what they had been told. Even Jane looked animated and hopeful at the prospects they had been promised in this new world.

Birch watched gloomily as Jane and Lauren smiled and laughed easily with each other. Their burdens had been lifted. Their weary journey was done and they were home. At least that's what they thought. Edwards, on the other hand, seemed subdued. His eyes were shifting between them and the door. Something about what he had seen in there had shaken him.

He looked thoughtful and worried.

The group was quickly herded out and thrust into the waiting elevator. The doors had hardly shut before they were plunging down to earth again. The two soldiers stood glowering at them as they guarded the door. Their hands were on their weapons but Jane and Lauren hardly seemed to notice. Birch looked warily into their stony faces. He didn't like what he saw there. Even Edwards had a strange, distant look to him. He wouldn't look at him. The false cordiality was wearing a little thin, and to Birch's knowing eyes they were simply prisoners being pushed from one place to another.

Birch cast a cautious glance at the men's guns. His mind was already racing, grasping for any hope of escape, but the truth was not encouraging. In these cramped quarters there wasn't a chance, and he imagined the guards would be their constant companions from now on. They had walked into this, but there wasn't any easy way to walk out. They would have to fight to get away. Soon they would be back in the enviro-dome. Then they would never get out. They had to get away before they got back. He just didn't know how.

They were soon at ground level again. They were marched through the doors and into the waiting vehicle at the front of the tower. Their truck sped quickly away on a route returning them to the house they had left hours ago. It had felt like a prison to Birch before, but now he knew that it was he shuddered at the thought of going back. How could he escape?

He watched the idyllic landscape passing before his window and considered the options. The germ of an idea came to him, but he doubted that it would really work. Still, it was something, and that was better than nothing, better than just sitting and watching their freedom disappear.

It was a simple plan, if you could call something so direct and so stupid a plan. He would wait until the guards looked distracted and then jump them. That was it. It wasn't smart; it wasn't even likely to succeed, but it was something, and that was the important thing, doing something. With any luck he would be able to grab one of their weapons and see what happened from there. Perhaps with hostages he could force their release. Then they would just have to see how far they could get. It wasn't a great chance, but then he didn't like the alternative. He would rather die escaping than become a genetic crop to be harvested by Michaels and his men.

He glanced around the compartment. There were two armed guards at the back, a driver and Edwards at the front, and Jane and Lauren next to him. It would be hard to overcome their advantages, but he would try. He wished he could warn Jane or Lauren, to prepare them for what was going to happen. Neither of them was looking at him, though, and it would have been too risky to get their attention. They would just have to find out when it happened.

Silently he watched for the moment; his muscles were coiled, prepared to strike. It didn't take long. The guards had seemed distracted from the very beginning of the journey, and the closer they got to their destination the greater their preoccupation became. Finally, as they were coming into view of the cottage, one of the soldiers turned completely to look out the window. Birch saw his opportunity and pounced on the man, wrestling the gun from his grip. Before he could react Birch had swung the butt end of the rifle at the second guard and sent his head smashing hard against the metalwork. The man crumpled to the floor, where he lay groaning. In another step he had advanced on the first guard and sent a thudding punch to his chin that felled him.

Jane leapt swiftly to her feet, her face contorted with fury and disbelief.

"What are you doing?" she screamed. "Have you lost your mind? How can you do that after all they've done for us?"

She had advanced on Birch, but he pushed her aside

"We need to get out," Birch answered evenly and pointed his gun at the driver. "Open these doors, now!" The man nodded and pushed a button that sent them sliding up.

The new light streaming into the back of the truck was almost blinding, but in the seconds that it took for his eyes to adjust Birch instinctively knew that something was wrong. It was only as his vision cleared that he understood exactly what it was. It was everything. The whole city had been a lie, or at least a distortion of the truth. As he stepped out of the truck the beautiful view from the windows altered and shifted from the open spaces of nature, to a scene crowded with gray buildings and people. There were some elements that were the same; some of the buildings and other features were in the same place, but the beauty had drained away. After the illusion it was a shock. It was like looking at one of those pictures of a famous beauty without their makeup. It just didn't look right.

This was an alarming shift in reality. Jane and Lauren stood stunned. With no preconception of this they were confused. Birch had expected something, but Lauren and Jane were lost and bewildered in a land they could not comprehend.

As he stepped from the truck he was surprised by the number of people milling around and the strange buildings everywhere. They were in the middle of something. This was a busy place with families, and laughter, and music, and the smell of popcorn lingering in the air like a childhood memory. It was a place to be happy, but Birch was not happy. The ground was hard beneath his feet; the concrete was back. The grass had died and had been replaced by miles and miles of cold, gray cement that stretching out about them in broad walkways. People tramped along them from one building to another.

The buildings surrounding them were odd. They were constructed more of light and imagination than anything else. They reminded him of the protective domes they had used out in the mountains. These ones were transparent though, and from where he stood he could make out the forms of animals moving about under the observant eyes of the people gathering to watch. The animals were oblivious to it all. As they moved the scene around them changed. It was as though they were walking, but they were going nowhere.

It was the dome before them that terrified Birch most. There were no animals in it. It was an exact image of their home over the last few days, an idyllic cottage under glass for all to see. Nothing was hidden. Even interior shots could be seen on large viewing screens near the enclosure. It made Birch sick. He had suspected something was wrong, but even in his mind it hadn't been like this.

"Get out," Birch hissed at Edwards, taking care to conceal his weapon from the people passing by. "What is this place?" he asked hoarsely.

Edwards shrugged. "What does it look like?" he responded coolly.

Birch knew very well what the place looked like, and what it really was. It was a zoo! He didn't need Edwards' help to figure it out, but something in the tone of the answer was maddening. Furiously he pushed Edwards up against the side of the truck and mashed his face into the metal door.

"Don't try to be funny," he spat, "what are we doing here?"

"It's for your own protection," Edwards muffled voice could hardly be understood as his mouth was squeezed against the cold steel. "It's what we do for any Ares we catch, to try to rehabilitate them. It's the best way we can learn to help you."

"Learn to help us?" Birch let the irony of the words hang in the air. His voice was barely a menacing whisper, but his actions were beginning to attract attention. He pushed Edwards' miserable face deeper into the metal "Are you stupid, or do you just think we're stupid?" Birch continued, oblivious to the crowd gathering about them. "I don't know if I should kill you now or later."

"Major," Jane's voice interrupted. She was still holding a gun on the guards in the truck, but she was now gesturing behind him. By now a crowd of some twenty men had gathered near the truck and was moving toward him. Birch spun around, finally revealing his weapon to them. For a moment they hesitated before moving again in his direction.

The crowd only seemed to be increasing as he threatened them off with his gun. He fired a warning shot that scattered them briefly, but it only seemed to strengthen their anger and resolve. Their flinty faces hardened like cement and they rushed toward them. Among the shouting tumult a single angry word seemed to rise above it all: 'Ares'.

"I think you're about to find out what we've been protecting you from, Major," Edwards muffled voice sounded distant amid the din that surrounded them, "you might want to run!"

"Great!" Birch grunted as he pulled Edwards back into the truck. "Get us out of here," he shouted to Jane. With Lauren's assistance she had already thrown the driver out and taken over the controls, now she gunned the engine to escape the advancing throng; at least she tried to. Her first effort sent the truck lurching and coughing forward.

"Sorry," she mumbled and raised her hands in acceptance of her mistake.

"Just shut-up and get this thing moving," Birch barked as he shot another volley above the crowd. It didn't slow them at all this time, but in the next instant Jane was able to accelerate away with a screech of tires.

"You'll never make it," one of the guards smirked. "There's nowhere to go."

In that instant Birch exploded angrily. His face and eyes flushed a fiery red, "Thanks for your concern," he snapped, "but we'll just have to find that out for ourselves. We don't need you anyway so you don't have to stick around to see what happens." With that he grabbed the man and threw him through the open doors at the rear of the truck. The soldier rolled out and disappeared on the road behind them. A moment later the second guard had followed him, rolling and bouncing like a human ball on the pavement. Jane looked on in disbelief.

"What did you do that for?" she fumed. "There was no reason to do that!"

"We only need one hostage," Birch raised his rifle to point at Edwards. "He'll do fine. I think he's more important than a couple of guards, and he'll be less trouble. Besides, the other guy was giving me trouble. I don't like that."

Jane shook her head in disgust.

"You don't change," she complained. "You're wild, and one day you'll get us all killed for it."

Birch gritted his teeth and looked though the window. "Maybe, but I think I saved you today," he muttered.

# FORTY-SIX

It took a moment for Birch to remember that what he was seeing wasn't real. "Is there a way to turn this thing off?" he grunted to Edwards, gesturing toward the windows, "I'm tired of looking at happyland. Let me look at reality." Edwards nodded and pointed to a button on the front panel. Lauren hit it and the windows brightened.

The change was not sudden. It took a while before there was much difference except for the lightening tint of the glass. Slowly though the old forms melted away, to be replaced by the buildings that surrounded them. The road stayed the same, but everything around it was different now. Jane had been driving with the aid of a small monitor next to the driver's seat. Now, as the windshield cleared, she could see more easily and they picked up speed.

"Where do we go," she shouted over her shoulder, "where is the nearest exit to this place?"

"Wait," Birch responded as he turned to face Edwards. "You said this is the kind of thing you do to all the Ares when you catch them," Edwards shrugged noncommittally. "So, is that what you did with the Ares boy you picked up with me?"

"He is here," Edwards responded. "I can't let you get at him though, he's under our protection so I won't let you hurt him."

"I don't want to hurt him," Birch sighed, "I want to get him. We're taking him with us."

"Where?" Edwards asked doubtfully. "I don't think you realize the position you're in. You can drive around this spot for a while, but already the forces are after you and they'll put you back. There's nowhere for you to go."

"I think you're wrong," Birch muttered, "but even if you're right we're going to get him so tell me where he is." Birch had pushed Edwards into the corner of the truck and raised his hands menacingly to his face.

"Okay," Edwards sighed. He was thinking of his old life, of the things he had grown to hate. It was strange how vital and lovely they seemed to him right now. In the face of terror he wan-ted it all back, both the good and bad. He would recant, he wouldn't question anymore, if only he could get back to some sense of normality. For now though all he could do was go along with whatever crazy plans this madman from the past had and hope he would be rescued soon. Surely it wouldn't take long. Catching the Ares in the capital should be the easiest thing in the world.

"Get over to the eastern side of the compound," Edwards murmured, "he's in the general Ares enclosure." He directed them the rest of the way and soon the truck was skidding to a halt in front of one of the clear domes. This one was larger than most, and even from this distance Birch could see it was full. Pathetic figures behind the glass moved through imagined lives while the crowds watched. Birch couldn't see the boy.

"Open it," Birch ordered gruffly, but Edwards shook his head.

"It's not going to be that easy," he retorted. "I don't have clearance. I don't work here you know. I'm from the west, only local officials and high rankers can get in there."

"I guess we'll need the more direct approach then," Birch lifted his rifle and aimed at the enclosure.

"No, wait," Edwards voice was panicked and he reached for the gun, but Birch pushed him away and shot into one of the control arrays high above the dome. With a sound of shattering glass the panel broke loose and came crashing to the ground. The crowd scattered as screaming bystanders ran to escape the falling debris.

"Stop it," Edwards shouted, but Birch ignored him and fired again into another panel. It exploded in a shower of sparks that bathed the now fleeing crowd in a strange green light. The dome flickered and disappeared leaving the glass cage within. For the first time those inside could see their true surroundings. They stood blinking, staring dumbly at the world.

"That was pointless," Edwards shook angrily at the destruction around them. "You'll still never get in there, that glass is designed to withstand anything you can shoot at it. You may as well give up. With all that noise the authorities will be here to get you any minute anyway."

"We'll see," Birch muttered as he lifted his rifle and shot at the cage. Edwards had been right though; the glass remained undamaged.

"Great," Birch looked at Edwards with disgust, "let's try something different then." He threw Edwards back into the truck. Jane and Lauren followed him.

"I hope you know what you're doing," Jane added as they traded positions and he took the wheel. "I don't think we'll have long to get away from here."

"Don't worry," he revved the engine ominously, "I know what I'm doing." The tires spun as he reversed the truck away from the compound. "It's one of the oldest tricks, the smash and grab." He slammed on the brakes and they shuddered to a halt. From this distance he could pick up some speed before they hit the wall.

"Are you sure this'll work? That stuff could withstand a direct shot into it," Jane was sweating. "I'm not sure we'll get though!"

"I guess we'll find out," Birch grunted and gunned the engine. With a roar the truck lurched forward and hurtled toward the shimmering glass.

"You're crazy," Edwards was shouting. "You're not supposed to do this!"

"Sure," Birch smiled and bit down on his lip, "that's why we're doing it." The glass compound was now almost directly in front of them as they passed through the blur of bushes and shrubbery that were supposed to give this prison a decorative appearance. A moment later they were smashing into the clear barrier that kept these Ares in their false reality.

With a thunderous crash they burst through into the enclosure. The inmates simply stared at this new wonder that had thrust itself into their dissolving world. For that instant they stood motionless, astounded by the events that had sent everything literally crashing down around them. Quickly realization dawned in their minds and some of them, seeing the hole, dodged trough the gap before the rest of them made a rush for the breech and escaped into the zoo grounds.

Birch couldn't see the boy among any of the fleeing forms that passed him. He scanned the dirty, marked faces but none of them matched. "I thought you said he was here," Birch spat at Edwards.

"He is," Edwards answered sulkily. He pointed over to a small form huddled in a corner of the enclosure. "There he is." It was him. Shivering and alone he was slumped with his head in his hands. Birch walked over and started to lift the boy up, but the young Ares recognized him, panicked, and wriggled free. Swiftly he ran toward the gaping hole in the glass.

"Get him," Birch shouted to Jane as he chased after him, "don't let him out!" Jane had advanced a few steps toward him and lunged at the boy as he approached. She missed as he leapt over her outstretched arms, but as he landed she had grabbed at his foot and made him miss a step. He stumbled to the ground. He quickly bounced to his feet again, but that moments delay was enough for Birch to catch him. With a grunt he shoved the boy back to the ground and pinned him there.

"Great, you got him," Jane muttered. "Now what?"

"Now you get caught," Edwards smiled.

Through the transparent walls a line of vehicles could be seen approaching swiftly. "I told you you'd never make it," Edwards continued haughtily, "there's nowhere for you to go."

"We'll see," Birch was pulling the Ares youth to his feet and pushing him into the back of the truck. "Everybody get back in," he shouted over the roar of the approaching engines. "It's our last chance!" Edwards shook his head. This was pointless, but as long as Jane was waving that rifle at him there wasn't any choice. He'd be rescued soon enough, he just hoped Birch didn't get them all killed before it could happen.

By now a barricade of vehicles had formed outside the compound. They blocked their exit. There was nowhere to go. They had no choice; they had to go forward. Birch pushed hard on the accelerator and little flecks of dirt spun from the tires as they flew forward. He would rush for the other side. The compound was big and it took a few moments before the glass from the far wall came into view. By this time the barricade behind them had broken up and a twisting snake of trucks was slipping through the hole after them. Other vehicles had come crashing through the glass at points closer to them and were now rushing alongside them. Birch swerved the wheel to hit one, but the enemy's truck had instinctively dodged the maneuver and was inching ahead of them to block the way.

"Fire at them!" Birch shouted over the engine's roar. Jane had taken up the gun position and let loose with a barrage at the truck that had now pulled ahead. It exploded in a burst of orange flame and toppled over in front of them. Birch pulled hard at the wheel and sent their truck spinning in an effort to miss it. Their tires slid on the soft earth and when they stopped they found themselves facing the mass of approaching vehicles.

"We need to get out of here," Jane shouted, as the truck settled back on its wheels. She shook her head, trying to clear her addled brain.

"Really?" Birch snapped. "Thanks, but shut-up!"

"You would be better staying here," Edwards interrupted. "You can see they haven't shot at you, even when you have fired at them. They're just trying to help you, so just stop."

"No thanks," Birch was revving the engine again. "Nobody needs that kind of help."

They pulled away in a burst of speed and came fast to the clear, crystal wall at the other side. With a determined grimace Birch slammed hard on the accelerator and smashed through the glass, bursting through into the crowded concourse at the other side. People screamed, scattered, and cleared a way for the truck to rush on, away from their foes.

The three vehicles closest to them followed their example and crashed through the barrier to get at them. The strain finally seemed too much for the structure though, and with a thundering crash the whole dome of glass came down on the remaining trucks in a shower of crystal rain that cut and sliced through anything under it. Looking back toward the sound Edwards shook his head.

"Wow, you've really burned it now," his voice was pale and despairing. "Won't you stop?" No one answered his plea, but Lauren raised the rifle she had been keeping trained on him a few inches higher, as though warning him that he shouldn't try anything. He shook his head again and gazed hopefully through the rear windows. The trucks were coming. Only three had made it out, but they now chased their fleeing target with all speed.

It was a dangerous pursuit. People dodged into doorways and hugged walls as the fleeing truck sped by. An instant later they were forced back to safety again as the three vehicles chased after it. The gap was closing. Soon it would be over as they drove aimlessly along the maze of concrete walkways, seeking escape.

Inside the truck Birch sweated as he drove on. Finally he saw what he had been looking for, a gate to take them out of the zoo and into the outside world. But the gates were closing. Birch ignored that and sent the truck smashing through, sending crumpled metal flying into the air. The truck shook violently under the impact, but kept going into the relative freedom of the city streets. Behind them the pursuing trucks pushed aside the remains of the gates and hurtled after them.

"It's useless," Edwards shouted. "Where will you go? You could never make it back to the plains and there's nowhere to hide here. Every citizen will be looking for you. Just give up."

"No," Birch kept his eyes ahead but his voice was enough to tell Edwards his hopes of talking his way out of this were useless. "There is a way out," Birch continued. "When I met with Michaels, he said something about a Hypnos base here in Washington, at Metro station twenty-three. That's where we're going. Tell me how to get there!"

"What's the use," Edwards' voice was strained, "If you get there all you'll find will be a bunch of rusting, old equipment. That'll get you nowhere. Besides, it's a restricted area. Nobody's supposed to go there."

"Just get us there," Birch snapped. Turning in his seat he glared wildly at Edwards for a moment before looking again to the road ahead. "We'll worry about the rust when we get there."

Edwards sighed. He looked at the guns and the desperate faces around him. He knew the danger he was in. The trucks behind them seemed to have lost a little ground as they swung through the streets. They might not get caught for a little while and perhaps diverting Birch's attention to a futile escape plan would give them the time they needed to catch him. Without that hope Edwards worried that Birch might do something even more desperate.

"Okay," he muttered, "I'll lead you there, but don't expect it to do you any good."

"Fine," Birch answered, "Just get us there."

# FORTY-SEVEN

They raced through the city streets. Some of what they saw reminded Birch of their imaginary home in the envirodome. The world there hadn't exactly been a lie, but an exaggeration. It was clear that they were trying to achieve the things that the illusion had shown, but they hadn't succeeded. It was crowded in the bustling city of reality. The roads were all paved and the buildings had a less natural look. Most striking, however, was the color; it was like stepping from a Technicolor movie back into the drabness of reality.

Birch's driving continued at a wild pace. When Edwards gave a direction he waited until the last possible moment to make the turn. He screeched around the corners, hoping this would throw off the three trucks that persisted after them. This gained them a little space, but he knew it wasn't much, so when Edwards finally told him to stop outside one of the city's Metro stations he rushed to get the others inside as quickly as possible.

He couldn't get the Ares boy to move however. He just lay shivering in the corner of the truck A look of blind fear filled his eyes, and as Birch came to lift him out he snapped and growled like a wild animal.

"See if you can get him out," Birch shouted to Lauren and

Jane. He didn't have time for this.

Together the two women coaxed him out and soon they were all running to the entrance of the station. Birch reached it first, and as he looked back he caught sight of two trucks pulling up to the curb. He shouted for the others to hurry as their doors banged open and the heavy boots of soldiers clumped noisily to the ground. A moment later the men were pulling the guns from their belts, but Birch and the others had already disappeared inside.

Inside the station a great crush of people moved, herd-like through the turnstiles. Thousands of individuals, collectively forming a crowd moving swiftly toward the platforms, rushing for trains to take them home. Birch didn't see their individuality. He only saw them as a mass, an obstacle to be overcome in their dash for freedom.

"Where to?" Birch pushed his pistol into Edwards' back.

"We've got to get down to the lower levels," Edwards shouted over the sound of passing commuters and buzzing equipment. They ran to the turnstiles. "The base is down there." He pointed beneath their feet.

"Make sure you're right." Birch looked menacingly at him. "You wouldn't want to get it wrong."

"This is it," Edwards responded reassuringly. "They used part of the underground facility as a head start for digging out this station. Whatever's left is down there." He pointed again to the ground beneath them.

"Great," Birch spat, "let's get at it then." By now they had reached the barrier. A line of weary commuters filed through the turnstile, but instead of waiting his turn he pushed past the crowd and jumped over the metal posts blocking his path. He pulled Edwards behind him as he ran for the escalators. The others followed amid a tumult of angry, indignant voices. Soon they were all descending to the levels below. They rushed down the crowded escalator. Behind them the soldiers had reached the gate and were swamped by a sea of furious, complaining commuters.

Edwards knew it was only a matter of time. He would guide them as far as they wanted, but now that they were down here there was no way of escape. Already he had seen the cameras whirring and turning to face them in their dissent. Everything they did would be covered by those things. There was nowhere to run. Yes, he would guide them to the rusting relics of their history, but it would be the one thing that led to their capture. Back above he knew the troops would be radioing in reinforcements, setting up a cordon, and preparing everything to get these people back where they belonged. He only hoped there would be enough left of the old Hypnos station to keep them occupied until they could be captured. He didn't want to be around Major Birch when he realized that all of this had been for nothing.

Edwards led them deeper and deeper, away from the crowded walkways and into the darker service passages, and finally into a passageway of bare rock. For a time they could still hear the echo of the busy, industrious feet bustling above them. Finally even this died away and the silence of the earth surrounded them. Only the quiet clumping of their feet and the expiration of their own breath could be heard. It was dark now. They had passed beyond the area of electrical lighting and all they could do was hang on to each other and keep walking. It all should have been worrying, they were fleeing for their lives in the darkness, but instead Birch found peace. There was a healing silence- almost like the plains where he and Karla had sat among the tall grass and looked up into the dark sky to see the gleaming stars. He wished he could see them again.

The passage was narrowing. It made their progress harder. Birch was surprised. He imagined that the stars had come out for him as twinkling points of light glowed in the darkness above.

"What is that?" Jane was asking. It snapped Birch from the indulgent impression that they had all been for him, some kind of special remembrance of those days that would never return.

"It means we're getting close," Edwards answered. "This place still has a power source that keeps everything juiced up down here. You're seeing the reflection of that energy."

It was a beautiful wonder. Little pinpricks of colored light bounced from the dark stone and reflected around them; his mind was captivated by the sight. It filled him with an anticipation, like stepping through dark caverns toward a dragon's den filled with shimmering riches. In this respect the sight that met them as they entered the cave was a disappointment. There were no riches here. Edwards had been right, there wasn't any promising equipment left behind. The great cavern and the machinery within it, was dingy, dusty, and rusty. It was a perfect picture of neglect and decay. This was a forgotten history.

"Not much is it?" Edwards drawled.

"I'm not so sure," Birch was poring over one of the computer consoles. He had gingerly tried the power and was surprised when it immediately clicked and hummed musically in its startup sequence. This was very different to the dilapidated consoles in Denver, perhaps it was because it was military grade material, or maybe it was simply that moisture hadn't gotten into these computers the way they had with the others. Whatever the reason Birch felt lucky to see the menu appear, crisp and clean on the screen.

"What do you make of this?" he called over to Jane. She moved swiftly to his side and tapped away on the console.

"This is a control computer from the Hypnos missions by the looks of it." She continued working at the keyboard. "They must have moved all this stuff up to Washington after our time."

"Yeah, just like Michaels said," Birch mused. "It must have been pretty bad for them to move everything up here. This isn't exactly the ideal launch site."

Jane grunted an answer, but didn't look up from the screen.

"Well, see what you can find in the memory of that thing

that might help us. I was expecting more here somehow."

Jane nodded and kept working at the console.

Birch looked up to take in the rest of the cavern. Pieces of equipment lay strewn about. Some of them he recognized, others were alien to him. It was strange to think of this musty place as the last home of human hope. Now it had been replaced by Michaels' tower, but the ideas there were danker and mustier than this place could ever be. It was a return to feudal lordship. The reinstating of the old society of privilege, and this president held all the advantages because he made the decisions for everyone.

"I've found something, Major," Jane announced. "It looks like a manifest for each of the Hypnos missions. It's odd though."

"What?" Birch turned his attention to the screen.

"Well, the records are all here for the Hypnos missions, but everything's pretty sketchy. A lot of the information seems encrypted. None of missions are clearly laid out, but it looks like there were at least another ten after ours. The security measures go crazy from there though. It's like they didn't even trust themselves anymore. I'm running across all kinds of codes and counter-codes, all designed, not to keep outsiders from hacking in, but to keep fellow insiders out."

"That is strange," Birch looked worried, "was there some kind of conspiracy?"

"I can't really tell, but this is the weirdest thing yet," she tapped at the keyboard again and brought up a display of mission status. "Hypnos I and II are listed here; their missions both failed to find any suitable planets for colonization. I'm not sure if they tried to come back or not, that isn't clear, but they both failed."

This news was almost a relief to Birch. He wasn't the only one. He wondered if they tried to get back, and if they did what happened to them. At least his failure seemed less heavy to him now.

"That's not the weirdest thing though," Jane continued,

"it's what they've got listed with our mission." She pointed to the screen. Birch read the green letters flashing on the black background: 'mission successful: colonization process begun.'

"Mission successful," Birch echoed. "Michaels was right. They sent people up to that rock." Lauren looked up from where she was guarding Edwards and the boy.

"They couldn't do that!" she blurted. "We didn't lay any of the groundwork they needed to survive on that planet. It would have been suicide."

"Nevertheless, they did it," Jane reported evenly, "and it looks like some reports came back from the colony. Sounds like things started off okay there, though it's been silent now for a long time."

"They shouldn't have lived at all," Lauren persisted. "They wouldn't have had the ability to last long without our work being done."

"That's not what it says here," Jane gestured to the screen. "I don't understand it any more than you, but that's what it says." She fell silent. For a time she stood glaring at the computer screen, as though trying to read some foreign language that she could almost comprehend.

"What's the matter Jane?" Birch followed her gaze down to the screen.

"It's asking for you," she pointed down at the monitor. "It wants you to report." Birch hesitated for a moment before he looked. Indeed the computer was requesting his personal ID code. "I'm not sure how it knew you were here," Jane warned. "I wouldn't give it anything. Something isn't right. This computer seems to be at war with itself. Everything I've tried to do on it seems hard; it's like I'm coming between two distinct personalities. It keeps putting things on the screen; then pulling them off again. Trying to show me stuff, then removing it. I'm not sure what it's up to."

"Let me get this straight," Birch smiled, "you're telling me that we've got a schizophrenic computer here and you wouldn't trust it?"

"That's not quite the way I'd put it," Jane huffed, "but I know something's wrong. It doesn't seem right. I'm just not sure you'd want it to get a hold of your personal information. Remember, you're the one who told us to keep as much of that away from these people as we could."

Birch nodded, but a frown crossed his face. "Nice advice," he muttered, "but we don't have time to play it safe." A faint sound from further up the tunnel seemed to punctuate his thought. "We don't have time. You and Lauren better look around and try to find another way out of here, I'll work on this computer a minute longer and see if it can help us at all."

Jane nodded and sulkily left the terminal. Birch was glad to have her out of the way. He turned his attention back to the computer.

The screen still flashed with the prompt: 'Birch, Major Thomas- personal ID #'. For a moment he hesitated, the green icon appeared and disappeared, like the opening and closing of a door. Finally he decided. He punched in the code and an instant later a red light shot from the terminal and scanned him. He fell back in shock.

"Major!" Jane leapt quickly to his side. "Are you okay?"

"I think so," Birch managed to mumble. Physically he had felt nothing, but something had happened. That computer had looked inside him. It was looking for something he couldn't explain, and he didn't know if it had found it.

Then nothing happened. Birch understood what Jane had meant about the computer. It had been swift and efficient up to this point, but now it seemed to stall and delay at this last moment, as though it were fighting between two separate and distinct instincts. Finally one side won out and the display read, 'Clearance complete: Engine warm up sequence begun. Opening bay doors.' Birch blinked at the screen, unsure of exactly what this meant.

A sudden metallic creak from the far wall answered the question. Slowly it moved aside, and to Birch's astonishment the gap behind it revealed a spacecraft, not like their old ship, the Hypnos III, but sleek and shiny, like something out of proper science fiction. This was not the junk of reality. It was unlike anything he'd ever seen before. This must have been what they had developed in the last days before the government fell, the last hoorah for humanity and its noble dream of space travel. Now perhaps it could be born again to that purpose. It might help them escape.

The noise from the passageway was growing louder now. From the sound of it the men chasing them had brought reinforcements. He knew this was their last chance; they had to run. These men were coming to take them back to their gilded cage. Birch would never go back to that. He would prefer to die. He took one last look down at the screen and shouted to the others.

"The ship's engines are warming up," he bellowed. "Get up to the cockpit as fast as you can! It looks like we'll have company any minute now, hurry!"

They all ran for the ship. Lauren prodded Edwards and the boy toward the flight elevator.

"Don't take me," Edwards was pleading. "You can't have any other need for me now. I don't belong out there! I've done all I can do so why don't you let me go?"

His pleas went unheeded. They entered the flight elevator.

By now the first of the soldiers had entered the cavern and was running toward the ship. Birch pushed the button and they slowly rose into the air. A few shots from Birch and Jane had stopped the first men, but another two had reached them before they were more than a few feet off the ground. The first one leapt immediately onto the rising platform, but had been shoved off just as quickly again by a swift kick from Jane. The second man had lost his footing and held onto the floor of the elevator cage by his fingertips. It was only a moment later that he too fell to earth where they both lay winded.

Birch watched as they steadily rose higher up the side of the ship. It was too slow. Already some of the men below were working on the computer, trying to override the launch sequence. Another group were clambering up the stairs that wound around the elevator as an emergency exit.

It was the third group that worried Birch most. These men were at the bottom of the elevator shaft trying to stop their assent. A moment later they succeeded as the cage shuddered to a halt. Without pause Birch flung the cage door open and ordered everyone to jump to the staircase.

Birch was the last to jump, but just as he was about to leap to safety the elevator lurched again and started a quick dissent. For a moment he felt himself floating before gravity caught him and sent him smashing hard against the steel floor. Groggily he climbed to his feet, aware that if he reached the bottom he would never escape. With great effort he lifted the cage door again and jumped for the stairs.

The momentum of his dissent sent him hard into the metal staircase. His gun fell from his hands to the ground far below. At least he had made it, but he had lost a lot of ground. The others were now well above him and clambering fast toward the access door of the ship. He had to hurry, but a thudding punch to the side of his head told him that he had other problems to worry about.

Birch's fast trip down had brought him level with the soldiers running up the stairs. Now the first of them had reached him and was trying to force him back down. Birch kicked hard at the man's knee and sent him toppling backwards, but he knew this would only delay them.

He was quickly on his feet again and running up the stairs. Every few moments it seemed that another set of hands was grabbing at him from behind, but he would kick out again at the rising forms and send them thudding into each other. They would land in a pile of confusion, tumbling headlong down the narrow stairway, but each time they rose again. They were relentless, and Birch knew eventually he would be overcome.

From here Birch could see another, more worrying development back on the ground. The elevator had finally arrived at the bottom and soldiers were getting in. They were going to cut them off at the top. If they made it they would all be trapped on the stairs. Perhaps even Jane and the others wouldn't get there in time, but there wasn't anything he could do about that. All he could do was climb.

Birch made slow progress. His legs hurt and his lungs burned. He had gained little ground on the enemies below as they harried his every step. Above him he imagined that Jane's group would be getting close to the doors by now, but he couldn't tell. At least he'd slowed the soldiers on the stairs enough to give them a chance. There wasn't anything he could do about the elevator though. It had passed him a moment ago, baring its load of muscled troops. They had stared sullenly at him as they passed inches from his face. Only the metal of their cage separated them. Soon they would be at the top and they all would be trapped..

He had almost given up, but still he hopelessly pressed on. In his struggle to survive he hadn't noticed the form descending to him. He was startled when soft hands clasped his arm and pulled him away from another attack. It was Jane. She lifted her rifle and sent a shot down that scattered their pursuers.

"What are you doing?" Birch had snapped as she bent down to help pull his weary legs up.

"It looks like I'm saving you," she answered coolly.

Birch shook his head. "You're second-in-command, you have other duties. You should be getting ready for the take-off; you're putting the others at risk by helping me."

"I guess you're right," Jane responded, "but sometimes people have to help others in spite of what the regulations say. Sometimes you just have to do what's right." Her eyes fixed on Birch's for an instant. There was a deeper meaning there that he didn't care to understand. He looked away.

"Besides," she added mischievously, "we need a pilot."

"Great," he answered gloomily and heaved himself up. "Now give me that gun!"

He pulled the rifle from her hands and, without hesitation, pointed it at the main cable of the elevator and fired at point-blank range. The shot exploded the wire and sent it coiling like a snake to the ground below. The counterweight broke loose and fell to the ground, sending the other cable swiftly up with the sound of grinding metal. It was only an instant later that the elevator above them began a sudden plummet to earth.

Birch watched aghast as the cage of men slipped past them. The stony faces of these mechanical soldiers contorted with fear. Like the Ares boy in the woods they had seemed unreal, malicious, even demonic. It hadn't mattered if he hurt them, but now he saw that it did, and it made him sick. He stared as they hurtled to the ground. They landed with a grinding thud that shook the tower. It swayed under the impact and almost came away from the side of the ship.

"Come on!" Jane shouted. "We haven't got long!"

Birch nodded and started up the rest of the stairs. The last part of the climb was agony for him. The stairs swayed wildly and he found it hard to keep his footing, but Jane helped and finally they were both crawling into the cockpit. The door was slammed behind them. It wasn't more than a minute later that rough hands were pounding on the glass and attempting to open the door from outside. Birch hurried to the pilot's seat and set the countdown for five minutes, hopefully enough time for him to look around and get some idea of the controls on this ship. It was new to him.

"Launch in T- minus 5 minutes and counting," a monotone voice announced in the cabin, and was echoed through the speakers about the cavern. The reaction outside was instantaneous. The pounding on the cockpit window stopped as panicked soldiers fell over themselves to get down the stairs and away from the coming explosion of the lift-off. At the bottom a few men were still gathered around the computer, trying to override the launch.

"T- minus 1 minute," the voice announced.

The roof of the cave now seemed to have peeled away as natural daylight broke through. By now most of the men had left the stairs and were throwing themselves toward the entrance. Even the men at the computer had given up and were running for their lives.

"Thirty seconds to launch." Inside the cabin Birch was sweating again. He could see the blue skies above him but he didn't know where they would go beyond that. All he really knew was that they had to escape. They had to get away.

"Ten seconds," he looked around at the faces of the others. Edwards looked angry, sullen, and scared. The Ares kid still looked like a ghost of himself. Lauren was hard to read as ever, and Jane had a look that he interpreted as an, 'I told you so.' Their return hadn't turned out as he had hoped. She thought all this proved her right, but he knew her way hadn't been any better.

It was strange. So much had happened. He thought of the people he was leaving behind. The missing faces in the crew hurt, and these new ones didn't replace them. This wasn't any kind of crew he would have chosen, but now as he looked again at them he remembered that he could be wrong. He had been before.

"Launch sequence initiated," the engines roared and burned the now empty chamber to cinders as the ship launched into the empty sky.

www.ingramcontent.com/pod-product-compliance
Lightning Source LLC
Chambersburg PA
CBHW020325180626
46812CB00001B/56
* 9 7 8 0 6 1 5 9 6 8 4 9 0 *